Obsession

Series:
Louisiana Secrets   Book Two

Patti Corbello Archer

Copyright

 Dedication

This book is dedicated to you and all readers who enjoy a love story dripping with romance, passion, and suspenseful thrills.

Where there's Always a Hero.
Always a Heroine.
And always desire.

Introduction

Welcome to *Obsession* – book two in my Louisiana Secrets series. The main story takes place in eastern Louisiana. It weaves like the Mississippi River through Baton Rouge, close to St. Francisville, and into Angola Prison.

You will find extraordinary characters and incredible relationships. As always you will find attraction. Passion. Mystery and suspense. Great interaction. Actions and thrills.

But most importantly, you will enjoy another wild love story dripping with sex appeal and desire.

And the story begins…

Patti Corbello Archer

Louisiana Pronunciations:
Atakapa (Uh-tak-uh-pah)
Calcasieu (Kal-Kuh-Shoo)
Atchafalaya (Uh-Cha-Fuh-Lai-Uh)

Obsession

Chapter 1
Baton Rouge, Louisiana

"Look at him!"

Twelve pair of eyes in the jury box followed her pointing finger. They stared at the defendant.

Prosecutor Samantha Rutledge said, "Don't be deceived by the way J.J. Jones looks in court today. Dressed in a suit. Clean. Neat. Quiet. But instead, think about what he looked like that night. Raging. Hunting knife slashing at his wife, covering them both in blood. Hate spewing from his eyes and mouth." She paused. "And then, as he watched her bleed to death at his feet, he spit on her."

The jury saw the picture in their minds. They believed every word.

She said, "He's not a civil human being. He's a murderer. A killer. And that's why the twelve of you stand in the gap for her. To find him guilty of first-degree murder. And to give his wife the justice she deserves."

Then walking back to her seat in a courtroom filled with people still reeling from that image, Samantha turned and told the Judge, "Your Honor, the Prosecution rests."

The angry gurgle warned her, and Samantha glanced just in time to see a wad of spit flying straight at her. Quick on her feet, she jumped back, and it landed right where she stood a second before. Everyone in the courtroom gasped at the disgusting behavior while the defendant's attorney reprimanded his client.

The judge sighed as he looked at J.J. Jones, and said, "Bailiff, remove the defendant from the courtroom. And Mr. Jones, for the record, your behavior is appalling. No one appreciated your atrocious manners toward the prosecutor."

Spontaneous claps broke out in the courtroom.

Looking at Samantha, who stood composed and impeccable as always, the Judge said, "Prosecutor Rutledge, on behalf of the rude defendant, please accept the court's apologies."

Strikingly beautiful. Petite. Blonde, and blue-eyed, Samantha nodded, and said, "Thank you, Your Honor."

Whispers spread amongst the spectators as the defendant glared at her while officers led him out. He looked exactly the way you would think a human monster would look. Eyebrows bent inward in a vicious scowl. Lips drawn back in a tight grimace. Hate spewing from terrifying dark eyes. Clenched fists. Spit hanging off the edge of his chin. If he hadn't looked guilty before, he did now.

Once he was gone, the defense gave their closing arguments. Not that it helped much with the case against Jones — and then court was dismissed. Samantha knew the trial was basically over. Evidence presented. Witnesses testified. Arguments presented. It was the jury's turn to deliberate and determine if Jones was guilty of the first-degree murder of his thirty-five-year-old wife, Tia. Thereby forfeiting his own life with the death penalty.

Brian, second chair Assistant District Attorney, said, "Quick move."

She said, "Right. I expected an outburst. I didn't expect spit."

Liz, her paralegal, whispered, "That was gross. Ugh. Don't step in it. We don't know what germs he carries. He's a nasty animal."

Samantha grimaced at the floor, and said, "It's such a shame I couldn't just slap him. It would have been much more satisfying for me."

Brian laughed and said, "I wish! But we all know he will get much more than a slap. The jury is bound to convict. They hate him already."

Then gathering their files, they headed to the elevator.

Samantha said, "Liz, would you please bring my files back to the office? I have a couple of errands to run during lunch."

***

2

On the way to the parking garage, Samantha groaned. Her feet were killing her. She had been in high heels for hours. She had to wear them - and the taller the better. At only five-foot-two, she needed the extra height. And although she was petite, her toes still complained unmercifully about being compressed in tall, very fine leather.

Climbing in her blue SUV, she kicked off her heels and wiggled her toes. And with a relieved sigh, started the engine. Now that her feet weren't screaming for attention, she thought back to her closing arguments and felt confident the jury believed the evidence given. And the spit attack had turned out to be the exclamation point to her speech. An unexpected bonus. She was sure he was prison-bound.

And while she expected a short jury deliberation, there were only a few work hours left today. And tomorrow was Friday, the July 4th holiday. Courts were closed. So, hopefully, they would have a verdict by Monday afternoon.

Her phone dinged. Checking the text, she smiled.

***

Sean: Heard the trial ended. Jury still out?
Samantha: Yes. Hope to hear something by Monday.
Sean: You'll get him.
Samantha: I saw you on the news, FBI Agent Man.
Sean: Any time a mother and child is found alive is a good day.
Samantha: I'm proud of you.
Sean: Who is this? And what did you do with Samantha?
Samantha: Very funny.
Sean: Seven o'clock dinner still on?
Samantha: Yes, feed me.
Sean: I aim to please.

***

Samantha put the car in gear, driving out of the garage thinking about Special Agent Sean Nash. He was crazy sexy. Literally. FBI.

3

Intelligent. Tall, dark, sensuous, and lick-your-lips handsome with Native American heritage.

They'd met through his brother, Dakota, who married one of her best friends, Gabrielle, over a year ago. And Sean had been on the hunt for her since then. He wanted more from her. A lot more. But she just couldn't. And she didn't know when she could. So, they shared steamy, but short-lived embraces, as she struggled with what to do about it.

Her cell rang – the boss.

***

She answered, "Yes, sir."

The District Attorney said, "Great job on the Jones trial."

"Thank you. I'm confident the jury will convict – with the death penalty."

"They will. He slit his own throat when he slit hers."

"Yes, he did."

He asked, "Are you going out of town for the July 4th holiday?"

"Yes, sir. Do you need me to work the long weekend?"

"No, take the break. You need it. You have depositions and discovery due next week, along with sentencing when the Jones jury reaches a verdict."

***

After the call, she focused on maneuvering through the packed highways in Baton Rouge. Holiday travel had obviously already kicked off. She was headed to the boutique where she ordered her swimsuits. Fun ones. Sexy. Eye-catching. Vintage or movie star style. And the black and white one-piece she picked out would do the trick. She had plans to hang out on Gabrielle and Dakota's new sailboat tomorrow in Lake Charles. No bikini for her though. Not since she had been sixteen.

After picking up her bathing suit, and zipping through a couple of drive-throughs, she had cash for the weekend and a Wendy's salad and tea for lunch. When she was next in line to turn onto the highway, she noticed the black sports car pull up behind her again.

She had seen it several times. Was he following her? Always feisty and bold, she turned to let him know she saw him. Abruptly, he roared around her and disappeared. She shrugged and headed back to the parking garage.

Twenty minutes later, she parked at work and gathered her purse, salad, and tea. Holding her phone, she walked, heels clicking on the concrete, toward the elevator. She heard fast footsteps and turned to look behind her. The sound stopped and she didn't see anyone. In a couple of moments, she hit the elevator button and the doors opened. Stepping inside, she hit the up button to the D.A.'s floor. Just before the door closed, a man's arm shoved through the crack. Startled, she screamed, unable to see the man. But the door forced him to remove his arm, and it closed.

Shocked, she thought, how odd. Everyone in this building knew the elevators were quick. There were too many deadlines and court cases to have sluggish elevators. The guy would have another ride in a second. He must be new here.

***

Late afternoon, Samantha shifted in her desk chair and rubbed her neck. She needed a break and went to the kitchen for a cup of coffee.

She looked in her paralegal's office and said, "Hey Liz, I wanted to remind you I'm leaving before six-thirty p.m. today. Have a good holiday weekend and I'll see you Monday."

Liz said, "Yes, ma'am. And I wanted to tell you, you rocked closing arguments today. He really lost it."

She said, "Right. That alone made the spit part worth it."

Just before she got to the kitchen, Suzette stepped out of her office and leaned against the doorframe. Samantha stopped again.

Suzette smiled and said, "I heard you left Jones wounded and in trouble today."

"Why Prosecutor Driscoll, no blood was evident on the defendant."

They laughed.

Samantha said, "Let me grab some coffee and I'll join you for a quick chat. I still have plenty to do before I leave for the holiday."

Suzette had been on staff with the D.A. several years longer than Samantha. She was an attractive brunette in her late thirties and single. Friendly. Smart. And the women enjoyed lunches and conversations from time to time. But that was as far as the friendship went since they both worked long, hard hours.

In a couple of minutes, Samantha carried her coffee in Suzette's office and perched on the arm of the sofa. She asked, "Do you have plans for the weekend?"

"No. I'll probably go to a movie or out to eat, but that's about it. I want to wear shorts and flip flops all weekend."

"I hear that! My poor toes are on strike."

They nodded in joint commiseration.

Suzette said, "I presume you have plans for the long weekend. I heard you talking to Liz."

"I do. Sean is picking me up for dinner. He just finished the case with the FBI on the mother and child kidnapping out of New Orleans that's been in the news. I'm catching a ride with him tomorrow to Lake Charles for the weekend. We plan to enjoy Dakota and Gabrielle's new sailboat."

Suzette whistled and said, "That sounds like a good weekend."

"I'm looking forward to it. I haven't seen them since the Pirate Festival in early May. Did I tell you Gabrielle is pregnant?"

"That's terrific! She's one tough, beautiful lady. You've been friends since LSU, right?"

"Yeah. We were roommates at LSU with Jade and Zoe. Those were fun days. We only thought we knew what work was. And speaking of work, I better get back to it. Have a good weekend."

Samantha's desk phone rang when she walked back in her office. She glanced at the clock. Just before five p.m.

***

She answered, "Prosecutor Rutledge."

The judge's clerk said, "The Jones jury has reached a verdict. Court will reconvene at ten a.m. Monday for sentencing."

Smiling, Samantha said, "Thank you."

Hanging up, she thought, now that was quick. He was one guilty dead man walking.

***

At six p.m., her phone alarm went off. She put away her work. Locked her desk. And headed to the restroom to freshen up before Sean arrived.

Looking in the mirror at her black pantsuit and white blouse, she sighed. She had to do something to look less like a lawyer. Off went the jacket and she untucked, then unbuttoned her blouse, revealing a silk V-neck undershirt. After shaking her long blonde hair out of the bun, she pulled it into a high ponytail. Then slipping on long earrings, touching up her makeup, adding her trademark red lipstick, and a spray of perfume, she was ready.

When she stepped in the hall, Sean was leaned against her office door. He smiled that sexy smile of his.

She grinned, and said, "Well, look at you, Agent Man. We match tonight."

Sean's gaze roamed Samantha. She was pure red-hot woman. Shapely in every meaning of the word. Gorgeous eyes…lips…long blonde hair. Smart. And feisty was his cherry on top. She was everything that made him burn. And she knew it.

Samantha smiled at his expression, then took her time looking him over. Six-foot-two inches of lean muscle. Long black hair that brushed his shoulders. And that face. So fine…

He stepped closer as they finished their eye inventory, and teased, "Hey, killer. I bet you ate him up in court."

She grinned, then boldly pulled his lips to hers. And in less than a second, he pulled her tight, taking lead on the kiss. He had to. Because she wouldn't let it last long. She never did. Ten seconds –

fifteen maybe – sometimes thirty. And he was right. A few breaths later, she pushed back and looked at him.

He said, "I guess this means you missed me while I was out of town."

She unlocked her office door, and said, "I'm not telling you."

"You forget. I'm an agent. I can tell. I know you missed me."

"And that means what exactly?"

"You tell me."

She sidestepped the issue, and said, "Like you didn't miss me."

"I did. Why don't I show you?"

"Why don't you take me out for dinner like you promised, Agent Man. I'm hungry."

Chapter 2

The man in the shadows watched Samantha and the guy walk out of the D.A.'s office toward the parking garage. He lifted the binoculars and kept his eyes glued on her. My, my, he thought, she was all grown up now. He felt the rush. It had been so easy to find her. One quick search on the internet for Samantha Rutledge, and Prosecutor Rutledge popped up. Technology was amazingly helpful.

She unlocked a blue SUV and put her briefcase in the backseat while the man waited for her. Then they walked about ten parking spots away and got into a black SUV. Shadow Man smiled as they drove away. Excellent. That meant she would be back later for her car.

Just before he stepped out of his hiding place, a dark-haired woman dressed in a suit walked out of the elevator, heels clicking. She looked to be in her mid-thirties. Fairly attractive. Slim. She stopped at an expensive white Jeep parked right next to Samantha's vehicle.

And minutes later, she left, heading north. He glanced around and pulled the gray hoodie over his face, then stepped out of the shadows. He slipped into the parking garage. In moments he slid an envelope under Samantha's windshield wiper. He chuckled and disappeared.

Down the road, the man unlocked a black BMW and got in. His blood was pumping. He never got over this feeling. Ever. Not since Samantha. He groaned in desire and started the car.

Chapter 3

Sean parked outside the Little Village Italian restaurant in downtown Baton Rouge and glanced at Samantha. He knew she would comment on his choice of restaurant. There was no doubt about it. Nothing slid by her.

She looked at the couples in the windows cozied up in candlelight, and said, "What are you up to, Sean? Wanting a little intimacy tonight, are you?"

He didn't answer and walked around and opened her door. He intended to let it play out. She sat there looking at him and didn't move.

He offered his hand and said, "Scared, Counselor?"

She slid her fabulous legs over and stood, then said, "What are you up to?"

He slid an arm around her waist to lead her inside, and said, "To feed you. Just relax and enjoy your Italian food."

They settled in a sweet corner table by the windows. It was a beautiful evening overlooking the Mississippi River. Candles lit. Music in the background. Romance dripped off everything.

Sean decided to take her mind off controlling the situation, and said, "How long do you think the jury will deliberate?"

She exclaimed, "I can't believe I didn't tell you! The jury already has a verdict. We are due back in court Monday at ten a.m. for sentencing."

He smiled and clapped softly, then said, "You did it."

Her expression heavy for a moment, she said, "He needs to be off the street, Sean. He liked killing her. I hate that she went through that."

The waiter interrupted them to take their order. Sean was grateful - he didn't want Samantha's thoughts to get heavy. He had other plans for tonight. Long overdue ones.

After the waiter left, Samantha grinned, and asked, "Aren't you thrilled to start a month's vacation now that your case is over? I'm so jealous."

"You won't be jealous while I'm sweating at the ranch. And on that note, I can't thank you enough for finding the place for me. I love all twenty acres of the hilly forests; pastures, and my sweet part of Thompson Creek. St. Francisville is a beautiful area of Louisiana. It's perfect for me. I owe you."

"No, you don't. I was happy to help you. It took almost a year to find the right place. Seeing the look on your face is thank you enough."

He smiled, and said, "Then I'm glad you decided to stay at the ranch tonight – at least you can enjoy it too."

"I know! It's been, what...a couple of weeks since I've been there? We have crazy schedules. What time are we leaving for Lake Charles in the morning? I hope that I will have a little time to enjoy the ranch before we head out."

"We'll have plenty of time to look around - don't worry. And be sure and check out my décor and layout in the house for me. I need a woman's perspective. As a single guy, I might be missing the mark somewhere."

She gave him a *yeah right* glance knowing the house was perfect, and said, "It's a dream place – and you and your house aren't lacking anything. You are single because you want to be. Women are mesmerized when they see you."

He stared at her for a moment, then said, "Are you mesmerized when you see me?"

The blow landed. She leaned back in her chair, and said, "I plead the fifth."

He said softly, "That won't work anymore."

"So, that's what tonight is about?"

"You can't be surprised."

Watching him, she said, "What do you want, Sean?"

"I want you to spend more time with me. Let me in."

She sat quietly for a bit, then said, "I've never let anyone but you this close."

"I'm aware."

She leaned forward and said, "Aware of what?"

"Do you really believe I can't tell?"

She didn't answer him.

He continued, "You have a secret. A big one. When are you going to tell me what it is?"

She glanced away and said, "I might have more than one."

"I don't care how many you have. I want more time with you."

"Why?"

"You know why. This isn't a game anymore. We have something special going on and you know it."

She asked curiously, "You're such an alpha male. Why have you let me control the romance between us?"

"You only controlled the amount of physical contact. The romance grew on its own."

"Then why did you let me control the physical contact, Agent Man?"

He put his elbows on the table and said, "Because you need to be in control. Why is that?"

She ignored his question. Contemplated how to handle the conversation. She had known this day would come as their relationship grew.

She said, "What if I do agree to spend more time with you? What will you want from me?"

He didn't let the smile show on his face. But he was right. She was ready. He responded, "For you to let your walls down. Give us time to linger together in our personal space. This conversation is not about sex, Samantha. I'm talking about us enjoying what we have face to face. People dream about relationships that feel like this. I want us to make a way for what we could have. Don't you?"

He picked up her hand and said, "We've known each other a year. We both know what's happening. You know what type of man I am. You know my family. My job. That I'm a Christian. I moved to be near you. You helped me find a home. I know you like touching me. Kissing me. You know me."

She looked at him intently but stayed silent.

He could see her mental processes turning and pressed her. He said, "What is it that you need to know about me that you don't already know? Talk to me. Ask me."

She glanced out the window for a few seconds, then looked back at him. She said, "Will you stop when I say stop?"

Her question hit him in the gut with a fireball. But without delay, he said, "Every single time."

She nodded. She believed him. And he knew it.

He said, "Who didn't stop?"

"No. I'm not going there yet."

He nodded – but wanted to kill whoever had hurt her so badly.

Samantha saw the fury flash in him. He was an FBI agent after all. Then she taunted him and said, "So you think you can handle me?"

That was her way of saying yes.

Smiling, he said "Test me."

After dinner, Sean drove Samantha back to the D.A.'s office to get her vehicle. There was an envelope under the windshield wiper. She pulled it out and opened it. It said one thing: *I'm back.*

She said, "It must be a prank," and showed it to Sean.

He said, "Do you usually get notes like this?"

"No. It's probably just someone from the office messing with me."

Sean glanced around the shadowed parking garage. He didn't like the idea of someone at her car for any reason.

Chapter 4

In downtown Baton Rouge, a big guy sat in an upscale bar. Tall. Muscular. Nice-looking. Short brown hair. Wearing expensive slacks and a dress shirt. He looked wealthy. Confident. Direct. Smart. He kept his eyes focused on a brunette woman in a suit that sat at a small table overlooking the busy street.

The bar was an attorney hangout and he pegged her for an attorney - like him. He'd been here for an hour, and she had been here when he arrived. And since she didn't seem to be in any hurry to leave, she might be open to company. Which meant it was time to make his move. She wasn't the type that usually interested him, but the opportunity was too good to pass up.

He motioned the bartender and pointed to the lady, then passed him two twenties. The bartender nodded, fixed the drink, and gave it to a waitress to deliver. The brunette looked surprised at the drink and glanced around the room. His cue.

He smiled and walked toward her.

She smiled, trying to appear casual instead of surprised, and said, "Thank you."

"You're welcome. May I?" as he motioned to the seat next to her.

She waved her hand toward the seat, and said, "Please."

He sat, and introduced himself, "My name is Wells. You looked deep in thought; I hope I'm not intruding."

"No, not at all, Wells. I'm Suzette. I'm just unwinding after a full day."

He began a friendly conversation and before long knew she was an attorney – a prosecutor. No doubt, intelligent. A touch of an introvert. Thick brunette hair. Not beautiful but classy. Neat. He bet she hadn't had a date in a year. She was ripe for someone like him.

She said, "Do you work in Baton Rouge?"

"I will. I moved here a short time ago. I'm a defense attorney – opposite sides of the aisle you might say."

She laughed and said, "Well, welcome to Baton Rouge. I'm sure we'll run into each other in the courtroom at some point."

He gave her a slow smile, and said, "I'm hoping for something more regular than that. Rather than a game of chance."

"That's direct."

"Why not? You see my interest. Why delay getting to know each other? You know time off from law work is hard to come by."

She agreed, and said, "Absolutely. Long hours and stress. Hence, my stop here."

He lifted his glass to her and said, "Hear, hear!" Then said, "Do you socialize often with the attorneys at work?"

"Mostly as a group. But another female prosecutor, Samantha, and I sneak away sometimes for girl talk, venting, and laughter. No offense, but we listen to men all day."

He laughed. Bingo. Keeping the plan rolling, he said, "Let's quit talking shop. Since tomorrow is the 4th of July, how about we share a picnic and watch the fireworks along the river?"

She said, "As long as I don't have to wear heels, I would love to."

Much later, Wells watched her walk to the bathroom. He loved being a predator.

Chapter 5

After leaving the parking garage, Sean followed Samantha to her apartment to get her luggage for the weekend. Because of the note on her car, he insisted on clearing her apartment before she entered. Then satisfied it was safe, she finished packing for their trip to Lake Charles.

He'd only been inside a few times to pick her up. That's it. They never lingered to watch a movie. Never cooked together. And never even kissed here. Now he knew why. But since she was occupied, he took his time looking around.

He picked up various nuances of her personality. She liked cozy furniture. Rugs. Romantic settings – including snow in the mountains based on her pictures. She liked Louisiana culture. And self-defense which was no surprise, being she was a fencer and carried a pistol.

He looked through her music. He expected Salsa – but not the oldies with the deep groove or body rubbing tempo. She was full of secrets. Her book choices were expected. Law. Ministry. Fencing. Mystery and suspense. No romance novels – which was telling based on what she said at dinner. Unexpectedly he found literature on gymnastics and the FBI Academy. That came out of nowhere. Interesting.

He checked her fridge. Sparse put it mildly. Cheese. A few fresh fruits. Veggies. Bagels. And she had several takeout boxes.

She called down the hall, "I won't be much longer, feel free to get a drink or snack in the kitchen. Well…if you can find one."

He said, "I notice you don't cook much."

She stuck her head out of the bedroom, and said, "So the takeout boxes in my fridge gave me away?"

"Oh yeah."

After a couple of minutes, she called for his help, and he walked in her bedroom. She was sitting on the edge of a suitcase larger than her, trying to close it. He laughed and walked over to latch it.

He said, "How many outfits did you bring? This weighs a ton."

She squeezed his arm muscles acting impressed, and said, "I like choices. Lots of them. I'm lucky you're strong."

He laughed.

She said, "I'm sorry it's taking me so long."

"I'm on vacation, remember? I've got all the time you need."

"Rub it in."

He laughed, and said, "I'm occupying myself, take your time."

"You're wasting your time profiling me. It won't tell you much."

"You'd be surprised what it tells me."

Leaving her to finish, he walked out on her fourth-floor balcony. Nothing soft and cozy out here. No plants. There was a nice chair and small table. He could imagine her quick mind gazing out across the city, contemplating the strategy to win whatever case she was working on.

Samantha joined him before long dressed in jeans and a tank top. Her blonde hair hung well past her shoulders. Beautiful Caribbean blue eyes and long lashes. Lips full – usually red but right now, natural. She smiled as he studied her.

Without looking at the city, he said, "You have a nice view here."

She raised her eyebrows and said, "Which view do you mean?"

He lowered his mouth to hers. Softly. Coaxing her lips open. He didn't rush. Just let her feel him without the passion.

Then smiling, he said, "Call that a late dessert," and went to pick up her suitcase.

Samantha watched him walk away, her lips tingling. That had been slow and deliciously sexy. She had limited him for so long. No…limited both of them. But she hadn't had a choice – till now.

Being safe opened a whole new world. And she sure knew she wanted him to do that again.

***

In thirty minutes, they were on Highway 61 headed north out of Baton Rouge toward St. Francisville. Once they crossed Thompson Creek, Sean took the next right. He drove east into the woods for about ten miles and turned through a gate. The long driveway was more like a country road. When he pulled into the clearing, motion lights popped on.

Samantha clapped, and he laughed.

His new house was a two-story barn style with a wing on each side. It had double entry doors and large windows. The front porch went from one side of the house to the other and was decorated with rockers and plants.

They grabbed their bags and headed to the porch. Sean opened the front door and turned off the alarm. The lights came on inside.

The master bedroom and bathroom were in the loft upstairs. The left wing consisted of three bedrooms and a large bunkroom that slept four. The right wing was a chef style kitchen and dining area. The center was open with two moss green velvet sofas. A beautiful, patterned rug. Leather easy chairs with pillows. And a low sofa table. Under the loft was Sean's large office, and a cozy seating area with a fireplace.

Sean said, "It even smells like home now."

"It's a great home. It looks like you."

Teasing, he said, "I look like green velvet?"

She thought about how sensual he was. Smooth. Vibrant. Silky touch. He saw her expression change as she looked at him. Unguarded feelings flickered in her eyes. Ahhhh, he thought. So, velvet did remind her of him. Intriguing. But there was so much she hadn't seen from him...yet. But she would.

He smiled and said, "Now, no argument, but as my honored guest, I yield the master suite to you. I will sleep down here."

She opened her mouth to argue, and he said, "Come on, Samantha, let me offer this to you. You found this place for me. I am grateful. I want you to have the best that I have to offer."

She walked into his arms and hugged him. A real hug. The first. Sean was captivated by her gesture and gentleness. He held her. Breathed her in. She was opening to him, one step at a time. Finally.

She stepped back, and said, "Thank you."

He said softly, "My pleasure. Now, let's put your things upstairs."

After they got her settled, he brought some of his clothes downstairs and changed.

When he came out, she asked, "Can I see your horse now?"

"Sure, I have a surprise to show you at the barn."

She grabbed his arm, pulling him, and said, "Well, hurry up then!"

His barn was a walk-through building with horse stalls and storage on one side, and equipment and tools on the other side. Upstairs was a loft apartment in the event a groom was hired. But Samantha only had eyes for the horses. She gasped as she walked to the two stalls – seeing the new horse.

Sean's horse was a Morgan. He had a rich brown coat and long black mane and tail. His name was Bear. He was eager to have her attention and danced around. Samantha greeted him and rubbed his neck - then reached for the white Arabian mare.

He said, "What do you think of her?"

"She's gorgeous! When did you get her?"

"A couple of days ago."

"What's her name?"

"Whatever you want - she's yours."

She stared at him. Mouth open. Stunned. And said, "I can't believe you bought me a horse. Why?"

"So, we could ride. So, you could love on her. Besides, she reminds me of you. Shockingly beautiful and graceful."

Moved beyond words, she hugged him again – head against his chest.

Holding her there, he said softly, "You're welcome."

Stepping back, she said, "You've shocked me."

"You shock me all the time."

Laughing, she glanced at the mare, and said, "I think I want to call her Sugar."

"Ahh. Sounds perfect…it fits both of you."

She said, "Thank you seems insignificant. She's a fabulous gift. I love her already."

He smiled and she glanced at his lips. Suddenly they were all she could think of and touched them softly.

When they opened for her, she felt the heat within, and said, "Sean—"

And that's as far as she got. His lips covered hers. His heat claiming her as he pulled her tight. She responded fully - their fit perfect. But this wasn't what the horse had been for. This was what he had waited almost a year for. Real surrender. After a several long moments, she stepped back and met his eyes. Awareness and intimacy were now alive and well.

He cupped her face, and said, "I have to be honest with you…you taste…so good to me. And I'm really hungry for you. I have been for a long time."

Deep passion flashed through her at his words. His honesty and intent arousing. She blinked at the impact, and he saw it in her eyes. His lips lowered to her neck, trailing up, and her head fell back. He kissed her again. Taking her mouth with a hunger too long denied.

The next time, he was the one that stepped back. Because he wanted her desire to set the pace – not his. He wanted to keep her in her safe zone.

Watching her, he said, "Tell me, Counselor, do you feel safe?"

Eyes sparkling, she grinned, and said, "Do you?"

And he laughed.

An hour later they sat on the stairs overlooking the den.

Sean said, "Do you want to take a ride in the morning before we leave for Lake Charles?"

"Yes. Let's race."

"Do you think you can beat me?"

"Silly question."

He chuckled; well aware she would fight to the death to win.

Then they sat silently for a little while. Her smile faded as she stared out the front window - lost in thought as she remembered what she wanted to forget. Sean saw the shift in her body language. Tense. Fingers curled into fists. Not blinking as she gazed at nothing. He knew she was thinking about her secrets. No doubt about it. She caught his intense gaze and tried to play it off as she smiled at him. It didn't work. He waited. Watching her. Not giving her a way out.

She shrugged and said, "Ok. I get it. As an agent, it would be hard for you having this mystery staring you in the face. I know it would be for me as a lawyer. But let me ask you something. Have you ever been afraid for yourself, Sean? No, wait. Afraid isn't the right word. Terrified beyond comprehension is a better description. Like dangling over a river of molten lava. Like knowing a predator is about to eat you alive. Have you experienced anything like that?"

He grimaced internally at what she meant, and said, "No. But I hate that you have."

"Yeah. Me too. And it's made me a complicated person. Two people almost. One public. Brave and fighting for others. But one private. Fearing the fear that's not imaginary."

"Do you want to tell me yet?"

"No. I just want you to know that this…with us…is priceless to me. Being vulnerable is not a place I visit with others, if you know what I mean."

"I do. And I don't receive your gift lightly. I value it. I get where it comes from."

She nodded and said, "It's so much easier being tough. Feisty. Independent. A champion for others."

He said, "That's why some survivors make fierce warriors. Even with battle scars."

She nodded, then unexpectedly flipped the mood on him, and said softly, "You really have a way about you, Sean. I like that you read me. Know things that I don't tell you. Almost like you read my mind. I have to say it's sexy to the brilliant degree."

He smiled and said, "And you changed the subject very effectively I might add."

She grinned and said, "Thank you. I have skills too…but am I lying?"

"No, Counselor. You're not. And I like that you like, what I do to you. Most especially since it's just beginning."

A short time later she said goodnight and headed upstairs. Sean watched her walk into his bedroom and shut the door.

He smiled and whispered, "Welcome home, Samantha."

***

Samantha got ready for bed and climbed under the chocolate down-filled comforter. She almost disappeared in the fluffy mattress. She laid there for a moment and smiled. She smelled the pillow…hmm Sean. Then glanced out the window at the moon above the trees. Her mind spun from tonight. She knew Sean was deeply attracted to her. Maybe he wouldn't mind when he found out she was spoiled goods. Worse than he even thought. And maybe one day…he would love her as much as she already loved him.

Chapter 6

The next morning, Sean poured Samantha a cup of coffee when he heard his bedroom door open and close. He glanced up to see her running downstairs. A beautiful sight to behold. A tiny blonde powerhouse, hair flying, wearing jeans, a sports shirt, and a fabulous smile. He smiled and pushed a cup of coffee toward her.

She noticed his grin and said, "What?"

"You're a morning person."

She quipped, "Aren't you?"

"Let me ask you a question instead."

"When do you not ask questions, Agent Man?"

He put his coffee down and stepped in front of her. He said, "What kind of person do you think I am first thing in the morning?"

She looked at his handsome face. Sexy body. Long finger-combed hair. White T-shirt and jeans, and said, "Really hot?"

He laughed and said, "How about affectionate?"

"I've never heard of an affectionate morning person."

Sean said, "Hmmm…like this," and sensuously wrapped her in an embrace that was both a hug and a snuggle. He nuzzled her neck and massaged up and down her back. Samantha was enraptured by his touch and closed her eyes. She melted into him. After a little while, he stepped back and softly kissed her.

Knees weak, Samantha whispered, "What did you do to me?"

He laughed and said, "Come on, your horse is waiting," and she pulled him to the barn.

23

Before long, Sean saddled the horses. He was just about to give Samantha a leg up when her phone rang. She glanced at the caller.

***

Samantha answered, "Hi Jade, I'm with Sean. Are you on the way to Lake Charles?"

Jade said, "Hey guys! We just left New Orleans. Do y'all want to ride together?"

Sean nodded yes, and Samantha said, "Sure."

Jade said, "We'll be there by ten a.m."

Sean said, "Perfect. We're heading out for a ride now. Do you have directions to the ranch?"

Angel said, "We do. See y'all in a little while. Have fun on the ride!"

***

Sean gave Samantha a leg up on the mare. He stepped back and looked at the picture she made. Long blonde hair. White Arabian with long white mane. Stunning. Then he mounted his stallion and spun him in a circle as Samantha laughed. They were both ready to run.

He pointed down the long stretch of pasture to the north where a red barn stood, then said, "First one to the barn wins – ready? Go!"

They leaned low and gave the horses free rein. In no time, they were flying. The mare was fast and slowly edged ahead of the stallion. The stallion pressed to beat the mare. The finish line drew closer as the old barn loomed ahead. It was exhilarating. Then it was down to the wire. At the end, the mare surged ahead and passed the side of the barn first.

Samantha screamed and raised her arms in victory. Sean laughed. She was one feisty beauty. After high fiving her, they talked and rode along the creek. Then just as they were heading back into the woods, Samantha's phone dinged with a special ringtone she had set.

She glanced at Sean and said, "Do you mind if I check an email? I've been waiting on this information."

"Go ahead."

***

She quickly opened the email:

To: Samantha Rutledge
From: Chicago Investigations
Re: Maxwell Chance

Message: It appears Maxwell moved back to Baton Rouge last month. Address unknown. He's under the radar and not using credit cards. He has visited Angola – Louisiana State Penitentiary several times. He is single and drives a black BMW. Driver's license picture attached. Let me know if you need any further information.

Steve Langley

***

Samantha knew she was going to be sick and slid out of the saddle. When her feet hit the ground, she threw up. Sean dismounted and ran to her. Rubbed her back. She threw up again. Once the spasms passed, he handed her a tissue and bottled water. She rinsed her mouth out. Finally composed, she looked at him.

Alarmed, he said, "That was so sudden. What's wrong?"

"I'm so sorry. I must have eaten something that made me sick."

"Try again. You haven't eaten yet. What was the email?"

"Just work."

She was lying to him. Sean knew fear when he saw it. He pressed her and said, "Talk to me. What was on the email?"

"No. I'm not ready to talk about it."

Her statement was like the *not now* response she gave him last night at the restaurant.

Insistent, he turned her face to him, and said, "Do you mean to tell me that email is connected to what you won't tell me?"

25

She shrugged and held her ground – not ready to dig into the past for herself. Or Sean.

He said, "This *thing* has affected your life. You can't even bring yourself to talk about it. It makes you throw up. And now someone is leaving messages at work – remember your car? Samantha, it's past time to talk about it. You know that."

She looked away. She just couldn't do it.

Determined, Sean said, "Answer me this, Samantha. How many cases have you prosecuted because the victim ignored the warning signs?"

She groaned and said, "I can't say it. I just can't."

Ok. She gave him something to work with.

He went a different route and said, "Was it a crime?"

"Yes."

"Was it reported?"

"Yes."

"Was there a trial?"

"No. He pled guilty."

Sean said, "You know I need to know everything to be of any help to you. I want to pull the file and read the case."

Relieved, she nodded.

Sean, knowing she was safe with him, and that he would get his answers soon, said, "Ok. Then we'll talk afterwards."

She said, "But…there are things not in the case file."

And then he knew. He said, "You're in danger, aren't you?"

"I could be."

He said curtly, "When were you going to tell me?"

"I planned to ask you for help once I had more information. It just got ahead of me."

He ran a hand through his hair, and said, "Ok. We'll go to Lake Charles as planned. You need to unwind obviously. And we'll be with friends and family today. But by morning - your friends will step into their professional roles. No argument. Understood?"

She nodded.

He said, "Where's the email?"

She handed him her phone. He read it and forwarded it to himself.

He touched her face, and said, "You're with me 24/7 until this is resolved. I've got you."

They rode back to the barn and unsaddled the horses.

After giving them treats, Sean said, "I hired a part-time groom to take care of the horses when I'm out of town. You'll meet him so you need to know he's got a record. A felony. He killed the man that killed his little sister. He literally happened upon the crime scene and the guy was still there. It was awful.

"His name is Kerry Hart, and he had a perfect behavior record in prison. And believe it or not, he's a pianist. Shocking, since he is a giant of a man. A handsome black guy with bright blue eyes. I'm impressed with him. We click as friends. I think you'll like him too."

Able to imagine a brother's rage and grief coming upon that scene, she found sympathy for him. He was both a victim and a felon.

She said, "I can't wait to meet him."

They headed to the house and hauled suitcases on the porch before Jade and Angel arrived.

Samantha and Jade had a lot of history. As college roommates, they were more like sisters. Family. Always there for each other. And Angel was Jade's business partner – although everyone but Jade was aware he had other plans in mind for her.

Fifteen minutes later, they arrived, and Sean gave them a quick tour of his new ranch. Samantha caught Jade giving her a probing look. Intuitive. She knew there was an issue. But as an investigative reporter and private investigator – she should notice things like that. But Samantha refused to engage with her silent questions. She had to hold her off till tomorrow or late tonight at the earliest. She didn't want to do it now.

***

They loaded up and headed to Lake Charles. Sean rode upfront with Angel. The girls rode in the back. Samantha asked how their investigator business was going. Angel and Jade fist-bumped and took turns sharing shocking as well as hilarious encounters with clients and criminals.

Then Angel pointed at Jade. She nodded and said, "We jointly purchased an old Victorian three-story house for a home and business. It has towers, turrets, and dormers. Even some stained-glass inlays. It's fabulous but needs remodeling. The plan is for the business to be on the main floor. Angel would live on the second floor. And I would take the top floor.

Samantha said, "That's a terrific idea! Cost and time effective for sure. I'm impressed."

Sean said, "I love those homes. Great personality. Congratulations."

Angel said, "Thanks. Each floor will be a fully functioning unit. Jade wants more of an open floor plan for her flat. I want an open kitchen and den-style study. But I want a private gym and bedroom."

Jade said, "We're supposed to move in soon. I'm thrilled!"

While they were talking, Samantha looked Jade over – a truly gorgeous woman with Russian and Latin heritage. Almond-shaped brown eyes and olive skin. But today…she was vibrant. She had more makeup on. Sultry. Glossy lips. Heavy liner. And her long dark hair was loose instead of braided for comfort. She wasn't in her usual sporty clothes either - but more feminine in a crop top and jeans. Who could blame Angel for wanting her? And how could Jade not know?

Samantha glanced at Angel. Not quite as tall as Sean, but he had muscles on top of muscles. Latin. Short black hair. Intense green eyes. He had a direct and masterful air about him; being a former marine, that wasn't surprising. A great guy. Bold, sexy, tough, and smart.

Jade caught Samantha watching them and crossed her eyes to break the contact. They giggled.

Sean began to share some of the more humorous side of his work stories with the FBI. All of their professional lives were intense, so they needed this down time. They laughed the rest of the way to Lake Charles.

***

On the Calcasieu River in Lake Charles, Dakota was in his office on the main floor of their log cabin. He heard Gabrielle, coming down the hall.

He said, "Hey, beautiful! Sean, Samantha, Jade, and Angel will be here in thirty minutes. Are you ready to go to the marina?"

She walked in his office, and he whistled.

Laughing, she twirled, dark hair spinning, and said, "Do you think it's too flashy to ride in a boat?"

He said, "Number one. It's a sailboat. Flashy is allowed. And two. No. You are perfectly delicious and nothing else matters."

She had on a cotton candy pink one-piece swimsuit covered in sequins. Every inch of it. And the back dipped low exposing her tattoo – a tropical explosion of flowers and greenery that rose from her lower back to her shoulders.

Dakota walked around the front of his desk to show his admiration and ran his hands over all the sequins before giving a long kiss of approval.

He said, "It is possible however, that you could be a boating hazard for all male boat captains."

Gabrielle grinned and released his ponytail. She loved his long black hair down. Then touching her stomach, she prayed his Sioux genes would show up in their baby. All their babies. She wanted their children to be tall, dark, and gorgeous like their daddy.

Several minutes later, Dakota had just loaded the last box in his SUV when Sean and his group drove up. Sean got out first, and fist-bumped, then half-hugged Dakota. Obviously, they were brothers. Hunks to the bone. And the youngest, Adam, who was off on a mission trip to Brazil, was said to be the biggest head-turner of them all.

Dakota shook hands with Angel, and the men began to talk boats. Gabrielle came outside, and the women hugged and laughed.

29

Everyone was excited about having a great day on the water in the new sailboat. And then tonight, they would kick back and watch the 4th of July fireworks extravaganza.

Before long they piled in Dakota's SUV and headed to the marina. Sean rode up front with Dakota. Angel grinned and got in the back with all three gorgeous women. His kind of backseat ride.

***

Sean texted Dakota on the way down the road: Samantha's in danger. Meet me late tonight.

Dakota checked the text without a word. His hands tightened on the steering wheel in response. FBI Special Agent Dakota Nash was a profiler for special cases. This would be one. They would meet.

***

In thirty minutes, Dakota pulled into the marina driveway and parked. Everyone gathered their bags and followed him down the long dock to the last sailboat. A real beauty. A forty-foot, white Catalina yacht with red, white, and blue sails. The name of the boat was The Cat. Gabrielle's nickname.

The boat was amazing. It had comfortable seating for eight on the back deck. The cabin below had a modern kitchen, large dining booth, bathroom, shower, and bedroom.

Once all the supplies were aboard, the men headed back on deck. The women stayed below to change into bathing suits meant to impress. After all, sailing the lake was a social event not to be taken lightly.

Gabrielle came out of the bedroom first in her cotton candy pink sequined one-piece. Sexy female from head to toe. Jade changed into a red one-piece with a low back and shear ruffled wraparound that was Salsa all the way. Samantha stepped out in a retro black and white halter one-piece. High cut on the sides. Low cut in the back. Movie star quality.

30

They took selfies. Grabbed sunglasses. And headed to the deck. All three men turned when the door opened, then wolf-whistled in total appreciation. The women posed.

***

Sean lounged across the back of the boat and patted the seat next to him. Wind-blown hair. Faded denim cutoffs that rode low on his hips showing tight abs and muscles reaching well below the waistband. Sunglasses and a sexy smile. Killer hot.

Giving him a sultry look over the top of her sunglasses, Samantha sat by him and opened the sunscreen.

She said, "I'm not olive skinned like all of you. I would be a lobster in no time."

He whispered, "I love lobster."

She smiled, and he reached for the sunscreen, and said, "Please, let me…"

And after saturating her back and arms, he pointed to her legs.

Grinning, she said, "I'm pretty sure I should do my legs."

"But just think how much more I could rub at one time."

"That's exactly what I'm thinking."

***

They enjoyed the ride as Dakota steered the sailboat down Contraband Bayou. Across Prien Lake and the Calcasieu River, till they sailed into Lake Charles. It was a beautiful day with dozens of vessels on the water. Many boaters hollered and waved at Dakota. He had developed quite a following since playing Jean Lafitte at the Pirate Festival a couple of months ago. Gabrielle had her own fans too since learning she was Jean Lafitte's real descendant. But that's another story.

Sean noticed something on Dakota's hip when he bent over to pick up a rope. He walked behind him and touched the waistband of his shorts.

Dakota grabbed his hand and said, "Hey. Hands off."

Sean said incredulously, "Is that what I think it is on your hip?"

Dakota said, "Mind your own business," and Sean burst out laughing.

Gabrielle grinned, knowing Dakota couldn't get out of this now. The others said, "What did we miss?"

Gabrielle called out, "Dakota, the cat's out of the bag," and laughed at her pun.

Jade said, "What is it?"

Gabrielle walked up behind Dakota, then pulled down the edge of his shorts. There on his hip was the tattoo of a cat. Beautiful. Sassy. Obviously, a reference to Gabrielle. Jade and Samantha cheered at the romantic gesture.

Angel said, "Hey man. I would tattoo my woman on my hip. I think it's great."

Gabrielle said, "It was a gift for me. Isn't she the cutest cat ever?"

Dakota groaned over the hated description cute, as Sean laughed, ribbing Dakota.

Samantha leaned over with a sexy grin, and slipped her fingers inside Sean's waistband and said, "I don't know Sean, I think a tattoo would be a great gift to get from your man."

Sean's eyes went from her eyes to her fingers in his shorts, and back to her face. Smiling, he said, "We are going to…get into this…discussion again. No doubt about it."

***

After making a few rounds on the lake, Angel said, "Jade, how about a little Salsa dancing?"

"Here on the boat?"

"Why not, we can shorten our steps."

Jade heard most of the boats playing music, and said, "Ok. I'm game."

Angel asked, "Hey Dakota, how about some Salsa music so Jade and I can dance?"

"Sure! Go for it."

Angel picked a playlist and plugged it into a speaker. Drawing Jade to her feet, they posed. Sultry. And when the music started, he pulled her against his chest while she wrapped one leg around his hip and leaned in. Offering. Fiery. They spun and began to dance the spicy routine they had danced many times.

Angel felt Jade's body mold with his. Sexy. Bold. Teasing. And decided he was tired holding back. After the next set of spins, he pulled her against him, and she leaned back - baring her throat to him. But today he took advantage of the routine and licked up her shoulder and neck to poise above her lips like he would kiss her.

He smiled at her wide-eyed glance as her body tensed, but she didn't miss a beat. Hanging in there, she teased, and slid her hands all the way around him — but now her mind was racing. What was he doing? But knew that was a stupid thought. She knew what he was doing.

Angel touched her with new intimate moves. Suggestive. Aggressive. Making himself very clear. Their eyes meeting. Their bodies sweating. Sliding. Then he lifted her and held the position. Draped in the cover of her gorgeous hair. Both breathing hard. Then she slid down his body to land at his feet. They panted and looked at each other. He winked. She didn't know if her knees would work to get back up.

Then it sounded like a ballgame with all the claps and yells around them. Angel helped her stand and they looked with amazement at all the boats that had drawn close to watch them dance. Angel slipped an arm around Jade, and they bowed.

Voices called, "Encore, encore!"

Angel shook his head no, and they waved to their fans. Good naturedly, boats revved their engines and continued cruising the lake. Angel and Jade turned to their friends, who stared at them in complete amazement.

Gabrielle said, "There is no way you are just business partners. I don't care what you say."

Angel kissed Jade's hand and leaning close to her, whispered, "Not anymore."

***

Afterwards, everyone went downstairs for snacks and drinks. In minutes they trailed back on deck. Jade and Angel stood alone in the kitchen.

She said, "So, what was that?"

"You know what that was."

"But you know I don't—"

"I know you do. But you have some notion we can't because of the business."

"I trusted you to understand."

"I do understand. But things change. You're just nervous."

She snapped, "I am not."

He stepped closer. She stepped back.

He said, "You proved my point. But when we dance, you let go. I want you to let go now."

He watched the struggle on her face as he pulled her in his arms. He said, "Tell me you aren't attracted to me."

"I don't think about that at all."

"Liar."

She blushed at his truth.

He whispered, "Don't you want to know what a kiss between us will be like?"

She looked at his mouth and hers went dry. She licked her lips.

He said, "I'm going to take that as a yes," and pulled her mouth to his.

The shock from his mouth connecting with hers, was like fire in her belly. Jade had never felt anything as wonderful as him and wrapped her arms around his neck. Letting go. Lost in feeling him. Angel groaned as she ignited - and devoured her lips. Caressed her. Held her higher, tighter, and hotter. He knew he would never get enough of her.

Several powerful kisses later, he licked the taste of her on his lips.

Breathless, Jade said, "I take it, this means you want to date now?"

"I want a whole lot more than that."

***

After lunch, the ladies decided to sunbathe. They climbed on the cabin roof and laid out their towels. Wrapping their hair in messy buns, they basked in the very hot Louisiana sun.

The guys asked Sean about the drones he was inventing.

Dakota said, "What's your goal? To sell your patent to the FBI or be a manufacturer?"

"I haven't decided yet."

Angel said, "Won't you need an attorney to work that out?"

"Yes. I have a gym buddy who's an attorney. He's working with me. Jonathan Remington."

Thinking about the earlier text warning, Dakota glanced at Sean, and said, "Did you tell Angel about tonight?"

Angel said, "What about tonight?"

Sean said, "I didn't, but now is good."

Angel waited.

Sean explained, "Samantha is in danger. I'll know more later tonight."

Angel and Dakota both said, "What type of danger?"

"She found out today that a man from her past is back in Baton Rouge. She got physically sick. Terrified. And that's not Samantha. She refuses to fill me in on the details but told me I can read it. That tells me the level of fear she's in. So, based on the name in her email I sent for a copy of the case. It should be in tonight. So, until we know she's safe again, she's with me. And here…I'm sending you the email she got."

The guys read it.

Angel said, "Do you have an idea of the type of crime?"

Dakota said, "Violent."

Sean said, "Probably sexual in nature. She's hiding something traumatic. She said the whole truth isn't even in the case file. Which means, only she can tell us what no one else knows."

35

Chapter 7

The ladies finished sunbathing and went downstairs to freshen up. When they returned on deck, Gabrielle curled up in Dakota's lap.

She said, "Have you heard about a gender reveal party?"

"Sure. Do you want to plan one when we find out what the baby is?"

"We're having one today."

Astounded, and completely ignoring everyone around them, he said, "You mean you know and haven't told me?"

Touching his face to calm him, she said "I only found out yesterday. I wanted to surprise you."

"Just tell me, honey. Boy or girl?"

She said, "You have to guess oh brilliant one."

Exasperated, he said, "You've got to be kidding me."

"Come on, Dakota. I am giving you the biggest hint I can. You can do this."

"What hint?"

"It's in your lap."

He looked at her sitting in his lap. Pink sequins. He laughed and yelled, "It's a girl! I'm going to be a girl dad!"

***

As afternoon turned into evening, it was spectacular on the lake. The city lights sparkled on the water along with all the boats. And where the lake merged into the river, the large Interstate 10 bridge rose high above the festivities to reach the towns of Westlake and Sulphur on the other side. Spectators lined the beach, the Civic Center seawall, the park and waited everywhere that offered a clear view of the sky.

Dakota said, "Fireworks will start in about thirty minutes. Make yourself comfortable!"

He killed the engine and dropped anchor. The boat rocked gently on the waves. It was romantic, even with thousands of people around the lake.

***

Sean whispered, "Come with me," and Samantha followed. They climbed on top the cabin and found a secluded spot hidden in shadows.

He kissed her shoulder and said, "I wanted you to myself. I find I'm getting stingy as the day wears on."

"So…what do you want to do with me?"

He pulled her in his lap, and said, "What would you like me to do?"

She turned, wrapping her legs around his waist as their lips met. On fire at her intimate position, he groaned and pulled her closer. Harder. He tasted her groans and felt her nails bite into his back. His desire raged at the passion her trust had released. He wanted her. Forever.

Holding her face, he said, "Surely you know I'm in love with you. I have been for a long, long time. You're mine. Say it…"

She whispered, "I feel like I've loved you forever, Sean. Hiding it and hoping one day…"

And the kiss that followed was all things magical. Then cannons shot fireworks high in the sky - exploding. They both jumped, laughing. Then snuggled and watched the sky light up. Just like them.

***

On the back deck, Angel watched the flicker of fireworks light up Jade's face. She felt his gaze on her and tried to act casual, but with all the romance sparking on the boat - it was impossible.

Angel put his arm around her and said softly, "Come on. Enjoy the fireworks with me. You're as nervous as a cat. Quit worrying about when I'm going to kiss you again."

She said, "Stop playing with me or I'll push you overboard. Besides, you don't know that I want to kiss you."

And she refused to look at his lips. Fought it. Hard.

He grinned and tucked her under his arm, then said, "You do, but I'll give you a break. Just relax with me. Get used to the idea of my hands on you."

She finally relaxed in his hold, enjoying his company the way she always did. But inside she was a mess. Her organized life was crumbling under his lips. But then again, did she really care about her rules? He tasted better than she had ever dreamed.

***

After the fireworks, they headed back to the dock – in major boat traffic as everyone else on the water headed back to their docks as well. It would be a long while before they made it back home.

***

Almost two hours later, they drove up to the cabin. The ladies went to shower. So, with them occupied, Dakota led the way to his office. He motioned for Sean to use his desk. Sean signed in on the computer, and the case files on Samantha were ready for him. He started printing. But left evidence and crime photographs on the computer, linked to the large TV to review as a group. He dreaded having to go over the pictures. He'd already seen it was a nightmare. No wonder she was terrified.

Once he finished printing, he said, "We're ready to review. The only thing left is what Samantha hasn't told us."

The guys heard the ladies in the kitchen and joined them. It was time to fill them in.

Samantha met Sean's gaze when he walked in the room. He wrapped her in a hug.

He said, "We have your case ready to review. Are you ready for this?"

"No. But do it anyway."

He nodded and they turned to face the others.

Gabrielle and Jade felt the tension in the room. Saw the signs of trouble on the faces around them.

Gabrielle said, "Dakota, what's going on?"

He glanced at Samantha, giving her the lead.

Samantha said, "Gabrielle. Jade. I was a victim in a criminal case as a teenager. I never talk about it. Ever. And that's the only reason you don't know about it."

Shocked, they stared at her in disbelief – trying to fathom this new truth among them.

Samantha continued, "I received some information today on a dangerous man. I believe he's returned for me. The guys need to read my case and determine the next step. I'm sorry for the cloak and dagger – and for messing up the weekend."

Gabrielle said, "We don't care about the weekend. Jade and I will stay with you while they work. You are all that matters."

At eleven p.m., Sean, Dakota, and Angel walked into Dakota's office and shut the door. Samantha watched the door close. Solemn. Aware that the past she tried so hard to forget was about to be exposed. Discussed. And become part of her life now. Which would change things. Truth always does. But then again, it was time to face the beast.

Gabrielle and Jade didn't chat to fill the silence or ask questions. They pampered her instead. Gave her the spa treatment and painted her fingernails and toenails. Brushed and braided her hair. Made her fancy coffee. Sat with her on the porch.

Every hour or so, Angel came out for more coffee for them, and returned to the office.

About two a.m., Samantha walked to the front window and looked across the Calcasieu River at Gabrielle's family home. Samantha thought of the danger Gabrielle had been in last year. Bad. Terrifying. But the task force had saved her. A nightmare with a good ending. So that's what Samantha wanted now - a good end to her nightmare.

She glanced at Gabrielle, and said, "What made you so strong when evil stared you in the face?"

Gabrielle looked across the river with her, remembering, and said, "Dakota prepared me. He reminded me that God had equipped me with skills that I needed to survive. He reminded me that it would never be over for any of my family if I didn't fight."

Samantha said, "I was crazy proud of you. Scared for you, but proud."

"Fear changes to courage when it's time to fight. And you're a warrior now. Whoever is out there...is in trouble this time. Believe that."

At three a.m., the women sat on the staircase not far from Dakota's office. The door opened, and Sean stepped out. He took Samantha by the hand and led her outside. When the door closed behind them, he picked her up and held her. Face buried in her neck as she held on to him. The fury and pain in him swarmed like bees. He could only imagine what she had struggled with all this time. It all made sense now. All of it.

Samantha was sad for his inner turmoil. But she also felt relief knowing that no matter what - he had her. He loved her. And he would fight for her. He sat with her in a rocking chair. Tucking her tight in his embrace. Protective and ready to kill dragons.

He could feel her slight trembling and groaned. She was small even now...and to think at sixteen...it was a miracle she had even survived. Hiding her face in his neck, Samantha's tears began to fall. Sean felt them and wanted to kill the man that hurt her. A dozen times. A hundred. But he knew that even then, it would never be enough.

In time, they found peace in each other's arms. Samantha heard the night sounds. The river. The crickets. Owls. She smiled...the sounds of life. She looked at Sean and he kissed her so sweet.

He said, "If I could take it from you, I would."

"I know."

"Are you ready to tell us the rest of it?"

"Yeah. Let's get started."

They went back inside, and the others were waiting in the kitchen.

Samantha hugged Gabrielle and Jade, then said, "Please, go get some sleep. I need to finish this with the guys. Thank you for being exactly what I needed tonight. I love you."

She turned to the guys and said, "Come on. Let's do it."

And Sean smiled for the first time in hours. Prosecutor Rutledge took charge.

In the office, they had set up a large dry erase board with a drawn picture of the crime scene. A collage of the picture evidence was up on the TV. Samantha looked at what was visible. The waterfall. Her best friend dead. And then her...naked and critically wounded. And a photo of a man in handcuffs. An identical twin. Now she contemplated what they didn't know. She asked for a red and black marker and another dry erase board.

They got what she needed and watched her. She drew the large outline of a man's body on the second white board.

She said, "Spencer confessed to killing Mary Beth, and my attempted rape and murder at the waterfall. However, I don't think it was Spencer at the waterfall."

And there it was. Maxwell – Spencer's identical twin. They listened as she laid out her case.

She explained, "I was sixteen years old. Barely alive when I was rushed to surgery. I had been so sick I almost didn't make it to the sentencing a couple of months later. I lead to this - no one asked me identification specifics. Ever. That said, after Spencer was sentenced, Maxwell attempted to apologize to me for his brother.

"I was horrified since it was like looking at the other one. I realized he liked my fear and the look in his eyes changed. He snarled, 'I almost had you. I'll be back.' And since I was already an emotional and physical mess, I was worse after.

"I don't know why I never told anyone what he said. And I don't know why no one asked. The only thing I can think of is that under the circumstances, it was creepy for everyone because they both looked like the criminal."

Sean and Dakota glanced at each other. They convicted the wrong twin.

Sean said, "Spencer's quick confession obviously hid any question of identity for those in authority. It was all over the news – a shock to the community. But that's no excuse. Evidence wasn't verified. Not even by the defense. So, let's talk identification. What evidence specifics can you recall during the attack?"

Samantha walked to the body outline and using the red marker, drew a line on the lower right side of the abdomen. She said, "Rescuers made it to me barely in time to prevent the rape, but his pants were down. The scar was clearly visible to me. Probably an appendectomy scar."

Then she drew a double red line on the right forearm and said, "He tried to shove his arm in my mouth to stop the screaming. I bit him. Hard. Blood went everywhere. He would have to have a scar. A deep one."

They nodded. Scars were great evidence. Irrefutable if the other brother didn't have them.

She said, "One more thing. The only item missing from the crime scene was my panties. Pink. I'm assuming he took a trophy."

They all knew Maxwell had them.

She continued, "Confirming scars should be easy for us with Spencer in prison. They're required to keep a record. If we're lucky, Maxwell's medical records might mention if he has any. The bad thing is, we can't compare DNA between Maxwell and Spencer since we all know twin DNA differences take extensive research. And results aren't even allowed in court yet as forensic evidence.

"But..." she paused. "What if he kept doing it and there are other victims? Other DNA opportunities."

Dakota said, "A serial killer?"

"He was young when he attacked me. Vicious. Savage. Wild. With a raging hunger. What if I was just his first? A hunger like that doesn't just fade."

Sean looked at the evidence and said, "Is there anything he said during the attack? Anything that was a weird thing to say?"

She looked at the pictures of her broken body at the base of the waterfall, and said, "He rambled about me being blonde. He wanted me because I was a blonde...everywhere."

Sean knew information like that was hard to share. But she did it.

He said, "I think you just found a way to search for victims. He's obsessed with blondes. And...unfortunately, you're right. It's doubtful that he stopped with you. It probably made it worse."

She said, "I found out years ago, he had moved to Chicago. Once I became a lawyer and thought about what he said, I hired a private investigator. Knowing where he was, helped, and I didn't have to be afraid I would run into him. But he said he would be back, so it was always in the back of my mind. And he isn't a tall gangly nineteen-year-old anymore."

She pointed at his picture on the screen. "He's a big guy. Muscular. Tough. An attorney for heaven's sake. He's why I have a concealed carry permit now."

Dakota said, "Ok. He's back. So, we'll keep you covered. Now we need to search for other victims and check your theory."

Sean said, "Maxwell would never expect that."

Angel said, "In that case, he would feel invincible. His brother in prison for the first crime, and other victims back around Chicago."

Samantha said, "I hope I'm wrong, but I don't think so."

Sean said, "You need to be an agent, Samantha."

Dakota said, "Yep. She has FBI written all over her."

Sean said, "Speaking of FBI," and picked up the phone.

***

The phone was answered on the first ring, "Director Washington here."

"Sir, this is Sean Nash. I'm in a meeting with Dakota, Prosecutor Rutledge from Baton Rouge, and Angel, a Private Investigator from New Orleans. Somethings come up. We have an old case that may not be solved, which leaves a serial killer in Louisiana. He just moved back from Chicago."

"Give me the outline."

"Prosecutor Rutledge is the live victim. It involves a murder, and attempted rape and murder from twelve years ago. An identical twin is in Angola prison. The actual offender is believed to be the other twin. And we believe he's returned for Samantha. He has a blonde obsession. There could be a trail of unsolved blonde cases around Chicago. And to make it worse, he's an attorney now, which opens a lot of doors for him. Dakota just emailed you the case file, the suspect's info, and new evidence we need researched."

"Ok. It's a go for surveillance on the twin not in prison. Find him. Follow him. Dakota you are back on duty. Sean, you are in charge."

The Director said, "Prosecutor?"

"Yes, sir."

"I remember you from Gabrielle's case. We will get him. Stay with the team."

"Thank you, Director."

"Sean and Dakota, keep me in the loop and go to bed. You will be busy tomorrow."

44

Chapter 8

The next morning, deep in the woods north of Baton Rouge, the heat woke Shadow Man out of a sound sleep. He stomped naked over to the window air conditioner and banged on it a couple of times. The AC slowly rattled back to life. The landlord was lucky he had told him how to make it start up again.

He looked through the filthy window at his black BMW sitting outside. It certainly looked out of place in the middle of nowhere but hiding was necessary for now. All because he had a dark hunger for blondes. Twelve years ago, Samantha had opened his eyes to the woman of his dreams. That's when he learned how to feed that thing inside of him.

Deception had become simple through the years. He didn't look the part. That helped. He had money. That really helped. But the surrogates only tided him over, they never quenched the hunger. Memories of Samantha screaming under him at the top of the waterfall stirred the craving in him. He had come back to Louisiana to finish what he started.

It wouldn't be long.

Chapter 9

On the river in Lake Charles, Sean heard whispers in the kitchen. He opened his eyes to see King, Dakota's Bengal cat, staring at them from the top of the sofa where it lounged, flipping his tail. Samantha shifted in the crook of his arm, and he drew her closer, rubbing her back. Snuggling to kiss her neck.

She whispered, "Agent Man..."

His lips settled over hers in response. Then more voices came down the hall. So, kissing the tip of her nose, he said, "How about coffee?"

She stretched and smiled.

He said, "I'll be right back," and headed to the kitchen.

But Samantha scooped the cat in her arms and followed him. She stopped next to Dakota at the snack bar. He glanced at her, impressed at her inner strength, but still concerned she was ok.

To fire her up, he teased, "How tall are you anyway?"

She pinched him.

Dakota yelped and rubbed his arm. He said, "Well, you woke up on the feisty side of bed," and glanced at Sean with a wink.

Samantha knew he was picking and grinned.

Angel and Jade rounded the corner, and Jade said, "Morning! How's everyone?"

Gabrielle said, "Dakota and Samantha are sparring."

Angel said, "Who's winning?" Then noticed Dakota rubbing a red spot on his arm.

He said, "Never mind. Evidence noted."

Jade smiled at Samantha, and said, "You ok this morning?"

And Samantha realized that last night's sorrow was gone. And yes, she was good. Strong. Ready. And thrilled to be here with them.

She nodded and said, "I am. Really." Then asked, "Gabrielle, can we go to your place this morning? I need to talk to you and Jade so we can get past this and enjoy ourselves."

"You bet! One girl-talk coming up!"

An hour later, the guys readied a couple of Jet Skis for the women to ride across the river. They roared off and in less than a minute, coasted onto the sandbar.

***

Dakota turned to the guys and asked, "Who votes for bacon and eggs then a trail ride?"

Angel said, "Sounds like vacation to me."

Sean's stomach growled. He said, "Just cook, Dakota. Cook."

***

The ladies tied up the Jet Skis and walked uphill. The two-story house was mounted on twelve-foot piers. It was white with unpainted cedar storm shutters. Acadian style. There were decks on both floors. Once inside, they found a comfy spot to sit and talk.

Samantha faced them, and said, "Here goes. The case the guys reviewed relates to the scars on my stomach. I told you years ago it happened in an accident. But it was way more than that."

She stood and walked as she talked, "I was on a gymnast team in high school. One weekend we talked the coaches into taking us on a field trip. Something different. Exciting. And we didn't go far, just to the Angola prison craft fair and rodeo, north of St. Francisville, along the Mississippi River.

"The area where the craft fair was held was packed with public shoppers buying beautifully crafted items made by the prisoners. It was a strange feeling to be near special prisoners allowed to man their booths. While other prisoners were required to sell from behind a fence. But…it was cool. Interesting. Really fun.

"At least until two guys followed us around. Identical twins that were older than us. Tall and skinny. It was kind of flirty-funny at first but then got creepy. Weird. And the coaches ran them off by threatening to call the police. They disappeared and I forgot all about them.

"After we left Angola, we stopped by Woodriff Falls for a long hike before we headed home. I had always been fascinated by waterfalls and we had fun exploring. Taking pictures. Laughing. Cutting up. Just being young.

"When it was time to go, we followed the coaches down the trail toward the van. There were fifteen of us. Mary Beth and I brought up the rear. And like kids will do, we snuck off and ran back to the waterfall just so I could snap another picture."

She stopped and turned to the window, her mind traveling back to that day. She said, "Mary Beth and I were standing at the top ledge of the waterfall, talking while I took my picture. Then she screamed. I turned to see one of the twins from Angola running toward us. I froze in shock - wondering what he was doing. And Mary Beth charged him."

Her eyes filled with tears as she said, "And with no effort at all he slung her over the edge to the rocks and water below."

Gabrielle and Jade gasped in horror. Mouths covered. Eyes wide. Minds incredulous at the vicious mental picture.

Samantha ignored the tears sliding down her cheeks, and said, "As I watched Mary Beth fall, I screamed. Then he had me. Began to rip off my clothes. And to cut the story short, in moments I was totally naked in the woods with a crazy man. We fought. He dropped his pants. And then our group came screaming out of the woods just before he could rape me. He jumped up, enraged like I had never seen before, and threw me over the falls."

Tears of disbelief and despair trailed down Gabrielle and Jade's faces. Silent pain for Samantha evident.

Samantha wiped her face and sat on the coffee table in front of them, and said, "The cops were at the hospital when I woke after surgery. Mary Beth had died in the fall. I had broken ribs. A broken leg. A million cuts and bruises. And four abdominal puncture wounds from being impaled on a small tree.

"The twins were picked up since the group recognized the guy from Angola. Spencer confessed and pled guilty. He was sentenced to life in prison, no parole, in Angola. After the sentencing hearing, the other twin made a comment to me that I didn't quite grasp fully at the time. But now…I believe…the wrong twin is in prison."

Gabrielle said raggedly, "No!"

Jade said, "Do you know where he is?"

Samantha said, "Yes. Sort of. I found out yesterday he's back in Baton Rouge. A lawyer, believe it or not. So…here we are. And I don't want to talk about it anymore. We all need a break. Laughter. Sarcasm. Jokes. Man talk. Please. Let's head to your trails."

Gabrielle said, "Come on!"

They grabbed something to drink and hit the garden trails filled with multi-level decks, treehouses, pot plants, obstacle courses, and swings. It didn't take long for laughter to echo through the woods. They made it halfway down the trail and climbed onto a large deck. They talked and laughed, and as usual, the talk turned to men.

Samantha said, "Jade, something seriously spicy was going on between you and Angel during the Salsa dance yesterday. Do you always dance like that?"

"Not exactly."

Gabrielle said, "What does that mean?"

"His touch was much hotter."

"You can say that again!"

After laughter eased, Jade said, "It's hard to explain. It just became more than dancing."

Samantha said, "Has he kissed you yet?"

"Not till last night."

"Well, how was it?"

"Passionately delicious. I know what it means now to get knocked off your feet."

Laughing, Gabrielle said, "I bet a hundred bucks he's just getting started."

"Yeah. Well, no bet needed."

Samantha turned to Gabrielle, and said, "You are the only one married. Was saving yourself till the honeymoon...really hard?"

They screamed in laughter. Then Gabrielle finally found her breath enough to answer, and said, "Perfect word choice. And yes, it was. But it gave back anticipation. Passion. Intimacy. And a desire for each other that spanned beyond the moment."

Then Gabrielle's phone rang, and she laughed.

***

She answered as the girls listened to a one-sided conversation, "Hey, Dakota."

Pause. Then she giggled and said, "I'm not surprised."

Laughing, she said, "We're having a great time. In fact, I was just talking about you."

Pause. She burst out laughing and said, "Well no, I kept that to myself."

Pause. "No. Keep riding. We're having fun."

***

After the call, Gabrielle said, "They can hear us all the way across the river."

Samantha said, "They want to know our secrets."

Jade said, "No doubt at all."

Gabrielle pointed at Samantha and said, "Ok, your turn. You who have left men floundering for years; how did Sean manage to get beyond your barrier?"

"Amazingly, he waited a year, letting me flirt and retreat all that time. But Thursday night he drew the line – and laid it out there. We...debated you might say. And I trust what he told me."

Gabrielle said, "Because you love him."

"I have for a long time."

Jade said, "There's no doubt he loves you."

Smiling, Samantha said, "And he's very, very, good at it."

50

A short time later, a silver car flickered through the trees as it drove down the driveway, then stopped at the house. Gabrielle, Samantha, and Jade jogged out of the woods toward the car. A woman with long copper hair got out and opened the back door.

Gabrielle called as they drew closer, "Hi there!"

The woman turned with a child in her arms. Smiling, she said, "Hello!"

Samantha glanced at Jade, and they said *wow* with only widened eyes. The woman was gorgeous. Silky copper hair. Dark eyes that were almost ebony. Fair flawless skin and an amazing smile that stopped you in your tracks.

Smiling, Gabrielle reached her, and exclaimed, "My goodness. You and your son are beautiful!"

And the little boy was a bundle of adorable. Olive skin. Straight dark hair. Dark eyes. He looked to be about three years old – and looked nothing like his mother.

The woman laughed and said, "Thank you! A greeting doesn't get any better than that. And right back at you! All of you."

As Samantha and Jade occupied the little one's attention, Gabrielle, said, "What brings you way out here on the river? I don't get a lot of people driving by, are you looking for someone?"

"Actually, yes. I'm looking for you."

At Gabrielle's surprise she continued, "I'm Raven Macawi. And this is my son, Lance. I have quite a story to tell you."

"Well, come on in. Let's visit where it's cool. You have no idea how much we love a good story."

Samantha and Jade settled with Lance at the table with snacks, paper, and colors so the two women could talk. Gabrielle handed Raven a soft drink and motioned to the seating area.

Raven said, "The only way to begin the story, is tell you that our grandfathers were very close friends."

With a hint of puzzlement, Gabrielle said, "Which grandfather?"

"Your ancestor. Pirate Jean Lafitte."

Chapter 10

Shocked, Gabrielle exclaimed, "What! Who's your grandfather?"

"The Atakapa warrior, Wolf."

Moved to tears, Gabrielle wrapped her in a hug. Heart overflowing with wonder. It had come full circle for Lafitte and Wolf after all these years - through their granddaughters.

Wiping tears, Gabrielle said, "How did you learn of me? All I knew of Wolf was his name."

"I've known the story of them all my life. But I didn't know about you until the news report last year. Then I researched and even read the book Dakota wrote."

"But how did you learn the original story to begin with?"

"After Wolf died, your grandmother wrote a letter to my grandfather's family. My ancestors passed the story down as a song through the generations. Eventually the Atakapa tribes left Louisiana and scattered, joining other tribes to survive. Wolf's family headed north. They settled and married into the Sioux nation."

Gabrielle glanced at Lance, who was as dark as his mother was fair.

Raven smiled and said, "My father's an Irish preacher. I look like his side of the family. My mother's half Sioux – a nurse. They met at a hospital in Minnesota. They are missionaries overseas now. But in keeping with tradition, my mother taught me many of the songs of our people. Including the one of Wolf and your family. I will begin teaching them to Lance too. His father was also half Sioux."

Gabrielle sighed at the 'was.'

Somber for a moment, Raven said, "My husband was Beau. Beau Macawi. He died on a camping trip before Lance was born."

"Oh, Raven. That had to be so hard. But looking at Lance, you've done a wonderful job of raising him. He's happy. Healthy. You're an incredible mother."

Raven noticed Gabrielle lay a hand on her stomach, and asked, "When are you due?"

Surprised at the question, Gabrielle said, "How..."

"I'm an RN; I saw your protective movement. It's automatic when you're expecting."

They shared the smile of mothers, and Gabrielle said, "She's due close to Christmas."

Lance interrupted and wanted to go play outside, so they headed downstairs. Walking downhill toward the water, Gabrielle pointed to the log cabin on the other side of the river and said, "Dakota and I live there."

Raven said, "Log cabins are great. There are many up north. Your Acadian place here is wonderful too. My goal is to find a place for Lance and me on the river. I want to raise him here in Louisiana."

"That's exciting! We can help you."

Then pulling out her phone, she said, "Let me text Dakota that you're here. His brother, Sean, and Jade's partner, Angel, are with him. They'll want to meet you."

In minutes an engine started, and the men rode across in a bay boat. The women waited at the sandbar, laughing as Lance tried to get in the river. Repeatedly.

When the boat landed, the men joined them, grinning themselves at the wriggling little boy in the red-haired woman's arms.

Gabrielle said, "Guys, be prepared for a shock. I'd like you to meet Wolf's granddaughter, Raven Macawi, and her son, Lance."

Exclaiming in surprise, the guys introduced themselves, intrigued at this turn of events. After shaking hands with Raven, Dakota noticed the little boy's awestruck stare.

Raven said, "I'm sorry, Dakota. Sean. Forgive us for staring. Your features are strikingly Native American, although I had read that. It really is amazing."

Dakota smiled, and said, "Ah. You read the book."

"I did." Then her son pointed across the river at Gabrielle's shepherd on the dock and said, "Momma! Sunka!" and squirmed to get down.

Recognizing the Sioux word for dog, Sean said, "Your son is Sioux?"

"He is. From both his father and me. I'm Sioux and Atakapa from my mother. This red hair came from my Irish father. Rarely does anyone recognize the Indian in me."

Sean said, "But I bet anyone that looks deeper will know."

Nodding, she smiled – indeed they would. Then her son touched Sean's hand.

Sean knelt and said, "Hi."

Lance's dark eyes roamed Sean's face. His little hand softly touched his cheek, then he glanced at his mother and said, "Look Momma. Like daddy."

Raven swallowed the quick lump in her throat and squatted beside him. She said, "Yes, sweetie. Like his pictures."

He nodded, then distracted by a frog, ran to play.

After a confirming glance with Gabrielle, Dakota said, "You're a widow?"

"Since before he was born."

Her words held an unspoken wealth of meaning.

Gabrielle touched her arm, and said, "You know, Raven, I haven't asked, "Do you have a place to stay?"

"Sure. I have reservations in a hotel until I find the right place to rent or lease. Long term, my goal is to buy or build a place on the river. This was just my first stop. I couldn't wait to meet you."

Dakota winked at Gabrielle's quick glance at him. Yes.

Gabrielle said, "Please stay with us. It would give you time to find a place, and us time to get to know each other. We would love it!"

Before long, they were all back across the river. Dakota and Gabrielle helped Raven and Lance get settled inside. Angel and Jade took off on the Jet Skis. And Sean and Samantha stood on the deck and watched them disappear around the bend.

Sean put his arms around her and said, "I finally have you to myself. I've shared you with one, two, three…wait, six people, a cat, and a dog. Just today."

She smiled teasingly and said, "Ah, what do you want to do with me this time?"

"Be careful how you frame the question, Counselor. You're looking at a very hungry man."

She said, "Let me rephrase. Show me what you want, Agent Man."

He kissed and lifted her as she wrapped around him. Groaning, he took all he could get - but wanted more than he could have. Samantha was lost in him. His feel. His touch. His strength. He drove her wild.

After a long while, he looked at her. Flushed cheeks. Breathless. He said, "You're so mine."

She tightened her legs around him and whispered, "I can't believe I made us wait so long. You feel—"

He groaned, hands squeezing her hips. But this was getting too hot. And too public. They were on the dock. Boats could pass. The others were just in the house.

With hungry eyes, he said "We've got to cool this down. Give me something else to think about."

As she slid down to stand on shaky legs, she said, "Then…how about we go for a ride on the stallion."

Touching her well-kissed lips, he said, "We'll still be hot in the saddle, but I want that ride."

Passion's flame eased off as they readied the stallion. They mounted and rode quietly through the woods along the river. Sean's arms held her against him. Her hands covered his. Love intwining them in emotional and physical intimacy. Safe. Beautiful.

Sean could tell Samantha's talk had gone well with Gabrielle and Jade. She was relaxed. Happy. And the power of the past was crumbling off her. She would find she was much larger than what she had feared, and way more powerful now.

Samantha closed her eyes in a moment of sweet bliss. Her world had completely changed in two days. While it had begun with a paralyzing fear of rape, now she embraced...no, wait...encouraged passion with Sean.

Sean stopped the stallion at the top of a bluff, and they looked down the river. Wrapping his arms around her, he said, "You seem adjusted to all you've been through in the last couple of days. But...if you want to talk about anything. Vent. Share. Explain. Or just tell me anything, I'm here, a good listener."

"Good listener doesn't begin to describe you. You can read me. And that's cheating."

Smiling, he said, "So speaks the prosecutor. Come on, we both have our skills. But don't evade the question. Is there anything you want to talk about? I won't harp on it, but right here, right now, I want to open the door, ok?"

Samantha knew he meant her medical records. Her inability to have children. Her scars to prove it. But she knew he knew, so that was enough. She wasn't hiding it from him, but she was not talking about it. Ever. That part of her could never exist and she wasn't going there.

She turned in the saddle and looked at him. Direct, she said, "You know what happened. You helped me face the terror. Loved me enough to fight for what we have. So, for now, that's all. Can you handle that? Leaving the rest where it is?"

"We'll go at whatever speed you need, Samantha. Nothing else matters to me."

An hour later, the black stallion raced across the field as they returned. Their laughter carried on the wind. Sean pulled to a stop near the barn at the same time Jet Skis slid to the dock. Both couples waved at each other.

They joined up and Jade said, "Hey, I'm positive we saw Dragon not far from here."

Thinking of the huge beast, Samantha said, "Ugh. The alligator of nightmares. What did you think of him, Angel?"

"I can't help but be impressed at the sheer size of him. He has survived a long time. And I was extremely grateful to be on a Jet Ski – faster than him in the event we suddenly appeared tasty."

Sean said, "Right. We'll never know how many people he has helped...let's say, disappear over the years. Gobbled up like secrets along the river. At the bottom of the river. Or in the belly of the beast."

Jade said, "That thought's terrifying. I love the river. I do. And all activities *on the* river, I am good to go. But not in it. I prefer to swim in a pool. Blue. Clear. Nothing waiting to eat me."

***

That night for dinner, Dakota and Gabrielle arranged for a wiener roast. The guys got the firepit ready and the chairs setup around it. The women laid the hotdogs and fixings out in the kitchen. Sean lit the fire at dusk, and in a little over an hour, they had cooked, eaten, and cleaned up the kitchen.

Everyone relaxed around the crackling fire as the southern night embraced them. Crickets chirped. The river lapped the bank. Owls hooted. And Lance chatted to the dog as they laid next to each other on the ground.

Dakota glanced at Raven. As an agent, he was curious. Well, more than curious. It was highly unusual for a woman to take her child and leave family and friends to travel far away for a new life. Around strangers, even though it was an ancestral area. And she

57

didn't offer anything else about herself. He looked at Sean and nodded to Raven. Sean nodded. He got it. He had questions too.

Gabrielle caught the unspoken communication between the brothers and added her own warning glance at Dakota that clearly said, stop it. Don't quiz her.

Dakota gave her the agent look and turned to Raven. He had to know. They were in their home and would be in their lives now.

He asked, "Raven, what made you decide to move to Louisiana?"

"I've always been intrigued with the stories, swamps, and wetlands. The food even. I don't remember a time when I didn't want to come here."

"I'm sure your family and friends didn't want you to leave."

Gabrielle warned, "Dakota."

Raven said, "No, Gabrielle. He's right to question me. I expected it from a family with FBI agents. I'm not offended. What do you want to know, Dakota?"

"Are you running from something?"

"You could call it that. After my husband died, I had trouble with a man that insisted I marry him. It was a difficult time, but he's no longer in the picture. And my parents are in Africa. So, we needed a fresh start. New people. A new life. It's not healthy for Lance and me to live only with memories."

And not one person around the fire disagreed with her.

Dakota said, "I understand. What about the man you had trouble with – where is he?"

"In prison. He won't be getting out."

"Good to hear. That takes care of my concerns. I appreciate you understanding. And let me assure you, we're glad you're here."

Samantha offered, "You'll love Louisiana. And I'm at attorney, so if I can help you with anything at all, just say the word."

Gabrielle said, "And I will help in any way you need. Including giving Lance a new friend to play with in December."

Raven said, "Thank you. All of you. It's more than a pleasure to be here. I'm thrilled."

Sean said, "Well, let's call it destiny then. Welcome home. I know your grandfather is proud."

Lance interrupted with a squeal, and Raven watched her son run as fast as his little legs could carry him.

She scooped him up and he asked breathlessly, "Momma, pleeease play the drum. Please. Please. Please."

Her heart melted as she looked into his beautiful pleading eyes. He loved the drums. She didn't have the heart to tell him no.

Glancing at Gabrielle and the others, she asked, "Do you mind if I play the drum? Lance loves to dance around the fire, and I haven't played…well, in a long time. He misses it."

Thrilled, Gabrielle said, "Yes, of course! I can't wait myself!"

Lance followed Raven all the way to her car and back, whooping in excitement. Dakota and Sean smiled. This would be a rare treat since men usually played the drums. Raven sat in her chair and placed the leather drum between her knees.

The rhythmic beat took over the night. Lance began to do little stomps and turns around the fire. Obviously, doing what he had seen many times. Dakota and Sean glanced at each other, then stood, removing their shirts, and joined the little one. They danced.

Samantha stared at Sean. Gabrielle stared at Dakota. Their strong bodies were sweaty and bold in a magnificent way. Graceful power. Long hair swinging. Sexy. Warriors.

A good while later, drumbeats faded to silence, and the three Sioux warriors stood proud before the fire. The story told. Lance lifted his arms to Dakota to be held, and he picked him up. Raven closed her eyes, aching at the need of her son for a father. Tears dripped in the firelight.

Gabrielle touched her hand, and whispered, "God brought you here for a reason, Raven. All will be well. You'll see."

Sean walked toward Samantha, took her hand, and led her into the darkness. Once hidden from the others, he kissed her. Hungry. Wild. The beat still going inside of him. He licked her shoulder. Her neck. Lifting her up when her knees buckled. He buried his face in her stomach wanting her so bad he could taste her.

Chapter 11

Later that night, at Maison Lacour French Restaurant in Baton Rouge, Suzette laughed as she gazed at the handsome man sitting across from her. Who knew he would show up at her favorite attorney bar Thursday after work, much less, that they would hit it off so quick?

Seeing her smile, Wells reached across the table and squeezed her hand. Inwardly, he groaned - ready to go home. But he needed her. So, here he sat. He looked at his plate of grilled filet topped with crawfish tails in a spicy red butter sauce and picked up his knife. Glancing at Suzette dressed in cream silk and pearls, he wondered what she would look like splattered with blood.

They smiled at each other, and he took a bite of the steak - imagining.

Chapter 12

The next morning in Lake Charles, Samantha woke to shoulder caresses and neck kisses. She groaned and stretched in enjoyment as she glanced at Sean. He smiled and slid under the covers.

She burrowed in his arms and said, sleepily, "You snuck in my room, Agent Man."

Growling at the feel of her warmth, he said, "I used stealth."

She kissed his neck and whispered, "Your touch…kills me."

Pulling her face to his, he said, "Not exactly the word I would have chosen."

"Who cares, just kiss me."

He glanced at the side of the bed. She looked to see why. Little Lance stood there watching them. She squealed and ducked under the covers.

Dakota laughed.

Sean glanced at the door where Gabrielle, Dakota, and Raven stood.

Dryly, Sean said, "May I help you?"

Gabrielle grinned, trying not to laugh.

Appalled at her son's invasion of the couple, Raven said, "I'm so sorry, Sean. Lance followed you down the hall."

Sean picked up the boy and said, "Are you hunting me, little warrior?"

"Yes! I hunt you!"

Samantha laughed under the covers and stuck her head out.

Lance wanted down, so Sean set him on the bed. He crawled to Samantha, and touched her hair, mouth open in amazement.

He said, "Big white hair."

Everyone laughed while Samantha grabbed Lance and tickled him.

Then she climbed out of bed, and with as much dignity as possible, said, "Now, if all of you would please excuse me while I dress…"

Sean snatched a kiss on his way out.

Later, Samantha followed the smell of pancakes to the kitchen. Dakota opened his mouth to pick at her again and Sean elbowed him in the stomach. Samantha rewarded Sean with a sexy smile. Then turned mean eyes on Dakota. Everyone laughed.

Angel said, "I feel like I'm in the audience of a sitcom. Thank you for a front row seat."

Samantha gave Angel a warning glance, and he laughed, hands up in surrender.

Jade said, "You better stop. She pinches hard."

Gabrielle said, "Behave, all of you. It's Sunday. Go sit down, pancakes are on the way. Lance's request."

They had just finished their last bites when four phone notifications dinged. Dakota, Gabrielle, Sean, and Samantha glanced at their phones.

Sean said, "Why would we receive the same text?"

***

They read:

Dear Honored Guest,

You are cordially invited to join Esquire, Jonathan Remington, Thursday, July 10th at seven o'clock in the evening for his Baton Rouge mayoral race fundraiser dinner. It will be a formal black and white affair aboard the American Harmony Riverboat.

The night will be an exciting opportunity to share support for a man that stands for the values of our great city. Please join us and bring a guest for fine dining, jazz, social hour, and a message for the future of Baton Rouge.

Please R.S.V.P. to J. Remington & Associates, 225.764.2000 extension 8.

***

Samantha exclaimed, "It's Jonathan's campaign! I've known him literally my whole life."

Gabrielle said, "I'm excited for him. I remembered him from LSU with you. But he also reached out to me last year after my attack. A super guy."

Dakota said, "He is. I've worked a few cases with him and will certainly support him."

Sean said, "He's impressive. We're gym buddies. He's also my personal attorney."

Samantha said, "Then come on. Let's all plan to go. It's what…only five days away."

After they agreed, Gabrielle and Samantha high-fived and said, "Formal dress up!"

Late morning, as the task force, they met in Dakota's office for a final review on Maxwell.

Dakota said, "We have full FBI authority to 1) Keep Samantha safe from Maxwell by any means. 2) Find and watch him. And 3) Search his past for possible rape/murder victims - while at the same time, determine if the wrong twin is in prison."

Sean said, "Samantha, we need to meet with the D.A. after you are finished in court tomorrow. He needs to know about Maxwell, your safety concerns, and possible work limitations."

She said, "I'll message him about a meeting."

Sean glanced at Angel and Jade, and said, "As investigators, are you able to work at the ranch with us on the task force?"

Samantha said, "Wait. Why at the ranch?"

"We need to limit your exposure to Maxwell. We'll have more control in a secluded location than in the highly populated areas of Baton Rouge – like your apartment. We can get what you need from your place tomorrow. After that, I'll be your bodyguard until Maxwell is no longer a threat."

Angel motioned to Sean and said, "Jade and I will make a few calendar changes so we can work from the ranch. But we do need to gather our equipment from New Orleans and meet you back at the ranch. Say...mid-afternoon. We can push it."

Dakota said, "We all need to remain clear that the research angle for Maxwell is confidential until evidence is found. Which means, even when we find him, he is free to come and go as he pleases. We research and watch him until there is an actual criminal case. And, Samantha, can you come with me to Angola to see his twin? We need to ask about the scars and find out why Maxwell is visiting him after all this time."

"Sure. Whatever you need."

Sean said, "I'll need twelve hours to program the drones for surveillance and security. Hopefully, we will have eyes on him soon.

Angel said, "So what's the FBI intel plan on the serial angle?"

Sean said, "The FBI is digging into blonde victims around the Chicago area for the past twelve years that fit a similar victimology on Samantha's attack. They'll forward the info. We will search through it for a link to Maxwell."

Everyone nodded. The task force was a go.

Dakota's phone rang as they headed toward the den. He didn't recognize the number.

***

He answered the call, "Dakota Nash."

A male voice, heavy with accent, said, "This is Dr. Ramos with the hospital in Sao Paulo, Brazil. Your brother, Adam, was in an accident."

Dakota's heart skipped a beat. He hit speaker and grabbed Sean's arm.

He asked the only question that mattered, and said, "Is he alive?"

Sean's gaze locked with Dakotas in alarm, and the others froze at the unexpected question.

The Doctor said, "He's alive. He fell off the side of a mountain trying to help a patient. His right knee was badly broken. Then while he was on the ground, an anaconda attacked him."

Everyone groaned, and Dakota asked, "What's his status?"

"He went through surgery two days ago. His right leg has pins, and he will need physical therapy - but he should get back to normal. Our concern is the snake bite damage. It bit the foot on the broken leg. He didn't need anti-venom, but anacondas have a vicious bite with teeth like razors. The foot is ripped up and inflammation may take a long time to abate. But he is stable enough now to fly home. Can someone come get him? He may need care for a while."

"I will leave today. May I talk to him?"

"He is sedated – but don't let that alarm you. It keeps him comfortable, and from hurting himself."

"Will you tell him I'm coming?"

"Yes. And I want you to know, the medical mission group he was with saved his life. He wouldn't have survived the trip to the hospital without them."

"Jesus."

The Doctor said, "Exactly."

***

Dakota and Sean stepped into a grateful-he-was-alive hug after the call. Gabrielle and Samantha joined them.

A few seconds later, Dakota frowned thinking of the case, and said, "Sean—"

Sean said, "Stop. Just go get him. Don't think about anything else. We have the task force plan. Angel and I can share your part and I can get more agents if we need them. Tell Adam I'll see him when he returns. And keep in touch."

Dakota turned to Gabrielle and said, "I need you to call Mom and Dad to come. I will bring Adam here to our house. We'll get whatever medical care he needs. And once he's settled, I'll meet Sean in Baton Rouge."

Raven interrupted, and said, "I'm a registered nurse. I can take care of whatever medical needs he has."

Dakota and Sean sighed in relief, and group-hugged her, grateful beyond words.

Then Sean pushed Dakota toward his office, and said, "Go schedule your flights and pack."

As Dakota disappeared around the corner, Gabrielle touched Sean's chest, and said, "We've got things here. My parents will help Raven and I get ready for Adam until your parents arrive. Just please take care of Samantha. Keep Maxwell away from her."

***

In less than an hour, Angel was driving back to Baton Rouge. Sean, finally quiet with his thoughts of the accident, prayed as he looked out the passenger window. Adam wasn't FBI like Dakota and him. But he was an amazing man who wanted to save the world and rescue everyone. He was truly the best of them. A picture flashed through his mind of Adam broken on the ground in the jungle. In unimaginable pain as he watched a giant snake attack him. Sean's stomach twisted. A second later his phone dinged with a text.

***

Dakota: I leave Houston at four p.m. Will get to Adam by two a.m.

Sean: Let me know when you see him.

Dakota: Mom and Dad will be here by morning.

Sean: When do you and Adam leave Brazil?

Dakota: Nine a.m. tomorrow. In Houston by eight p.m. In Lake Charles by eleven p.m.

Sean grimaced: Hard trip.

Dakota: Yeah. I'll see you Tuesday.

***

Sean glanced at the others, and said, "Dakota will have Adam in Lake Charles by tomorrow night late. I just want him home."

66

Angel said, "Yeah, I get that, man."

Samantha leaned up from the back seat and slid her hand down Sean's shoulder to rest on his chest. She felt his heartbeat. He laid his hand over hers. A few minutes later, he began to talk about the case. He had to protect the woman he loved and catch a killer.

They crossed the eighteen-mile-long twin Interstate 10 bridge over the Atchafalaya Basin early afternoon. And the Mississippi River bridge in Baton Rouge thirty minutes later. Then turning north out of the city, they followed Highway 61 to the ranch turnoff.

Sean glanced at Angel and said, "What time do you think you'll make it back to the ranch?"

Angel said, "Between four and five, depending on traffic."

"Ok. I've got to program and test the drones. They need to be running by morning at the latest."

Samantha said, "When we find Maxwell, how do you operate surveillance?"

"We'll station a surveillance team at a distance, camouflaged. I'll use several drones of different styles and sizes. The goal is to watch and not engage. Maxwell shouldn't know we're there. I just work with the situation based on how it plays out. It isn't always by the book. I have flexibility to fly them where I want."

Minutes later, Sean and Samantha watched Angel head back down the driveway to New Orleans. They heard singing in the barn.

Sean said, "Let drop our bags on the patio. That's Kerry. I want you to meet him."

"Oh my gosh, his voice is amazing."

"He's shocking in a lot of ways. You'll see."

Just then, a big man – no, a huge man in jeans and a red shirt walked out of the barn. He stopped singing when he saw them and smiled.

Sean said, "Hey, Kerry. How's it going?"

Kerry's shockingly deep voice said, "I figured you'd be rolling in pretty soon," and he glanced at Samantha with a grin.

Sean motioned to them, and said, "Samantha, meet Kerry. Kerry…Samantha."

Smiling, Samantha looked at Kerry's dark black skin and bright blue eyes, and said, "Hi! I've heard some great things about you. And your voice is fabulous."

Flashing a stunning smile back at her, Kerry leaned against the fence and said, "Thank you! I've heard some pretty amazing things about you as well. Glad to meet you. And Sean, you weren't exaggerating one bit, she is one gorgeous woman."

Sean winked at Samantha's quick grin, and said, "Oh yeah."

Samantha turned a quizzical gaze on Kerry. Sean chuckled. He knew the questions would come.

She asked, "How tall are you?"

He laughed, looking at her petite frame, and said, "I might ask the same question about you."

After they laughed, he said, "I'm only six-foot-six. What about you?"

"I am five-foot-two, but I act much taller – you'll see."

After more laughs, Samantha eyed him again with blatant curiosity.

She asked, "Where did you get those crystal blue eyes?"

Kerry shrugged, used to the question, and said, "No one will tell me."

Samantha laughed delightedly, then said, "We're going to be great friends."

He chuckled and high-fived her. Gently.

Sean smiled. He knew they would hit it off. He said, "How are the horses?"

Kerry said, "Beautiful and healthy. I think your stallion likes the new mare a great deal."

Sean chuckled, and said, "I just bet he does."

Then changing the subject, Sean said, "Kerry, I need a favor. A big one."

Without hesitation, Kerry said, "Name it."

"We think Samantha's in danger. A joint task force has been set up to work from here at the ranch. But this morning we found out

Adam was severely injured and had surgery in Brazil. Dakota is about to fly out to bring him home."

Kerry's big brow furrowed, as he said, "Man. That's rough news all the way around. I'm glad to see Samantha is safe with you. But is Adam going to be alright?"

"Yes, thank God. Though it will take time and medical care. As for the task force, you need to know that the two private investigator friends that just dropped us off, will be returning later today. Angel and Jade. And the favor is that since Dakota is out for a few days, I need another man I can trust here at the ranch. To keep an eye out for trouble that may come calling."

They fist-bumped as Kerry, said, "I got you. I'm your man."

"Thanks. There's room to sleep in the house or in the barn apartment. Whichever you prefer."

"Perhaps I would be better served out here. I'm a light sleeper, and the horses would warn me if something was close."

Sean said, "Good thought. Keep something handy in case you need a weapon. I wish I could give you a gun, but we know that's not possible because of the felony."

"Don't worry about a gun. I'm big as a tank. I'll keep a few things handy as a weapon in the barn."

"Ok. And no argument, you eat meals and hang with us. Anything you need is in the house, so make yourself at home. Just holler when you come in, so I know who's inside. You know where the key is."

"Man don't worry about feeding me. I'll grab a few things. I'll be fine with snacks."

Samantha drawled, "Right...you grew that tall just nibbling."

Kerry chuckled, and said, "There's that sassy prosecutor you told me about."

Samantha glanced at Sean with raised eyebrows, and said, "Really? That's how you described me?"

"Come on...you know I'm into sassy."

Kerry laughed with them, and said, "Just in case you want to know, I'm a good cook. How about I man the stove for meals?"

Sean said, "That's the best news I've had all day!"

In minutes, Sean was in his drone workroom/office with Samantha.

He said, "I prefer you to work in here with me where I can see you. My desk is yours. Help yourself. Let me know if you need anything."

"No problem. I'm quiet, so you won't even notice I'm here. I'll start work on the prison interview."

She glanced at all the monitors, laptops, and technical equipment on the walls and counters around the room. Dozens of drones were lined up like a small army. She glanced at Sean and remembered Dakota's nickname for him – Drone Master.

She said, "You're brilliant."

He winked and said, "Drone Master sounds cooler."

Late afternoon, Samantha stretched, cramped from working on her computer. She turned to look at Sean. All his computer monitors showed her. A drone hovered nearby staring at her. Several more sat with a blinking green light on his workbench.

Samantha said, "I'm being stalked."

Sean grinned and said, "They're amazing to work with really. Flying robots that obey my every command."

Samantha said, "Anything?"

"Anything they are built and instructed to do." Then picking up a controller, he said, "Stay still. Close your eyes. And listen to my voice."

Grinning, she closed her eyes.

He said, "Imagine me close to you. Touching distance."

She felt the hair by her neck move but she didn't hear anything.

Continuing, he whispered, "My lips are close. I'm breathing on you," and a gentle puff of air blew on her neck. Almost like a breath.

She gasped and opened her eyes. Sean stood in front of her, but a drone hovered near her left ear.

Smiling, he picked the drone out of the air, then nuzzled and kissed the same spot on her neck before returning to his bench.

He said, "I can fly it that close to someone and they never know."

"That's unreal. Do all the drones have the same technical abilities?"

"Just the basics. I've created adaptations for special search and rescue drones that I want to try out today."

"That's remarkable."

"It's a work in progress. The only negative is that steering or directing keeps me behind the scenes since I determine their next move. At least until more people can man them, or I teach them to problem solve."

"I'm in awe."

He slipped his arms around her and whispered, "Awe...works for me."

A door opened and shut, and they heard, "It's me!"

Sean kissed her softly, then said, "Hey, Kerry, we'll be right out."

They joined him in the den and Kerry said, "I just came to see if there is anything I can help with."

Sean said, "Actually...yes. I'd like to make test runs on my drones and could really use both of you. It would save me lots of time. Then I want to get some eyes in the sky as quick as possible. We don't know where the bad guy is yet. And I don't like that at all."

Chapter 13

Wells killed the car outside Suzette's townhouse in Baton Rouge. His head pounded with a raging headache. He hadn't pegged her as a chatterbox and would prefer to shove her out the car door and drive away, but he had to suck it up for a few more days. That made her a very lucky woman. Now anyway.

So, he smiled and walked her to the front door like she expected.

She faced him with a smile, and said, "I can make us a quick cup of coffee before you head home if you like."

"You read my mind - thank you."

She unlocked the door, disarmed the security system, and motioned to the den.

She said, "Please. Make yourself comfortable. It won't take me long to make the coffee."

After glancing around the room, he didn't see anything impressive about her taste in homes or decor. Then he noticed a long-haired white cat curled up in the corner of the sofa. He jumped at it, scaring it half to death, and it hissed and ran up the stairs. Grinning he sat in the warm spot where the cat had been.

Suzette returned to the den with their coffee and sat on the sofa facing him. He took a sip and glanced at her silently. Oddly. She felt a sudden twinge of unease. Where had that come from?

Wells said, "I need to tell you something…well, terrible."

She tucked her hair behind her ear, a habit when she was uncomfortable, and said, "What do you mean, terrible?"

Leaning wearily against the back of the sofa, he ran his hand through his hair, and said, "My brother is in prison for murder."

Surprised. No, shocked really, Suzette gazed at him with compassion – understanding his use of the word terrible now. Incarceration of any kind was always hard on the family. She touched his hand in understanding.

Wells continued, "He killed a woman and attacked another a long time ago. It was as bad as you can imagine. It has taken me years to sort it all out in my mind."

She nodded. They were both lawyers. She got how bad it must have been.

He said, "But that's enough of that. I didn't mean to end our day like this. I just figured you would rather know. Let me make up for it - we can go out for dinner tomorrow night—"

Suzette interrupted him, and said, "Wait – that reminds me! I have a work dinner tomorrow night with the D.A. and other staff attorneys. Please, come with me. I would love to introduce you to them and break you into Baton Rouge law socially."

He smiled and slipped his arm around her, and said, "I wouldn't miss it for anything. Thank you."

She melted. He kissed her softly, then walked to the door. He stepped outside and glanced back at her.

He said, "Be sure and lock the door behind me. It's not safe these days."

The door closed and she locked it. Then leaned against it. She couldn't wait till tomorrow night.

Chapter 14

Angel checked the time. They'd left New Orleans an hour ago and were about to take Highway 61 northbound out of Baton Rouge toward the ranch. The traffic bottle-necked suddenly by Southern University and he hit the brakes, then maneuvered swiftly out of the crazy traffic.

Jade watched Angel's quick response. Hands firmly on the steering wheel. Capable. Strong. And remembered his touch and kiss on the sailboat just two days ago. She bit her lip and glanced at him. Black hair. Green eyes. Luscious Latin. She was in trouble and wanted to kick herself. Or maybe not.

He caught her unguarded gaze and pulled into the Made to Go Truckstop parking lot. Pulling behind a group of trees, he stopped.

She said, "What—"

Glancing at her, he said, "Stay right there," and got out of the car.

She watched as he came around. She got out just before he reached her, and he never slowed down; he was kissing her before his arms were all the way around her. Pressed against the car.

Jade couldn't believe she was doing this in public - but wrapped her arms around him even as she thought it. Angel swore she was honey. Pure sweet honey. When he finally lifted his lips, he was ready to start over again.

She said, "Angel…I…listen…we've got to stay focused. For work. I mean it."

He kissed her, silencing her, then whispered, "This is work. I am focused. We're multitasking. Besides, you wanted this. You can't lie to me. And this is only kiss two anyway."

She felt him against her. Lingering there. Making his point. It was so much more personal than any Salsa they had ever danced.

She whispered, "This is way more than a kiss."

"Oh, honey, you bet it is."

***

About twenty-five minutes later, they turned into the ranch driveway. When they rolled to a stop, the door of the house opened and Sean, Samantha, and a large black guy stepped out.

Sean was pulling a cart with equipment on it and waved. He said, "Hey there! Great timing. We're just about to field-test the drones."

Angel said, "I have been dying to see this."

Sean said, "Come meet Kerry. He takes care of the horses when I'm gone and will give us a hand protecting Samantha for a while."

Jade looked up at the mountain of a man and said, "Wow. You're impressive. I'm Jade. Blade sisters with Samantha."

Kerry, smiling, raised his eyebrows, then said, "Hi Jade. So, tell me, what is a blade sister?"

Samantha and Jade slipped an arm around each other, and Jade explaincd, "Samantha and I, along with two other friends, are fencers."

He whistled and said, "That's about the most amazing thing I've heard."

Angel introduced himself and said, "So, Kerry, have you done any wrestling or pro football?"

Kerry chuckled and said, "I get that question a lot. But no, I'm a musician. I play the piano and sing."

Samantha said, "And wait till you hear him sing. If you think his size is impressive…"

Kerry said, "I appreciate that. But…" and he glanced at Sean, who nodded.

He looked at Angel and Jade, and said, "You need to know more than that about me. I'm not comfortable until you do. I'm a felon. I killed a man who murdered my little sister fifteen years ago. I served twelve years in Angola for manslaughter. I live in St. Francisville now and keep to myself for the most part. I happened to run into Sean, and the future is suddenly brighter. I promise I'll do anything to keep Samantha safe during this time."

Samantha high-fived him and her hand disappeared in his huge one.

Angel shook Kerry's hand, and said, "Many a good man has made a tough, life-changing choice. I'm sorry about your sister. And we are proud to have you on the team."

Once Angel and Kerry hauled the luggage inside, they joined the others looking at Sean's cart.

Sean said, "We are going to test four drones. You are my test victims. On the first test, the drone is going to plant a tracking device on you with adhesive. Then you will hide, and I will see if the drone is able to track you. When it does, we will communicate through the drone. And lastly, there will be a pouch for you to check underneath the belly of the drone."

Angel sighed in adoration and said, "I really, really, really, need one – or two of these."

Grinning, Sean programmed a drone to search for each tracking device, then said, "Make sure the drone has access to the top of your chest."

They did and each drone acted like an air pistol and blew a tiny tracker that stuck on their skin.

Sean said, "Now go hide. I'll give you ten minutes and send your drone after you," and all four took off.

Sean's controller screen was split into four windows, and he could see the tracker for each person moving away from him. Once all the tracking devices were still, he sent out the first drone.

***

Kerry and Samantha paired up and ran toward the creek. They found a hiding place by the bluff. Samantha was laughing at Kerry's joke when the drone dropped right in front of her – like a spider. She screamed. Kerry laughed at her, then his drone did the same thing to him.

Both drones hovered facing them. Silently. Then an LED panel lit up with green letters that read, "Got you. Press the white button and remove the object from the net."

They found candy bars.

***

Angel and Jade took off on a four-wheeler into the woods. Angel climbed a tree and sat on a low limb. Jade was hidden in a bush behind the four-wheeler. They were talking about renovations when Jade saw Angel startle and grab the branch to steady himself. A drone hovered in front of him. Then Angel glanced at Jade about the same time she squealed as a drone stalked her in the bush.

Green letters scrolled across their LED panels that said, "Gotcha. Press the white button and remove the object from the net."

Cookies.

***

Back at the house, Sean was pumped. The communication and tracking systems worked perfectly. The two drones from the creek returned to him first and then he heard Kerry and Samantha coming.

She poked him when she got close and said, "That was totally awesome, but you scared me."

He chuckled and the last two drones returned to him with the four-wheeler in hot pursuit.

Angel said, "I almost fell out of the tree."

Everyone laughed, and Samantha could see the satisfaction on Sean's face.

She said, "Good results?"

"Not to pat myself on the back, but yes."

Angel said, "Very cool, Sean. Very cool, man."

Sean said, "The four of you saved me a lot of time. I owe you!"

Samantha said, "Hey wait a minute. Sean, how come you haven't told me you're a runner? Kerry said you're super-fast."

He said, "It's normal to me. I've always been fast. I rarely think of a reason to mention it. I came close to going the Olympic route but chose the technical field instead. The FBI snatched me up. And now I'm behind a computer. Go figure."

Samantha said, "Well, I want to see you run."

Angel squatted like he was at a starting line, and said, "Come on, I'm game. No big deal if I eat dust. Show me what you've got."

Sean squatted next to him, and said, "Come on, muscle man. First one to the red fence and back. Kerry, say when."

Kerry said, "Don't get your feelings hurt, Angel."

Angel said, "I'm good. Go for it!"

Kerry yelled, "When!"

It wasn't an equal race by any means. Sean flew. Angel finally just stopped and watched him run. He turned to look back at the others. Kerry grinned and shrugged an I-told-you-so. Samantha's mouth was open in shock. She walked into the yard and watched her man fly. Jade whistled.

Sean returned, laughing, and gave Samantha a sweaty kiss.

Impressed, she said, "You are so hot – pun intended."

He winked.

Angel said, "I have never, ever, seen anyone that fast. You are the man. I think I'm gonna call you Flash."

Sean said, "Funny. But I can't be two superhero's – I'm already the Drone Master."

After he cleaned up, they got to work. Kerry began dinner as the task force set up camp in Sean's office. Before long, the FBI began to forward the first few unsolved cases of blonde victims around the Chicago area, and everything they found on Maxwell.

They sorted the documents as they came off the printer. Empty victim boards were set up, ready for evidence and details of the projected victimology. They all knew it would be hours and days till all the intel came in and was reviewed. This was just the beginning.

Sean handed Samantha the file on Maxwell. She wanted him. She sat by the blank profile board and began inspecting his life. Piece by piece.

It was close to nine p.m. when Kerry called, "Dinner's ready."

Glad to take a break, they filed into the kitchen where amazing aromas had teased them for over an hour. It smelled like a Mexican feast. Kerry chuckled as they eagerly targeted the food bar.

He said, "Welcome to fajita night. Sean keeps a great stocked kitchen so enjoy the benefits."

They piled plates with fajita mixtures and grabbed a soft drink, then settled around the table. After their first bite, they realized Kerry rocked the kitchen. There was little conversation as they filled their stomachs.

The ladies finished eating first and began to tell stories of college. Eventually the men stopped going back for refills and joined in the conversation. With bellies full and tension eased, laughter flowed from exaggerated or embarrassing tales.

Kerry enjoyed their stories, but it made him think of things best left forgotten in his life. Things had played out in a way no one ever imagined, and he had made his peace with it.

He thought about the fencing and said, "Does anyone have pictures of the fencing?"

Angel got to his phone first, and said, "Here, I recorded their fencing exhibit at the art show last year. There are plenty pictures of them before and after the video. Help yourself."

Kerry scrolled through the pictures as he shook his head in amazement. Then watched the video. Stunned, he looked up and caught Angel's gaze. The women were a fencing ministry.

Angel nodded, knowing the impact of the women teaching about the armor of God. He said, "Powerful, isn't it?"

Kerry glanced at Samantha and Jade, and said, "You can pray for me any day, anytime, anywhere," and they smiled.

Sean said, "Ok everyone, let's burn some energy. Take a walk outside. Whatever you want to do, then we've got to dive back into research. It's getting late."

Samantha said, "Come to the barn! I want to show you the Arabian mare Sean got for me. She's gorgeous! I call her Sugar."

It was a beautiful night. The stars carpeted the sky as they walked to the barn. There was a light breeze. Night sounds of owls, wolves, and other nocturnal animals carried through the air. Including the occasional flutter of bats after bugs drawn to the outdoor lights. The horses whinnied hearing their approach.

Jade gasped when she saw the white horse and glanced at Samantha.

Samantha said, "Right! She is a beauty."

They all took turns appreciating the stunning horse. Then Sean's stallion snorted for his missing attention. They didn't leave him out. It was after ten p.m. when they headed back to their research.

Samantha looked at the profile board on Maxwell. His picture was at the top. His hair was brown now – and short. He was no longer fair but tan. No longer lean and lanky but a big muscular man like Angel. He had dead brown eyes without an ounce of warmth, and an intense gaze that gave her goosebumps.

His history indicated that he moved to Chicago with his parents after his twin, Spencer, had gone to prison. They had been seniors in high school when the attack happened. Their parents died in a freak car accident before Maxwell started college less than a year later.

After law school, he was hired by a local law firm and stayed on staff till a month ago. He was the perfect example of dependable, intelligent, honorable, loyal, and successful. His personal life was nil. He wasn't married. Relatively no social media. No serious relationships. Quiet. Went to the gym faithfully and drove a black BMW.

His finances seemed normal for his choice of career and his credit was excellent. He rarely used credit cards. The only thing still pending was his medical records.

She pondered and made notes on the board. He worked hard as an attorney. Worked hard in the gym. And then nothing. No hobbies. No sports. No nothing. No women. There was no way he worked that hard for nothing. He lived the secret life of a psychopath. He worked hard to enjoy his secrets. And she knew what they were. They just had to find who his victims were - and stop him from making new ones.

Sean walked over to study her work. He said, "You know it's him."

"Yes. He's too perfect in the light of day. So, if he doesn't use credit cards, how will you track him? He's got to use cash to stay off-grid."

He said, "True. But he can't hide from cameras and videos. He still has to buy gas, food, a place to live, and find blondes."

Samantha said, "A true predator in every sense of the word."

Then she turned to look at the victim boards and said, "Wow."

They had already located a few victims from the first FBI batch that fit the victimology. Samantha's stomach churned at the suffering of these women just because they favored her. She grimaced.

Sean put an arm around her, and said, "You've got to get some sleep. We need to leave early to get you to the office for court in the morning."

She said, "Let me just glance over the victim boards you've started."

They watched her look at the victims and skim the details listed under their pictures. The boards were lined up by date reported missing - beginning twelve years ago.

Samantha's brow creased in concentration. She asked, "What's the cause of death?"

Sean said, "Strangulation."

She said, "What about the dump sites?"

Sean paused, hating to remind her about the waterfall attack, then said, "He tossed their bodies off of bridges, gullies, and cliffs."

Stomach on fire now, Samantha said, "Ok, I think that's enough for me tonight. I'll see y'all in the morning."

Sean escorted her upstairs. He said, "You ok?"

She shrugged and said, "I will be. I'll take a shower and get right in bed. I promise."

He knew she wasn't ok, but it was the nature of the beast.

Hugging her, he said, "Leave the door cracked so I can hear if you need me."

Heading downstairs, he hated all this for Samantha. And he wanted Maxwell behind bars or underground. He knew which he really preferred.

Samantha dressed in sporty pajama shorts and dried her hair. Then climbed into Sean's fluffy bed. She tossed and turned. She just couldn't relax. Her brain wouldn't shut up. First the case. Then the memories. She left the bedroom and sat at the top of the stairs where she could hear them working. A little while later, Sean stepped out of his office and looked up and saw her.

His heart ached. He said softly, "Baby..." and led her back to bed.

She said, "I can't sleep."

He said, "Roll on your stomach."

And he began to massage her back, her shoulders, her arms, and her legs. She closed her eyes and focused on his touch. Gentle. Rhythmic. Warm. Safe. Loving. Sean felt her muscles begin to loosen and kept massaging till she was sound asleep. He kissed her head, covered her up, and prayed all the way downstairs.

Angel and Jade went to bed around one a.m. so Sean took a break. He grabbed a cold Gatorade and walked out on the patio with a drone. He sent it skyward for a thermal scan of the area. He watched the monitor and relaxed. No humans on the scan. No large animals. No danger.

He went back inside and looked over the victim boards. He reviewed, and reviewed, and reviewed the boards again. Something kept niggling the back of his mind and then it hit him. They needed to line them up by *dates of death* and compare *places last seen*. He started working on that.

His phone rang. Dakota.

***

Sean answered, "How is Adam?"

"Alive, drugged, and his leg is a mess."

"And that is supposed to heal and be normal?"

"The doc said it would take time, but the tissue will heal. It'll be scarred but healthy skin."

"Have you been able to talk to him?"

"Not much, but he saw me and tried to talk."

"How are you?"

"Better since I've seen him. I catch Z's here and there. I'll be fine once I get him home. We are leaving the hospital at six a.m. to head to the airport. He'll be in a wheelchair. I pray he sleeps the whole way home. What's the update on Maxwell?"

"We're beginning to receive and sort victim documents. We meet the D.A. tomorrow and see Spencer on Tuesday at Angola. We're good. Just get home safe."

"That's what I say. We'll talk later."

***

Scan hung up and rubbed the back of his neck.

Angel asked, "How's Adam?"

Sean turned and saw Angel leaning against the doorframe, and said, "With Dakota now. They'll leave in a few hours."

"Glad to hear it."

"Get some sleep, Angel. I think I'm going to crash on the sofa for a few hours. I did a drone scan and no one's in the woods. Kerry's keeping an eye out from the barn."

Angel said, "It would take an idiot to tangle with that man."

"Yeah. Or a psycho."

83

Chapter 15

Just after seven a.m., Sean poured a cup of coffee from his second pot of the morning. He hadn't slept much. Normally his training allowed him to shut his mind off to rest, but it didn't work. With Maxwell out there, Samantha's safety on his mind, and Dakota bringing Adam home - he quit fighting sleep and got up almost two hours ago.

Taking a sip, all at once, Angel rounded the corner. Kerry came in the back door. And his phone dinged with a text – Dakota.

***

Dakota: About to get in the air. Adam's drugged for the trip.

Sean felt the pain as he looked at a picture of Adam in a wheelchair. Pale. Way too thin. Long straggly hair and a beard. His leg wrapped and immobilized. He looked like a war prisoner.

Sean: I hope he sleeps all the way home.
Dakota: I second that. I'll keep in touch.
***

Sean handed his phone to the guys, showing them the picture.
Angel said, "Dude. Makes me hurt for him."
Kerry said, "Poor guy. He's been through the ringer."

A little over an hour later, Samantha and Jade laughed as they came downstairs. Samantha was dressed for court in a charcoal gray silk pantsuit and black heels, with her blonde hair pulled back in a low bun. She looked every bit the gorgeous, intelligent prosecutor she was. None of the weary memories that had haunted her last night showed on her today.

Sean whistled and headed for a hug.

Grinning her sexy, sassy grin, she said, "Morning, Agent Man," and walked into his arms.

He kissed her, and said, "Morning, Counselor."

"Have you heard from Dakota yet?"

"They just flew out of Brazil." He showed her the picture of Adam.

She moaned and said, "Ouch. I feel for him. But I know Raven will have him cleaned up and cared for in no time."

After giving Sean a sympathy hug, she handed the phone to Jade.

Jade sighed, handed the phone back to Sean, and said, "I'm with Samantha. He'll be in good hands soon. And home."

Sean nodded, and with a glance at Samantha, said, "I'll go dress for court. Be down in fifteen minutes," and he jogged upstairs.

Samantha and Jade looked at each other incredulously. Samantha said, "Fifteen minutes. That's ridiculous. I protest the injustice."

Jade said, "My feelings exactly."

In fourteen minutes, Sean came downstairs in a gunmetal pinstripe suit, white shirt, and tie. Tall, dark, handsome…and really hot. Samantha whistled as everyone laughed.

She said, "I love it when you dress up for me."

"The feeling is mutual, gorgeous."

Then, he said, "Angel and Jade, I made some research changes last night. Go ahead and change the victim boards to include the additional victimology. And intel is sending Maxwell's expenses this morning – and hopefully medical records on the twins."

Glancing at Kerry, he said, "Continue to make security passes around the property, ok? I'll get drones set up later."

Kerry saluted.

Calling his boss as they headed to Baton Rouge, the Director answered, "Sean. Give me updates."

"Samantha and I are on our way to the District Attorney's office now. And Dakota and Adam are on the way home from Brazil. As for Maxwell, unsolved cases are beginning to arrive from Chicago and we're comparing victimology. The plan is to meet with Samantha's boss today. Head to Angola tomorrow. And hopefully have Maxwell under surveillance soon."

"What do you need?"

"I need a surveillance detail to monitor Maxwell once we find his location. I need another detail to watch Angola in case he continues to visit there."

"Done. A detail will be enroute to Angola after we hang up. A detail is ready for surveillance on Maxwell once he is found. And remind the D.A. to keep this under wraps. Until we have a clear tie to Maxwell, he's a free man. We don't need any leaks or threats to warn him."

"Yes, sir. On more thing. After we leave Angola tomorrow, I need to take an overnight run to Lake Charles to see Adam. Samantha will be with me."

"Got it."

Then the Director said, "Good morning, Samantha."

"Good morning, sir."

"Stay with Sean. We'll get Maxwell. And tell your boss we've got you."

***

Thirty minutes later, they walked into the office. And Samantha was shocked that it took ten minutes to reach her office door after weaving through the female staff greeting Sean.

Unlocking her door, she said, "That's totally ridiculous."

"Come on. I'm a likeable guy. What do you expect?"

"And your looks have nothing to do with it. Good thing you'll be in my office to protect me, or they wouldn't get any work done."

He said, "Ahhh, but will you?"

Grinning, she walked inside. Sean sat in a wingback chair in the corner so he wouldn't disturb her. He worked silently on his phone, with an ear tuned for sounds in the hall. He glanced at Samantha every few minutes.

Samantha pulled out the Jones case, reviewing documents she would need in court today. Then, called in her paralegal and gave her a few instructions. Following that, she messaged her boss to remind him of their private meeting before lunch with Sean. He reminded her of the staff dinner tonight.

She groaned, and Sean said, "What is it?"

"I forgot I have a staff dinner tonight at The Gregory after work. Will bringing me be a problem for you?"

Grinning, he said, "You, and steak are never a problem."

Smiling, she stood with a folder and said, "At least I come before the steak."

After he chuckled, she said, "I need to run next door to talk to Brian."

Sean followed her to the door and waited with a view of the hall. He could hear her talking next door. The hall was clear.

She popped out of Brian's office a few minutes later and whispered, "bathroom."

He followed her toward the kitchen, right next to the bathroom, and grabbed a cup of coffee. Then stood by the kitchen door watching the hall. He saw Suzette walk out of her office and head toward Samantha's door. She paused when Samantha wasn't there. He was about to call her name, but she turned and saw him.

Smiling, she said, "Morning, Sean. I just wanted to tell Samantha something personal. I'll catch her later."

He said, "Hi, Suzette, she should be back in her office in a few minutes. I'll tell her."

She gave a nod and returned to her office.

Sean sipped his coffee and played the scene back in his mind. Something happened in Suzette's life. She was more attractive today. Bubbly. Like a woman in love or maybe she won the lottery.

Samantha came out of the bathroom, and Sean said, "Suzette was looking for you."

She said, "Thanks, I'll check in with her."

He grinned and raised his cup of coffee in acknowledgement. He would wait where he was.

Samantha knocked as she stepped in Suzette's office and then stopped. She said, "You're glowing today. What happened? And don't lie to me."

Suzette laughed as she shut the door, then said, "I had a great holiday weekend. In fact, I've invited a guest to our staff dinner tonight. I wondered if you and Sean would sit with us. He's a new attorney in town and I want him to connect."

"How fun! Of course, we will. What's his name?"

"Wells. And no more questions. I can see them piling up in your brain. Ask him yourself tonight – he'll enjoy it."

"I can't wait to meet him!"

***

Just before eleven a.m., Samantha and Sean headed to the D.A.'s office for their appointment.

Smiling, he motioned them to have a seat, then said, "Okay, let's get this clandestine meeting underway. And give me the bulleted version – I'm hungry."

As their chuckles faded, Samantha said, "This relates to the case where I was a victim at age sixteen and my friend was killed."

A frown creased his forehead and he said, "Why?"

"I believe the wrong twin is in Angola."

Abruptly, he said, "Explain."

"They charged the twin who confessed. I was young and critically injured. No one questioned me on identification of the attacker since they were identical. But…truth is, the one that

88

attacked me had scars. Two. One on the right abdomen. One where I bit his arm. This needs to be checked."

His brow creased. That was a big red flag.

She continued, "My private investigator confirmed Friday that the other twin, Maxwell, moved back to Baton Rouge recently. He's an attorney now. I think he's going to come after me."

Expression grim, he said, "I'm shocked you had a private investigator on him. Why – without confirmation on the scars?"

"He made a comment to me in court after his brother was sentenced. No one else heard, and I was a mess emotionally and physically. I didn't really get his point at the time – but he said he'd be back for me. The last few years I began to keep tabs on his location."

The D.A. nodded. Red flag two.

Samantha glanced at Sean, and said, "This brings us to the next element. We think there's a possibility Maxwell could be a serial killer."

The D.A. stood and faced the window. Red flag three…his mind rapid firing on the nightmare being exposed.

Sean said, "The FBI has begun the investigation and a task force is in place. Unsolved blonde rape murder victim cases are being gathered from the Chicago area where he's lived. We are also working on the scar identification issue between Maxwell and his brother. My director wants time to work the investigation without Maxwell knowing. He's got to be a free man until evidence is found. This is top priority. We want both, Samantha and the public safe – but we don't want him to disappear or panic."

The D.A. faced them and said, "I understand. The Attorney General will have to be in our loop. Where is the task force stationed?"

"At my ranch north of Baton Rouge. Samantha is under our protection 24/7 and working with us to put the case together. I will be her security. The director will call you."

"Keep me informed of updates." He looked at Samantha and said, "Don't take any chances with this guy. After court, disburse cases as needed to other prosecutors. I presume Sean will be with you at the staff dinner tonight?"

"Yes, sir."

Sean handed him Maxwell's current photo and file information. The meeting was over.

***

At three p.m., Sean followed Samantha and the prosecutor team to court for the sentencing hearing of J.J. Jones. They stepped off the elevator on the 5th floor and headed to Criminal Courtroom 8C. The team settled at the prosecutor's table in the front, closest to the empty jury box. Samantha, as lead counsel, had the aisle seat.

Sean took an aisle seat on the back wall by the main entrance. He checked the room and watched the people. There were a dozen long rows on either side of the aisle for spectators and family. A wooden rail divided the legal proceedings from visitors. Two bailiffs were up front near the side doors.

Others began to arrive and be seated. The court reporter, clerk, and judge's assistant entered the room and sat near the bench. Several people filed into the row directly behind Samantha and she turned to greet them. Undoubtedly, the victim's family.

On the defendant's side of the aisle, people filed in behind defense counsel. They were solemn and nodded at the attorneys in front of them. Sean knew that this was more than likely not going to be a good day for them. And neither the victim's family, nor the defendant's family, made any contact with each other.

A few press reporters arrived and positioned themselves for the best viewpoint. Moments later the bailiff opened a side door, and two deputies escorted the defendant inside. He was seated between his attorneys, and the deputies stood against the wall.

Sean noticed the defendant's sour look and rigid posture. Jones was an angry man. Imposing. And looked like he still wanted to kill somebody. Not a good sign. Sean glanced at Samantha.

The Bailiff said, "All rise," and everyone stood as Judge Lawrence entered the courtroom. The court officer handed the judge an envelope. After he reviewed it, he addressed the courtroom with instructions for the verdict portion of the trial. The judge had the bailiff bring in the jurors and they filed solemnly into the juror's box.

The judge asked the head juror if they had reached a verdict. She told him yes and handed a document to the court officer. The judge looked at it then passed it back to the court officer, who began calling out each count of the indictment against Jones, including the jury's verdict. In the end, J.J. Jones was determined guilty on all counts, including first-degree murder, with penalty of death.

Cheers erupted from most of the spectators, while several members of the Jones family sobbed and embraced. Then following protocol, the judge called each juror by name to confirm the verdict and punishment rendered. They concurred and the jury was thanked and dismissed.

Jones hissed a comment to his counsel just as the judge instructed him and his counsel to rise. They stood. Sean stepped out of the pew and watched Jones. Concerned. The guy's body language shouted explosive.

The Judge said, "Mr. Jones, you have been found guilty of the charges read before the court. You are hereby sentenced to imprisonment until the time of your death by lethal injection."

Heavy sobs broke out from his family.

The Judge continued, "Bailiff, please remove the defendant from the courtroom and see that he is transported immediately to the Louisiana State Penitentiary."

With a growl, Jones shoved his counsel to the floor, and barged toward Samantha. Sean yelled a warning as he ran. Screams echoed around the room. By the time Jones crossed the center aisle, Sean went airborne and kicked him with both feet in the side. Jones flew, then slid, landing with a thud against the judge's bench. Still and silent.

Sean turned to Samantha, who was wide-eyed in the lap of the victim's father. She leapt up and Sean stood with her as the judge banged the gavel for order. The deputies surrounded Jones and cuffed him, but he wasn't moving.

The judge leaned over the bench and looked at the defendant on the ground, then looked at Sean.

He said, "Prosecutor Rutledge, please introduce the gentleman to the court."

Samantha straightened her clothes and said, "Your Honor, may I introduce to the court FBI Special Agent Sean Nash."

The judge nodded like it made sense now, and said, "Agent Nash, while I abhor violence in my courtroom, I thank you for the speediest rescue I have ever seen."

The courtroom sounded like a cheering ballgame, so the judge banged the gavel again, and said, "Bailiff, escort the prisoner to the hospital for clearance, then on to the prison. Court dismissed."

Samantha and her team were the last to leave the courtroom. A bevy of excited reporters waited with questions – but saying no comment, they stepped on the elevator.

When the doors closed, Samantha grabbed Sean's arm, and said, "I heard you call out to me, but as I turned, you had already kicked him. Sean! You flew. Horizontal."

Brian said, "It happened so fast. The yell. The kick. And the victim's father yanking Samantha out of the way."

The paralegal sighed, and said quietly, "I just need a vacation. Please. With a bonus."

Everyone was still laughing when they returned to the D.A.'s office. And since news travels fast in the same building, cheers awaited them as the doors opened.

The D.A. shook hands with Sean and said, "You'll make national news no doubt. I'm glad you were there to stop him."

Sean said, "Jones looked like a powder keg ready to blow. I just watched him."

Samantha glanced at Sean with a grin, then back to her boss and said, "He's quick. You have no idea. Did you hear the guilty verdict?"

"I did. Justice was served. And deserved."

After that, Samantha worked with her paralegal and transferred cases to other attorneys for the next few weeks – taking it as personal time off.

An hour later, they were in the parking garage headed to Sean's SUV. He said, "We have more than an hour before your staff dinner. Do you need to pick up anything to bring to the ranch?"

"Yes. I would like to run by my apartment since it isn't far from the restaurant. Check mail. Tell the doorman I'll be out for a few days. And grab more clothes since we have the political dinner Thursday."

"What about the lonely take-out food stacked in your fridge?"

She elbowed him and said, "That won't win you any brownie points."

Chuckling, he said, "What will?"

"I already owe you for the fabulous massage you gave me last night. I never did thank you."

In one smooth move, Sean slid his hand behind her neck and stopped, pulling her face close to his.

He said, "You fell asleep. That was the thank you. My bonus was knowing it was my hands that did it to you."

She looked into his dark eyes and felt the sizzle all the way down her legs. He watched the impact and looked at her mouth.

She wet her lips, then whispered, "And…what can your hands do now?"

He kissed her hard. Then carried her the few steps to his car, pressing her against the door. A car started not far away, interrupting them.

He bit her lip lightly and said, "Does that answer your question?"

***

93

Shadow Man watched from a hiding place not far away. He was aroused after watching them. Needing release as they drove away, he raked his key deep into the door of a shiny black Mercedes. The grinding of the metal and the ugly damage felt good. That's what he had in mind for Samantha.

He pulled out his burner phone.

Chapter 16

Once they got to her apartment, Samantha changed into a black jumpsuit and slipped on ankle-strapped black stiletto heels. She had just turned on the vanity mirror when Sean called from the den, "Are you dressed?"

"I'm touching up my makeup. Come on in."

He appeared in the doorway and leaned against the frame, watching as she tilted her head back with parted lips, and freshened her eye makeup. His eyes roamed her - appreciating her slight grin because she knew what he was doing. He loved the curve of her. The fan of her blonde hair across her back. The sexy spread of her legs as she leaned forward. The tease of shoe-straps that begged to be undone. She was flaming hot and knew it.

She glanced at him in the mirror when she picked up the red lipstick. Heat radiated from him clear across the room. She felt it in her belly. She looked him up and down. Broad shoulders. Flat stomach leading into firm powerful thighs. Native American gorgeous. She loved the look of him.

Raising her eyes to his, he headed toward her. Shrugging out of his jacket, he tossed it on the bed. She waited…her body reacting to his pursuit. Her toes curled. Eyelids lowered, sensuous. Breath quickened. Leg muscles clenched.

Meeting her gaze in the mirror, he took the lipstick from her and laid it down.

Voice deep and hungry, he said, "You might want to wait a minute on that." Then slid his hands down her sides and knelt, turning the stool to put him between her legs.

He started at her feet and ran his hands sensually up her legs till he reached her thighs, then picked her off the bench – holding her at his waist. She wrapped around him like a female lion as their lips met. He groaned at the feel of her as she purred and tightened her legs.

A few moments later, he met her hot gaze, and said, "There's no question what I want."

"Tell me anyway."

Squeezing her thighs, he said, "Marry me so I can show you."

Smiling, she whispered, "Yes…" and kissed him.

He couldn't get close enough and growled. He said, "The minute this case is over, lets elope. Run away with me to Switzerland. I can't wait any longer than that."

"So, hurry and finish the case…"

A few kisses later, she remembered the staff dinner, and gasped. They were going to be late.

***

Thirty minutes later, Sean pulled into the restaurant parking lot. It was packed.

Samantha said, "I'm glad they reserved a room. This is unusual for a Monday and I'm starving."

"You haven't eaten much today."

"You were distracting me."

He laughed as his phone rang.

***

She grinned as Sean answered, "Director. I expected your call."

He listened, then chuckled and said, "Not at all, sir. You know I prefer behind the scenes – Jones just didn't give me a choice."

Glancing at Samantha, he said, "She's tough. And no, I won't let her out of my sight."

***

Walking toward the entrance, Samantha said, "I forgot to mention that Suzette invited a guest tonight - a new attorney she met. She wants us to sit with them. I look forward to meeting him. I don't think I've ever seen her this taken with someone."

Sean said, "That explains the change I saw in her today."

As they entered the foyer, the D.A. had just arrived too. He motioned them to follow him. The hostess escorted them to the private room. The sound of conversation and laughter made them smile as the door opened. Cheers and clapping broke out as they walked in. Sean was still the hero of the hour.

No one was in a hurry, so they visited from group to group in the lovely room. Elegant lighting. Beautiful windows. A large mahogany table set with formal dinnerware. And background music.

Samantha caught a glimpse of Suzette talking to a big guy and two other prosecutors. She headed her way. Sean was still trying to get away from the long-winded wife of one of the older attorneys.

Smiling, Samantha greeted and hugged Suzette, then said, "You look wonderful in red – my favorite color! Sorry we're late. I got tied up."

Suzette said, "No problem! We haven't been here long," and she motioned behind Samantha.

Before Samantha turned, a hand slid up her side pressing firmly into her breast. She jerked away and spun. And for the briefest of seconds, her world tilted. Her mind spun with a million thoughts on how to handle this. Her heart pounded. Stomach clenched. Then she blinked, and rage made the decision.

Mentally lethal now, her eyes narrowed as she said threateningly, "If you ever touch me again, I will kill you, Maxwell. Do I make myself clear?"

Wells held up both hands truly surprised at her vehemence. But he was totally excited by it. He said, "Isn't that a bit harsh? I'm amazed you even recognized me. It's been years since we've seen each other. What's with the anger?"

Sean hit him. Women screamed and scattered. Maxwell regained his balance and wiped the blood off his split cheek. The look he aimed at Sean was vicious.

Sean said, "Unless you have a death wish, keep your hands off her. She's off limits. Do I need to make it any clearer for you?"

Suzette tried to fathom why the world had suddenly gone crazy.

The D.A. stepped into the fray and told Maxwell, "You shouldn't be here. Please leave."

Suzette exclaimed, "Sir, wait. He is my guest!" Then turning to Wells she said, "Why are they calling you Maxwell?"

"It's my given name. I also go by Wells."

Suzette motioned at the disturbance, and said, "What is all this?"

Samantha said curtly, "Let me answer. His twin brother is in Angola for killing my best friend, and then trying to rape and murder me. My encounters with him and his family have been unpleasant."

Shocked, Suzette looked at Maxwell. His words repeating in her mind as she thought about what he'd told her about his brother.

Sean said, "Maxwell, I'm FBI Special Agent Sean Nash. Let's go. I'll escort you out. Now."

Maxwell glanced at Suzette. She nodded to him, and looked at the D.A., then said, "I'll go with him. I'm so sorry for the trouble, sir. And to you, Samantha."

They left.

Sean followed them outside. They got into a white SUV, and he memorized the license plate. Watching them drive away, he knew Maxwell set this up. He wanted Samantha to know he was here. That was good, and bad.

Just before Sean joined the dinner again, the FBI responded on the vehicle. Maxwell had a rental car. He had given a false address on the application and paid cash. Dead lead. But no matter. Between Suzette's connection, and their research, they'd find him. Especially since he was eager to get up close and personal with Samantha now.

As Maxwell left the restaurant, he watched the FBI agent fade in the rear-view mirror. He had already learned the guy was FBI on the news report today. That made the game a little more fun. He glanced at Suzette, and she glanced at him. He felt like he was on the witness stand.

Suzette's mind was busy trying to sort and formulate all the probable reasons for what had played out tonight. But plainly, Wells…no, Maxwell…had known who Samantha was and that she wouldn't be pleased to see him. So why did he put himself in such a humiliating position? Why hadn't he told her he knew her?

Maxwell wiped a drop of blood from his cheek again, then licked it off his finger.

He said, "I should have told you I knew her. But why do I have to be defined by my brother? I didn't even know she would recognize me. Nor did I have an inkling I was an issue for her. Twelve years is a long time to hold a grudge."

"I think the word grudge is a bit casual for the crime don't you think?"

"Maybe. But the fact remains, the one who attacked them is in prison. I refuse to cower in shame for his crimes. I'm not rude to her because my brother is rotting in prison. That's the truth of it."

Suzette couldn't fault his argument.

He said, "Suzette, I'm not going to grovel. I'm an attorney too. We will all meet publicly in the years ahead. Even in court. Everyone will have to get over it. But you and I, that's a different matter. I think we could have something together. So, am I worth the challenge you might face?"

She looked hard at him and glanced out the window. He waited for her response.

She said, "Of course I don't blame you for your brother. But I do expect you to be wiser in dealing with my colleague on the sensitivity of the matter. It's not Samantha's fault either."

He nodded, agreeing with her argument.

"However," she said as he pulled into her driveway, "I'm not afraid of a personal challenge. *If* you are honest. Don't lie – even by omission again – and I will stand by you and see how we…play out."

He said softly, "I'm glad. I look forward to…us." He touched her face and said, "I'm sorry I embarrassed you. Forgive me?"

She smiled, and her eyes softened. She nodded.

He reached to open his door to walk her inside, and she said, "Don't. I'll be fine."

So, he leaned over and kissed her gently, then watched her walk away. Remembering something, he lowered his window and said, "Are we still on for the political riverboat dinner this week?"

"Yes. We'll work it out somehow."

A few miles away, Maxwell pulled over and stopped. He checked his phone. Samantha hadn't checked the text he sent after gouging the Mercedes in the parking garage. Shadow Man smiled. He only needed a few more days.

***

It was close to nine p.m. when Sean and Samantha pulled up to the ranch. Kerry walked out of the barn. Angel and Jade stepped out of the house.

Jade hugged Samantha and asked, "Are you okay? I about passed clean out when I saw that guy try to attack you on the news."

"I'm good. My bodyguard here made quick work of Jones."

Angel said, "You can't hide now, Flash. The whole world knows how fast you are," and Sean laughed.

Kerry said, "That really was the coolest move. You didn't even mess up your suit."

With laughter ringing through the night air, they headed inside.

After the ten o'clock news, everyone poured a fresh cup of coffee and met in the office for task force updates. Five of the twelve victim boards were filled with information fitting the victimology. Samantha's heart hurt. She wished she had been wrong about the serial killer angle.

Sean said, "We met with the D.A. and he's on board. However, the news report is not the only shock of the day."

Jade said, "What do you mean?"

Samantha said, "Maxwell showed up at the staff dinner tonight. It was a shock. He was there with a co-worker and groped me. I threatened to kill him. Sean hit him. And the D.A. kicked him out."

There was barely a second of shocked silence before they all asked questions at once.

Sean held up his hands to stop them, and said, "I escorted them out. The vehicle he was in turned out to be a rental. Dead lead. So, we need to know where he is staying. Like yesterday. He knows who I am now and will find out where I live easy enough."

Frowning, Kerry said, "Why don't I take a ride around the property and make sure nothing looks suspicious."

Sean said, "Thanks. And as soon as I'm caught up here, I'm going to send up a drone to check."

Kerry headed out, and Sean said, "Did you find anything in Maxwell's finances possibly relating to his secret activities?"

Jade said, "Yes. He rarely writes checks, but one cleared his bank recently for a house rental in this area. I'm thinking it's an older landlord. The elderly still use checks a good bit for record keeping."

"Where's the house?"

Angel said, "We're working on it. We only have the owner's name and contact information for you. None of their information is online. I'm getting property records. And as for credit card expenses, there's a few from his move back to Louisiana for gas and food. He must pay cash for most things – or have black market credit cards."

Jade said, "I did some digging for online service fees here in Baton Rouge. A few were for personal information on Samantha."

Samantha said, "No surprise there."

Sean said, "I need to get a security detail out here. He'll presume you're with me when you don't show up at the apartment. But he won't know about the case, which is the goal."

Angel said, "You still headed for Angola tomorrow?"

"Yes, and on to Lake Charles after that."

Jade said, "One more thing came in. Maxwell and Spencer's medical records. Maxwell had his appendix out before the waterfall attack. Spencer still has his."

Samantha took the folder, and said, "No surprise there either. I knew it was him."

A half-hour later, Kerry returned to the house.

He said, "A black BMW was parked down the road. He took off when he saw me come out of the woods."

Sean said. "Did you—"

Kerry said, "I texted you the number."

***

After Sean security scanned the area with the drone, he called the director.

"Sir, contact has been made with Maxwell. We need a security detail here at the ranch. He knows who I am and where we are."

"Give the team an hour to get there."

***

The black BMW left the ranch behind. The huge black man had startled him coming out of the woods so quickly. Obviously, he seemed suspicious, but no matter, he knew Samantha and Sean were there. That's what mattered. Maxwell smiled. The best part was - his place was only ten minutes from here.

He hoped Samantha read her text soon. It made him raging hot to play in her head. He'd get in other parts of her soon enough.

***

Once everyone was back in the house, Jade said, "Stop. Everyone just quit working and listen to me. We need a fun break while we wait on the security detail. It's been a heavy day.

Especially for Samantha. Why don't we play a game? Unwind. Loosen up. Give your mind a breather."

Samantha plopped on the sofa, and said, "Yes! Do I get a chance to win?"

Jade laughed and said, "No, Miss Competitive. We are going to learn things about each other that don't come up in general conversation."

Angel said, "Oh. I get it. A nosey game. I'm game – pun intended!"

Sean sat by Samantha, and said, "Sounds good. One hour, then back to work."

Jade said, "Ok. Here it is. We take turns picking different questions for everyone to answer. Interesting ones. You pick the first question, Samantha."

Samantha said, "First question: What scares you?"

Angel said, "I'll answer. Spiders. I hate them all. I saw the movie Arachnophobia and couldn't sleep for a week as a kid."

Jade crawled her fingers up his arm teasingly, then pointed at Sean, and he said, "Bees, wasps, and hornets all equally. I'm grateful I can outrun them."

They laughed, then Samantha said, "I stay away from them too. I'm not allergic but my body is sensitive with more than one sting. I usually keep an EpiPen somewhere around me."

Alarmed, Sean said, "Why haven't you told me that?"

"Because I was waiting on the game, Agent Man." They laughed.

Jade said, "Your turn, Kerry."

He said, "Hands down - scorpions. They are tiny monsters. They would make me scream like a girl."

Angel chuckled at that picture, and said, "Your turn, Jade."

She said, "Spit devils or walking sticks. Ugh. They look creepy and even swim. I had one dive after me in a pool before. I freaked out."

Samantha said, "I guess so. That's horrible."

Jade pointed at Samantha and said, "You need to answer your own question."

Samantha shrugged, and said, "For me, it's no surprise. Waterfalls," and everyone knew why.

Sean said, "Maybe you need to try to go again. With me."

"Not anytime soon. Let me think about it for the next hundred years."

Then pointing at Jade, Samantha said, "Next question, nosey."

Jade said, "What's something you really want to do?" and pointed at Sean to go first.

Sean said, "Be a pilot."

Samantha said, "Really! Can I be your stewardess?"

"Can I pick your outfit?"

Laughing, Jade said, "You're next Angel."

"I want to be a drone master like my hero, Sean."

Grinning, Sean said, "I always wanted an apprentice!"

They pointed to Samantha, and she said, "I want to be an FBI agent."

Sean said, "What?"

She put her hand on her hips, and said, "What. You don't think short people can be an agent?"

It took ten minutes for the laughter to die down.

They pointed to Jade, and she said, "I want to learn karate."

Angel said, "Really. Any special reason?"

"If I don't have my sword or gun, doesn't my body need to be my weapon?"

Angel said, "Excellent point."

Kerry was next. He said, "To play the piano again."

Sean jumped up and ran down the hall. In a few minutes he was back with a keyboard.

He said, "It's not a piano but it's yours. I totally forgot I had one."

Kerry was moved. Deeply. He took it from Sean and carried it to the counter and plugged it in. He played a few cords to test it. Then with no hesitation at all, he began to play and sing. Amazed, they watched and listened.

When he stopped, he said, "Thanks Sean. It feels really good to play again."

Sean said, "You're incredible. Have you ever played and sang publicly?"

"Chancy and I performed frequently as a duo."

Samantha said, "Chancy?"

"Someone special."

Coaxing him, she said, "And…"

"And then my sister died, and Angola happened."

Sean said, "What happened to Chancy?"

Kerry sighed and said, "I don't know. I sent her away when they sentenced me. She was devastated, but she didn't deserve the future ahead of me."

He pulled out his wallet and handed Sean a picture. A younger Kerry and a lovely laughing woman stood by a piano. They passed the photo around.

Samantha said, "She's gorgeous," and Kerry nodded. Solemnly.

Samantha flipped the picture over and the woman's name was on the back. Kerry Hart and Chancy Moreaux. She showed it to Angel and Jade, then gave it back to Kerry.

Samantha whispered to Jade, "Find her."

Jade and Angel went back to work. Kerry took his keyboard to the barn. And Sean and Samantha waited for the security detail.

Samantha said, "We need to find Chancy for Kerry."

"Let's see what we find out before telling them anything. We don't want to open a door that would be painful for anyone."

"I agree."

He bumped her shoulder, and said, "Are you serious about the FBI?"

"I am. How do you feel about that?"

"Impressed. You have strong instincts and powerful skills already. Are you thinking about behind the scenes or on the front line?

"Profiling. Put me out front. I'm not shy."

He said, "True. And I like the idea of you being FBI. I've never kissed an agent.

Then headlights flashed as the two agents arrived. They met everyone, got briefed on the situation, and headed outside to guard.

Once they were back in the office, Jade said, "Sean, I ran Maxwell's license plate on the BMW. It's clean."

Sean nodded, then noticed the glance between Angel and Jade, and said, "What else?"

Angel said, "We found Chancy."

"Where is she?"

"She's a music professor at LSU."

Samantha said, "Is she married?"

Jade shook her head no and pulled up a bio and picture of her from the LSU website. She was still easy to recognize. Just more mature. Confident. Classy. And still very beautiful. They read her bio. She was not married but had a sixteen-year-old daughter.

Sean said, "Did you find a picture of the daughter?"

Angel printed it and handed it to him. She had dark skin. Long black braids. And bright blue eyes.

Sean said, "Kerry has a surprise coming."

Chapter 17

Late that night in Lake Charles, Dakota lifted an unconscious Adam out of the wheelchair and laid him on the bed. The flight from Brazil had been long and the pain meds had come way too close to wearing off completely. The pain shot Raven had given him in the car when they drove up had already knocked him out. He was in awful shape, but at least he was home.

Dakota motioned his parents, and said, "Go ahead and take a few minutes with him. Then we'll get him cleaned up."

A few minutes later, the others left the room. Raven knew it was time to take over. Make decisions. Give instructions. And keep Dakota busy.

She said, "We need a dishpan, a trash can, soft cotton rags and antibacterial soap. We need to remove all his clothing and burn them since we don't know what germs they carry. Don't touch his hurt leg until I can read the doctor's instructions. And if you would help me bathe him in bed this first time, it would be best. Although he's thin and weak, he's a big man."

Dakota was grateful she knew what to do and left to get what she needed. Raven put her phone on the bedside table and set the alarm for his next pain shot. He couldn't run behind. Not at this stage of pain. She began to review the doctor's orders from Brazil.

Dakota returned with the supplies and a large trash can. Raven gently cut off everything on Adam but leg bandages. She heard Dakota's moan at seeing his brother's wounded body. Then he began bringing her warm rags. They bathed him from head to toe. Once he was clean and examined, Dakota brought in a pair of shorts with one leg cut so it would fit over the leg bandages.

Raven's heart ached for Adam's suffering. Besides the broken leg, surgery, and bite damage, he had cuts, bruises, scrapes, gouges, rashes, and insect bites over much of his body. She checked his hair and didn't find any wounds on his scalp. Dakota brought her a brush and ponytail holder, and in minutes, she had Adam's long black hair neat and in its usual ponytail.

She said, "Do you want to shave him or shall I?"

"I will." And he returned shortly with what he needed.

Raven reviewed the remainder of the medical instructions from the doctor while Dakota shaved Adam. She paused a time or two and watched as Adam's face was revealed. She could tell he was a good-looking man. Sculptured features. Laugh lines. Long lashes and a beautiful mouth for a guy. Wow. She focused again on the medical documents.

Dakota finished and said, "Now he looks more like himself."

She glanced up again. The resemblance to Dakota and Sean was remarkable.

Putting the medical records aside, she said, "Ok, now it's time to take a look at that leg."

She removed one thick layer of packing at a time. Adam began flinching with discomfort at the parts that stuck but didn't wake. She finally removed the last bandage and threw it in the trash. The knee surgery looked good. Not pretty, but no evidence of infection. The stitches were clean and in place – especially after all the traveling. But he would need to get that knee to rehab soon to keep maximum flexibility and strength.

She said, "He'll need a local doctor immediately. I will run out of pain medicine before noon tomorrow."

Dakota nodded and messaged Gabrielle.

Raven looked at the anaconda bite. The razor teeth had ripped the skin of his foot. Swelling was up the leg. The bruising was black, red, yellow, and purple. It would be extremely painful for days. The hospital in Brazil had cleaned it well and stitched what they could, but it still had areas that were raw, ragged, and angry. It would take aggressive care to calm the furious reaction going on in his foot.

She gathered the creams, medicines, and cleaning solutions, and said, "Next is the hard part for him. He will have breakthrough pain as I clean and care for the open wounds on his foot. His knee is painful as well, but nothing like the foot. I need you to hold him steady, so he doesn't hurt himself. We may need your dad to help you hold him down."

Both men returned to the room.

Raven said, "Fold a sheet and put it across his chest, binding his arms. Dakota, climb on the bed and straddle his good leg and hold the sheet across him. Be aware that Adam may wake up or even pass out from the pain. The liquid will burn terribly so I will work as fast as I can. Mr. Nash, please just help Dakota with what he needs."

Both men looked like they'd rather tread barefoot on hot glass but got into position.

Raven said, "Now," and as they held him, she poured the solution on his foot. Adam screamed in pain. The men fought to hold him until he finally passed out.

"Just stay in position," Raven said. "I'll be a few more minutes."

She cleaned, added medications, and rebandaged the foot and knee – propping pillows under both. He moaned a few times but didn't wake again. Then they removed the dirty sheets.

When she finished, he was clean, bandaged, and sleeping. She checked his vitals and laid out his next dose of medicine. Dakota cleaned everything and brought in a pitcher of water and a straw.

He said, "What's the schedule?"

"He'll need my twenty-four-hour care for maybe two days. He's young and strong so he may bounce back more quickly than others would. Now that he's off the hospital intravenous dosage, he'll start staying awake longer. But he'll also feel the need for the next pain dose before it's due. And he'll need to start drinking liquids as soon as possible. Then food."

She showed him where the urinal was, and they both knew Adam wouldn't like the loss of personal privacy. He would never remember the bath. Raven decided to wear scrubs to make it more professional for him as he woke. Dakota stayed with him while she left to change.

When she returned, he said, "You need breaks. You can't work around the clock. Lance will be upset."

"By tomorrow afternoon I should be able to take longer breaks. Until then, I can run in and out, and nap in the chair closest to him. Once he's awake more, he'll need company to keep him occupied. Men are generally impatient patients."

Nodding in agreement, he said, "Alright. Oh. Gabrielle found a doctor. But he can't get here till noon tomorrow."

Raven nodded. That meant Adam would be an hour with minimal pain meds. She would have to spread the doses out enough to try to help.

***

Close to two a.m. back on the ranch, the task force looked at the six blonde victim boards that linked to Maxwell. Half of the victims they projected already. Plus, they still had nineteen Chicago cases to review.

Sean said, "All six of them were killed in April of various years."

Sighing, Samantha said, "His obsessive repetition will hang him. He didn't even try to hide the connection to the day he attacked me and Mary Beth."

"He's one crazy dude," Angel said.

Sean said, "And they were all last seen at truck stops on Interstate 55 outside of Chicago. We're waiting on truck stop videos. It will take a while."

Angel said, "As far as my expense review goes, it looks like Maxwell was in the general vicinity those days. That's not extremely helpful – but it doesn't rule him out."

Samantha said, "Any phone pings?"

Sean said, "No. But I have an idea. Let's check medical records and see if anyone was infectious or contagious."

Samantha said, "Got it. I'll check his now."

She reviewed Maxwell's medical records and he seemed healthy. His only surgery was when he had his appendix out the year before the attack on her.

Minutes clicked by as the others researched. One by one, the victims' medical records revealed nothing.

Till finally, Sean said, "Victim ten had HIV. She was killed two years ago."

Samantha said, "Maxwell hasn't been to the doctor in three years. He could have HIV and not even know it."

Then the security detail interrupted with a radio check-in. All was well.

Sean said, "Ok, everyone, we need sleep. It's late. I'll stay downstairs on the sofa.

Everyone noted their stopping point. Samantha picked up her leather folder containing notes for Spencer's interview at the prison tomorrow. Her phone was underneath. She hadn't checked it in hours. Skipping social media altogether, she scrolled through texts for anything urgent. She saw an unknown and opened it.

***

I'm gonna spread those legs wide, blondie. Real soon.
***

Shocked, her stomach heaved as those words jumped from her memory. She leaned on the desk, head down. She didn't know whether she wanted to scream, cry, or break something.

In two steps, Sean had his arm around her, asking, "What happened?"

She handed him the phone. He read the text, and she saw the fury flash across his face.

Voice tight, he said, "I'll make him pay for that. I promise."

"You know Maxwell sent it."

"I know. And I'm sorry - we can run the trace, but we already know it's probably a burner phone pinging around Baton Rouge. He won't do it at his house - and researching to find him buying the phone doesn't get us closer to finding him."

She said, "I would absolutely shoot him if he came for me. I really would."

He held her face and said, "You do whatever you have to do to protect yourself. We all will. But you know he did this to get in your head. Don't read texts you don't know the sender. Or let me keep your phone. He's not going to stop – you know that, right?"

She nodded, kissed him softly, and went upstairs - with her phone. She could ignore Maxwell. At least until he was in her crosshairs. Then he was all hers.

Sean watched Samantha shut the bedroom door and his phone rang. Dakota.

***

Sean answered and Dakota said, "We're home. I helped Raven with him. Be glad you weren't here. But for now, he is clean, bandaged, and sleeping."

Sean felt the relief. Adam was home. Safe. He said, "Have you talked to him?"

"Nothing I would call communication, but Raven said he'll be better soon. You have no idea what a God-gift she is. Calm. Smart. And totally in charge. Though when Adam is better, he will have a fit that we let a beautiful young woman tend to him. And yes, I'm a die-hard Raven fan now as you can tell. I'm sending you a new picture of him."

Sean's phone dinged and he looked at the picture of Adam asleep, clean, shaved, and safe. He said, "Thank you, God."

Dakota said, "Maybe he can talk to us by the time you get here tomorrow. The doctor will be here at noon."

"We'll be there."

"Gotta go. See you tomorrow."

***

Late that night in Lake Charles, Adam moaned. Raven opened her eyes and saw him in the lamplight. The clock showed four-thirty in the morning. He grimaced and she knew it was getting

112

close to time for his pain shot. But she wanted to see if she could get him to drink some water and talk a little.

She stepped to the side of the bed. His color was good. She touched his forehead to check for fever and his eyes partially opened.

She smiled and said, "Hi, Adam."

He blinked and groaned again.

"Are you thirsty?"

He nodded and she held the straw to his lips. He took a few sips and looked at her again. Hoarsely he said, "Where am I?"

"At Dakota's."

She barely heard, "Thank God."

She wiped his face with a cool wet rag and asked, "Do you remember what happened to you?"

He licked his lips and said, "Some." Then grimaced, and said, "My leg is on fire."

"I know. It's almost time for your medicine but let me get Dakota. He wants to see you awake," and he nodded.

Raven ran down the hall and knocked. Dakota opened the door in seconds.

She said, "He's awake."

In seconds, Dakota touched Adam's hand. He opened his eyes but choked up. He was too emotional to talk.

After a few moments, Adam said, "Am I ok?"

"Yes, but it will take a long while for your leg to heal."

Adam nodded and groaned again.

Raven said, "Drink a little more."

He took a few sips, waking up even more, and said, "Who are you?"

"Right now, your nurse."

"You're gorgeous."

Dakota chuckled with a glance at Raven, and said, "Yeah, he's gonna be fine." Then said, "Adam, Sean will be here by noon. The doctor too. Mom and Dad are here."

Adam nodded, then grimaced, and said, "Are you sure they didn't cut part of my leg off?"

"It's all there. The anaconda did a number on you though."

"It was a monster. I tried to kick him."

"They had to kill him to get him off you."

"Good."

Raven handed the cup to Dakota, and he helped Adam drink a little more.

She asked, "Adam do you need anything other than pain medicine?"

"A hug."

Dakota laugh-snorted in response.

Grinning, Raven said, "Adam, are you flirting?"

"I'm trying."

Then Adam growled and strained. He said, "Are you sure the snake isn't biting me again? It feels like it's ripping my foot off."

Raven quickly gave him the shot and the snake disappeared.

***

In the woods north of Baton Rouge, Maxwell couldn't sleep and got out of bed. It was still dark. But the feel and smell of Samantha at the dinner tonight was enough to send the hungry thing inside of him berserk for more. He sat back on the dingy sofa in the cabin and scrolled through his pictures on the burner phone. The special ones. The April pictures of each year since that day at the waterfall. And he let the hungry thing look at his trophies.

Later, after a shower, he fixed a cup of coffee and stepped outside and gazed into the dark yard. Only the light of the window shining on the ground and first rays of dawn filtering through the trees touched the darkness. He was nocturnal like most predators. It made him want to hunt. The flickering shadows teased and reminded him of fun things to come. Though, daytime worked too. A true predator could always hunt.

He couldn't ever remember a time when this thing wasn't a part of him. Even as a boy, he enjoyed bringing pain to others. Even his twin brother. Spencer. Poor Spencer who wouldn't hurt a soul in the world, now locked away for something he would never have done.

Good riddance. He spit on the ground.

***

Just after dawn on the river, Adam woke Raven. Tossing his head. Panting. She figured he was in the middle of a nightmare and leaned close and laid her hand on his chest.

Not wanting to startle him, she whispered, "Adam."

No response. He was still lost in the throes of the dream, so she touched his cheek. He jerked, grabbing her, as his eyes opened in panic. She lost her footing and landed on the side of the bed.

She whispered, "Adam, it's ok, look at me."

He blinked to focus and saw her. Then realized he gripped her arms and quickly let go.

She said soothingly, "It's okay. You were just dreaming," and got to her feet.

Hoarsely, he said, "I hate that snake."

"Me too."

"Did I hurt you?"

"Not at all, I'm fine."

She picked up a wet washcloth, and said, "You're sweating," and began to wipe his face.

He put his hand over hers and said, "I've got it. Thanks."

She handed him the rag. That was a good sign. He wiped his face, arms, and chest, then handed her the rag. She gave him ice water and he drank quite a bit then leaned back against the pillows. He was much more awake now which surprised her.

He said, "Your hair is beautiful."

She forgot it was loose instead of in the ponytail she normally kept it in. Smiling, she said, "Thank you."

He grimaced as a spasm shot through his leg. She checked the time, and he had a couple of hours to go before she could give him the last injection.

She explained, "I have one shot left. We need to wait about two hours for the medicine to last until the doctor arrives at noon.

115

Your body is adjusting to not being on the intravenous dosage. I'm sorry."

He nodded; aware it would be a painful wait. He said, "Occupy me. Please."

"Do you feel like talking?"

With a touch of humor, he said, "A minister can always talk," and she smiled thinking about her dad who always bragged he could talk a mile a minute.

He said, "Besides, I'm used to visiting with women."

Raven laughed.

"Ugh. Sorry. Not quite the way I meant it to sound."

"It's alright. I figured you as a charmer."

He looked at her. Really looked at her. He was trained to see more than she wanted him to. Aware of his intensity, she avoided his gaze.

He said, "I'm tired of thinking about myself. Tell me about you. You don't sound like you are from Louisiana. Have you been here long?"

"No. I'm from Minnesota."

"You're a long way from the snow."

Laughing, she said, "True. But I don't mind Louisiana heat. How long were you in Brazil?"

"Almost a year. How long do you plan to be in Louisiana."

"I moved here."

"I don't see a ring. Are you married?"

"Easy there, charmer."

"That means no."

She didn't answer. Nurses went through this all the time with male patients, and she was used to drawing a firm boundary. But it's not like he wouldn't know about her soon enough from the rest of his family.

Before she responded, he said, "I'm not married."

With a quick glance at his hot looks, she said, "How did you stay single?"

"I could say the same about you."

"Touché."

He said, "Besides, I'm waiting."

"For what?"

"The right one."

She smiled, impressed that he was bold enough to admit it. Then he smiled. A knockout smile that flipped her stomach. He should be illegal with looks like that.

Leaning forward, he said, "Is it okay if I sit up on the side of the bed?"

"I think it will be painful with your foot hanging down."

Determined, he said, "Can I at least try?"

She nodded and showed him how to move himself. He moved slowly - grimacing at his painful idea. She helped him swivel and made sure his leg didn't touch anything. He finally sat on the side of the bed, and she put a pillow under his heel. She handed him cold water and he drank two glasses.

She said, "You'll need to use the bathroom now that you're drinking."

He frowned and said, "I should have considered that."

"You will need to use crutches and get assistance for a while, or you can use the urinal." She motioned where it sat close by.

"I'll pass. Crutches are fine."

He sat quietly as she checked some scrapes on his back. He didn't say anything when the throbbing intensified. He frowned. It was still bearable. The sharp stabs came a little later. He grimaced and looked at the ceiling trying to ignore it. Sweat starting to form.

From behind him, Raven saw his movement and said, "Are you hurting? I can do this later."

"I'm hanging in there. Go ahead and finish."

The razor-sharp pain came next. As it worsened, he got lightheaded and sweat rolled down his temples.

He felt her finish and said, "Raven…"

She heard it in his voice and ran around the bed. She quickly helped him lay back down. As she turned to grab the last pain shot, with gritted teeth he said, "It feels like…the snake… is back."

She hit the plunger on the syringe.

Chapter 18

Back at the ranch, Sean slipped into Samantha's room before her alarm went off. He slid under the covers. She purred as he pulled her toasty warm body against his. He caressed and groaned knowing that the last thing in this world he ever wanted to do was get out of this bed.

He said, "I'm your new alarm clock."

"You could make a fortune as an alarm clock."

He chuckled and kissed her, starting their day with some steamy snuggling.

Before long, she pushed him out of the bed and said, "Go now or we'll be late again. I hate to be late."

He watched her wink and stretch in his bed. He kissed her one more time and forced himself back downstairs, dreaming about Switzerland every step of the way.

In an hour, Samantha came downstairs dressed in a demure black pantsuit and pearl accessories. They were going to see a prisoner in Angola, after all. Not the place to attract attention. Been there. Done that.

Sean smiled and slid her a cup of coffee across the counter, dressed in a black suit as well. He winked at her, and she teased him with an up-and-down onceover.

Jade said, "What's up with y'all? You're hiding something."

Laughing, Samantha said, "I'm allowed to have personal secrets."

Jade pressed, "How personal?"

"I plead the fifth."

Angel drawled, "We aren't in court."

Sean said, "Good answer, Angel. I will remember that."

Samantha poked him and said, "Wait a minute, whose side are you on?"

He pulled her into a hug and said, "Come on, Counselor. It was a great answer."

They laughed, and Sean said, "But on a serious update, Samantha has begun getting texts from Maxwell. We've got to ignore them at this point and focus on the case. We don't want him to start looking over his shoulder."

Jade said, "I hate that guy."

Samantha said, "Me too."

Sean and Samantha hit the road for Angola. They needed to be there by eight o'clock sharp.

Sean said, "The warden confirmed our appointment with Spencer. You ready for this?"

"Yes. I sure hope he has secrets he's willing to share. Maybe he's kept them to himself because no one asked. Like no one asked me about identification marks."

"I'm with you on that."

They rode quietly, and Samantha watched the lush Louisiana countryside pass by. Then they rode through the beautiful, picture perfect town of St. Francisville with its many hills and antebellum landmarks. Now it was just twenty-three short miles to Angola.

She reflected on its history. Some called it The Farm. Others called it the Alcatraz of the South. Some, Angola. But regardless of its name, the Louisiana State Penitentiary was one of the largest, toughest prisons in the United States.

Once a plantation with slaves that came from Angola, Africa, it later became a prison. Then the state took it over. Known for years as the bloodiest prison of them all, fear of Angola was often used to intimidate those beginning to walk the criminal path. Because housing over six thousand inmates, most would never leave. Alive anyway. And escape was less than rare, with it bordered on three sides by the Mississippi River and swampland.

Glancing at Sean, she knew he couldn't miss the turn or get lost. Highway 66 ended at the gates to the prison.

Once on site, they rode the bus from the visitation center to the prison. They entered a room with tables and chairs and had a seat. It was not regular visitation day, so this was a special circumstance. No one else was in the room. In a few minutes, the door opened, and Spencer Chance walked in.

They couldn't help but recognize him. He was a thinner, pale version of Maxwell.

He shrugged congenially, smiled, and sat across from them. He glanced at Sean first, but focused on Samantha, and said, "I rarely have visitors. How can I help you?"

She said, "Mr. Chance, I am Samantha Rutledge, Assistant Prosecutor for East Baton Rouge, and this is FBI Special Agent Sean Nash."

Spencer got it then. She was a grown woman now. Sorrowful, he sighed and said, "Why are you here?"

"I know it wasn't you."

He shrugged and said, "No. Not the attacks, but I didn't warn anyone or explain afterwards, so I'm guilty either way."

"Why did you confess and take the fall?"

"You met Maxwell face-to-face in the middle of a rage - so that answers that question. Besides, he doesn't take no for an answer. He also threatened to kill our parents if I didn't."

She figured it was something along that line and said, "I didn't realize until after sentencing it might not be you. He told me something that day and it always made me wonder. It left a bad taste in my mouth and a strong measure of fear."

Spencer said, "He was always bad. I'm safer here."

She said, "He's after me again."

Spencer paled and said, "No."

"We need information from you."

"How do you know I have any?"

"How could you not?"

He nodded.

She said, "But he can't know about this meeting at all. Can you hide that - even when he visits you? We know he does."

"I won't tell him."

Sean said, "Samantha's attacker had an appendix scar, and we know you have your appendix. She also bit her attacker on the right forearm. He should have a scar. Have you seen it?"

"I helped him bandage it. He had his appendix out not long before the attack."

He held up his right forearm showing it free of scars.

Sean said, "Thank you. Will you sign an Affidavit to these facts?"

"Yes."

Sean asked, "Why did he go after Samantha and Mary Beth specifically?"

"It wasn't Mary Beth. It was Samantha. He always loved blondes, but he became obsessed with Samantha at the craft fair. It was just crazy. He scared me."

Samantha understood completely and said, "Why's he coming to see you now, after all this time?"

He smiled and said, "He sent me an anniversary card every year just to harass me. He wanted to make sure I hadn't saved them and keeps harping on it. But I told him I trashed them."

Samantha lost her breath for a second in dismay.

Spencer said, "But I lied."

Sean said, "You have them?"

"Every single one."

All three of them smiled.

Then between the guards and phone calls to the Warden, an hour later guards returned with a small box and handed it to Samantha. She put it in her purse.

Samantha asked, "What about you, Spencer? Do you need anything?"

"I'm fine. Really. I do woodwork that I enjoy for the craft fair. And I'm Christian now and get to help sick inmates. I've made good friends with other lifers. And let's face it, it could have been worse. I could have been with Maxwell."

They understood completely.

Spencer said, "So, don't fret over me. My parents are dead, and he probably killed them. Just stop him. And whatever you do, stay away from him."

"I will. And thank you, Spencer. I won't forget you."

Before long they were back in their vehicle. Samantha opened the box. Inside were eleven white envelopes all mailed in April of consecutive years. They looked at each other knowing the value of what they had. Samantha opened the first envelope. It was a simple anniversary card with a four-word message: *Remembering Samantha, Love Maxwell.*

In the bottom corner of the card was a ragged red heart. Every card was the same.

Samantha flipped through the dates, and said, "The only April missing is this year."

Their gaze met and Sean said, "Because he came back for you."

An hour later, the evidence was on its way to the FBI lab and Sean and Samantha were westbound on Interstate 10 to Lake Charles.

***

Maxwell pounded the steering wheel in the Angola parking lot. He had seen Sean and Samantha drive away from the visitor center. He was going to pay to have Spencer killed if he told them anything.

By the time he signed in and reached the visiting room as a family attorney, he was raging on the inside. The door opened and Spencer came in and sat down.

Maxwell said, "What did they want?"

"Who?"

"I saw them, don't be stupid."

Spencer shrugged and said, "No big deal. They had a question about some evidence."

"What evidence?"

"How do I know? I wouldn't talk."

Maxwell smiled and left without another word. Spencer chuckled on the way back to his cell.

Unfortunately, FBI surveillance didn't recognize Maxwell with red hair and a beard in a faded yellow car. He drove right past them.

Chapter 19

On the river in Lake Charles, a giggle woke Adam. He barely opened his eyes. A little dark-haired boy knelt on all fours in the bed staring at him with excited brown eyes.

Adam grinned at the look of wonder on the little one's face. He said, "Hi."

The little boy smiled with delight and waved. Then his eyes widened as he remembered and pointed at Adam's leg.

He said, "Ouch!"

Adam widened his eyes too and agreed, "Big ouch."

The little boy crawled closer and touched Adam's long hair, then said, "Like daddy."

Adam wasn't sure who daddy was, and said, "What's your name?"

He sat back on his feet, touched his chest, and said, "Lance."

Raven walked in the room and gasped at seeing Lance in the bed. She scooped him in her arms and said, "I hope he didn't hurt your leg."

"Not at all. I didn't even know he was in the bed till he giggled."

Lance said, "Mommy, he woke up," and Adam laughed.

"Did you help him wake up?"

Lance nodded proudly, and they smiled.

Adam said, "He's precious."

With a tender smile, she touched Lance's nose, and said, "Thank you, I agree."

With an understood question, Adam offered, "He said I look like his daddy."

"Oh. Goodness. I'm a widow and he's intrigued at the resemblance you, Dakota, and Sean have to his daddy's pictures."

Surprised at the reference to their Indian heritage, Adam said, "I hear a story in there somewhere. Tell me. Please. Especially if the rest of my family already know."

"Well, yes. They do."

He prompted, "I love stories."

She sat with Lance and began, "In Gabrielle's story, do you recall the Atakapa warrior named Wolf that helped Jean Lafitte?"

"I do."

"I'm Wolf's granddaughter."

Adam said, "Wow. Now, that's my kind of story. Keep going."

"After Wolf died, Serena sent a letter to his family explaining where he had been all that time. As years passed, my Atakapa ancestors left Louisiana and moved north. They married into the Sioux Nation."

Adam raised his eyebrows. Really.

She said, "My mother's Sioux and Attakapa – a nurse. My father's a white preacher. Irish."

Adam glanced at Lance.

Raven kissed Lance's cheek, and said, "I married Beau Macawi, a great guy, also part Sioux." With a slight pause, she said, "He died on a camping trip before Lance was born. So, Lance has never known his father, just pictures. And men with your looks fascinate him."

Adam touched her hand and said, "I'm sorry for the loss - for both of you."

She nodded and continued, "Then last year I saw the news report revealing Gabrielle's connection to Lafitte. I read Dakota's book. And made plans to move to Lake Charles as soon as I could. I got here yesterday. Gabrielle's house was my first stop. They kind of took us in - and then you got hurt. I offered to care for you since I'm a registered nurse."

"You left out a few parts."

"Like what?"

"Why your friends and family let you leave home to move here."

125

She said, "You sound like Dakota."

"And you sound like you have a secret."

"Sort of. I explained to Dakota and the others, after becoming a widow, and then having an issue with a man who wouldn't leave me alone, Lance and I needed a new start. And new memories."

Knowing she hurried through the explanation, he said, "Where's the man?"

"In prison."

"For how long?"

"Life."

"You don't want to talk about it."

"No."

Adam said, "Ok then. I'm willing to help you."

"Do what?"

He smiled and said, "Make new memories."

She couldn't help but smile. Mr. Charmer he was. Then Lance insisted on going to Adam and fussed when she said no.

Adam said, "Let him come. Really."

Lance crawled to Adam's shoulder and rubbed his hair. Adam removed the ponytail holder. Lance touched his short hair while looking at Adam's long hair.

Raven consoled him and said, "Your hair will grow, sweetie."

Lance curled up next to Adam, bliss apparent, and pain crossed Raven's face. Adam understood.

She said, "I'm sorry."

"Don't be. Let the men around you help him. God will make a way."

Then they heard a commotion in the hall, and someone knocked on the door. It opened, and Sean walked in. Raven picked up Lance – who waved at Sean as Raven stepped out of the way.

Sean said, "Hey there, little warrior!" Then he touched Raven's hand and said, "Thank you for everything. You know I mean it."

Then he quickly moved on to hug Adam as Dakota sat on the other side of the bed. Raven shut the door behind her.

***

Sean said, "You look much better than the picture Dakota sent me Sunday night."

Adam said, "I barely remember any of that."

"Do you remember what happened on the mountainside?"

"Parts of it. The medical mission team I was on got wind of a woman too sick to travel down the mountain. She lived in a hut on a deck of sorts perched on a ledge. She couldn't climb anymore because of a tumor growing on her spine. We made it up there and a medical helicopter hovered over the deck as we worked to load her in it.

"The helicopter foot bumped me. That was it. I was already at the edge and just went right over. I fell about two stories. I tried to aim my feet down to absorb the fall and remember seeing flashes of jungle on the way down. I don't remember hitting the ground, which I don't mind at all. I woke to a raging pain in my leg. And then panicked as bugs found me."

Dakota and Sean grimaced. What a nightmare.

Adam said, "I looked up at some point and saw the medical team trying to reach me. But then they began to scream and point. I glanced, and a large green anaconda was coming for me. Until then, I hadn't even realized I was half-in, half-out of a stream. I tried to kick him with my good leg, but he was on the bad leg side. My foot disappeared in his mouth, and he bit down. It felt like a hundred nail guns going off at once and he began to wrap around my leg.

"My memories are sketchy after that. I remember the team loading me in a helicopter basket and they knocked me out with meds. The rest you know from the doctor."

Dakota said, "He was great. I left a few hours after he called. Sean's on a case and couldn't leave."

"What case?"

Sean said, "We'll talk about that later. Let me enjoy how much better you are – and less hairy."

Adam said, "Oh. Right. The beard."

Dakota said, "That was quite a beard. I shaved you and Raven did the rest."

Groaning, Adam said, "I'm glad I can't remember that."

Dakota said, "She's amazing. She took charge when I didn't know what to do first. And in no time flat, you were clean, rebandaged, and sound asleep. She even brushed your hair and put a ponytail in."

Adam said, "And she's gorgeous too. God loves me."

The guys laughed and someone knocked on the door. Raven stuck her head in and said, "Adam, I need to clean your leg before the doctor gets here. Are you ready?"

"No but do it anyway."

She stepped in. And as Dakota and Sean stood, she said, "You don't need to leave."

Dakota knew what was coming. Sean didn't. Raven removed the bandages. And while Sean knew it would be bad, his stomach rolled at the ripped tissue on Adam's foot, the surgery, and the overall condition of his leg.

Raven picked up a bottle of liquid and said, "Hang on, Adam."

He closed his eyes and clenched the sheet in his fists. She poured the saline solution over his lacerated foot. He groaned hard and muscles bulged, his face red in a tight grimace. Sean and Dakota looked at the floor, straining with him. Beads of sweat formed on Adam's body as the pain racked him. His heart raced.

Raven said, "Just one more minute, Adam. We're almost done."

When she finished, Adam released his hold on the sheet and caught his breath. He felt like he had run through razor wire. Leaning back into the pillows, his muscles quivered. Exhausted. She draped a large thin pad over his unbandaged leg.

She glanced at Adam, concerned. He nodded and gave her a thumbs up. She handed him a cool washcloth, and he wiped the sweat off.

She said, "The doctor will have pain meds for you. He should be here any minute. After he leaves, how about a shower, some lunch, and a nap?"

"You are not giving me a shower."

Dakota and Sean burst out laughing.

Raven, hiding a grin, assured him, "Not me. Your brothers can help you. I just need to give you a few instructions."

When she turned away, Adam winked at Dakota and Sean. They laughed again.

A few minutes later, voices carried down the hall. Gabrielle stepped in with the doctor and the Nash's. The doctor gave a nod of acknowledgement to Raven, then went straight to Adam.

He said, "Hello, Adam. I'm Dr. Drummond. I know Gabrielle's family from church and assured them that I would be glad to treat you here at home till you're mobile."

"Thank you for the house call, Doc."

The doctor glanced at Raven, and she handed him the hospital orders from Brazil.

He scanned through them and said, "When was his last pain shot?"

"Eight a.m."

"Adam, I know it hurts something fierce, but let me take a look at the leg before we do medicine."

He lifted the drape off the leg and gave a long whistle. Then gently touched the foot, leg, and knee in various places. He checked for pulse along the leg. Looked at all the scrapes, bruises, bites, and small cuts on the rest of his body. Adam was trying not to show signs of pain, but they knew.

The Doctor said, "I've got to get you off the pain shots. I'll prescribe pills instead. Don't miss a dose because they take longer to work, but they will be effective. You won't sleep as much either. I'll continue you on antibiotics and anti-inflammatories until the wound and incisions are further along in the healing process. And I'm changing the wound cream.

"You need to get up on crutches today, so start eating and make sure you're stable. Do not fall. And you need to start knee therapy in two days. I understand Raven will continue with nursing care."

Adam glanced gratefully at Raven, as she answered, "Yes, sir."

The doctor pulled a packet of pills out of his pocket and gave Raven instructions. Then he handed Adam a handful of prescriptions that needed to be filled.

He said, "Do not put any weight on that leg until I clear it. No exceptions."

Adam said, "No problem. Just the thought hurts."

The doctor smiled and said, "I believe your leg will be fine. Your foot and knee will have scars but should function as God intended."

He shook hands with Adam, said goodbye, and Gabrielle escorted him out. Raven handed Adam two pills and water. He downed them.

She said, "Dakota or Sean, would one of you get these prescriptions filled, while the other one gets soup or a sandwich on the way? Pain pills are tough on an empty stomach and it's time to build his strength."

They headed out with their instructions.

Adam said, "You're good at being in charge."

"It's not that so much. I just know what's best for you right now. You need me to know that. Once I teach you how to care for yourself, you'll be in charge again."

He watched her sort through the supplies, and said, "What are your plans here in Lake Charles?"

She turned and leaned against the dresser, then said, "I'd love to build a place on the river. I'm also a photographer. Somehow, I'll fit all that together, including nursing."

"Sounds like building blocks to a new life to me. A new adventure is always exciting. And in case you didn't know, I'm quite an adventuresome guy. You have to let me help. I love the outdoors. And when I'm not chained to the bed, I'm handy to have around."

"Roaming the mountains of Brazil verifies that. And thank you for the offer. Will flirting be part of what you offer?"

He said, "I am afraid so. I'm a package deal."

She laughed and asked, "What about you? What are your plans? Will you stay with missions once this is behind you?"

"A different type of missions. Before my untimely cliff dive, I was contemplating something new as well. I want to start up a search and rescue operation here in southwest Louisiana. Being an avid hiker and survivalist, I think I'm a good fit for that. Besides, I can vouch that being lost, injured, or helpless is a bad place to be."

She took a serious look at him. Impressed that he could think of others while in need himself.

She said, "You're quite a guy, Adam Nash. That's a worthwhile endeavor on any level. Sign me up. I'd love to help as well."

"Do you offer flirting in your sign-up package?"

And Dakota interrupted them with soup and sandwich. She grinned and ignored the question.

***

Raven headed to the kitchen to look for Lance. No one was there. She looked outside and everyone was in the yard. Laughing, she walked toward them as Samantha tried to teach Lance tumbling. Sean saw her and waved her over.

Raven said, "I didn't know Samantha could do all that."

"Me either."

They watched as Samantha hopped to give herself momentum and jumped into a perfect straddle split. Little Lance eagerly tried to lift one leg and fell over. Everyone chuckled. Then Samantha showed Lance a forward roll and helped him do a few. He was thrilled.

Afterwards, Gabrielle insisted Samantha show them her skillset. She did a few backbends, walkovers, flips, splits, and jumps. Lance hopped. Rolled. And did his best to imitate her. She laughed and tickled him.

Sean thought again of her medical records. Her extensive abdominal damage. He hurt for her as he watched her enjoy Lance. She didn't want to discuss it and he wasn't pushing it. He loved her just the fabulous way she was.

Samantha joined them and Sean said, "I didn't realize you stayed active in gymnastics. That's quite a set of graceful skills."

"Thanks. It was a dream, and I grieved the loss of competing. But the workouts make me happy. Even still."

"I see that. You made Lance happy too."

Samantha smiled at Lance, then glanced at Raven and said, "I hear you've taken wonderful care of Adam. We're so grateful. I am always comforted by the calm power of a nurse."

"Thank you, but I'm glad to help him. He's a strong patient."

"And a fine one too."

Raven laughed.

Sean said, "Speaking of patient, Samantha, come with me to check and see if Dakota and Adam are finished in the shower. I want to tell him about the case. And Raven, don't worry about interrupting. You're the boss. Come in and out as you need to."

Samantha raced Sean to the house. He let her win - but made her work for it. She laughed, appreciating that he made her push. After all, wasn't that the whole point of a challenge? They headed to the kitchen for a snack and something to drink.

Gabrielle had set out a fabulous charcuterie board with slices of meats, cheeses, olives, figs, strawberries, blackberries, honeycomb, glazed nuts, special jams, peppers, and crackers.

Samantha dove in while Sean fixed the drinks. He watched her choose the exact piece she wanted and slowly put it in her mouth – and wiggled in delight at the taste. And did it again. He set the drinks down and just watched. Hungry, but not for food anymore.

She glanced up and caught his look. Smiled…and dipped her finger in the honey and opened her mouth. But before she could lick it off, he was doing it for her. His lips made quick work of the sticky sweet goodness, and her belly sucked in at the heat of his mouth.

Then he slipped a couple of fingers in her waistband and pulled her close. He dipped his finger in the honey bowl and she opened her mouth. He touched her tongue, and her lips closed over his finger claiming the honey. He groaned and sat her on the snack bar, kissing her, tasting sweet honey all over again.

A few steamy minutes later, he said, "I hope no one comes in."

From behind them, Gabrielle said, "Too late."

Sean groaned and Samantha giggled against his chest.

Little Lance asked, "Can I have a taste too?" and they laughed till they cried.

Still chuckling on the way down the hall, Sean knocked on Adam's door.

Dakota said, "Come on in."

Sean glanced at Adam in bed, fresh from the shower while Dakota sat drenched in the chair.

Laughing, Sean said, "What happened to you?"

Adam said, "It's my fault. I slipped. I don't have the hang of this one leg balance act yet, so he had to catch me and got a blast of hot water."

Samantha laughed at Dakota, then kissed Adam on both cheeks, and said, "I'm glad you're home and on the mend. You scared us."

"Right. It scared me too – and it's good to see you. You're even more beautiful than when I left."

Dakota interrupted them as he asked Sean, "What's that blob on your shirt?"

Sean glanced down at a drop of honey. Samantha giggled and Sean scooped it up and licked it off his finger.

He said, "It's honey," and winked at Samantha.

Dakota said, "That just great. You're making out in the food."

Sean said, "Get over it and buy more honey. You're running low."

After the laughter faded, Dakota looked at Adam and said, "Sean and I need to fill you in on a new case. It involves Samantha."

Adam glanced at Samantha with a concerned frown. A case?

He said, "What's wrong?"

Sean said, "A quick outline is that Samantha was the victim of a violent attack at age sixteen. Her best friend was killed. An identical male twin confessed and is in Angola for life. But the wrong twin went to prison and the real killer has returned to finish what he started. But it's even more complicated than that. He's an attorney now and we suspect a serial killer. So, she's under FBI protection. The task force is based at my ranch, and we need to return in the morning. I just needed to come and see for myself that you're ok."

Adam said, "If Samantha needs me—"

Dakota said, "I get it – but no. We need you to stay here and get well – take care of that leg. Gabrielle and I will need to head to Baton Rouge too, but Raven, Mom, and Dad will be here with you."

Frustrated, Adam said, "Samantha…"

She said, "I can do this with their help, Adam. He'll go down. Please, work with Raven and get well. And thank you for caring."

Dakota walked to the door and called down the hall, "Gabrielle!"

Smiling, she came in and hugged him.

He said, "Adam, we do have some good news too."

"Thank God. What?"

"You're going to be a girl uncle by Christmas."

Adam yelled, "Hallelujah!"

***

It was almost midnight by the time everyone headed to their bedroom. It had been a full day. Samantha was about to climb in bed when her phone dinged. She glanced at the unknown number. No doubt it was Maxwell. Gritting her teeth, she knew there were so many things she would like to do to him. None of them pleasant. But they fell under the category of justice. One day he would get pay-back for all the women trophies under his belt. One day soon.

Sean knocked and stepped through her open door.

She said, "Hey, come in. I was about to head your way." She handed him her phone and said, "Psycho sent another text. I didn't look."

With clenched jaws, he read…

***

I'm going to make you like it. Then make you scream.

***

134

Fury flared so fast Sean knew there must be singe marks on his insides. But outwardly, he forwarded the text to his phone and deleted it on hers.

He said, "I know you're a pro at all this, but I wish you would let me hang on to your phone at night."

She knew what he was doing and hugged him. She said, "You keep it."

He led her to bed and said, "How about I stay with you tonight?"

She scooted over. He took his shirt off and slipped into bed, pulling her close.

After a soft kiss he said, "Get some sleep, baby. I'm not going anywhere."

***

North of Baton Rouge, Maxwell drove down the road near Sean's ranch. It was after midnight, but he couldn't sleep. Thoughts of Samantha made him toss and turn, so he figured harassing her might help. He glanced at the gun on the passenger seat. He was prepared for trouble even though they were gone. He had overheard Suzette mention on a call that they were out of town - but planned to be at the political dinner Thursday night.

He stopped near the entrance of Sean's driveway and tossed a red gift bag where it wouldn't be missed and drove away.

Further down the road, he removed his gloves. That bag, along with the texts he'd been sending were meant to invade Samantha's mind. Keep him with her. Stir her fear. Maybe even make her remember their day back at the waterfall. He smiled as he turned onto Highway 61 and headed home. It was all about the waterfall.

He had almost raped her back then. He literally couldn't have gotten any closer. But a group of people had ran out of the woods, screaming and yelling at him to stop. And it had been pure rage and frustration that caused him to throw her over the edge.

Then he'd ran, planned, and decided his brother could get him out of trouble. Make it all go away. Because he wasn't ready to stop. He was just getting started. No blonde would be safe. And then later, when he found out Samantha had survived, he knew it wasn't over. Not by a long shot.

***

As taillights faded away back at the ranch, an FBI agent stepped out of the trees toward the bag. He texted the license number, then radioed the others he was coming in. Angel waited on the porch.

When the agents arrived, they joined Jade in the house. Angel called Sean.

***

Sean slipped out of bed and hurried into the hall to answer the vibrating phone.

He said quietly, "Yeah."

"You had a night caller toss a red bag in your driveway a few minutes ago. The agents brought it in. We have gloves on, are you ready for us to open it?"

"Go ahead."

Jade cut the bow and opened the bag. She tilted it and a plastic bag with puzzle pieces slid out.

Angel said, "It's puzzle pieces."

"Put it together."

They spread the pieces out trying to determine the image. Jade began to snap a few pieces together, not sure what the picture with hair was yet. One agent whispered to Angel, who stopped Jade.

She said, "What's wrong?"

Angel said, "Hang on a second, Jade. Sean, the sicko left a zoom view of a woman's V."

Jade jerked her hands away, and said, "Ugh."

Sean growled softly and said, "Send it to the lab. I doubt they find DNA but try anyway. He's texting too. Ramping up. We need evidence to arrest him. I would like to ram it down his throat."

The fax machine rang, and Angel said, "Hang on, the fax is printing."

136

Entering the office, Angel picked up the fax and said, "They found Maxwell's rental location. I'm forwarding it to you. He's only ten miles from here."

"Ok. I'm calling the director to get eyes on him now. Samantha and I will be home in the morning. Great job everyone."

***

About two hours later, Sean's phone vibrated with a text:

Surveillance: We're in place.

Maxwell is here. Alone is seems.

He has four vehicles.

BMW and three rentals.

We'll be eyes only.

Sean: Got it. I'll be there tomorrow.

***

At Suzette's house in Baton Rouge, she turned off the lamp and headed to bed. It was almost three a.m. but she had been determined to read the case on Maxwell's brother. It had been a terrible crime and she was horrified for all that Samantha had suffered.

She stopped at the window and looked outside. No moonlight. It was cloudy. Creepy, after reading all the attack information. She sighed at the dilemma she faced. Maxwell's classification in the case was a relative. And a witness to the meeting of the victims at Angola's craft fair. That's it. Not even a hint of any crime, deceit, or involvement. An innocent man. A family victim.

Climbing into bed, she snuggled under the covers, grateful for safety. But in all honesty, she was grateful too for a chance with Maxwell. What could that hurt?

Chapter 20

Early the next morning in Lake Charles, Adam heard movement and opened his eyes. Dawn peeked through the window shades as he watched Raven walk across the room and look outside. Her long red hair hung down her back like silky fire. She raised her arms and stretched, amazingly graceful.

She turned around and caught him watching her. She smiled, then yawned, and apologized.

He said softly, "You need a good night's sleep in a real bed."

"I'm used to this. I nap pretty good when you're asleep."

She neared the side of the bed and laid a soft hand on his forehead, then cheeks. And said, "No fever. Very good."

He adjusted to more of a sitting position, wincing a bit at the movement of his leg, and said, "I'm curious."

He turned the lamp on to see her expression, and asked, "Have you dated since Beau passed?"

While she decided whether to answer, he said, "Is it that big of a secret?"

"No. But why? What difference does it make?"

"It makes every difference. One relationship touches the next. Even for friends. Don't you think we'll be friends? Close friends even. My family loves you. Won't I?"

"Are you asking as a minister or as a man?"

"You can't cut me in pieces. I'm always a man."

"I'm not trying to be difficult. I'm just…private. It's been tough. But no. I haven't dated." And trying to shift the conversation, she said, "I presume you date."

"Why?"

"You're single. A charmer."

Smiling, he said, "I socialize rather than date. I learned from past difficulties to handle it wiser. One-on-one time will come with the right woman."

She said, "I get that. That's why I keep it simple and avoid all of it."

"Then how will you find the one for you?"

"Maybe he'll knock on the door."

With a grin, he said, "Or be a patient from Brazil."

"Cute."

***

Down the hall, Sean smiled at Samantha still sound asleep in his arms. She smelled wonderful. Then he smelled coffee and started sliding out of bed. Her eyes barely opened.

He kissed her softly and said, "I'm grabbing us coffee. I'll be right back. Stay comfy." She smiled and dove under the pillow.

He chuckled and headed to the kitchen. He heard his parents talking as he walked down the hall. As he rounded the corner, Dakota came in from outside. And Gabrielle waved as she rocked Lance in the den.

He said, "Morning everyone."

His Dad said, "Morning Sean! What time do you and Samantha need to leave? We'll start breakfast shortly."

"I just came to grab us a cup of coffee. We need to be on the road by eight-thirty a.m. or close to it. And thanks, breakfast sounds wonderful."

After giving them a hug, he fixed two cups of coffee and headed back to Samantha. When he stepped in and shut the door, she squirmed in bed. He set the cups down and slid back under the covers. She curled up against him and he groaned softly, wrapping around her.

Voice husky from sleep, she said, "Thank you for staying with me last night."

"I was up and down a few times, but I didn't want to leave you. I behaved myself. Sort of. But if you keep moving like that, I might get in trouble now."

"Then give me coffee and I won't tempt you. Maybe."

***

Before long, everyone in the house was in the kitchen. Even Adam, escorted by a closely watching Raven. Lance was running and jumping, thrilled to see his momma. Then he stopped close to Adam's leg and pointed. He limped like Adam and laughter filled the room.

Dakota turned on the big screen TV and called out, "Does everyone know we have an action hero in the house?"

Gabrielle laughed as Dakota hit play on the DVR. Samantha grinned as the courtroom with J.J. Jones filled the screen. The whole news video played as Sean yelled, ran, and slung himself through the air and kicked the defendant across the room.

Shocked, Adam glanced at Sean, his behind-the-scenes brother, and said, "Where did that come from?"

Dakota said, "Samantha happened to him. The wild warrior finally came out of the drone room."

***

Less than an hour later, Sean pulled onto Interstate 10 headed back to Baton Rouge.

He said, "I got a few messages during the night. They found Maxwell's rental house and started surveillance last night."

Samantha fist-pumped, and said, "Yes! That's great news!"

"It is. I'll need to get over there with the drones when we get home. And…now for Maxwell activity."

"That sounds ominous. What now?"

"After he sent you the text last night, he took a drive by the ranch and tossed a present in the driveway. It was a picture puzzle. Disgusting as it turned out. Take my word for it, you don't want to know."

"Tell me anyway."

After a pause, he said, "A zoom shot of a woman's V."

Samantha grimaced in revulsion, and said, "He's hell in the flesh! He's going to get his. And I'm going to enjoy watching what justice does to him. I mean it."

Still appalled after the conversation, she ignored the landscape flashing by her window and thought about the puzzle. She couldn't imagine walking in a store with items like that or even ordering it online. The dark side of life was so ugly when exposed to the light. Deadly. Meant to erode and destroy what was meant to be beautiful. She couldn't help but think of all his victims. She vowed to avenge them. Champion them. And thought about the FBI Academy. Her dream.

Sean gave her space for a while, then said, "You don't talk much about your growing up years. Tell me about some of your adventures. Your parents."

She smiled, shifted a bit to face him, and said, "It was just Mom and me. Tiffany Rutledge. She was my everything. Brilliant, beautiful, about my size and coloring. She opened my world up to knowledge. Dreams. And always encouraged me to believe I could achieve anything if I worked hard. Including gymnastics.

"She was amazing, Sean. A political science professor." Then she sighed and said, "She found out she had skin cancer after my attack and died just before my high school graduation."

Sean slipped his hand around hers.

She squeezed it and said, "And Jonathan Remington stepped in at that point to help guide and support me. He had grown up with my mom. Best friends for as long as I knew. Even after he married his wife, Sara. We were family friends. Jonathan's three sons, Luke, Jessie, and Devon are like brothers to me. Without the Remington's, and Gabrielle, Jade, and Zoe, I wouldn't have had a family."

Noticing there was no mention of a father, he said, "And your father?"

She shrugged, and said, "I know next to nothing. She said he couldn't stay with us. But she never complained about him. Never spoke about him in anger. He just wasn't there. I never knew him. I don't even know his name."

Sean said, "We could do some digging if you want. I know Angel and Jade would be glad to help you. Do you want to know who he is?"

"I guess if I had an emotional hole in my life, I would. But I never lacked for anything, so I didn't dwell on it. Thanks for offering. I'll…think about that."

"What about your faith. When—"

"In college. Gabrielle insisted on bringing me with them to church. And before long I started following Him myself. I don't have the lifelong Christian language and experience long-term Christians do, but I know He loves me, and I love Him. But…I have a feeling I'm labeled in the feisty group of believers."

Sean laughed and said, "No doubt, hot stuff."

She said, "When did you believe?"

"I was young. I grew up strong in my faith until college. I stumbled big time doing my own thing with meaningless relationships. I had to recommit myself to move on."

She said, "I get that. Being a Christian single is not an easy road. Was there anyone special?"

"Not even close."

She nodded, and said, "Well…you already know my story about men. Fear always kept me from going too far. But…I've kissed a lot of men."

He looked at her and said, "You thought you should make that clear?"

She unbuckled her seatbelt and leaned to slide her hand across his tight stomach. Feeling his muscles clench, she whispered, "But those were the shortest kisses in history. No one ever made me feel the way your touch does. Ever."

Sean pulled into a picnic rest area in the Atchafalaya Basin. He got out of the car and motioned her to follow him. After a searing kiss, he led her to the most private table he could find and made her feel that way again.

Cheers and whistles followed them back to the car.

142

***

Back at the ranch, Angel stopped the video feed and rubbed his face. His eyes were tired after watching truck stop videos most of the night. He had made Jade go get a few hours of sleep. Glancing out the window, the brown stallion and white mare ran wild and free in the corral. Jumping. Racing. Nipping at each other. He didn't blame the stallion. That was one fine mare.

He stood and stretched, then walked in the kitchen to start another morning pot of coffee. Jade stood in front of the coffee pot, barefoot, in low-rise lounge pants and a tank top. She made him ache in half a second. She turned at the sound of his footsteps – meeting his gaze. Her sleepy eyes and full lips did him in.

Without a word, his mouth covered hers. Starving. They had been so busy in the case. Distracted. Concerned. But it was getting harder to not make this part of the day. Desire fired through Jade as she opened to him. Clutching him. Wondering what in the world she was going to do with this thing between them.

Kerry cleared his throat to make his presence known. They hadn't seen him in the easy chair by the door.

With a grin, Angel asked casually, "How about some coffee?"

Kerry said, "I don't know. It looks like you might need something cold instead."

They laughed.

Angel said, "I'm glad you're here, we wanted to talk to you. But…I got sidetracked."

"I noticed that."

Jade said, "Let me change, I'll be right back."

Angel watched her walk down the hall. His longing evident.

Walking up to get a cup of coffee, Kerry said, "Does she know you love her?"

"Not a clue."

"You keep kissing her like that and she'll figure it out."

"You sound like a man that knows."

Kerry nodded and said, "A long time ago, my man, a long time ago."

143

They were both drinking coffee when Jade came back in the kitchen. She glanced at Angel, then sat at the table.

He joined her and said, "Come sit for a second Kerry, we have some news for you."

But a knock on the door interrupted them. Jade smiled on her way to the door and opened it. She was early.

The woman said, "I know I'm early, but I couldn't wait any longer."

Jade understood and motioned her inside. The woman walked in and locked eyes with Kerry. He slowly stood and stared. Shocked. Speechless. She was dressed in jeans, a pink top, sandals, with long dark hair, and loving brown eyes. Chancy.

She smiled and said, "Hi, Kerry."

He swallowed still trying to believe his eyes and find his voice. He said, "How did you know I was here?"

Chancy glanced at Jade.

Kerry glanced at Angel and Jade, then said, "I guess this was the good news you were about to tell me?"

Angel said, "It was. So now, I think Jade and I will take a walk."

In a second, they left out the back door.

Kerry walked toward Chancy, not quite sure what this meant after all these years, and said, "You really wanted to see me after all I did to us?"

She touched his chest and gazed up at the man she had loved forever. With her heart in her eyes, she said, "Not a day passed that I didn't want to be with you."

Emotion swamped him. Disbelief, as she wrapped her arms around him. Still unsure how to respond, he said, "I don't deserve you, Chancy, but God help me, I love you so much I ache."

She kissed his chest and he groaned, warning her of his struggle. He whispered, "Chancy…"

"Stop fighting it, Kerry. You're free to love me now."

And picking her up, he kissed her with a ragged hunger hidden for years. She yielded. Surrendered. And offered, as she hung on to her passionate giant.

Deep voice even huskier as he kissed and talked, he said, "Oh…Chancy…you…taste like heaven."

Breathless, she said, "I was thinking…the same thing."

Carrying her to the sofa, they sat, and he said, "I just can't think. It's like a dream. Does this—"

A knock on the door interrupted him. He looked up to see a tall girl, dark like him, with long braids and sunglasses. She knocked again. Impatiently this time. He glanced at Chancy with a question on his face. She smiled and stood, drawing him to the door. His mind spun at what was happening.

Chancy opened the door and the girl said, "I'm sorry Mom, I couldn't wait either."

Then she removed her sunglasses, and said, "Hi, Daddy. I'm Misty."

His heart exploded as he stared into crystal blue eyes, and scooped her up in a hug, daring to believe this was true.

Angel and Jade watched the reunion as they walked to the barn.

Wiping happy tears, Jade said, "I bet we'll be guests at a wedding soon."

"Oh yeah."

***

A couple of hours later, Sean and Samantha drove up to the ranch. They saw the extra vehicle, and Kerry with two women on the patio. Jade and Angel walked outside to meet them.

Samantha asked, "Is that…"

Jade said, "Yes. And it was the most amazing thing ever."

Sean smiled as Kerry led his family to meet them. Samantha didn't wait for the introduction but went straight in for the welcome hugs.

Several minutes later, Kerry said, "Samantha, I hear it was your idea to find them."

"I just beat the others to the idea. It would have happened anyway."

145

Heading inside, Sean and Samantha went to the office for updates. Victim boards lined the walls. And though the connection to Maxwell was still circumstantial at this point, they were getting closer to a direct link.

As it stood now, they were 1) reviewing truck stop videos, 2) waiting on lab reports for the anniversary cards, and 3) about to begin drone surveillance.

After they were up to date on all the details, Sean and Angel packed the drones while Jade showed Samantha the map to Maxwell's house.

"It's crazy," Samantha said. "He's a mere ten minutes from here. We could have run into him anytime. That gives me the creeps."

"I hear that. And he keeps a lot of vehicles, so no one recognizes his car. He has four at his house right now. He certainly does not want to be found."

Picking up a gray case, Sean said, "I'm going to head outside to set up a security drone here at the ranch. It will have visual and thermal capabilities. Continuous feed. Then my office will have a full view of the surrounding area."

Angel said, "Bring it on Drone Master."

Sean laughed as they headed outside.

They reached the base of an old fire tower in the woods. Sean knelt with the case and pulled out a three-legged, triangle shaped drone with a helicopter style rotor blade. Setting it on the ground, he opened the control panel. The drone powered up quickly and a tiny green light blinked. He flew it up the side of the closest post until it reached the top. Watching his monitor, he backed the drone into position. A quick pop sounded.

Sean said, "Ok. The drone is secure to the post and can see 360 degrees. Now, for the recharging station."

Once in the barn, Sean headed to several shelves in between a set of cabinets. He bolted a solar powered triangle base with antennae to the top shelf.

He said, "The drone will be offline when it is recharging. But it's quick. And it's programmed to continue this routine until I give it a different command. Let's test it."

Picking up the control panel, he called the drone. In seconds, it swooped through the door and docked on the station. Sean saluted it and sent it back out. Angel fist pumped.

In the house, Kerry visited with Chancy and Misty while he seasoned prime Angus beef to grill hamburger steaks. His world had just burst wide open with dreams again. Love. Passion. And a future with the women he loved. He had a lot of planning to do.

The patio door opened, and Sean led the group inside.

Kerry said, "How did it go?"

Sean said, "Perfect. But now I'm going to need to borrow you for a bit of training. Sorry ladies."

Chancy said, "Oh. No problem. We'll walk out on the patio for a while."

Kerry followed the task force to the office. Sean turned on the large monitor and after a few keystrokes, the drone view from on top the fire tower appeared - overlooking the house, yard, barn, driveway, and into the woods.

Sean explained, "This security screen will now remain on. Each of you need to know how to manage what you want to see. Thermal or camera view."

Kerry and Angel grinned. Yeah baby.

Sean pointed to the screen showing a clear view, and said, "This is normal daylight view." Then he hit a green key and said, "This is thermal view. Heat. You would be looking for human shapes or large animals. Danger. See the image of the women on the patio?"

Everyone nodded, then Sean hit a yellow key and using the controller, zoomed in on them.

He said, "You can't see their features, but it helps you determine size and shape. Are they standing. Lying down. Running. Climbing.

That type of thing too. Take a few minutes to practice while I load my equipment. And Angel, why don't you come with me to Maxwell's this trip?"

"You got it."

"Dress in black or camo," and Angel left to change.

Instructing the others, he said, "You know the FBI security detail is here. But still, Samantha and Jade, stay armed. And Kerry, I know it's bad timing, but I think it's safer if Chancy and Misty aren't at the ranch until Maxwell's in custody. We don't want him to even see them or know they exist."

***

Kerry joined Chancy and Misty and explained the situation.

He walked them to their car, and said, "I'm sorry about this. But I need both of you safe. At least we can keep in touch by phone."

Chancy said, "Be careful, Kerry. And please stay out of harm's way. We've waited so long."

"I know, baby. And that reminds me, when you get back home, would you run an errand for me?"

"Anything."

"How about stopping by the courthouse for a marriage license?"

Misty screamed in excitement while her mom was soundly kissed by her dad. Everyone ran outside expecting trouble. Then grinned.

Kerry said, "You're all invited to a wedding as soon as this is over!"

After cheering for Kerry, Sean winked at Samantha. She batted her lashes at him. They had a wedding around the corner themselves.

***

Fifteen minutes later, and ten miles away, Sean and Angel parked deep in the woods. Two black SUVs were already there. Sean texted the surveillance agents they were headed toward them.

Sean pointed south and said, "Maxwell is on the next road. We'll hike about a mile to join the team."

They grabbed an earpiece, radio, and put a small, but powerful, pair of binoculars in their pocket. Picking up his drone case, Sean motioned silence and they took off. It was two p.m.

The landscape was pure wilderness. Hills. Woods. Ravines. Streams. And dense vegetation. They worked up a sweat on the summer jog dressed in camo. Before long, Sean glanced at his GPS watch and stopped. He pointed and Angel looked at the screen. They were close to the other agents.

As they topped the next ravine, Sean saw the camo net blocking the view in front of the surveillance tables. Two agents sat in front of equipment. They turned with a thumb's up. Sean led the way into the work area and looked through the camo net window toward the cabin in the distance. Three vehicles were parked alongside Maxwell's black BMW.

The tall agent whispered, "He's been inside all day."

Sean nodded, and said, "I need to get trackers on those vehicles now."

He opened his case and removed a search and rescue drone. After he loaded trackers and adhesive in the proper compartments, he motioned Angel to stay. Then checking the area, he moved closer for better visual while the other agents went into defense position.

He chose a tree with low branches about forty feet from the road, then climbed to be higher than the vehicles. Once settled, he removed the four-footed drone from his backpack and picked up the controller. Flipping it on, the drone flew on a mission course above the trees toward the house as they watched their monitors.

The drone lowered before leaving the tree line and skimmed just above the ground. It reached the driver's side of the black BMW and landed. Then crab-walked under the rear car wheel well. It blew a sticky tracker underneath.

Sean stilled as the door to the house opened. Maxwell walked out, muscles evident, dressed only in LSU shorts and flip flops. No weapons visible. He neared the BMW, and his phone rang. They listened.

***

With a few choice cusswords, Maxwell pulled the ringing phone out of his pocket. Then in a deceptively friendly tone, said, "Hey Suzette, I was just about to call you."

He laughed with his voice, but not his countenance, and said, "Do you like Mexican food?"

Pause. "Great! I'll pick you up from work about six p.m. if that's ok."

Pause. "Perfect. I'll meet you in the parking garage."

Pause. He laughed again and said, "I look forward to it. See you in a little while."

He hung up and spit on the ground. Obviously aggravated. And going back inside, he slammed the door.

***

Sean got back to work. He walked the drone under the next vehicle, a white car, and planted another tracking device in the same location. He did it for the blue truck and silver van as well. Then brought the drone back to him.

He whispered in the radio, "Scout drone next," and pulled out a gray four-footed drone. Smaller, with a camera extension. Sean flew it high above the trees toward the house and checked the complete structure. Roof. Walls. Windows. And doors for access inside.

Once scouting was complete, he positioned the drone at the BMW and looked through the windows. Brown duffle bag. Gray hoodie. Black cap. Box of disposable gloves. A polaroid camera. Nothing in the other three vehicles.

The front door opened. Sean quickly landed the drone and walked it underneath the van. Maxwell walked out, leaving the door open. He opened the trunk of the BMW, then cussing, walked back in the house like he forgot something.

Sean flew the drone across the ground back to the BMW, then hovered next to the driver's side of the open trunk. He slid a camera extension inside. There were various professional uniforms and hats. Cops. Firemen, and Medical. Random jackets. Plenty of wigs. And a backpack with an Angola patch on it.

Sean heard "Move!" in his earpiece as Maxwell jogged out of the house with a knife.

Sean landed the drone and moved under the car to listen and watch. Maxwell dropped a bundle of something and leaned down to pick it up. Twist ties and a roll of duct tape. No surprise there. Tools of the trade.

They listened as Maxwell hummed and cut something up in the trunk. Sean turned the drone. The front door of the house was still open. He walked the drone away from Maxwell. Skimmed around all the vehicles and flew into the house.

He only had seconds to hide. He walked the drone underneath the sofa. Against the wall. And faced the front. Locking it in stealth mode, it sat – ready for instructions.

Maxwell walked back in the house and shut the door.

Chapter 21

Sean climbed out of the tree and headed back to the surveillance camp. The men fist-bumped his covert move.

He whispered, "It was too good an opportunity to pass up. I'll look around the house after he leaves. But we have a two hour wait – maybe more."

Angel watched him prepare the next drone, wanting one so bad he could taste it.

***

Back at the ranch, Samantha and Jade helped Kerry with the horses.

Samantha said, "Kerry, what are your plans now that you'll be married with a family?"

"We're talking about it. Chancy and I always planned to open a piano dinner club in New Orleans. But…we'll have to wait and see what's best for Misty."

"A piano dinner club sounds perfect. I'll come!"

Jade said, "Angel and I bought an old Victorian house in New Orleans to turn into flats and a business, so we'll be frequent guests if you open one."

"You better!"

A few minutes later, Samantha said, "I'm going to take a walk down to the creek and enjoy the freedom since Sean has eyes on Maxwell. I won't go far."

Jade said, "I'll check for new intel first and then come join you."

Kerry glanced toward the bluff hiding the creek and said, "Just make sure both of you stay armed. Holler loud if you need me."

***

Samantha climbed down the bluff, kicked off her sandals and wiggled her toes in the sand. Smiling, she waded into the clear, shallow creek and headed toward the bend. The locals had warned them that Thompson Creek filled up fast with heavy rain, but there had been no rain recently. So, enjoying herself, she listened to the sounds around her. A light breeze. Birds. Trickling water. Totally peaceful. What a treat after all the commotion of the last few days.

She checked behind her to see how far she had waded. That was far enough. She turned and headed back. After only a few steps, she heard loud splashes behind her. She spun and a black bear was charging her. It roared.

She grabbed the gun out of her waistband and backing up, aimed, and fired. Once. Twice. She hit him. It stumbled and fell then clambered up and continued after her - madder than before.

She screamed and ran. He roared again. She couldn't take a chance another bullet wouldn't stop him, so screaming for help, she scrambled up the bluff. Hearing the growls. Knowing it wasn't far behind her.

Reaching the top, she kept screaming as she ran across the yard. She saw Kerry running full speed toward her from the barn. Jade ran out of the house, pistol in hand. The bear rounded the top of the bluff and quickly gained on her.

The FBI agents ran through the woods toward the screams and hit the clearing in time to see the shocking scene before them. And ran. But Kerry reached Samantha first. All he had time to do was lift her away from the bear and sling her onto his back.

Samantha hung on as the bear charged Kerry. He kicked it with everything he had. And the force of the big man's blow knocked the bear aside, but it got up and lunged, swiping long claws toward Kerry's side.

153

The agents and Jade couldn't find a clear shot with the twisting and turning of Kerry and the bear.

Samantha hung on with every muscle in her body as Kerry hit the bear. Upside the head over and over. Hard. The bear shook its rattled brains and lunged to bite. The FBI agents ran into the fight. Shoved guns into the animal's side and kept shooting till he dropped. Dead. Mouth open. Claws bloody.

In slow motion, Kerry dropped to his knees. Samantha slid off and held on to him. He was breathing hard. Bleeding. Samantha was in shock. Shaking. Jade dropped to the ground beside them and tried to see their wounds.

The oldest agent texted Sean.

***

Bear attack. Kerry protected Samantha. Kerry hurt.
Sean: Coming.
***

Before long, they heard Sean roaring down the driveway. He slid to a stop - jumping out, Angel following. Samantha and Jade ran to meet them in the yard.

Samantha leapt into Sean's arms. Holding her tight, he said, "Are you hurt?"

"No. But Kerry is," and pointed to the patio.

Sean quickly headed his direction. Kerry stood. Sean saw the wound on his arm. And dried blood all over him. A towel was wrapped around his waist. He saw the look in Kerry's eyes and knew how bad it had been.

He said, "I can't thank you enough. That's crazy courage. Come inside. Let me check your injuries. Did anyone call an ambulance?"

Kerry said, "I told them no," and the door closed behind them.

***

Jade's tears had dried on her face, but Angel saw her anxiety. He pulled her in his arms and said, "Are you hurt?"

154

"Just shocked. A bear attack is not something you think to prepare for."

Angel looked toward the agents, and then they all turned to look at the dead bear lying in the yard.

The youngest agent said, "I've never seen anything like it, Angel. Samantha came over the top of the bluff screaming and running, long blonde hair streaming behind her. Then the bear lunged over the top after her. Kerry was already heading across the yard. That big man was pumping those legs hard - straight toward her. It looked like they would run right into each other. But as he reached Samantha, he slung her on his shoulders, and she held on like a cat. And he fought that bear without a weapon."

The oldest agent said, "Not hardly. That big man was the weapon. He saved her life before we killed the bear. He's my new hero."

***

Reaching the bathroom, Samantha gathered rags. Sean pulled out the first aid kit as Kerry carefully removed his torn shirt. They winced at the raw rips on his arm, waist, and stomach. Jagged, but shallow, with dry and seeping blood. It had to be terribly painful.

Sean asked, "Are you injured under your jeans?"

"Pretty sure it's just bruises. Nothing burns."

Sean looked closely at the wounds, and said, "I'd prefer if a doctor checked you out. This is not a normal wound."

"But they aren't deep. If I hadn't been as big and strong as I am, I would look a lot worse. But if we clean it, put antibiotic ointment and bandages, it'll scab in no time. I've had worse than this in prison and I heal quick."

Sighing, Sean said, "I give it till morning. If it's worse, I insist on the emergency room."

"Deal."

Sean said, "But we've got to clean it good and that will be painful. Animals have nasty bacteria and diseases, and you have a wedding around the corner."

With a touch of humor, Kerry said, "Yeah, well there were nasty bacteria and diseases in Angola too."

Grinning, Sean said, "I hear that. But come on. Stand in the tub and let me pour this over the wounds. I'm sure it's going to burn. Bad."

"Don't worry about that. At this point, air burns. Just go for it."

In thirty minutes, the wounds were clean, treated, and bandaged. They walked onto the patio where everyone waited. Kerry couldn't help but grin at their expressions.

The oldest agent said, "You are now the Black Avenger. I will forever tell of that fight."

After their laughter faded, Sean began to hear the tale of what happened. The screams. Gunshots. Roars. Claws and teeth. He glanced over at the dead bear while it played in his head. Death had been inches from Samantha. And Kerry. Samantha saw it in his eyes and slid her arms around him reassuringly.

About that time, Dakota honked as they came down the driveway.

Everyone headed toward the SUV. Dakota got out and walked over to the dead bear.

He glanced at Sean, then noticed the big black man's bandages and said, "I guess you are the one that met up with this bad boy."

"Yeah, about an hour ago."

Dakota knew that had to have been a nightmare.

Sean said, "What Kerry isn't telling you is that he got between Samantha and the bear. She was hanging onto his shoulders as he fought it with his bare hands."

Dakota and Gabrielle looked at Samantha. Stunned.

Samantha said, "It was bad. And he's a real hero. He snatched me right out of the path of that bear."

Shaking Kerry's hand, Dakota said, "Even a man your size would have needed a massive amount of courage to do that. Thank you. I'm grateful – and impressed."

Kerry glanced at Samantha and said, "Who wouldn't brave a beast to save her?"

Once everyone was back inside, Sean led Dakota to see the victim boards. Eleven dead women were projected as the serial victims. Dakota scanned all the linked details on each victim. Then scanned Maxwell's stats before turning to Sean.

Sean said, "Surveillance detail is at Maxwell's house. I've put trackers on all four vehicles there. He's a fan of rentals. Only the black BMW contained items of interest: a camera, wigs, uniforms, twist-ties, duct tape, and a gray backpack with a large Angola patch. Most of which are in the trunk he left open for a few unguarded minutes.

"And fortunately, he left his front door open too. So, I flew the drone in the house and hid it under his sofa - where it waits for me now."

Dakota laughed and high-fived him. He said, "That's brilliant. Stealthy. I expected no less from you."

Smiling at Angel's fist-pump behind Dakota, Sean said, "So, I need to get back to surveillance."

Dakota said, "Ok then. Let's go."

Sean said, "Angel, I need you here since Kerry's wounded. And everyone needs to stay near the house or barn. Security detail will be close by. And I'll let you know if any of the trackers show Maxwell headed this way. Keep check on the drone security."

Minutes later, Sean and Dakota prepared to leave. Sean gave Samantha a quick kiss before climbing in the SUV.

Lowering his window he said, "Keep your phone and gun on you, Counselor. Watch those truck stop videos and stay safe. No more hikes."

***

As Sean drove away, Kerry walked to the barn calling Chancy.

The phone rang a few times, then breathlessly, Chancy answered, "Hi, honey!"

He said, "I love hearing that again."

"I love saying it again. Is everything okay? You sound tense."

157

Kerry laid it out there and said, "We had some trouble this afternoon."

Heart pounding at his tone, she said, "What trouble?"

"A bear chased Samantha from the creek into the yard. The FBI killed it."

Horrified at the thought, she gasped and said, "Please tell me she is okay!"

"She wasn't hurt, just scared out of her mind."

She paused, feeling that inkling of unease, and said, "What aren't you telling me?"

"I got between her and the bear. He would have killed her."

She began to cry.

He said, "Chancy, listen, I'm going to be fine. Honestly. The wounds aren't deep, and Sean and Samantha patched me up. I don't even need stitches."

"Where are the wounds?"

"On my stomach, side and arm."

She groaned, "Kerry…"

He said, "Baby…it's ok. You'll see."

"Send me pictures. I mean it. I want to see for myself, or I'm coming back out there."

"I hear you. The next time they change my bandages I'll send you pictures. Please don't come. Not yet. It's too dangerous."

Raggedly, she said, "I love you. I need you with us. All in one piece."

"And I love you. I'll be there as soon as I can. Just a few more days."

She said, "Then sing to me. Now. Like you used too. I need to hear your voice."

Kerry glanced back at the house. Angel and Jade were on the patio. He walked through the barn and leaned against the fence, then sang *Unforgettable*. Chancy hit speaker on her phone and listened as his voice filled her room. After a few moments, she joined in, and they sang for lost years and new dreams.

Neither knew that Misty listened outside her mother's door. Happy tears streaming down her face at finally being able to hear her parents sing.

At the log cabin in Lake Charles, Raven put the last bandage in place on Adam's leg. She glanced at him. His face was still pinched with remnants of pain, but he was hanging in there.

He blew out a quick breath and said, "The foot pain is not near as raw. It feels more like hot coals now instead of lava. That makes a big difference."

"Yes, it does. Each day will be better. By the weekend it may be closer to hot ashes."

He grinned and said, "Encouraging. I have that to look forward to. Now please, reward me. Let's go outside. I'm tired of being in the bedroom and I need to get better on crutches anyway. Who's here right now?"

"Your parents. They are cooking dinner. Gabrielle's parents picked up Lance to play with the twins at their house."

"Ah. So, I can have all your attention."

She rolled her eyes.

He said, "Come on. Help me up."

"No. You're flirting. You can do it."

Chuckling, he swiveled, grabbing his crutches, and slowly stood. The blood rush filled his leg. Ouch. She rewarded him with a big smile. She knew that was not a pleasant feat with a raw foot and a surgical knee.

He said, "That's one killer smile you've got there."

She pointed to the door, ignoring his flirting, and said, "Keep going."

Before long, Adam leaned against the porch rail and looked at the river. He said, "This is what I'm talking about. Outdoors. Fresh air."

She sat in a rocker and smiled, completely understanding what he felt. She had been there.

He said, "Talk to me. Tell me new things about you. Do you have any hobbies or special interests?"

"A few. I play the drum."

"What kind?"

"A native tom-tom."

Intrigued, he said "Really." He glanced at her hands and said, "You're so gentle. I don't see you beating the drum. Do you dance too?"

Not wanting to elaborate, she said, "I do. Now it's your turn to share. What do you enjoy?"

"I'm pretty good with a bow and arrow."

Smiling, she said, "I can't wait to see you shoot. You should be able to balance well enough before long. Is your bow and quiver here?"

"Yes, and my horse. The paint." He pointed to the corral where Dakota's black stallion and his brown and white paint grazed.

Her face softened and she said, "He's gorgeous. I love to ride."

He said, "Me too. I hope it isn't too long before I can get on a horse."

Raven said, "Hmmm. Not until you get a protective boot. You need that leg too much to take chances."

He didn't answer so she glanced at him. He was watching her.

Adam was entranced as her long copper hair danced in the breeze, framing her gorgeous face in the sunlight. For a few seconds Raven got lost at the look in his dark eyes. Penetrating. Sexy. Awareness teased them.

Breaking contact, she glanced across the river at Gabrielle's place and said, "I plan to shop for land on the river soon. Would you like to get out and ride around sometime? It'll get you out of the house and help me find a new home at the same time. It's important to get Lance and I settled. A place to call home."

"Come on. I'm game for a ride now."

She grinned and said, "Your first therapy session is tomorrow. You should have more physical freedom once that starts. They'll teach you what you can and can't do. You might be in a cast or boot soon – giving you more mobility. Freedom's coming."

***

North of Baton Rouge, Sean and Dakota turned south on Highway 61 and headed to the turnoff for surveillance. Sean keyed in a cell number and hit speaker.

The Director answered, "What's with the wild stories about bears and sneaky drones coming from Louisiana?"

Sean said, "Wild is a perfect word for it. We've had an unusual day. But Dakota is here now so we'll get him in on the action. We're joining surveillance shortly."

Dakota said, "Afternoon, Director."

"Glad to have you back on board, Dakota. Adam getting better?"

"He's healing amazingly fast actually. It might have something to do with his gorgeous nurse."

Chuckling, the Director said, "Smart move. Now, get to work. Find evidence and keep in touch."

***

Sean led Dakota through the woods to the surveillance camp. And less than five minutes after they got there, Maxwell walked out. He headed to the blue pickup and took off down the road. Then before the dust even cleared, he roared in reverse back to the house. After screeching to a stop in front of the door, he ran inside for a few seconds, then left again.

The team watched the tracker reach Highway 61 and turn toward Baton Rouge.

Sean called out, "All clear."

Able to talk freely with Maxwell gone, Dakota said dryly, "Well now…that could have been messy if we had jumped the gun and walked out."

The guys chuckled.

Sean climbed the same tree as before and activated the hidden drone inside the house. Underneath the sofa, the drone lit up and their monitors showed a shadowed view of the room.

Sean said, "Here we go."

He walked the drone to the center of the room then raised it a few feet in the air. He rotated it 360 degrees to see the interior of the house. It contained a small kitchen with a back door. A living room where the sofa was. A small hall with a bathroom on the left and a bedroom on the right.

Now that he had the layout, he searched for evidence. Not that there was much to see. Nothing was out of place in the living room or kitchen. Maxwell was obsessive about clean for sure.

Then Sean glanced at the tracker on Maxwell's truck. Surprisingly, it was turning around. What was he doing? Watching closely now, Sean called Angel when the tracker turned off Highway 61 toward his ranch. Dakota called the security detail.

***

Angel answered, "Hey, Sean."

"Maxwell's tracker shows his blue truck heading down the road toward the ranch. Make sure the women are armed and in the house. Keep me on speaker. Dakota called the agents."

Angel barked orders and killed the lights. They waited.

Sean said, "He turned into the driveway and stopped."

Angel said, "Got it."

Samantha's cell phone dinged. She groaned.

Angel said, "Samantha got a text."

Sean said, "Samantha, hand Angel your phone."

She did. Angel read the text and sent it to Sean.

Sean felt the text vibrate, and said, "He's backing out and leaving. Coast clear. And Angel, delete the text from her phone."

"Done."

"Ok. I've got to go."

***

Sean opened the text: I'm gonna eat you alive.
***

Sean growled and had to shake it off. He was in the man's house. This is what he had to think about for now. He glanced at

162

the tracker and the truck was miles from here, so he got back to work. He had a couple of hours at best – and steered the drone down the hall.

The bathroom was squeaky clean. Either he was a germaphobe or the cleanest guy he'd ever seen. The only thing personal in the room was a shaving kit that sat neatly on the shelf. No wet towels, rags, or water drops in the tub. Very odd.

He crossed the hall and hovered in the bedroom doorway. The double bed was made. Neat. One closet in the room - door closed. One book open face down on the bed. A controller of sorts next to the book. Six moving boxes were stacked in the corner - two stacks of three. The top lid on one of the boxes was askew. He flew close. Law books. He looked around the room.

No clothes lying around. No shoes tossed on the floor. No change or pocket items on the dresser. No trash in the trashcan. Other than the bed, nightstand, and dresser, the only unusual item in the room was a large television. Way too large for this room – or this house for that matter. Obviously, Maxwell brought it with him. Red flag.

One of the agents said, "Looks like he really likes that TV."

Sean moved the drone closer to the TV and looked around it. No cable. Not out here in the woods. And no satellite outside. There was only a computer game box - a brand he wasn't familiar with - connected to the TV. He doubted it was even American made. The edge of a game stuck out of the machine. He zoomed in. The title was *Blonde Bait*. His blood ran cold.

Dakota said, "That ain't good."

Sean turned the drone to the items on the bed. He hovered over them, then zoomed in on the controller. Same make as the game box. He moved closer to the book. It was a law book. What was the connection between a law book and playing a sick game about blondes?

The book was partially raised off the bed on the other side. He flew over the book and landed on the bed – and zoomed in. There were small gaps in pages throughout the book. Like thick bookmarks. The gap closest to where Maxwell had the book opened showed something sticking out. Shiny cloth. Black. He clicked on the spotlight. It didn't clarify what the cloth was.

Then the tracker caught his eye. Maxwell had left Baton Rouge. He was coming home early.

Chapter 22

Fifteen minutes later, Sean flew the drone back to the living room. As he backed the drone under the sofa, Maxwell's headlights flashed down the road. Sean sat still in the tree watching the truck. The surveillance team went silent and pulled weapons – spreading through the trees.

***

Maxwell drove down the dusty road checking off tasks in his mind. All the pieces were in play for his game. He should be screaming in ecstasy by the weekend. He just needed to catch Samantha vulnerable, and they would disappear.

Until then, thanks to Suzette, he might have another up-close-and-personal opportunity with her at the political dinner tomorrow night. Even though they couldn't sit with the D.A. staff, he would still see her. Watch her body. Maybe smell and touch her.

He hungered to see the widening of her eyes. The flash of fear. Fire ate him when she did that. But now there was rage in her too. Fire on fire. A crazy hot battle. He couldn't wait to see how tomorrow night played out. Or…when he finally had her all to himself.

He pulled in the driveway and got out of the truck. A large snap echoed in the woods behind him. He turned. Watched. Listened. It had sounded like a branch breaking. Not unusual in the woods, but…he pulled his gun and walked toward the trees.

He didn't hear anything as he neared the tree line. The moon flashed a little light, but he didn't see any movement. He walked several more feet into the woods and tapped the gun barrel against his thigh. He walked further. And listened. Predators learned early to wait.

Sean glanced down. Maxwell stood under the tree he was in. The team was dead silent, but he knew their weapons were beaded on Maxwell. But a shootout wasn't the plan. Not without concrete evidence. After a few moments, Maxwell shrugged, and headed back to the house.

Sean heard sighs in his earpiece, and Dakota said, "Almost a gunfight, cowboys. Sean…"

"I'm heading back."

***

Back at the ranch, Samantha sat up and rubbed her neck. She'd been in one position too long watching truck stop videos. Looking around, Gabrielle, Angel, Jade, and Kerry were engrossed in videos too.

She noticed fresh blood on Kerry's side and said, "Hey Kerry, blood has seeped through your bandages. Why don't we change them and make sure everything is ok."

He nodded and hid a grimace as he stood. Soreness was working its way through his muscles.

Angel said, "I'll come help," and followed them.

Supplies were still on the counter. Kerry pulled off his shirt and Angel unwrapped bandages while Samantha got the supplies ready.

Kerry said, "I promised Chancy I would send her pictures proving I hadn't lied about the wounds. She threatened to come check for herself if I didn't."

Samantha said, "My kind of girl!"

The guys chuckled, then Angel said, "You realize she isn't going to like the pictures either, right? You might have to sing her another song."

Kerry laughed - he should have known they heard him earlier.

166

Once all the bandages were removed, Samantha inspected the wounds. Angel grimaced.

Kerry said, "Right."

Samantha said, "You really need something stronger for pain."

"No. This isn't the time to be fuzzy headed or drowsy. Besides I'm too big for a regular dose."

Angel said, "Good point. Hey - hand me your camera, I'll take the pictures."

***

Once they were done, Kerry texted Chancy the pictures.

Kerry: Don't be upset. Here are three pictures.

Chancy: What! How big was that bear?

Kerry: Not little.

Chancy: Those are huge claw marks. I can't imagine the pain.

Kerry: Not all that bad. I'll just end up with battle scars and a campfire story.

Chancy: Why didn't you shoot it?

Kerry: I'm a felon. No guns.

Chancy: Baby, I'm sorry.

Kerry: Don't be. Today's the happiest day of my life.

Chancy: I need to kiss you for that.

Kerry: In a few days, you'll get what you want. Now sleep good, honey. Gotta go.

***

It was late when Samantha, Gabrielle, and Jade showered and changed for a long night. Angel tried to get them to go to bed. They refused but pulled a few mattresses to the den. Angel nodded. He preferred them close anyway.

Kerry watched the security monitor in Sean's office. Angel brought a computer in the den and reviewed videos where he could keep a close eye on the doors and windows. The agents texted all was quiet outside. And he knew Sean would let them know if Maxwell was on the move.

***

It was almost midnight when Sean turned on the drone in Maxwell's house. In stealth mode, Maxwell wouldn't hear it. Now he had to make sure he wouldn't see it. So, he side-walked it as far as possible under the sofa. He could see down the hall.

Maxwell walked naked from the bathroom to the bedroom, brushing his teeth. In a moment, loud music started playing. No. More like a computer game than regular music. They all knew *Blonde Bait* was about to play.

And for the next hour the agents listened to the foulest language. Most vicious acts. Terrifying screams. And sounds of...lust coming from down the hall. It was like hearing demons through an open window to hell.

Then finally, Maxwell turned it off and his lights went out.

***

On the way home, Sean said, "I'll tell the team what we found tonight - not what we heard. I'll put that in my formal report. Everyone can imagine it anyway from the name of the game. He's a rabid animal in skin. He needs to be eliminated or locked in a dungeon."

Dakota said, "Agreed. So, when we get back, let's get on the truck stop videos and try to find the needle-in-a-haystack backpack with the Angola patch. Forensics should have some DNA in a couple of days on the anniversary cards. Whoever finds confirmation of his connection to the victims first, will kick off the arrest warrant. Research can continue after that."

Sean picked up his phone and keyed in a number.

He said, "Director, I have an update..."

***

When they arrived back at the ranch, Sean updated the task force.

168

Samantha, brow creased, thought about the law books they saw. Especially the one on the bed with the bookmarks. She knew that as an attorney, Maxwell would constantly refer to law books. She did. But she didn't have a set at home. Not with computer access. That didn't fit.

She said, "Sean, can I see the law book on the bed with the bookmarks?"

He nodded and downloaded the video, making sure she would not hear the game. She looked at the book. Just a normal law book. As the drone flew over the book and zoomed in on the obvious bookmarks, she leaned closer. Then she counted them. When Sean joined her counting, they knew. Twelve bookmarks. One was Black. But there were only eleven victims. What were the bookmarks?

She pointed at the controller next to the book, and said, "Did he watch anything when he returned?"

Sean turned off the video and said, "I'm not discussing what he watched. You can read it later in a report."

She prepared to argue, and he said, "Stop. I'll never tell you."

And with that, she knew it was bad.

She touched him softly, and said, "Ok. I'll let it go. But I need to know more about the bookmarks if you're able to get more video on that."

"You have an idea. What is it?"

"I'm going to check and see if we have the colors of the victim's missing panties."

Later, Samantha brought Sean the color list of victim underwear.

He said, "You're good."

"Let's face it, I have insight on this case."

"True. But your mind has to be able to problem solve in a very unique fashion. You were born with that. And speaking of that, did Suzette respond to your warning to be careful?"

"No. Not yet. I just hope she listens."

About two a.m., Sean glanced at Dakota and Angel pouring over video footage. They had insisted Kerry get some rest. He argued. But lost.

The security agents had split their detail. One kept an eye on the security monitor inside - while the other patrolled the tree line. And they swapped every hour.

Sean went back over the video list. They had rewatched videos for five victims so far – beginning with the first. Backpacks with Angola patches were seen in three of the videos with large men. Same male shape but with different hair, uniforms, or style. Classy. Country boy. Sporty. Even a priest. Maxwell was one smart serial killer.

***

By six the next morning, Sean and Dakota were back with surveillance at Maxwell's place.

Sean set up in a different tree this time and sent a drone out to scan the backyard area. All was quiet. Then he lowered it for a quick view in all four vehicle windows. Nothing new. Recalling the drone, he clipped it to the tree for later use.

He said, "It's a go."

Inside the house, the drone silently powered up. Audio picked up snoring. Sean side-walked the drone and looked down the hall. Clear. He moved the drone into the open and flew high till it hovered in the open bedroom door.

Maxwell slept facedown, snoring like a freight train. Naked. He really was a big guy. Powerful. His left arm was on top of the pillow by his face, and his right arm hung off the side of the bed. Covers were kicked to the side.

The drone entered the bedroom. Sean looked for the book with the bookmarks as he flew around the room. Only the game controller was on the floor. Phone on the nightstand. No clothes visible. No shoes. Where was the book? He flew closer to the head of the bed and caught a glimpse of the corner of the book. It had slid behind the pillow.

Backing away from the bed, Sean landed the drone on the floor. Maxwell's arm hung right in front of the drone. Samantha's bite scar clearly visible. Fury distracted him for a hard second.

Then clenching his jaw, he gave the arm a wide berth, and walked the drone under the bed. A minute later, he zoomed in on the top edge of the book. It had fallen, bending pages. Only some of the bookmarks were visible. He zoomed more. The bookmarks were obviously cloth. Some shiny. Some with patterns. And he knew Samantha was right. They had to be panties.

The bed shifted as Maxwell obviously turned over. Sean stilled the drone and listened. Snoring stopped, but a loud noise echoed in the room. He shook his head, ignoring the chuckling in his ear. The joys of surveillance. He waited to see if Maxwell would go back to sleep. No. He rolled and sat up on the side of the bed and yawned. Then walked to the bathroom and peed forever.

Sean backed the drone as far as he could to keep it from being seen under the bed. Maxwell flushed and headed back toward the bedroom – dropping what was obviously a pair of pink panties on the floor.

Then a warning light flashed on the drone controller. The battery had less than five minutes. There wasn't anything Sean could do at this point but transmit the data.

***

On their way back to the ranch after noon, the director called. Sean answered, "Yes, sir."

"That was extraordinary drone work as usual. And it looks like Samantha's idea on the bookmarks was right on. They'll be full of DNA."

"And more nails in his coffin."

"Exactly. Are you expecting him to be at the political event tonight? I know the lab is on the final stages of testing the anniversary cards."

"He'll be there. Hopefully we get the results when we're with him."

While the guys reviewed more videos in Sean's office, Samantha and Gabrielle flipped through party dresses. They still hadn't made up their mind what to wear for the dinner tonight.

Jade watched them, reminded of college, and said, "Samantha, which one are you thinking of wearing?"

"Hmmm. I think the short off-the-shoulder black lace sheath and bolero."

"That's a hottie. How can Sean watch for Maxwell if you distract him?"

Samantha laughed and said, "He multitasks very well. What about you, Gabrielle?"

She shrugged and said, "I couldn't zip my black tulle dress from mom's wedding. My waist is filling out with the baby," and she patted her tiny bump with a smile.

Jade pointed to a floor length black halter dress. She said, "Try that one. It will show off your tattoo and all sorts of other body parts Dakota is sure to enjoy."

Gabrielle slid her hand across the fabric agreeing, then glanced at Samantha.

She said, "Are you sure you're ready for Maxwell tonight? You know he'll be lurking somewhere."

"I expect a confrontation. I just don't see how he can accomplish much in front of a room full of legal professionals. I mean, he's a lawyer. He'd be damaging himself if he exposes who he really is."

Jade said, "Well. He might be intelligent. But obsession lowers his wisdom level to gut craving. And all he wants is you. So, stay alert."

***

Leaving the girls to dress, Jade jogged downstairs. Angel caught her eye as he stepped to the patio door to take a break. He motioned for her to follow. It had been way too long since some one-on-one time with her.

They walked to the barn since there was little privacy with the FBI patrolling and the drone watching. As they stepped out of view, Angel pulled her close. Holding her. Just wanting to feel her against him. Warm. Smelling so good. Jade hadn't expected this type of embrace from him and yielded easily, sliding her arms around him. Feeling his strength. Receiving his gentle desire to just be near her.

He rubbed her back and softly nuzzled her neck. She was melting. Trying not to - but failing. He made her feel so good. She caressed his back.

Angel said, "Kiss me..." and she lifted her lips.

He caressed her mouth with his. Coaxing. Loving on her. Then captured her. Backing her against the wall of hay so he could press closer. His hands molding her like a potter. Lifting her for closer contact.

Breathless, she said, "Angel..."

"I know. You feel so good, Jade."

"But..."

"No but."

"But wait...I want to know..."

"Know what?"

"Is this...the only reason...you agreed to be my business partner?"

Looking at her, he said, "Jade. Wait a minute. Let me ask a question. Why did you agree to be my Salsa partner when we first met? And later ask me to be your business partner?"

"Several reasons. You're a great dancer. Intelligent. Skilled."

"Right. And my passionate touch when we dance – my body touching yours – and my interest in you had nothing to do with it."

She flushed. Guilty. Then said, "But I..."

He trailed his lips close to hers, and said, "I'm going to kiss you again..."

"Don't...play games with me."

He said, "Who's playing?" and kissed her.

***

173

Sean and Dakota met in the den before six p.m., both dressed in a black tux. Sean's wavy black hair brushed the top of his shoulders while Dakota's straight black hair hung below his. Jade whistled at the gorgeous brothers and fanned herself.

Angel and Kerry laughed.

Kerry said, "I'm thinking women will not be listening to the speaker tonight. They'll be eyeballing both of you."

Sean said, "Just wait till you see Samantha and Gabrielle. I doubt anyone will be listening to the speeches."

After the laughter faded, they heard the door open and giggles. Gabrielle appeared at the top of the stairs in a floor length black halter dress. Slit way past one knee. Long dark hair braided and hanging in the front. With her amber cat eyes and red lips, she was exotic to a T.

Everyone whistled and Dakota met her halfway up the staircase. Looking her over, he said softly, "Why don't we have an early night instead."

She kissed him, running her hand across his chest and said, "Not a chance, handsome. Just enjoy the view for a few hours."

He chuckled and escorted her down.

Angel and Jade smiled at Kerry's wow expression. They were used to seeing the gorgeous couple.

Jade said, "Just wait Kerry. Check this out. Turn around Gabrielle."

Gabrielle smiled and turned.

Kerry said, "No way..." and stared at a tattoo that went from her waist to her shoulders.

High-fiving Kerry, Gabrielle glanced at Sean and said, "You can go on up, Samantha's putting heels on. Be prepared brother-in-law..."

Sean walked to the open door. Samantha saw him and posed. Her blonde hair was braided. Smoky eyes. Deep red lips. Diamond loop earrings. Her dress was black lace. Mid-thigh. Off the shoulder. Bare legs. Black stiletto heels with ankle bows. He growled dramatically and gave her a spin.

Smiling, she ran her hand down his chest, stopping at his pants.

The look he gave her was hot. He whispered in her ear.

Gasping, she said, "I can't believe you said that."

"That's what happens when you play with fire. I'm ready for you."

Dakota hollered upstairs, "Hurry up!"

Then catcalls and whistles came from the group as they joined them downstairs.

Jade said, "Girl. That dress did not look like that hanging in your closet."

***

At the dock in downtown Baton Rouge, the majestic American Harmony riverboat sat proud on the Mississippi River. The sound of jazz coasted on the waterfront breeze.

Sean pulled up for valet service. The landing was packed as they joined the guests headed inside. Impressive was the proper description of the people. Silk. Lace. Sequins. Diamonds galore. Class and elegance. Important guests. Political powerhouses. There was no mistaking the tone of the night.

They checked in at Jonathan Remington's guest table and were directed to the second floor where the dinner event was being held. Excited, Samantha smiled and squeezed Sean's arm as he led the way. Dakota and Gabrielle followed.

They exited the elevator onto the second floor and walked toward the dining room. Spectacular black and white decorations filled the room. A smiling hostess escorted them to their table.

As they walked across the room, Jonathan Remington waved and joined them. He gave Samantha a warm hug first - and they talked with the familiarity of a long-term relationship. And Sean stared. Shocked. He couldn't believe he had missed it.

Jonathan turned and said, "Sean, thanks for coming! I'm glad you were free to make it."

Not revealing anything, Sean smiled, shaking hands, and said, "You know we support you. Let us know if there is anything we can do in the days ahead."

He laughed and said, "Be careful. Don't offer – I might take you up on it!"

Then Jonathan looked at Samantha and said, "Be sure to see Sara and the boys, they look forward to seeing you tonight."

"I will! I miss them. I'm sorry I haven't visited in a while."

Jonathan motioned to some tables up ahead, and said, "Not that anyone will sit much during the social hour, but these tables are for the D.A.'s office. Be sure and enjoy yourselves. We'll connect more later."

Then he moved on to visit with Dakota and Gabrielle. Sean's phone vibrated. He noticed Dakota reaching for his phone too. Surveillance text.

***

Maxwell just left in the BMW. Headed to Baton Rouge.
***

Sean glanced at Jonathan again as he moved to another group to welcome guests.

Dakota said, "Hey, I know that look. What's up?"

"Jonathan is Samantha's father."

"How do—"

"Watch them. You can't miss it when they're side by side. It's the first time I've seen them together or I would have known long ago."

"She doesn't know?"

"Her mother wouldn't talk about her father. At all. Obviously because she already had a close relationship with him."

"You're going to tell her."

"I'm going to make sure he tells her. There's no reason for her not to know."

"When are you going to confront him?"

"Before I leave tonight."

176

"Well…that just made the night more interesting than it already was. And…" He glanced at his watch and said, "Maxwell and Suzette should get here in thirty minutes or so."

"Yeah. I'll tell the D.A. if you want to tell the security officers to be on alert."

***

A little later, guests began dancing. Sean winked at Samantha and nodded to the dance floor.

He said, "Come dance with me. You can't wear black lace and heels like that and not expect some hands-on activity."

Smiling, as they walked to the dance floor, she said, "Then my plan was successful."

He slid his arms around her, pulling her snug against him. Intimate. His. He held her there as they moved to the music.

Thinking about their elopement, he drawled, "So, Counselor, tell me. What would you like to do in Switzerland?"

"Stay in bed with you."

Desire hit him, and he responded with a gaze dripping sexy. He said, "Who said we will only use the bed?"

Tingles climbed her body. Her lips parted in surprised impact. He tightened his hold, knowing it. Lowering his lips, he kissed her.

Next to them, Gabrielle said, "Hey…easy does it. It's getting steamy in here, don't you think?"

After a couple of songs, Sean led Samantha on the deck. It was a beautiful night. Dusk was setting across the western sky and lights from the boat and city flickered in the river. The bridge lit the background. Picture perfect.

Sean said, "Maxwell and Suzette will be here before long. Dakota and I will keep him in sight. Make sure that neither you nor Gabrielle go anywhere without us nearby. You do realize he's going to try to get close to you at some point?"

"I do. Hopefully it'll be verbal only."

"If he can control himself. Otherwise, if there's a scene, we'll handle it. Do what you have to do."

177

"I don't want to mess up Jonathan's night."

Sean tilted her chin and kissed her softly. He said, "I promise, Jonathan won't care about anything but you."

Back inside, a speaker announced dinner would be served in twenty minutes. They had just gotten seated when Sean and Dakota got another text.

***

Maxwell reached the riverboat.
***

Sean said, "Stay alert. He's arrived."

Samantha nodded. At least she would know he was in the room. But she was determined not to give him the satisfaction of watching him or showing fear. Sean and Dakota would let him know soon enough they were watching him.

Gabrielle whispered, "Too bad we couldn't bring our swords," and Samantha grinned - that would have been great.

Jonathan stepped to the podium and welcomed his guests. After several moments of comments and sharing his appreciation for their attendance, background music came on and dinner carts rolled in with plates of filet mignon covered in crab sauce. Blackened red snapper. Scalloped potatoes and steamed broccoli with mushrooms. Wedge salad topped with blue cheese dressing and candied pecans. Platters of warm bread and seasoned butter. Cups of pecan pie cheesecake with praline drizzle. A southern feast.

Appearing casual, Sean and Dakota watched the entrance as they ate and socialized. Samantha picked at her fish and salad as she laughed and visited – until she noticed Sean and Dakota's gaze focus across the room. She glanced at the main entrance. Maxwell stood with Suzette at the oversized double doors.

Two thoughts crossed her mind. One, how ironic it was to have to act normal in a room full of lawyers, judges, and police, when the man who wanted to kill you was in the room. And two, Suzette

178

looked more beautiful than Samantha had ever seen her look. Dark hair in a bohemian styled ponytail bun. Black and white floral strapless floor length gown. Sparkling jewelry. Barely-there heels. She was absolutely lovely.

Sean watched as they passed by, headed to the rear of the room. The D.A. glanced at Sean and Dakota. They knew trouble was here. Samantha sighed in sorrow for Suzette. Obviously, she had arrangements to sit with another law firm. The D.A.'s staff passed quick glances amongst themselves. It was an awkward public moment.

***

Suzette noticed the D.A. and staff. She waved casually in greeting as they passed, trying not to notice the interest it caused in the room when she didn't sit with them. She knew tonight would be uncomfortable because of her decision to stand by Maxwell. She glanced at him as he pulled out her seat. He seemed excited now that he was here. For some reason that didn't comfort her at all.

***

Following dinner there were guest speakers from various organizations. Law firms. And political allies that lifted Jonathan up as the man to lead Baton Rouge into a new era of commerce and justice. And by the time he stepped to the podium with his wife and sons, the room erupted into cheers as everyone stood to their feet.

Almost an hour later, the political portion of the evening was over, and the party continued. The band kicked off a new set of jazz music and special requests. Movement filled the room as partying guests headed to the dance floor. Other guests said goodbye since tomorrow was Friday – a workday – and probably court for many of them. And the ones wanting to socialize swarmed in groups to take advantage of a room full of colleagues.

***

Maxwell watched Suzette disappear down the hall to the bathroom. With a smile, he turned to find out where Samantha was in this throng of people. Ah. There she was. He stood.

***

It was a social wave at the D.A.'s tables. People came from all over the room to congregate. They were friends tonight – not opponents from across the aisle in court.

Samantha stepped away from Sean to hug a friend from another law firm. Sean glanced toward Maxwell and Suzette. They weren't at their table. He quickly looked back at Samantha. She was in lively conversation with a group a few feet from him. He wondered if Maxwell and Suzette had slipped out the door.

He raised his hand for Dakota's attention and motioned to Maxwell's table. Dakota saw Maxwell was gone and looked at Samantha. She was maybe four feet away. Surrounded.

Sean tried to catch Samantha's attention to no avail. Too much commotion. He watched the faces around her for Maxwell.

***

Maxwell walked along the wall weaving through guests, keeping his eye on Samantha. She was petite – but a blonde beacon as far as he was concerned. He zeroed in on her and made sure to stay near tall men as he traveled. Hidden in plain sight. As he neared the area closest to Samantha, he noticed that some of the crowd behind her stepped away to join a different group of people. Now Samantha's back was to a table with several open chairs.

Glancing at Sean, he ducked below the crowd, dropped his keys on the floor, and slid into a chair not far behind Samantha.

***

Samantha laughed at yet another crazy tale from court. They would never run out of stories. She glanced at Sean, and he motioned for her. She nodded, then someone bumped into her. She stepped backwards to get out of the way and caught a glimpse of a man at the table behind her as he leaned over to pick up a set of keys on the floor. Making sure not to step on his hand, she moved away. A hand went up her dress.

Chapter 23

Samantha screamed and spun as hands grabbed at her underwear. It was Maxwell. Furious at his disgusting touch, she slammed her forearm into his face. He growled, jerking back as blood spurted from his nose. Everyone screamed and scattered. Dakota yanked Samantha out of the way, and Sean dove across the end of the table for the tackle. Both men hit the floor. Chairs flew. Dishes fell off tables. Women ran away. Men ran toward them.

Gabrielle drew a shocked, but furious Samantha aside. Sean and Dakota flipped a raging Maxwell facedown pulling his arms behind his back. Riverboat security quickly cuffed him.

Dragged to his feet, Maxwell taunted Sean as he said, "I got me a good feel, Sean, since you were late to the party. Do you know she gets into rough, hot action?"

Sean hit him. Hard. Maxwell's head flew back and down he went. Lights out.

Pulling Samantha to him, Sean said, "Are you hurt?"

"Just a scratch. I'm glad he made out worse."

He looked her over, and said, "Where are you scratched?"

"Don't ask."

He got it – and his eyes went black with fury. Jaw tight. He had seen Maxwell pull away from the bottom of her dress.

She said, "You defended me, Sean. Watching you knock him out was enough. And he's got more coming. I'm good with that. Let's let it go for now. This is a win tonight. He's going to jail."

***

Suzette stood there. Stunned. Appalled. Shaky, as she collapsed at a table staring at Maxwell on the floor in cuffs. What happened for the few minutes she was gone?

***

In seconds, sirens neared the riverboat and the police boarded.

The D.A. said, "Charge him with sexual assault of a prosecutor, causing a public disturbance, assaulting a federal agent – and anything else you can think of. Get him out of here. Drag him if you have to."

As Samantha answered the policeman's questions for the report, Dakota nudged Sean and said casually, "It's tough when it's personal. Maxwell's lucky you only hit him. I saw your face."

"I want him dead. I admit it."

"I get it. I've been there, believe me. When Gabrielle was in danger, I wanted them all to die twice."

When Samantha finished with the police and joined them, she said, "I'm going to talk to Suzette. She's in shock. And I still need to apologize to Jonathan."

Sean said, "Why don't you talk to Suzette, and I'll talk to Jonathan."

"Ok. But be sure and tell him I want to talk to him before I leave."

***

Sean caught Jonathan's eye in a group of guests - and waived him over. They walked on the deck for privacy.

Sean said, "Samantha and I are sorry for the commotion."

"That's nothing. I care about Samantha."

That was exactly the response he expected, so Sean said, "Why doesn't she know you're her father?"

Not surprised, Jonathan smiled. He said, "I knew you saw the resemblance tonight. But it's not what you think. I've always

183

wanted to tell her. Her mother wanted to wait for the right time. But as the years passed, the right time never happened. At least I was able to be her surrogate father or uncle so to speak. I've always loved her. My wife and her half-brothers love her."

"I understand. I'm in that line myself."

"I thought so. And thrilled to hear it."

Sean said, "Being her father, I have some news you are not going to like. She's under FBI protection. We are working two cases that involve Samantha and the man arrested here tonight."

"What the— Who is he?"

"He's the identical twin of the man in Angola for attacking her twelve years ago. The wrong brother is in prison."

Jonathan paled and said, "No."

"And it gets worse. He returned to Louisiana to finish what he started, which brings up case two. Samantha's instinct had us do some digging. It seems he became a serial killer after the first attack. Eleven victims are dead around Chicago. And if that isn't bad enough, he's an attorney now."

"How close are you to a warrant?"

"Any moment. She's with me 24/7."

"Get her to my office in the morning. We need to at least file a restraining order."

***

Samantha joined Suzette after another co-worker walked away.

Suzette said, "I heard what happened. What's this all about? It doesn't make sense."

"I can't say. But you aren't safe either. Stay away from him. Leaving town is even better. The D.A. knows what's going on and we're worried about you."

"Maxwell used me to get to you?"

"All I can say is that appearances with Maxwell are deceiving. Go somewhere, Suzette."

She nodded, and said, "I'll get a flight and leave tomorrow. I'll go stay with my sister in Georgia."

"Good. Now, no argument, let us bring you somewhere tonight. Preferably not home alone."

She said, "I'd appreciate the ride home. And don't worry, I'll just be there overnight. I've got to pack."

***

Jonathan waited till Samantha finished her conversation, then crossed the room. She smiled and stepped into his hug while he swallowed the lump in his throat. She had been through so much in her life. He had decided to tell her in the morning who he was. The time would never be right - but she needed to know. Especially now.

He said, "Sean's going to see that you get to my office in the morning for a Protection Order against Maxwell. We can't have him free to harass you at his whim. Is eight good for you? I want to get the order filed before I'm due in court. I insist."

"Eight is fine. You're the best - and thanks. I'm so sorry about the commotion tonight."

"Don't be. You're ok and that's all I care about."

He pointed to his wife and sons, and said, "If you have a minute, would you tell them hello? They want to know for themselves you're ok."

***

A short while later, Sean, Samantha, Dakota, Gabrielle, and Suzette stepped off the riverboat. Sean's phone vibrated with a text. The D.A.

***

Found out Maxwell is out on bail. Left in a cab.
***

Sean showed the text to Dakota, then messaged the surveillance team, task force, and security detail with the update. Maxwell was

185

on the loose again. Without a tracker. He checked the time. Ten p.m.

By ten thirty, they dropped Suzette at her house. She insisted.

At ten forty, the director called.

***

Sean answered, "Yes, sir. We're headed back to the ranch."

"We've got DNA confirmation. The warrant was issued to pick up Maxwell. All eleven anniversary cards confirm his DNA and each victim. He drew the hearts with their blood. He's one sick, smug…" and trailed off, wanting to call him a lot worse.

Samantha closed her eyes. Sick. Gabrielle moaned at the horror of blood hearts.

Sean said, "We'll have to find him again. You got my message that he's in the wind now?"

"Yes. Keep your eyes peeled for him. He's not done. Additional agents are headed to his house and yours. At least now, local law enforcement is watching for him too."

***

Before long they were back at the ranch. Sean gave everyone the update on the warrant and told them extra agents were on the way.

Angel said, "What now?"

Sean said, "Watch and wait. He'll either make a move or be found. Except now we don't know what he'll be driving."

***

Close to one a.m., Samantha texted Suzette to check on her. She knew she would probably be packing or unable to sleep.

***

Samantha: Did the D.A. let you know about Maxwell?

186

Suzette: That he's out on bail - yes.
Samantha: You ought to get a patrolman to ride by until you leave.
Suzette: Don't worry. I'm ok. My security system is armed.
Samantha: Be careful. Please. You don't know him like I do.

***

Sean knocked and stuck his head in the bedroom door. Samantha sat in the bed with her phone. Intense. He put her phone in his pocket and sat on the bed.

She said, "I think we need a patrolman to ride by Suzette's house till she leaves for the airport. She doesn't know what he's capable of. Her lack of concern is stressing me."

"I'll make a call. Now you need to rest. How about a massage?"

"I love your touch, but no. This is one of those times I need to think. I might even take a long soak in the tub. I need to work all this out in my head. Think about what he might be planning. Be prepared."

"I know."

Frowning, she said, "He had to know tonight would fail. But he did it anyway."

"He wants you more than any risk."

"While that's not encouraging, it makes it clear he's running wide open now. Will make mistakes. Take wild chances. Out of control. That makes it worse. He might even be planning a suicide kill – which means he has nothing to lose."

***

Just before dawn the next morning, Sean checked his office computer at the ranch for the tracker locations on Maxwell's vehicles. Nothing had moved. He glanced at the security monitor. Multiple thermal images moved through the woods around the ranch. Six agents were out there. Suddenly, a seventh image appeared by the road near the end of his property.

Sean radioed, "Someone's by the road west of the house – barely in my camera range."

187

Agents talked in the radio, and their images headed that direction. The figure just stood there, then suddenly turned, and ran till they disappeared off the screen.

Sean radioed, "He's off my radar."

Sean knew Maxwell had either heard someone in the woods or got spooked. He was a starving predator. He couldn't stay away from Samantha.

A little over an hour later, Sean heard the door upstairs and glanced up. Samantha jogged downstairs in white jeans. A black lace spaghetti-strap top. Carrying a white jean jacket.

He met her at the base of the stairs and opened his arms. She slid right in and wrapped her arms around him. He snuggled - she smelled delicious. She sighed as he massaged her back and nibbled her neck. Then cupping her face, he settled his lips over hers.

His phone rang. Surveillance at Maxwell's.

***

He hit speaker and answered, "What's going on?"

"A black Ram truck roared down the road toward the house – did a quick U-turn and roared off. I'm sure it's Maxwell. He smells trouble."

"But now we know what he's driving."

***

After the call ended, Samantha said, "I need to leave now to meet Jonathan in time to sign the Protective Order before he goes to court."

Sean called Agents Kent and Sylvester – his bear-killer agents.

When they came inside, Sean said, "I need you to take Samantha to Baton Rouge to an attorney's office. And I found out Maxwell may be driving a black Ram truck. Treat any threat the way you did those bears. Lethal force."

They nodded and glanced at Samantha.

Sean said, "Is your gun in your purse?"

"Yes."

He said, "You do exactly what they tell you to do. No arguments. Just immediate obedience. Understood, Counselor?"

"I get it. And we shouldn't be gone long just to sign a paper."

But Sean knew better. She was about to meet her father.

As they drove away, Sean and Dakota headed to Maxwell's house. They were going in.

***

Agent Kent pulled onto Highway 61, turning south to Baton Rouge. Both agents kept an eye on traffic around them while Samantha called Suzette.

***

Suzette answered, "Hey."

"Sorry to bug you. Just wanted to check in. What time do you leave?"

"After lunch was the earliest available flight."

"Can you go wait somewhere else? I hate for you to be home alone."

"The house is locked up tight and I plan to leave early. I promise."

"Ok. Keep in touch."

Suzette said, "Are you telling me – by not telling me - that he is like his brother?"

"Just go as soon as possible."

"I will. But you're scaring me."

"Good – leave, ok?"

***

While Samantha was on the phone, Agent Sylvester, in the passenger seat, said, "A black truck is coming up on your side of the road, Kent."

189

The agents watched in the mirrors as it neared the SUV.

When Samantha hung up her call, Kent said, "Lay on the back seat, Samantha."

Unaware of possible danger, she hesitated.

He said "Now!"

She quickly laid down. Heart pounding. Agent Kent braked as the black truck neared the car so it would pass by them fast. And with a quick glance, they saw a man with long hair singing and beating his steering wheel like a drum. Music blaring. The driver never even looked at them.

Watching the truck continue down the road, Agent Sylvester said, "All clear."

Samantha sat up, thinking it was just like the movies. Wow.

Further up the road, the black truck put on its blinker and made a left turn.

***

Maxwell laughed as he made the turn and watched the men escorting Samantha drive toward Baton Rouge. He pulled behind an abandoned building where he had a good hidden visual of the road. They would be back. His practice run worked well. He kicked back in the seat and took off the wig.

***

Once they reached Jonathan's law firm, Samantha pointed out the entrance. Agent Kent parked and both men checked the area before they opened her door.

She looked up at Agent Sylvester, the youngest, and said, "I feel like a movie star with all this fuss."

"You look like one too."

Samantha laughed and looked at the older agent. She said, "Does he say that to all the women you protect?"

Kent glanced at Sylvester and said dryly, "That's a no. And he better be careful. Sean has a mean right hook."

190

Inside the law firm, the receptionist greeted Samantha and offered the agents a seat. They shook their head no. Silent. Imposing.

Grinning, Samantha explained, "It's ok. They're with me."

She said, "Certainly. Right this way," and led them to a large corner office at the end of the hall.

Jonathan met Samantha at the door with a smile. After a hug, he said, "Come in," and nodded to the agents. They positioned themselves on either side of his door as he shut it.

Samantha grinned and Jonathan said, "Impressive."

She said, "Sean insisted they bring me. We've had some trouble as you saw last night."

"I heard. And Sean's a smart man. Especially when the trouble involves someone he loves. Right?"

She smiled and said, "Absolutely."

Jonathan motioned to the sofa, and said, "Let's talk for a few minutes."

As they sat, she asked, "Was last night successful for you? The community and legal support I saw was huge. Don't forget, I would love to help any way I can."

"Thank you! And yes, it was successful. It's hard to believe the election is a month away." Then he waved a hand and said, "But enough about me. Are you alright? That was a vicious attack last night."

"I'm fine. Really. The contact with him was short thank goodness. I hate that it disrupted part of the evening."

He looked at her beautiful face. It was time. He said, "Don't give it another thought. Your safety. Your wellbeing is more important to me than anything you could imagine."

She stared at him. Felt the shift in the room. It now had a very personal feel. What was he saying? She said, "What in the world are you hinting at, Jonathan? Just say it."

Chapter 24

Jonathan said, "Sean saw it last night. Right away in fact."

"Saw what?"

"How much we look alike."

She blinked. No. He didn't mean what that sounded like.

He watched her expression as she wrestled with the notion, and said, "I'm years late telling you, but you're my daughter."

Her mind flickered like a kaleidoscope, flashing memories of growing up. He had always been there.

She fumbled the questions trying to take a mental foothold, "But you...mom...why didn't you...why didn't y'all..." and her voice faded away as she tried to figure out a lifetime in a second.

Touching her hand, he said softly, "Let me tell you a story. You know your mom and I had been close friends since childhood. I mean best friends. I was there for her. She was there for me. We got along perfectly. Shared secrets. Dreams. But we didn't date. We were just perfect friends. But in college, one night we wondered if we might be more."

Samantha could imagine the wonder of that moment and nodded.

He continued, "While it was beautiful, we realized it wasn't who we were meant to be. The love we shared for years was truly close, amazing. But as best friends. Then we found out she was pregnant."

She covered her mouth. Overwhelmed for a moment. Feeling their journey through his words.

He took her hands, and said, "And you became the best part of us. You were everything. But we couldn't marry, and your mom didn't want you to experience a divided life, so we decided to tell you when you were older. Until then, I was a great friend to her, a blessed uncle to you...but always, a daddy in my heart."

She burst into tears, and he wrapped her in his arms, while they both realized a dream come true.

A few moments later, he handed her a tissue.

She asked, "Then why didn't you tell me as I got older?"

"We planned to tell you early but were scared to hurt you. Then you got busy with gymnastics. When I was about to tell you, you got attacked. Then your mom got sick. It just was never the perfect time. When you went to college, I didn't want to throw you off course with an emotional upheaval. So, I waited. And here we are.

"But I want you to know that I've loved you since before your first breath. Afterwards, I rocked you. Fed you. Kept you. Watched your first step. And then I watched you grow into the most fabulous daughter any father could ever want."

Tears of wonder pooled and slid down her cheeks.

He said, "Your stepmother and your half-brothers have always known. We have always loved and supported you, waiting for the day we could tell you that you're a Remington."

He stood and said, "Come see."

Walking to the large wall mirror, they stood next to each other. He smiled as her eyes flashed back and forth, comparing. Seeing it for the first time.

She said, "It's shockingly obvious now that I know."

"Exactly. No one ever compared us till Sean did. Which doesn't surprise me at all. He knew at a single glance."

"My man's brilliant."

"And so are you."

A little later, she followed him to his desk to sign the documents. She noticed his family photos along the top of the credenza. Her picture was framed next to theirs. Her family. She looked at him and he smiled. Her father.

**

Sean and Dakota hiked through the woods and reached the surveillance camp at Maxwell's house.

An agent said, "No sign of Maxwell since he sped out of here earlier."

Sean said, "Then I'll get a security drone up before I go inside."

In thirty minutes, he mounted a security drone on the power pole like he had done at the ranch. Now they had eyes in the sky. The monitors showed six agents in the woods. Nothing else. He was good to go.

Sean motioned to the cabin and Dakota followed him to the back door. They popped the lock and entered. Taking pictures as they went, they headed straight to the bedroom. The book was partially shoved under a pillow. The game controller was by the TV. They got to work. Sean went for the book. Dakota headed to the TV.

Sean slid the book out from under the pillow. He opened the book to each of the marked spots. Bikini panties. He sighed. Eleven pair. Two were shades of pink. Three white. Two black. Three red. One blue. He took pictures and bagged the book and trophies. Dakota packed up the video console, controller, and game.

Sean opened the bedside table. A phone. Probably a burner. It wasn't locked. He went to texts and found the ones sent to Samantha. He went to photos – and growled. Maxwell had a neat library of all the victims during their rape and killing. It was horrendous. He deserved the death penalty. Too bad it was illegal to make him almost die – bring him back – and do it all over again for each victim.

**

Heading back to the ranch, Samantha replayed in her mind the conversation in her dad's office. It was unbelievable that in those few minutes she had a father, a mother, and three brothers. And

Sean had known immediately. She appreciated that he left it to her dad to tell her. How she loved her Agent Man.

Eventually, she paid attention to their location. Highway 61. The forests were thicker. Neighborhoods and the city far behind. Agent Kent was driving, and it was quiet in the car. They should be home in fifteen to twenty minutes. She wondered if Sean was still at the ranch.

Agent Sylvester said, "Kent, a black truck is coming up behind us."

Samantha quietly watched them keep an eye on the truck. They had been wary of several black trucks on the trip today, but none had been Maxwell. She listened.

Kent watched for a bit, then warned, "The driver is up to something. Samantha, pull your weapon. Lay on the seat."

She did and her heart began to pound.

Sylvester said, "He's coming too fast. Samantha, get Sean on the phone – and if there is any type of accident, get out of the car and run to the woods. Hide. Understand me?"

Samantha squeaked out a terrified, "Yes!" and grabbed her phone, fingers shaking as she keyed in Sean's number.

Kent said, "Hurry, Samantha! Keep Sean on the phone. Sylvester, call 911." Then he yelled, "He sped up - get ready, he's almost on us!"

Samantha heard the phone ring as she looped her purse strap around her neck. Then held the gun in one hand. The phone in the other.

**

Sean answered the call, "What's wrong?"

Samantha screamed at the sound of gunfire. A tire blew. The car started swerving all over the road.

Sean yelled, "Where are you?"

"Thompson creek…a…black truck!"

Another shot shattered glass and Sylvester slumped over with a blood spray. Samantha screamed again.

195

Kent yelled, "We're going to crash! Get out and run! Don't worry about us! Just run!"

She wedged the phone in her bra, held the gun, and hung on as the car went airborne. She floated in the air till it hit the ground with a jarring thud, then slammed into the trees.

***

Sean and Dakota ran out of Maxwell's house headed for the truck – shouting about the attack in the radio. He grabbed his drone case. Four agents ran out of the woods and followed them.

In a little over five minutes, wheels squealing, Sean roared toward Highway 61 as Dakota called the director.

***

Samantha found herself on the floor of the car after the screeching metal and flying glass finally stopped. She panted with adrenalin. Hair covered her face and her lip burned. She touched it. Bloody. She shifted to see if she was injured – but nothing else hurt.

She gasped, remembering. Maxwell! Slinging her hair back, she looked over the console and both agents were unconscious. Bleeding. Air bags deployed. She looked back at the road and saw a black truck pulling over by the bridge – it braked.

Her mind screamed run and she looked for her gun. She grabbed it from under the passenger seat and pulled the passenger door handle. Stuck. She slid out of the busted window and dropped to the ground. Ducking, she ran to the back of the vehicle and holding the gun with both hands, peeked around the end of the bumper. Maxwell jogged toward them. She knelt, aimed, and fired. He stumbled, grabbing the side of his head and ran behind the driver's side of the truck.

Samantha sprinted toward an opening in the woods and glanced back at him. He saw her. She fired again and he ducked as it shattered his rear window. He stood, gun in hand, and aimed low. She spun to run, heard a gunshot, and a searing pain burned across her right thigh. She glanced down as she disappeared into the woods. Blood ran down her white jeans – it had grazed her.

Maxwell cussed as he noticed all the traffic stopped at a distance. Great. A crowd watching the wreck and gunfight. Cops would be here soon. He had to get her before then - and ran down the embankment by the creek. In seconds he turned south, hunting her. Smiling. He was finally alone in the woods with her again. His body on fire for her, he ran and screamed her name.

Samantha had seen him head into the woods by the bridge. He was coming. She tucked the gun in her waistband, ignored the pain in her leg, and ran. She struggled in the hilly woods, covered with thousands of acres of ravines. Steep hills separated by deep valleys. The ground slippery with morning dew.

Maxwell screamed her name somewhere behind her. He sounded like a wild animal, and she tried not to panic. She fought to climb up the hills and slide down the other side. Her fingernails snapped as she grabbed for roots and limbs. Her jeans were smeared with colors of the forest - and blood. Her long hair caught on everything. Her sandals filthy – barely protecting the soles of her feet. She panted, strained, sweat, bled, and hurried as fast as she could.

Then time had no meaning as she listened to the sound of her name in his screams. Warning her. Threatening her. But also helping her gauge his distance. As he drew closer, she ran through the bottom of the ravines until she had no choice but to climb a hill. Then his screams were too close. She had to hide.

She had noticed in some of the sharp bends in the ravines there were large gouges in the hillside from rushing water erosion. She looked inside one. It was like a little dirt cave with a large panel of green moss flopping over it like a door. Hearing the crunch of sticks as his footsteps neared, she slipped inside. Ducking as far to one side as she could, praying there were no predators in the damp dark with her.

In barely a minute, he was in the ravine with her. She bit her lips to keep from panting or making noise. Not moving a muscle, she listened.

Maxwell's chest heaved as he stood there. Listening. Not hearing her anymore. He looked around, then climbed to the top of the hill. Nothing. He half slid, half fast walked down the hill and waited. He sniffed and smelled only trees, dirt, and mold. Where was she? He walked toward the corner of the ravine.

Samantha's hand tightened on the pistol in her right hand and pressed against the dirt wall. Her left hand against the other wall. She had nowhere to go but out. His feet stopped in front of the opening of her little cave. She got ready. Oh Jesus, help me.

Maxwell smiled when he got a whiff of her perfume. He noticed the hole in the hill and knelt, lifting the moss flap. Not able to see, he leaned through the opening and glanced left. Their eyes met.

Fury raced through Samantha at the look in his eyes. He reached for her, then jerked back when he saw her gun. The first bullet slammed into his upper shoulder as he yelled and fell back. The second grazed his thigh as he scrambled away. She followed him out. He pulled his gun while sliding down a dip in the ravine, but his bloody hand caused him to lose hold of it. He tried to grab her leg, but she jumped back and fired at his face. It jammed.

By the time he stopped sliding, she was already rounding the next bend. She flew. Gun in hand. Hair flying. Purse flopping. Her thigh on fire. And then she heard sirens in the distance. But she kept running. Tears falling now. Sean was coming.

***

Maxwell grabbed his gun and followed her. Silently this time. Bleeding, but the bullets had hit shallow and went all the way through. She wasn't that far ahead, and he had to hurry. Cops would be swarming in minutes.

198

Samantha groaned as she heard him coming. She noticed a thick cluster of blackberries and brush halfway up a hill. A few seconds before he rounded the bend, she covered her face and dove into the bushes. Then watched silently as Maxwell ran by and faded into the distance.

She pushed through the back of the bush, seeing the small wasp nest too late. They stung her several times as she crawled out, then ran back the way she came. Then it got hard to breathe. So, climbing a magnolia tree with good cover, she pulled her phone with shaking hands. With only flickering signal, she texted.

***

Sean slammed the brakes and jumped out of the truck next to the crashed SUV. The other agents doing the same. His phone dinged with a text.

***

Samantha: EpiPen. Bee stings.
Sean: Sending by drone. I'm following.
***

Sean pulled a drone and EpiPen out of his truck as two agents checked on Kent and Sylvester, and the other three ran to the black truck.

In moments, Sean had the drone airborne and the thermal screen on. It showed a small figure deep in the woods to the right. A larger figure ran fast further away to the right. He barked Maxwell's direction to Dakota and the other agents. Then following the drone toward Samantha, he ran.

The drone reached her in a couple of minutes. Sean spoke through the drone, and said, "The drone landed. I'm close to you."

Samantha tried to climb down, but losing strength, fell - landing near the drone. Grabbing the pen, she jabbed it in her good leg and

199

laid back on the ground, feeling the blessed relief come. Air. She heard Sean.

***

Maxwell realized he had lost Samantha but kept going since he couldn't make it back to the truck. From time to time, he thought he heard someone behind him, so he angled his direction closer to the road. He needed a new escape plan. And before long, he caught glimpses of flashing lights as they passed on the highway. He smiled. Traffic would be backed up for miles. Perfect.

***

Sean saw Samantha on the ground halfway up the hill, then radioed the others he had her. In a few strides, he hit his knees beside her. She half-grimaced, half-smiled, at the look on his face.

He breathed a sigh of dismay mixed with relief, and said as she tried to sit up, "Oh honey, don't move. Let me check you."

Besides the bloody lip and bleeding thigh, there were several bee stings. She was covered in blood spray, cuts, scrapes, dirt, and green smudges. She was a mess. But alive. He removed his shirt and tied it around her leg. She winced and tried to control her wild filthy hair.

He said, "Wait - let me. We've got to hurry and get you out of here."

He twisted it into a rope and dropped it under her shirt. He tucked her gun in his waistband. Put the drone and controller in her purse and draped it over his shoulder.

She stood, ignoring his warning, and wobbled. He scooped her up and carried her.

Not wanting to appear weak, she said, "I can walk."

"I think you've walked enough. I've got you."

About to argue, her eyes rolled back, and she went limp. Passed out. He took off.

200

Before long, Sean reached the ambulance and the EMTs got to work on her. Checking the tourniquet. Her vitals. Sean told them about her allergic reaction and the EpiPen.

Feeling better and refocusing, Samantha sat up. She said, "Where are Sylvester and Kent? Don't tell me…"

"No. They're alive. It looks like Kent has a broken leg and head injuries. Sylvester was shot in the shoulder and has a broken wrist. They'll be ok. They're worried about you."

Glancing at the black truck down the highway, she said, "What about Maxwell? Did you catch him?"

***

Dakota interrupted them with a radio call. He said, "Maxwell disappeared, Sean. Run the drone and tell me if you see him."

Sean stepped away and flew the drone south over the woods. After searching twice, he saw three images. Only three.

He radioed and said, "No. I only see the three of you. He's either out of range or in the wind again."

Dakota spun at the sound of screams toward the highway.

He said, "He's in the wind - and I hear trouble. I'll get back with you. We're headed to the highway."

***

Sean switched the drone to camera and watched the agents with the drone. He saw a small group of people kneeling by a man crumpled on the highway. Women were crying. One lady was physically sick in the grass. Others stared solemnly at the man. Dakota and two agents ran out of the trees toward the commotion.

Sean radioed him and said, "I've got eyes on you. I'm sending an ambulance."

In seconds, the last empty ambulance at the crash site sped southbound, down the northbound highway, passing all the stopped traffic.

Samantha said, "What's—"

Sean said, "Hang on," then answered Dakota's call.

Dakota said, "A seventy-three-year-old man's down. Murdered. Apparently had his car highjacked when he stopped at the end of the traffic line. Ten. Fifteen minutes ago. They're not sure. It's a blue car – but no one can agree on the make. I'm waiting for confirmation on what he was driving for a BOLO. It's got to be Maxwell. He must have crossed the median and headed south."

Sean glanced at Samantha as they loaded her in the ambulance. He said, "Got it. Let me know when you find out."

***

After Sean hung up, Samantha said, "It's Maxwell, isn't it?"

Motioning for an agent, he said, "Probably. An old man was murdered when his car got highjacked down the road. I've got to go. I'll meet you at the hospital. Stay with the agent."

The agent said, "I've got her. Go."

Sean thought of something and stopped the ambulance door from closing. He asked, "What time was Suzette leaving for the airport?"

She gasped, and said, "Oh no! Hurry, Sean! She was leaving later than expected today. He will go for her, I know it. Here, let me key in her number for you…"

Chapter 25

Sean sped down the highway toward Baton Rouge listening to the phone ring. His speedometer registered 90 mph. Suzette didn't answer. He stopped the call, waited a second, then called for the third time.

Breathless, she finally answered, "Hi, Sean. Sorry, I was moving luggage. Is Samantha, ok?"

"Suzette, you need to leave. Now."

"What's the matter?"

"Listen to me. Look outside. Do you see a strange blue vehicle anywhere?"

Walking to the window, she said, "No. Why? You're scaring me."

"Maxwell is a serial killer. I think he's headed to you. I'm on my way with the FBI and Swat. If you don't see anything suspicious, get in your car and head to the nearest police station. Stay on the phone with me."

She was stunned. Motionless.

She jumped when he yelled, "Now!"

Dropping the phone in her pocket, she ran for her purse and keys. As she reached the kitchen, the back door glass shattered and she screamed, staring at Maxwell through the jagged glass. Bloody. Filthy. The scariest man she had ever seen. He kicked the door open, and she ran screaming. He laughed and stepped inside. This was the best part.

Sean floored it - hoping he would make it in time.

Suzette ran upstairs to the sound of Maxwell's laughter. Her mind quickly ran through options. None. What good was a locked door? Minuscule. And she didn't have a gun. She just knew she didn't want to get cornered in the house with that monster. She ran in her bedroom and locked the door. Then wedged a chair under the knob.

She wanted out and ran on the balcony, looking over. Two stories. If she jumped and broke a leg, she would be nothing but prey in a trap. She looked at the fire escape ladder that went to the roof. Kicking off her heels, she began to climb. Maybe he would think she jumped and got away. She heard the door crash open and climbed faster.

***

Maxwell looked around the bedroom. Whispering Suzette's name, he looked in the closet. Not there. Under the bed. Nope. In the bathroom. No. He smiled. She was feistier than he had given her credit for. He walked on the balcony. Nothing but high heels. He looked over the edge. He was a little impressed at her ingenuity. Then he turned and saw the ladder, glancing up just as she climbed on the roof. He laughed and began to climb - wincing at the gunshot through his shoulder and leg. But no big deal. And his head wound had dried long ago.

Suzette heard his laugh and ran toward the front of the roof - seeing flashing lights coming down the road. Sean saw her on the roof before he reached her house. He squealed to a stop and ran. The house was surrounded in seconds, then filled with law enforcement. Sean led the way upstairs. On the balcony. And headed up the ladder to the roof. Maxwell might not be able to rape her, but he would still kill her.

***

Suzette backed across the roof watching Maxwell stalk her.

She said, "Why are you doing this?"

"Why not?"

"The cops will get you. They're everywhere. There's no escape."

"You'll still be just as dead. And I'll be breathing – and remembering all the good stuff we shared in these last minutes."

Behind Maxwell, Sean climbed on the roof; pistol aimed dead center on the psycho in front of him.

He said, "Wrong, Maxwell. Because if you make one more step toward her. Even a tiny one. You'll roll off this roof a dead man long before you touch her. Which sounds like a great ending to me. So, your choice."

Other agents climbed up, fanning the roof.

Maxwell heard them all behind him and knew he'd gone as far as he could with Suzette. He certainly couldn't win in a gun battle with the cops. And he'd be dead before he jumped. But worst of all, he hadn't had enough time to finish with Samantha. This was certainly not his best day. So, he'd have to go for his day in court. No problem. He was a lawyer after all.

He said, "Like any good gambler when you're outplayed, I fold."

And kneeling, he clasped his hands behind his head.

As agents rushed to handcuff and read him his rights, Sean sat next to Suzette. Her knees had buckled. Face wet with tears.

She said, "If you hadn't called…"

"But I did," he said, and put an arm around her. He said, "We need to call Samantha. She was scared for you."

"Where is she?"

"On her way to the hospital. But that's another story. So, do you think you can climb down?"

"Yeah. But how are you going to get Maxwell off the roof in handcuffs?"

"I could always push him."

***

Samantha looked in the bathroom mirror at the hospital. She had finally insisted on a few moments of privacy. They'd cut off her clothes to tend to the gunshot wound, cuts, scrapes, and bee stings. They did tons of lab work and watched her oxygen levels. And the needles hurt as much as the bees.

She sighed. She looked atrocious – but at least her wild filthy hair was tucked under a surgical cap now. The hospital gown she was in almost touched the floor. And her poor feet were a dirty mess but hidden in paper shoes. She'd scrubbed her hands clean, but her fingernails were awful. Jagged. Embarrassing. She clenched her fists to hide them.

She heard a knock.

Sean said, "How about a hug?"

She opened the door and jumped in his arms.

Catching her, he buried his face in her neck. After a moment of just feeling each other, he carried her past the nurse's station to her ER cubicle.

He sat on the bed with her. He kissed her. A few times. Very softly because of her lip.

He said, "How's your leg?"

"Better. Well, honestly, it burns. All of it. The leg. The bee stings. My lip. The cuts and scrapes. And my hair feels like a rat's nest."

"Have you ever seen a rat's nest?"

"What difference does that make?"

As he grinned, her dad walked through the curtain with one thing on his mind – his daughter. She disappeared into his arms and Sean stepped out of the way.

Samantha smiled at her dad's expression. Pained.

He said, "You got shot."

"It grazed my thigh. But I shot him three times."

He groaned and looked at Sean, and said, "Where's Maxwell?"

"He's getting checked out at another hospital for getting shot and falling off a roof. Then he's heading to booking."

"Falling off the roof? Or pushed?" FBI Director Washington asked, with a chuckle as he stepped around the curtain.

Sean shrugged, and said, "It was a forced jump into an air bag. I followed him down."

Grinning, the director glanced at Samantha and said, "I just wanted to check on you before I saw Kent and Sylvester. I'm glad you're going to be ok – and I'm impressed with your skills. That was no easy battle you fought."

He dropped a packet in her lap, and said, "I hear you might be interested in this."

After he left, the D.A. walked in. With a quick glance at Samantha's condition, he looked at Sean. He had almost lost two prosecutors today. He shook Sean's hand and stepped closer to Samantha.

He said, "I think you've earned some time off. We'll handle the interrogation."

"No, sir. I want to be in on it. I know more about him and the evidence than anyone. I insist…respectfully, sir."

The men smiled. She meant it. And had earned it.

***

Twenty-five minutes, and a dozen phone calls later, Sean and Samantha reached the ranch. The task force started with questions, but Samantha held up her hands to stop them.

She said, "I'm not talking till after I clean up. I love you, but case closed. I'm filthy."

Sean led her upstairs. She would be his wife in days, but he wanted to be there for her. Now.

He shut the door behind him, then holding her, said, "Let me help you. Pamper you. Please."

Touching his face, she said, "Define pamper."

"Put on a bathing suit, then let me help you clean and tend to the worst of it. Afterwards, you can shower. Alone."

She kissed him softly, and whispered, "You'll get wet."

He took off his shirt and grabbed for shorts while she changed in the bathroom. It didn't take long.

She called, "Sean...can you bring a chair with you?"

When he opened the bathroom door, his eyes met hers in the mirror. She had on a floral bikini but held a towel in front of her stomach. Like a shield. Thinking of the waterfall attack, he knew why. Not addressing it right away, he stepped behind her and smoothed the hair away from her face. It hung down her back tangled with mud and forest debris.

He said, "Shall I brush your hair out first since it seems to bother you the most?"

"Yes, please. I hope there's nothing in there with teeth. Or stingers. I've had enough of those already."

Smiling, he picked up the brush.

She said, "Why don't you sit. It'll be easier since you're tall."

He sat in the chair and guided her between his knees. She looked back at him. Acknowledging the new intimacy. He held her hips as they both experienced a sizzle.

Voice husky, he said, "If you want your hair brushed, face the front. I'm getting distracted, and what's in your hair won't stop me."

She faced the mirror. He pulled what he could out of her hair and began to brush. But it was too tangled with dried mud from the cave.

She said, "Why don't we get in the shower. We'll have to wash the mud out."

After she got the water the right temperature, she turned...and stared. Sean stood in the steady stream of water. Tall, dark, handsome, sexy...and wet. Her eyes followed the water rivulets traveling down his body. Then forgot about her hair.

His desire burned as he touched her lips. Wanting what he couldn't have yet. His eyes lowered to her body. Wildly perfect. Wet. Slick. Water touching what he wanted to touch.

Stepping close, he said, "I know you love me. I know you trust me," and his hands covered hers on the towel.

Her hands clenched tighter as insecurity washed over her. The scars. But he kissed her neck and trailed them to her lips.

He said, "Baby, don't think. Kiss me. Forget the towel. I'm about to burn up. You're gorgeous. Sexy. And scars don't change a thing."

At his words, she let go. Tossing the towel, he knelt, running his hands over the scars on her belly, then licked them. She gasped, knees buckling. He caught her and stood, pressing her against the wall as he proved his promise. Scars didn't matter at all.

A few passionate minutes later, he washed – brushed – washed – and brushed her hair till it was clean. He scrubbed her ticklish toes with a brush as she giggled and scrubbed her fingernails.

She said, "I never imagined you doing this kind of pampering."

He smiled and said, "I'm aiming for two weeks – no more than three - and we're off to Switzerland. Then I'll show you what else you'll like."

***

While Samantha showered, Sean dressed and joined the task force in his office. They packed and labeled the case documents against Maxwell to bring to the police department. They had to leave in about an hour.

Later, Angel put the last box in the SUV that was backed to the front door. Dakota was on the porch reading a text from Adam. Sean was in his office on the phone with the director. Kerry, Gabrielle, and Jade watched the news about today.

Samantha watched it too as she headed downstairs to join the others. Sean finished his call and did a double take when he saw her and whistled. Everyone looked, and Samantha laughed. She

209

was dressed in a tight black skirt. Stretchy leopard V-neck shirt showing lots of cleavage. Sexy black heels. And sultry makeup.

Gabrielle said, "What are you up to? You look ready to start a bonfire tonight. I barely see any evidence of what happened today."

"Sean pampered me. Very well, I may add. But to answer your question, I'm providing distraction for Maxwell. I always heard, *why bring an empty gun to a gunfight.*"

Dakota said, "Perfect analogy. That reminds me. Sean said the director gave you a packet at the hospital. Was it what I think it was?"

She grinned and said, "What do you think it was? I'll tell you how close you are."

"FBI Academy application."

"No wonder you're an agent."

Everyone started talking at once.

Grinning, Sean interrupted and said, "Wait! Samantha Rutledge Remington has more secrets to tell you."

Gabrielle frowned – catching the name change. Why Remington? Dakota grinned. Everyone else was puzzled.

Kerry said, "Hey…Remington. Isn't that the new mayor candidate's name?"

Samantha said, "It is. That's who I met for my meeting this morning. He shocked me too. It turns out that he's more than a family friend. He is my father."

Gabrielle and Jade squealed in excitement, then pulled up his picture on their phones.

Comparing him to Samantha, Jade said, "How did we ever miss that?"

Sean said, "It's probably been years since you've seen them together. And back then you were in college. Busy. Not focused on a family friend. But side by side, you can't miss it."

***

Less than an hour later at the police station in Baton Rouge, Sean, Samantha, and Dakota met with the D.A., FBI director, and the chief of police.

The Director said, "Sean, for the record, lay out the case against Maxwell."

Sean said, "It begins with the case involving Spencer, his brother, who we all know is incarcerated in Angola for the waterfall attack. We now have in our possession new evidence proving Spencer was not the attacker. We have:

- An Affidavit by Samantha providing scar identification on the twin at the waterfall.
- An Affidavit and photos of Spencer proving he does not have either scar referenced by Samantha. But stating that Maxwell does.
- A copy of Maxwell's medical records proving he has an appendix scar. And video footage showing the forearm bite scar."

Explaining, Sean said, "Spencer pled guilty at arraignment. And no one questioned Samantha about assailant identification since there were witnesses to the attack. Therefore, Maxwell slipped under the radar and let Spencer take the fall.

"This exposure has led to the discovery of Maxwell's serial kills in the Chicago area where he moved after Spencer was sentenced. We have:

- Pictures of the eleven victims and their victimology.
- DNA and fingerprint reports of anniversary cards he mailed to Spencer."

Then Sean pulled up video feed from the drone surveillance in Maxwell's house. He said, "We also have:

- Souvenir panties presumably from each victim – pending DNA confirmation.
- His cell phone with photos of all Chicago victims during the crimes.
- And a video game linked to the motive. Blonde obsession."

Sean continued, "FBI forensics are still gathering evidence at Maxwell's rental house and his vehicles. But..." and he laid down a clear bag with pink women's panties embroidered with the initial S. "These were collected from Maxwell when he was booked into jail today."

Samantha stared at the bag in disgust. Maxwell had carried them in his pocket. Literally on him. Unfathomable. Truly driven by obsession.

She looked at Sean, and said, "They're mine. He took them at the waterfall."

Sean had figured that and nodded, then said, "In closing, we also suspect Maxwell contracted HIV during the rape and murder of victim ten. However, he has no medical records after that time. We would need a blood test to prove it, but we could use the threat to bait him during interrogation."

He paused, and said, "And that is the meat of our case until the search warrant results are in."

After legal discussions, dozens of charges would be involved. Including, but not limited to eleven counts of kidnapping resulting in serial rape and murder, two counts of attempted murder of prosecutors, three counts of attempted murder of federal agents, and the murder of the high-jack victim. And on top of that, the waterfall case would be re-opened.

Sean glanced Samantha and smiled. Now for interrogation.

***

Maxwell was alone in a holding cell. He sat on a hard bench. Legs crossed. Head leaned against the wall like he didn't have a care in the world. He thought back over today's activities. Why had Samantha been so well guarded? It seemed excessive for only a few texts she couldn't prove were from him, and two public confrontations. Sean was armed. FBI. So, why did he need more guards on her?

Then at the crash he figured she would panic. But she had been armed. Aggressive. He contemplated and touched the bandage on his head. Sore. Her leg probably was as well. He only returned fire to slow her down, not kill her. Killing her, among other things had been the plan for much later tonight. Maybe even at the waterfall. Or, after a few days to make up for all the years he had waited.

A commotion interrupted him, and he glanced in the cell next to his. Two men sparred like tomcats. He shook his head in disgust and closed his eyes, returning to his reflections.

The smell of her perfume in the woods almost did him in. He wanted to take her right there – pumped at the realization of her fear. Her hiding. Her vulnerability. So, the Glock shot in his shoulder and leg had been unexpected. She had turned into a wildcat, and he lost her.

Which led to his plan to take his frustration out on Suzette. But she turned into quite the little adversary. But he would have had her if the cop stampede led by Sean hadn't shown up. Why had they shown up? What led them there with such force? It must have been Samantha's influence.

Oh well. It was what it was. His plans hadn't worked out. But he knew what was next on the legal agenda. Attempted murders of guards and prosecutors. Murder of the guy in blue car. Sexual assault. But he had all sorts of fun things he could come up with to get out of most of it – and be out of prison having fun in a few years.

So, what was his best play?

***

Sean neared the holding cell where Maxwell reclined. Apparently unconcerned, which didn't surprise Sean. Maxwell knew the legal game. Now they had to knock him off balance to get a rise out of him. To lead him into the ambush they had waiting for him.

Sean motioned to the officer to unlock the door.

Maxwell rolled his head to the side and smiled. Just to be annoying, he said, "What's up, Sean? Busy day?"

Sean said, "Just the normal sewer," and told the officers, "Chain him."

Maxwell laughed.

Sean led the way. They put him in interrogation and motioned for him to sit. The officers locked him to the floor.

Maxwell said, "I'm getting the special treatment. I'm honored."

Ignoring him, Sean walked out, and into the observation room where the director, the D.A., Samantha, Suzette, and Dakota watched Maxwell.

The Director said, "He thinks everything's about today. So, let's start from the past and confuse him a little bit. See what we can trigger."

Sean said, "He's playing it cool so far." Then he glanced at Samantha, and said, "You ok?"

She said, "Oh yeah. This is my territory now."

The D.A. said, "Let's get started and see how well he plays."

The director and D.A. went into the interrogation room.

Maxwell said, "Finally, some company. I was lonely."

The director ignored his comment and introduced himself. The D.A. did the same.

Amused, Maxwell figured Sean wanted some federal action on this for the FBI to be here.

The Director reminded Maxwell of his rights, and said, "Even though you're an attorney, we advise you to have assisting counsel. Do you want to choose someone or shall we?"

Maxwell laughed without answering. The director called for a court-appointed attorney. They waited.

***

A blonde female attorney arrived and asked to speak with her client alone.

Once they were alone, Maxwell said, "You're here for legal presence only. I'm an attorney. If you say a word during interrogation, you're fired. And let's get this going. I'm bored already."

She sighed, and waved them back in. He was going to be one of those clients.

***

The director and D.A. returned. The Director took lead, and said, "You tried to kill two of my agents in the crash today."

Hiding surprise, Maxwell didn't respond. Why did Sean have an FBI team on Samantha?

The Director said, "Put your arms on the table."

Maxwell ignored him. His attorney took a breath to speak, and Maxwell's warning glare shut her up.

The Director repeated, "Put your forearms on the table. I can force you to do it or you can do it yourself. You choose."

Maxwell had just enough chain to slide his forearms on the table. The D.A. and director glanced at his right forearm. The D.A. walked out of the room. Maxwell looked at his arm. The scar. They suspected.

The Director said, "I have a simple question for you. Have you had your appendix removed?"

Maxwell thought, bingo. They were tying him to Samantha and Spencer. She had to have seen the scar. He said, "You want to see it up close and personal?"

The D.A. walked back in with a box. His turn now. He pulled out a document and slid it across so Maxwell could see it.

Maxwell shrugged. It was the appendectomy he had as a teenager.

The D.A. said, "You tried to murder two of my prosecutors today. Why?"

Maxwell laughed and said, "You're funny. Do your own work."

"Spencer didn't know the answer either when we questioned him about it."

Everyone saw Maxwell's involuntary tensing. Maxwell growled in his mind - and shut down. Spencer had lied to him. They knew about the cards.

The D.A. left the room, and the Director tried to engage him, "I hear you've got an itch for blondes."
But Maxwell stared at nothing. Zero connection.

***

Behind the glass, Samantha said to the D.A., "You've got to let me in there. I can make him respond. Give me ten minutes. Pull me out if I can't get anything going."
The D.A. looked through the glass at a stone-faced Maxwell, and said, "Do it."
Samantha and Sean glanced at each other. She knew what she was doing. And followed the D.A. into the interrogation room. Sean didn't like it.

***

The interrogation door opened, and Maxwell heard high heels clicking across the tile floor. He turned to watch Samantha enter. The director noted Maxwell's response and leaned back in his chair to watch. The D.A. leaned against the wall.
Maxwell watched Samantha glide across the room – hips rolling enticingly – seductively. She turned to face him and slowly slid her hands down her body. Teasing.
She whispered, "Hi there, Maxwell."
He flushed and eyed her up and down. He wanted to eat her up. She gave him a few minutes to get a good look at her, then neared the table and leaned over to look at his forearm. He could smell her perfume. See down her cleavage. Sweat popped up on his neck and upper lip. His legs clenched. Samantha reached out a finger to rub the bite mark she had left there.
He jerked and met her gaze.

She saw the fire building and said, "Do you remember what I looked like the day I bit you here?"

He growled and tried to grab her. The chains held. She smiled. Gotcha.

***

Sean went to the door.

Dakota blocked it, and said, "Watch her work, Sean. Look at her skills. She was able to get his response when we couldn't. She knows what buttons to push. Watch her. Trust her."

Sean turned back to the window and forced himself to focus on what Samantha was doing and why.

***

The director got up from the chair and gave Samantha the lead. He leaned against the wall opposite the D.A. They would see how far she could push him.

Maxwell was losing it. His muscles were jumping from his agitation. He saw her body in the tight skirt. Boobs bulging out of her shirt. Blonde hair swinging. He watched as she slowly sat across from him. His jumpsuit was getting damp from body sweat. She looked delicious. And she was so, so close. Teasing. Focusing on him. Just him and her. He didn't care about the ones watching.

She said, "Do you remember the waterfall, Maxwell?"

His eyes flashed and she nodded.

She said, "I know. I remember it too. I remember you also have another scar lower on your body. Shall I touch it?"

He drawled, "You almost got to remember more than that if we hadn't been interrupted."

Boom. Smug confession.

Samantha ran her hands through her hair and asked, "Do you still crave what you didn't get from me that day?"

He jerked on the chain.

She said, "Ah. You do still want it."

He glanced at her hair.

217

She slid her fingers through it and said, "Sean likes it too."

***

In the observation room, impressed, Sean said, "She's good."
Dakota said, "Oh yeah."
Suzette said, "All I can say is wow."

***

Maxwell's eyes narrowed when she mentioned Sean. The anger began.

She pressed him and said, "You've met Sean. My man. He touches—"

"Shut up."

She said, "How did you find my cave today?"

Maxwell blinked. She'd switched gears, but he wanted to talk about today anyway. He smiled and said, "I smelled you. I almost had you in my hands."

She stood, turned away, and said sassily, "Hardly. I shot you twice."

Maxwell's face turned red. Jaws clenched. The D.A. swallowed the chuckle as he watched her work him.

Samantha turned to the director and said, "Can Sean come in for a moment?"

The Director nodded into the two-way glass. Sean came in the room a second later, looking at Samantha for a lead.

She motioned him to stand in front of the mirror with her and whispered in his ear, "Touch me as we whisper. Fire him up."

Samantha ran her hand down Sean's chest and got closer. Sean whispered in her ear and slipped an arm around her waist. He lowered his lips like he might kiss her. Maxwell slammed his fists on the table. Samantha ignored him and lifted her lips.

Maxwell growled, "Get your hands off her."

Sean kissed her and Maxwell tried to flip the table. Sean touched her lips and walked out the door.

218

Samantha walked back to the table and said, "Now, where were we?"

Maxwell's eyes were dark with evil when she looked at him.

He said, "I'm going to rape you over and over before I kill you slow."

The director and D.A. stilled.

Samantha said, "Isn't that what you usually do?"

***

In observation, Dakota said, "Here we go."

Everyone was glued to the scene in the next room.

***

Maxwell's nostrils flared. Hate radiated from him.

Samantha said, "I bet you don't even remember the date you attacked me at the waterfall."

"April 21."

She pulled out the bag of anniversary cards. He watched her lay each card across the table in front of him.

She said, "Spencer was so sweet to me the day I visited him. He gave me his most treasured gifts from you."

Maxwell screamed in rage. Samantha disregarded his scream and pulled out a picture of each victim and matched it to their anniversary card.

She leaned across the cards to face Maxwell and said, "Don't you want to see their faces again? Or did your phone pictures help you remember them?"

Maxwell wanted to kill her. Bad. He looked at the cards. The pictures. And his mind raced through options until he finally latched onto an intriguing idea.

He forced himself to calm down and said, "So I'm guilty. I enjoyed every single minute of it. I get off on those thoughts any time I want. Including you, blondie."

Shrugging, Samantha said, "Were you aware that victim ten had HIV?"

He blinked. Finding number ten in his memories.

She said, "Did you get sick after killing her? Maybe flu like symptoms such as a fever, rash, mouth ulcers, anything like that? We haven't found a medical record on you after she was killed. Have you been to the doctor at all?"

He said menacingly, "If I didn't have these chains on..."

Samantha nodded. She knew. She remembered that look. She reached in the evidence box and pulled out the bag with her pink panties from the waterfall.

He growled, "Give...me...those."

She said, "I don't need them, I wear French lace panties now," and slung them across the table as she walked out of the room.

Chapter 26

Nicole Anderson watched her client, then picked up a pile of notes she had attempted to pass him during the interrogation.

She said, "That didn't go well. Now what's your plan?"

"I go to the arraignment hearing and plead guilty. They'll try to force a trial."

"You don't need me to tell you that you're looking at the death penalty – several times over."

"I have HIV. I'm guilty. What does it matter?"

"Don't you want to fight at all? At least stretch your time with appeals?"

"No. Meet me at the hearing and do what you're told."

She said, "The judge is going to wonder why you're so determined. He'll question you."

"I don't have to want to live in prison."

She said, "Fair enough. I'll see you Monday. Shall I reach out to anyone for you?"

"Find me a blonde."

She stood, ready to get out of the room. Away from him.

He said, "How long is your hair?"

Walking toward the door, she said, "I don't answer personal questions. Again, I will see you Monday in court. Let me know if you change your mind so I can actually do my job."

***

Back at the ranch, celebration steaks sizzled as Kerry plopped them on the patio grill, the aroma of seasoned butter filling the late-night air. Stomach growling, Sean walked to the door and watched the women and Angel line-dance in the den. Music competed with their laughter.

Dakota joined him at the door and said, "This was a good idea. Samantha deserved a celebration for her victory today."

Sean said, "You got that right. She's bounced from one blow to another today, wiped the dirt and blood off, and took Maxwell down. Hard. And looked gorgeous as she did it. She's incredible."

"She's got great instinct. Fearless skills. I sure enjoyed watching her work him."

Angel joined them outside and said, "I got a whiff of those steaks and lost my groove. You are the man, Kerry."

Sean said, "What's in that butter? I can smell what it will taste like."

Kerry chuckled and said, "Secret recipe. Wait till you taste it."

Sean noticed his bandages from the bear attack were smaller and said, "How are your wounds?"

"They're fine - as long as I don't meet up with another bear anytime soon."

Sean said, "Hopefully not," then paused for second and said, "Would you like to have a wedding here tomorrow?"

Kerry locked gazes with him and said, "You're kidding."

"No. I'm not. It would mean a great deal to me if I could do that for you two. Everyone would love it. Besides, I plan to continue this celebration all weekend. A wedding tops the list."

"You bet we want to! I can hear Chancy scream already."

The guys laughed, then Sean said, "I even know a minister that can come."

He looked at Dakota and said, "Don't you think we can get Adam and Raven here for the weekend? Adam needs to get out of the house anyway."

"He'd be glad to do it. He's been couped up way too long."

Then Dakota opened the patio door and yelled over the music, "Announcement time!"

222

Sean said, "Kerry, you better call Chancy quick. And let Misty know she can stay with us while you have a honeymoon. We'll make sure she has a good time."

Kerry pulled his phone and headed across the yard. Dakota took over the grill.

The line-dancers filed outside, and Samantha said, "What announcement?"

Sean said, "We're going to celebrate all weekend. And throw a wedding for Kerry and Chancy tomorrow."

The night exploded with female screams of excitement.

When he could finally hear again, Sean chuckled and said, "Let's get a houseful. Invite who you want. We have no work till court on Monday.

***

Kerry waited for Chancy to answer the phone. Impatiently.

She answered, "Hi, Kerry! How is Samantha?"

"Doing better than you could imagine. But I called for something else."

"What?"

"Do you want to go on a date tomorrow?"

"Sure! What do you want to do?"

"Marry you." She gasped. He said, "Noon - at the ranch. Are you ready?"

She danced, laughed, and screamed all at one time, then said, "Of course, I'm ready! And Kerry...I have everything. Our rings. Even my wedding dress."

"Chancy...I love you. What did I ever do to deserve you?"

"You love like no other. It's always been you."

"I'm here, baby. The waiting is almost over."

***

Kerry found Sean coming out of his office.

223

Sean saw the smile on his face, and grinned. He said, "It looks like the wedding is confirmed."

"That's putting it mildly. And we're both grateful. I don't know how to say thank you…or repay you, for your kindness and belief in me."

"Sometimes there's a connection between people. Unexplainable. You just know they're meant to be in your life. Like family. Look what you did taking on a bear for Samantha without a thought. That's how it works. I mean that."

Sean pulled an envelope out of his pocket and handed it to Kerry.

"What's this?"

"An offer."

"For what?"

"I heard something about a piano dinner club. I hoped you would accept me as a silent partner. The only thing I want is a good table when we go."

"You don't have to do this. Chancy still has the money we saved for the club. Over two hundred grand."

"Good – you'll need it. Now open it."

Kerry pulled out a check for fifty-thousand-dollars.

***

It was late when Sean escorted Samantha upstairs. Everyone else was asleep. He slipped fingers in the pockets of her shorts and backed her toward the end of the bed. Laying her back, he nudged her knees apart, and leaned over her.

Slipping her hands under his shirt, she said, "I like you putting me to bed."

He kissed her hard as he lowered some of his weight on her, and said, "Soon I'm going to get in bed with you and not get out."

"How soon?"

"I made reservations for our flight to Switzerland."

"How long is the flight?"

Rolling, and bringing her on top of him, he squeezed her thighs, and said, "Ten or more long, long hours."

"And the wedding?"

He groaned with desire as she bit his shoulder, and said, "Immediately. Nothing else happens till you're mine. If I can survive till then."

***

Kerry barely slept. It was still dark when his eyes opened for the hundredth time. He glanced at the clock. Five-thirty in the morning. He rolled out of bed and slipped on jeans. That was long enough. He was too pumped to stay in bed. Alone. But not for much longer.

Back in prison, he had spent hours, days, then years, aching because he wasn't Chancy's husband. But he had already experienced what it was like to have all of her. Just one time. In his arms. His bed. As love and passion held the reins. They had been impatient – and way too weak for a few hours one night. Not long after, he found his sister dead, and killed her killer. When he shut Chancy out of his life and went to prison, he hadn't known she was pregnant.

Now there was today. And Misty. God had been merciful. He was about to have a wife and a daughter. His family. And friends like family. And self-respect again. He texted Chancy.

***

Sing with me today.
Chancy: What song?
Kerry: At Last, by Etta James.
Chancy: Our song. I'll be there soon.
Kerry: Hurry.

***

Everyone hit the ground running at dawn. There was plenty to do to get ready for a wedding, guests, and lunch. After one cup of coffee, work began. The plan in motion was for food to be ready by eleven-thirty. Wedding at noon. And lunch would follow. The menu was bar-b-que ribs, brisket on a bun, a baked potato bar and tossed salad.

By seven a.m. the ribs baked; they would be grilled later. Baked potatoes roasted in slow cookers. Then the ladies set up décor for the impromptu wedding. Angel and Jade took a quick trip to St. Francisville for three bakery cakes to build a quick cake tier. Sean and Kerry arranged the room with the keyboard for procession entrance. And it was done.

***

In the barn apartment, Kerry checked the time. It was eight forty-five. He was dressed in a blue silk suit that had a sheen to it. White shirt. No tie. And he had made sure to double wrap his bandages. His suitcase was ready and waiting. It was time. He headed to the house and watched for his bride.

***

A few minutes later, Chancy arrived – and her heart skipped a beat when Kerry walked out of the house. Handsome. Vibrant. Powerful. Her man. She stepped out of the car and disappeared in his arms.

He said, "Oh, baby…you are so beautiful."

Smiling, she said, "Thank you, but wait until you see me later."

Touching her lips, he said, "I'm tired waiting," then leaned down to kiss her.

Misty squealed from the other side of the car, "Stop! You can't kiss her yet! You haven't said your vows. You're not even supposed to see her!"

For an intimate moment, Kerry and Chancy smiled at each other. Remembering their first time. His arms tightened – pressing her close. Wanting her. Loving her. Their gaze said it all. Thank God for second chances.

The others stepped outside and heard Misty's comment. Laughing, they joined them at the car and helped carry in their bags. The master bedroom in the loft became the bridal suite and they showed Misty to her room downstairs for the next few days. They had just gotten them settled when a horn blew outside.

Adam and Raven were here. Dakota and Sean were the first ones out the door. They headed to the passenger side as Adam maneuvered to get out of the car with a medical boot and crutches. Angel and Jade greeted Raven on the driver's side.

***

Watching from the porch, Chancy said, "Wow. That's what I call three good-looking brothers. Hot family genes."

Kerry laughed and watched the driver get her little boy out of the back seat.

He said, "The driver is Raven – his nurse and new friend of the family. Man, look at that head of red hair. She's a looker."

"And I bet she's the perfect incentive for him to get well faster."

"Or not…and get her to hang around longer."

They grinned as the group made their way on the porch.

Shaking hands with them, Adam said, "I see a couple ready for a wedding today."

Kerry said, "Yes you do! Thank you for coming. I can't tell you how grateful we are."

"I'm honored to be a part of it." He contemplated Kerry's size, and said, "I feel like I shrank."

Laughing, Kerry said, "I get that a lot."

Adam looked back for Raven. She was carrying an excited Lance toward the porch. He motioned her over, and she joined them. The kids quickly took center stage as Lance reached out and wiggled his hand in Misty's many braids.

Misty laughed, then ran her hand down Raven's long red hair. She said, "What color is this? Most red hair I see is not this color."

Raven said, "Mine is more copper."

"Well, it's awesome, and I want this color. Mom…"

A black Jeep drove up. Gabrielle's brother got out.

Smiling, Gabrielle ran to give him a hug, and said, "Blaze! I'm glad you made it home in time to come today!"

Adopted by her parents from foster care over a year ago, he was no longer a skinny, angry teenager. He was a healthy young man now. Good-looking. Above average height. Brown hair. Light blue eyes, with a gorgeous smile. He was sporting the expected soldier haircut.

She said, "When did you get out of boot camp?"

"Yesterday."

"Well, the timing was perfect!"

Sean called out, "Come on. Let's bring the party inside! We have a wedding in less than two hours."

***

As the crowd went inside, Adam led Kerry and Chancy to a private sitting area. He settled in a chair, and said, "Sorry, I needed to get off this leg. Besides, I wanted to visit with you. Sean gave me a rough draft of your story, but would you like to share anything? Today is for you."

Kerry glanced at Chancy. She nodded for him to begin.

He said, "We've loved each other since we were young. Before our twenties. We had the rings. The wedding planned. Her dress bought. And exciting plans for our future. But then I was arrested for killing a man I found standing over the body of my little sister."

Adam imagined the horror that must have been, and said, "I'm terribly sorry. How traumatic for you and your family in so many ways."

Kerry nodded and continued, "I had never been a violent man. My size intimidated most people, so they avoided trouble with me. But when I saw the bloody knife...I lost it. I swung. Hard. He flew backwards – dead before he hit the ground. They said I broke his neck and he died instantly. And then, life as I knew it disappeared. Family shattered. Our wedding gone. Our singing plans gone. My freedom gone. In a flash it was all over – replaced with a cage.

228

"However," and with a glance at Chancy, he said, "The night before it all happened...Chancy and I...made Misty. And then she found out she was pregnant after I was denied bail. She tried to see me, but I refused, insisting she move on. I didn't want her waiting for a felon. And she didn't want me to suffer finding out through a letter."

He slipped an arm around her, and said, "After fifteen long years, I told the story to Sean and the others. The rest you know. That's when I learned of Misty."

Adam, impressed at the couple who had stood the long difficult test of time, said, "That's quite a powerful love story. New beginnings. Second chances. I can only imagine what God will do through the two...no, three of you."

***

Thirty minutes later, a white SUV drove up and Sean pointed it out to Samantha. She smiled, pulling him with her.

He said, "You go first. This is a special moment. I'll join you shortly."

Smiling, Samantha walked out the front door. Across the porch. Down the steps. Right into the arms of the Remington's. Her family.

Lots of hugs, tears, and smiles later, her dad asked, "How's your leg?"

"The bullet graze isn't bad. I promise. The bruises and cuts are tender – but on the mend. Interrogation last night made me feel a whole lot better."

Smiling, he said, "I bet it did. I wish I had seen it."

"Well, I happen to have the clout to get you access to the video from the D.A."

After the laughter faded, Samantha's brothers decided to get in on the action. Picking as usual, the youngest said, "The oldest child shouldn't be the shortest."

Samantha grinned and glanced at her dad. She said, "Did you tell them?"

"I saved that for you."

With a hand on her hip, she smiled at her three brothers, and said, "If I'm tough enough to start the FBI Academy at Quantico – I'm tough enough to be the oldest sibling. The boss."

They were stunned at the word FBI. Then cheering, the boys picked her up, passing her around. Laughing, Sean joined the group.

***

A little before noon, Samantha watched Kerry practice at the keyboard. He smiled as she walked up.

She set a small black box on the ivory keys, and said, "I know you haven't had time to shop for Chancy. I'd be honored if you would accept this for her - as a gift from you. It's something I know she would love. Please, let me do this for you."

Moved deeply by her thoughtfulness and generosity, Kerry touched her cheek with a tenderness many wouldn't expect from a big man.

He said, "Thank you for doing that - for both of us. You're quite a woman. Sean is a very lucky man."

She kissed his cheek and climbed the stairs to his bride.

***

Upstairs, Chancy's mind swirled with memories of Kerry. His touch. His mouth. His passion. She glanced at Misty across the room and took a deep breath. She had to get it together - it was almost time. Her hair was done. Her makeup ready. Her dress touching her skin. Reminding her...

Someone knocked.

Samantha said, "Chancy?"

"Please, come in."

Smiling, Samantha walked in and gasped at the sight of Chancy. She said, "Oh my gosh...you're exquisite."

Chancy was dressed in a white slip wedding gown with spaghetti straps. Scoop neck. The back draped all the way to her waist. Her long dark hair hung in deep waves past her shoulders. She was gorgeous. Vintage. Elegant and sexy.

Misty said, "Daddy's going to want to kiss her for sure now."

As giggles faded, Samantha glanced at Chancy, and said, "Is there anything I can do to help?"

"If you would open the door for me once Misty is in place, I would appreciate it. That's all really. I'll be ready."

When they were in place, Samantha nodded at Kerry, and he began to play. Misty walked out and stopped at the top of the stairs, and he smiled, heart full as he watched their daughter come downstairs. Once she was in place, he segued into playing *At Last*, by Etta James. Everyone looked to the balcony.

Gracefully, Chancy walked to the edge of the staircase and paused, meeting Kerry's gaze. Then one slow step at a time, she began to sing on her way to him. Kerry watched every move she made. Her body. Expressions. Heard every word. And began to sing with her till he stepped away from the keyboard, joining her – and the last note faded away.

Smiling, Adam said, "And that proves why we are here today. For a love that climbs to the mountaintop. Survives the valley. And climbs again another day. A powerful love. Lasting love. Real love. At last."

Then he prayed over them. Led the vows. The ring ceremony. And finally, they kissed.

As they turned and faced their guests, Adam said, "I now introduce to you, Mr. & Mrs. Kerry Hart!"

After congratulations, they cut the cake and took a few pictures. And in minutes, goodbyes were said. Then hugging Misty one more time, they were gone, dust following in their wake.

Down the road, Kerry pulled into a private trail he used often, and stopped the car. This was the first time they had been alone together in more than a decade. They reached for each other, and she kicked off her heels. Hungry lips met as he pulled her across the car. In his lap, they both groaned as hands and lips roamed.

Hot beyond belief, he tried to talk, "This is not…the right place. I just needed to…hold you. Taste you. Hurry, tell me where you want to go…"

Wild for him, she said, "I'm…tired waiting…"

In a second his seat dropped back. Her dress flew across the car. And the waiting was over.

Chapter 27

At the ranch, the bar-b-que feast was next on the agenda. A buffet line was set up. Tender ribs with a spicy sweet sauce. Brisket sandwiches. Hot baked potatoes with all the fixings. A bowl of marinated salad filled with cucumbers, grape tomatoes, red onion, avocado bites, olives, and hunks of mozzarella cheese. And once Sean pulled the toasted French bread drenched in seasoned butter out of the oven, Adam said the blessing. The sound of laughter and clanking dishes followed. It was absolutely perfect.

After lunch, Adam and Raven leaned on the fence watching the stallion and mare.

Brushing windblown hair out of her face, Raven said, "I love to watch them run. They are beautiful animals - nature at its best."

Glancing at her, Adam said, "No. Not from my point of view. You are nature at its best."

She shook her head with a grin, and said, "You just can't help yourself, can you?"

"What else should I say with a gorgeous redhead right next to me?"

"Maybe talk about the horses."

"Ok. Let's talk horses. I'm ready to ride anyway. Come with me."

She glanced at his leg in the medical boot and said, "You would have to be perfectly careful not to use the leg. I mean it. You don't want to—"

"I know. I know. Then double with me to make sure I'm careful. You are my nurse after all."

She hesitated at the thought of sitting in a saddle with him.

He knew. Smiling, he said, "You know you want to ride. Come on. I bet Lance will want to ride too, so let him be your chaperone. Obviously, you don't trust yourself to behave when you are alone with me."

She sighed and gave him a look that said *men* – and he winked.

As Adam called across the yard for Sean and Dakota to come help them, Raven knew she should not get on that horse with him. Thigh to thigh. Tucked nice and cozy against his body. That was trouble. She had been through too much to rush or dive into any relationship – even with a man like him.

She had to focus on being a mother. Setting up a home. And deciding professionally what she wanted to do - and when. Ending up in his arms wasn't on the list. Not yet anyway. She planned on keeping them on the friend level - for as long as she possibly could.

Before long, they helped Adam mount the stallion, and Raven was settled in front of him, Lance strapped to her chest. Adam grinned at his brothers, then made a clicking sound and the horse headed out of the barn.

***

Dakota, Gabrielle, Sean, and Samantha watched them disappear across the pasture.

Gabrielle said, "Do you think passion is simmering yet?"

Dakota said, "If not, after this ride it will be."

Sean said, "I can't wait till he's in love. Especially with a stunner like her."

Samantha asked, "Why do you say it like that?"

"Adam's a passionate man. A hunter. Once he gets the scent, he won't quit. Ever."

Gabrielle said, "Sounds like a family trait to me."

Adam and Raven rode through the countryside. The woods. The hills. Listening to the sounds. Grateful for the summer breeze. Truly, eastern Louisiana at its best.

Raven closed her eyes for a moment, enjoying the sensation of riding again. She had missed it more than she realized. She needed this new life. This peace. This.

Adam thought about their current position. He was distracted by it way more than he should be. Their rubbing thighs were flat out hot. And her perfume filled his senses. He leaned closer and breathed her in. She felt his nearness.

He said, "Goodness, Raven, you smell good."

"Ah. You're a perfume guy then."

"Perfume on you."

"Adam…"

"Hmmm?"

"You're flirting."

"It's the perfect time, don't you think?"

The horse shifted going downhill, abruptly changing their position. Adam slipped an arm around her to balance them. Concerned about his leg, Raven laid a hand on his thigh and leaned down to look.

She said, "Tell me you didn't squeeze your leg."

The warmth of her hand on his thigh held his attention. His muscles tightened. She glanced back to see why he hadn't answered. Their gaze held - and awareness had its way. Each felt the touch of the other, and neither moved. Raven felt the flurry in her stomach and Adam got hot from the neck down.

She looked away and quickly removed her hand from his…firm muscular thigh. His hand flexed across her stomach as she sat back up. She groaned silently. Trouble. She knew it. And she knew enough about him to know there was little chance he would let this slide. He didn't miss anything – and addressed everything.

Adam enjoyed the feeling racing through him. Raven might act like it didn't happen, but he'd seen it all over her. No hiding it from him now. Nope. It would just get stronger. He smiled and rode quietly, arm around her, letting her get used to the idea. And after a few minutes of Lance's antics, the sexual tension eased, and they were laughing again.

Riding by the creek, Raven thought about the land she'd purchased along the Calcasieu River in Lake Charles yesterday.

She said, "It's still hard to believe I bought land on the first day of looking. Riverfront acreage can't be easy to come by, even though there are miles of river. Most of the land isn't habitable or accessible based on my research."

Adam said, "I know. I was as surprised as you. I figured we would look for months till you found the right spot. Gabrielle connected us to the right real estate agent."

"Why do you think the owner was selling the land? It's private. Already had a road. And there aren't neighbors for a mile or more. I know Sam Houston State Park isn't too far from there either. It's a gorgeous area."

"It is. And I can't imagine why he sold it. It was family land. Maybe the vast amount of property was too much responsibility."

"I guess. Well, I'm grateful."

"No doubt. The four acres you bought is a great space for privacy including area to expand. It couldn't be more perfect."

"Yeah. I don't want Lance to grow up in the city. I want to teach him about his Native American heritage and nature. Tap into what his strengths will be."

"I understand completely. But you'll need help. Animals. Security. A boat. Equipment. And it's too far out to be alone with him."

"I know. Maybe Gabrielle and Dakota know someone that might want part-time work."

"I already have someone in mind."

She glanced back and said, "You're kidding. Who?"

"Me."

"Adam! No! I can't impose on you like that. You haven't even found the place you want yet. You have plans too."

"Actually - I did find it. I bought the land I wanted."

"When?"

"When you bought yours."

"But we didn't look at any other land."

"I know. That's why I bought all the rest of the land he had for sale around you."

She gasped and said, "You did not."

He laughed and said "I certainly did. It was perfect for me too."

"You'll live next door? Is that what you are telling me?"

"You got it."

"I'm…surprised."

"I doubt that. We're friends…but we'll be a whole lot more and you know it."

She didn't respond. She knew. He was hard not to want. But she didn't have to make it easy for him.

On the way back to the ranch, he said, "I'm ready to get started on the search and rescue operation. I'll have plenty land for a house. Barn. Equipment. Animals. But keep the wilderness around us. I would love to have you on the team with me. Medical care saved my life in the field – and you're a fabulous nurse. What do you think? It wouldn't be full-time. Just as needed."

Thrilled, she said, "It never occurred to me. I would love to be on the team!"

"What about care for Lance when you're gone?"

"My former sister-in-law, Lance's nannie, is moving down from Minnesota once I'm set up. She'll live with us. She's amazing. Beautiful. And quite a woman. You'll enjoy her."

"I'm sure I will. Then, you'll be set. So…what about us?"

She didn't answer.

He whispered, "Ignoring it won't help."

"Ignore what?"

He laughed and said, "Have I mentioned I'm an excellent hunter?"

She got the innuendo, but acted clueless, and said, "And that means…"

"I'm coming for you."

She sparked. Red hair flying, she spun to look at him, and said, "Don't forget, charmer. I'm Indian too. You men aren't the only warriors."

Wham. He felt the blast. She was flaming hot, and he wanted to kiss her and taste all that right now. Smiling, he said, "Oh. I got you, Raven. I read you loud and clear. All I can say is, things are going to get hot. Get ready to sweat."

***

Late afternoon in New Orleans, Chancy walked softly down the hall to the kitchen. She started coffee and looked outside. It had been a magical day. She heard Kerry, then felt him step up against her. She laid her head back and looked at him.

He said, "I can't believe we made love in the car all the way to New Orleans. You were wild and wonderful. That gives me lots of ideas for secluded road trips."

She laughed and turned in his arms. Seeing his bandages with breakthrough bleeding, she said, "We need to check your wounds. I see blood."

"What wounds?"

Then he sat her on the counter. Reaching in the pocket of his pants, he said, "I have something for you."

He handed her a black box and said, "Before you open it, I want you to know that Samantha gave me this to give you – from me. She knew I hadn't been able to shop. And that in itself - is a gift. I wanted you to know. Now, open it. It's beautiful…like you."

Moved by the explanation, she opened the box and gasped. It was a diamond bracelet. Not one diamond. The bracelet was a solid row of diamonds. She looked at Kerry, stunned. He smiled and slipped it on her wrist.

She held the bracelet to the light, and said, "Who gives gifts like this to someone they've known less than a week?"

Smiling, he said, "Someone who knows how to love."

"They've done so much already."

"I know, but there's more," and he handed her the envelope from Sean.

As she opened it, he said, "It looks like we have a new business partner."

She screamed when she saw the fifty-thousand-dollar check.

∗∗∗

It was almost ten p.m. at the ranch, and the ones staying the night were winding down. They had celebrated all day. The wedding. The food. Music and more line dancing. Laughter. Horse rides. Games. And lots of joking around. Sean leaned back on the sofa; Samantha snuggled under his arm. Dakota and Gabrielle teased each other on the other sofa. Adam and Raven visited with Angel and Jade at the table about search, rescue, and investigations. Lance was sound asleep on a pallet by Blaze and Misty while they played a serious game of chess on the floor.

Samantha walked her fingers up Sean's chest and said, "How about you rock me on the porch, Agent Man?"

In moments, she was curled up in his lap outside.

She said, "Thank you for today. It couldn't have been better."

He slid a hand up her thigh and said, "Thinking about Switzerland, I respectfully disagree."

She giggled and said, "Do you plan on telling anyone we're eloping?"

"Just our bosses. Let's shock everyone else."

"Do you really think they'll be shocked?"

"Not that we get married. But they won't expect the elopement or the trip to Switzerland."

Laughing, she said, "I can't wait to get their reactions!"

"And I can't wait to have a signed marriage license."

Smiling, she said, "That goes without saying. But, speaking of marriage, it crossed my mind we haven't discussed financial plans at all. I wanted you to know that I have a substantial savings and investment portfolio. I also inherited my mother's house—".

He interrupted her and said, "Honey…finances are not an issue. You know I'm wealthy."

"Wealthy, by definition, can mean a lot of things. It's best to know what I bring to the table financially."

"Does millionaire define it better?"

"Ah. I see what you mean. But…I like our life as working professionals. I don't want it to change."

"I like our life too. And it doesn't have to change until we want it to."

She wrapped her arms around his neck, and said, "I can't wait to do day-to-day with you."

He slid his hands under the back of her shirt and whispered, "And I can't wait to do whatever you want, anytime you want it," and crushed her mouth to his.

***

Sunday morning dawned beautiful. Clear blue sky. Fanciful puffy clouds. And a smooth southern breeze. The three brothers drank coffee on the patio and watched the horses.

Sean rubbed the back of his neck.

Dakota caught the sign, and said, "What's on your mind?"

"After court, I'll be in Washington D.C. a few weeks. With Kerry married and adjusting to his new life, I can't leave the horses here alone."

"I can bring them home with me after court tomorrow. I think my stallion might like your Arabian mare."

The men laughed. Obviously.

Sean glanced at Adam and said, "Speaking of horses, that was a cozy ride with you and Raven yesterday. Is there anything you should tell us?"

"I can't imagine why you would think I need to tell you anything."

Dakota said, "He didn't answer the question."

Sean said, "Nope, he sidestepped it."

Adam laughed and said, "Having two older brothers in the FBI makes it hard to avoid a question."

Sean said, "Exactly. So, answer."

Adam grinned. They didn't know about the land he bought. But one thing at a time.

He said, "You already know Raven is gorgeous. If I think you need to know something else, I'll tell you."

Sean said, "Liar. You're hiding something."

"Hey. Watch yourself. Who do you think you're talking to?"

Dakota said, "Our little brother - who has eyes locked on a particular redhead."

Adam smiled. And still didn't answer the question.

***

Late that night, only Sean and Samantha were up. It had been another great day. Four-wheeler riding. Hiking. Horseback riding. A drone exhibition. A gymnastic show. Salsa dancing. And Adam amazed them with his bow and arrow skills.

Sean finished in the kitchen and headed to the sofa. Samantha came downstairs and laid where he could rub her feet.

After a few minutes, he said, "Do you have any thoughts on the arraignment tomorrow?"

"I just don't trust him. His cave-in so quickly during the interrogation bugs me."

"Me too. We'll stay prepared. Keep you covered. That's the plan. No matter what tomorrow holds, Maxwell is history."

***

In the jail cell, Maxwell thought of Samantha and smiled. A real smile. After the interrogation, he had realized what a worthy opponent she had become. She really knew him. She was the only one who had seen the *thing* in him and lived to tell anyone about it. To fight it. To slay the dragon. He had underestimated her and was proud in a way – because she knew her power now.

***

Samantha came downstairs the next morning dressed to kill in a fabulous red suit. Short skirt and jacket. Sassy red heels. Ponytail and red lips. Obviously ready to take on the world.

Sean gave her a spin and said, "Counselor! You look gorgeous. Bold. Victory looks good on you."

Smiling, she said, "Thank you, Agent Man - and I say we all make an impressive statement."

Jade, beautiful as always, was dressed in a black sleeveless dress and sexy heels. And Sean, Dakota, and Angel looked amazing in black suits. Handsome. Tough. Intelligent men.

Sean said, "That we do. You ready to finish this thing?"

Samantha nodded, and with a quick goodbye to the others, the task force headed to Baton Rouge. They had a court date with a killer.

***

Forty minutes later, Sean walked with Samantha into the 19th Judicial District Court for East Baton Rouge Parish. Dakota, Angel, and Jade followed. Samantha led them to a corner courtroom on the second floor with three entrances – one in the front and one on each side. She walked toward the prosecutor's table.

The D.A. greeted them, letting them know that the Attorney General would be in court today. Sean sat directly behind the D.A. in the aisle seat. Samantha sat next to him with Dakota on the right side of her. Angel and Jade sat behind them. Security officers were informed that FBI was in the room.

Before long, people poured into the courtroom. It would be packed because of the recent news reports. And because some, if not all, of the Chicago victims' families would attend. Sean watched the side door where Maxwell would enter.

Samantha glanced at her watch. Just ten minutes before court began. The side door opened. Two officers entered with Maxwell. He was dressed in a classy gray suit wearing front handcuffs. But for the cuffs, he appeared totally in charge and as professional as the other attorneys in the room.

242

His court appointed attorney, Nicole Anderson, stood to greet him. She wore her blonde hair in a ponytail and was dressed in a conservative blue pantsuit. Two other defense counsel were with her. The officers left Maxwell seated next to Nicole and joined two other officers against the wall.

Professional and pleasant, Maxwell greeted the attorneys at his table. Nicole leaned close and whispered earnestly to him for a few moments, all but begging him not to plead guilty.

He shook his head, and said, "I told you no. Do what I tell you. And smile. You look like you're about to throw up."

She tapped her ink pen on the table and glanced at the D.A.

Samantha watched. She was aware that Maxwell's guilty plea in a capital case during arraignment was frowned upon. Difficult even, in the event of a problem without trial decisions to back them up. Nicole turned and caught her eye for a second, then faced the front. Samantha knew this was a rough morning for her - given her client. Maxwell winked at Samantha and glanced around the packed room with a smile.

Soft crying and harsh whispers could be heard among the spectators now that he was in the room. Samantha sighed. Family members struggled when the accused was present. They couldn't help but suffer a myriad of emotions – all painful and forever locked in their memories. Glancing again at Maxwell, she did not have a good feeling in her gut. He was way to cheerful.

An officer at the side door said, "All rise," and everyone stood as Judge Collins entered the courtroom and headed to the bench. The court was now in session.

Noting the size of the crowd, the Judge said, "All visitors will remain seated, quiet, and respectful throughout the arraignment proceedings. Disruptions will not be tolerated. Officers will remove any offenders from the courtroom."

There was some grumbling, and the judge banged his gavel. He said, "That's my last warning."

Then he called on the prosecution to rise and identify themselves to the court. The D.A. stood and spoke. Next, was the defense counsel. Maxwell and Nicole stood. As counsel for himself, Maxwell identified himself and his team.

Following that, the judge explained Maxwell's rights to him, then called on the court clerk to read the first count against him. The process was simple. The clerk read one charge at a time, after which the judge asked Maxwell how he wanted to plead.

After each of the forty-one charges against him, Maxwell answered, "Guilty."

Once the last guilty plea was entered, the judge sighed and leaned back in his chair. He took a hard look at Maxwell and said, "It's a sad day indeed, when I have to listen to that horrendous list of charges. Vicious crimes. Murders. Rapes. Attacks. From an attorney no less."

Maxwell stood motionless. No response.

The Judge continued, "You have represented countless victims and clients as an attorney. Helped them seek justice. Yet today, you stand in my courtroom apparently proud that you're guilty. Like you think you deserve some type of respect. Honor. Or acknowledgement of your skill and intelligence. But all I see is a disgrace. A monster. A waste of a human life that had so much to offer."

There was still no response from Maxwell. But the judge was firing up the courtroom with his sharp rebuke and disdain.

The Judge looked over the list of charges one last time, and said, "Before I sentence you, is there anything you would like to say to the court?"

Maxwell nodded, and said, "Your Honor, if I may have a moment, I understand that the families here today would like closure. Vengeance. Retribution. Something to lay reason to the suffering of their loved ones. I would like to think my guilty pleas might make a difference somehow. That my willingness to suffer for my actions might help them with the pain of losing Alice, Callie, Donna, Ella, Giselle, Helena, Ziva, Lolita, Tracie, Sharonda, and Rebecca. But after a great deal of reflection, I believe that all eleven of them deserved exactly what I gave them."

Screams of rage and disbelief filled the room. The judge banged his gavel and yelled, but no one heard him. The crowd surged forward. Furious and ready to kill. Officers fought to keep the lynch mob from reaching Maxwell – who disbelievingly kept talking as his court appointed counsel tried to quiet him.

He said, "I enjoyed every tear. Every scream. The hot blood. The sex. All because they were blonde. Just like Nicole."

Then in one motion, he grabbed Nicole's ink pen and looped his handcuffs around her neck, yanked her tight against him, and stabbed her in the shoulder. Nicole screamed with the rest of the crowd.

Sean and Dakota rushed Samantha away from the danger. Maxwell drug a bleeding Nicole toward the bench, screaming at everyone to stay back. And pandemonium reigned as the officers lost total control in the courtroom. The judge and court staff ran. The D.A. called 911 as they ran out the opposite door. Spectators were both a wave of fear, and rage, running wild.

Pushing Samantha to Angel, Sean said, "Stay with Angel and Jade. We've got to follow Maxwell."

And with guns drawn, Sean and Dakota followed the blood trail through the side door. Angel ushered Samantha and Jade out of the courtroom, then cornered them behind a door so they wouldn't get caught in the stampede.

After the bulk of the crowd passed, he drew them with him near the side hall where Sean and Dakota had gone. They glanced around the corner.

Maxwell dangled Nicole in front of him – blocking his face from any head shots as he backed down the hall. The ink pen was now shoved partially in her neck as he threatened the cops to stay back. Nicole's weak screams were barely audible. Her feet dangled in the air with only one shoe. Blood everywhere.

Sean and Dakota took a few steps back – trying to stop the stab assault. But they were running out of time. Maxwell was headed to an open elevator. If he made it there, it would become a deathtrap for Nicole, or anyone else who came near him.

Samantha watched Maxwell. Obviously, he aimed to drag Nicole on the elevator. But when those doors closed, he'd kill her. Sean and Dakota needed a clear shot. Something to distract Maxwell.

Without warning Angel and Jade, she stepped out in the hall, and yelled, "Hey Maxwell!"

At the sound of her voice, Maxwell looked beyond the FBI and cops to Samantha standing at the other end of the hall. She smiled and posed for him, running her hands down her body – teasing. Whetting his appetite. Taking hold of his focus.

Sean and Dakota glanced at Samantha. She let her jacket drop to the floor and with that, they knew her plan.

Like a sexy runway model, she sensually walked slowly toward Maxwell. Distracting him from Nicole. From the FBI. From the cops. She wanted him to only think about her.

She said, "You don't want Nicole. Aren't you tired of all the blonde surrogates by now? Come on, you've got the real thing right in front of you. Let her go…take me…"

Other cops made noise as they moved in on the scene and Sean and Dakota yelled for everyone to back off – the FBI was in charge.

Samantha released her ponytail and blonde hair tumbled. She made a dance spin, working her hips, raising her arms – giving him a good view.

Maxwell's gaze was locked on her. Proud of her guts. Aroused. But he didn't release Nicole. He stood and watched.

She smiled and reached for the buttons on her shirt. With a quick glance at Sean, she began to unbutton. She had to make this good – she was almost half-way down the hall.

Maxwell wanted her to strip for him. To show him what he had seen at the waterfall all those years ago. He began to sweat.

Samantha brushed by Sean's shoulder as she passed him, and said, "Say when."

Two steps later her shirt hung open. Maxwell got an eyeful of red bra and lots of skin. He groaned in lust. Hands itching to grab her. He never even noticed Nicole had passed out – still hanging in front of him dripping blood on the floor.

Chapter 28

Samantha saw the shape Nicole was in. Bad. She had to hurry –
and let her shirt flutter to the floor. She posed in her bra, skirt, and
heels. Teased. Promised. Then began to walk closer, sliding her
skirt up her thighs, one inch at a time. Dancing. Giving him a
glimpse of what he had killed so many women for. Calling his
name.

Hot and hungry, Maxwell said raggedly, "Samantha…"

Eyes locked on him, Sean and Dakota began to inch forward,
following Samantha.

Skirt almost at her panty line, Samantha said, "What will it be
Maxwell? Me? Or her? Come and take me…"

Maxwell roared, dropping Nicole, and barreled toward
Samantha. Lost in his obsession. Cuffed hands reaching for her for
just one last feel…knowing…

Sean screamed, "Now!"

Samantha threw herself to the side, covering her head as she hit
the floor and slid into the wall. Gunshots rang out in a furious
cluster. Then after a second of silence, she heard the thud as
Maxwell's body hit the floor. She didn't look.

Sean couldn't get to Samantha fast enough. Dropping to his knees, he drew her into his arms, turning her face away from the scene.

Wrapping his jacket around her, he said, "Are you hurt?"

"I'm ok. Nicole?"

"EMTs are getting to her now."

"He's dead?"

"Finally."

She whispered, "I've never killed anyone before."

He saw the weight of it hit her, and said, "You saved a life. He made the choice."

As he drew her away from the body, first responders filled the hall. Dakota joined them and handed Samantha her blouse and jacket.

He said, "That was quite a bait-walk, Prosecutor."

"Is bait-walk a thing?"

Sean said, "It is now."

Angel and Jade joined them. Jade said, "Are you trying to give me a heart attack? Where in the world did that idea come from?"

Samantha said, "The guys needed a clear shot. A distraction. I had to make myself a tad more visible."

"You call that a tad?"

As they laughed, Dakota leaned to Sean and said, "You've got your hands full with her."

With a smile, Sean said, "Don't I though."

Once Samantha dressed, she wanted to talk to Nicole. Sean pointed to where the EMT's had loaded her onto a stretcher, and they headed her way.

Nicole's neck and shoulder were wrapped in bandages. Blood all over her.

She grabbed Samantha's hand and said, "I'll never know how you did that. He couldn't even function after he saw you. He would have killed me. How do I say thank you for that…"

249

"Just seeing you survive is more than enough. And promise me you will let this go, Nicole. Maxwell is gone. Don't carry this with you and clutter up your head."

Nicole nodded, trails of tears on her cheeks.

Samantha heard her name and turned. The D.A. and Attorney General walked toward them. The D.A. said, "Be prepared for what the news will air, Samantha. Reporters filmed what happened."

Samantha groaned and said, "I hadn't thought of that."

The Attorney General said, "No matter what you see on the news, there are no words for your bravery. I am proud of your instinct and sacrifice."

"Thank you, sir."

The D.A. was interrupted with a quick call, and said, "The press is waiting downstairs. Would the task force stand with us for the breaking news report?"

The task force walked out the front doors of the First Judicial District Court to see first responder lights everywhere. A crowd of reporters and spectators were gathered around the press podium. The D.A. motioned them to his side.

He stepped to the microphone and said, "Serial killer Maxwell Chance was arraigned today on a lengthy list of criminal charges. He pled guilty. However, at the sentencing portion of the arraignment, he caused a disturbance in the courtroom and took his female attorney hostage.

"FBI Special Agents Sean and Dakota Nash pursued him. But the hero of the day is Assistant Prosecutor, Samantha Rutledge, who offered to trade places with the hostage. Maxwell Chance was killed in that exchange.

"So, at this time I would like to introduce to you the task force that worked this case. FBI, Special Agent in charge Sean Nash and Special Agent Dakota Nash. From Southern Investigative Services out of New Orleans, Jade Louviere, and Angel Gonzales. And again, Assistant Prosecutor Samantha Rutledge of the District Attorney's Office.

"On behalf of Baton Rouge, we are grateful to all of you for your service. Thank you."

***

As the task force headed to their vehicle, everyone's phone began to ring. Notifications dinged. They laughed and began to answer their phones.

***

Sean answered, "Director."

"I got word Maxwell is dead. Is anyone else injured?"

"The hostage. She's on her way to the hospital but looks like she'll be fine."

"Do we owe Samantha a new suit?"

Sean laughed.

The Director said, "Between the bear attack, and the…what did Dakota call it? Bait-walk? Samantha is going to have a colorful beginning at the academy."

"Yes, sir. Indeed, she does."

Chuckling, the Director said, "Make sure you're in D.C. by tomorrow night. Let's get this case closed. Tell Samantha I need you for less than two weeks. Then I need her at the academy September 1 at nine a.m. sharp."

***

Dakota answered his phone and Gabrielle said, "Did I really just see Samantha strip on national TV?"

"Just partially. She kept on all the important pieces."

"She's a fabulous warrior. Sean better hang on to her."

Dakota glanced at Sean and Samantha, and said, "No problem with that. He's not going anywhere."

***

251

Samantha giggled at her caller ID and answered.

Kerry said, "Do you need a permanent bodyguard, Samantha?"

"It seems like it."

"I watched the news. Are you okay? That was crazy."

"I'm ok. It just kind of happened. He would have killed her."

"You saved a woman's life. I can't tell you how impressed I am. That was better than me fighting the bear. I won't even talk about the...exhibition."

Laughing, she said, "You are too funny."

***

Angel texted Jade sitting next to him in the back seat of the SUV: I've received three messages for investigation cases since the news bulletin aired.

Jade: I got some too.

Angel: We're going to be busy now.

Jade: That's a good thing.

Angel: What about time for us?

Jade giggled: There might time here and there.

Angel: We are way beyond that.

Jade: I know. I'm getting my head around it.

Angel: Hurry up.

***

Dakota said, "Really? You're sitting right next to me - an agent. Even a teenager could tell when one texts and the other responds. At least turn off the sound."

Everyone laughed.

***

Parking at the ranch, everyone headed inside. But Samantha turned around and returned to the car. She left her phone. Adam walked out on the porch to meet her. She blushed bright red thinking about the bait-walk and hid her face in his shirt.

She said, "I hope you didn't watch the news."

Giving her a hug, he said, "I watched it through my fingers."

252

She punched him on the arm.

He chuckled softly and said, "I'm just picking at you. But...I did thank God for your safety."

And the emotion from all of it hit her, and tears rolled.

Once she was composed, they went inside.

Gabrielle hugged her and said, "That was unbelievably brave. Were you scared at all?"

"No. I knew Sean and Dakota would stop him."

"I'm floored. What was going through your mind when you unbuttoned your blouse?"

"That I wished I had worn an extra shirt."

Everyone howled in laughter.

Raven took her turn and hugged Samantha. She said, "You are a true warrior. Such bravery should be rewarded."

Raven glanced at Sean. Point made.

A few minutes later, the task force left to change. Samantha dressed in blue jean shorts and a pink crop top. She ran downstairs and couldn't find Sean.

She said, "Has anyone seen Sean?"

Dakota pointed out the window behind her. She turned to see Sean on the white horse. Bareback. Bare chest. Buckskin pants. Watching her. Without a word, she walked outside.

Her gaze locked with his, feeling the potency of the moment. He was magnificent. And powerfully sexy. He reached for her. She grabbed hold of his arm, and he lifted her in front of him. Wrapping one arm around her, he kissed her neck, leaned forward, and the mare took off.

Samantha felt like they flew. Racing the wind. And riding bareback, she could feel the movement of the horse and the grip of Sean's body keeping them balanced. She didn't know what he had in mind, but she wanted this ride with him.

Sean knew where he wanted to bring her and turned into the forest. They began to climb a hill that would give them a decent view of the area. They reached the overcropping and dismounted. He drew her to the top, and they sat facing each other.

Holding a leather-sheathed hunting knife, he said, "What you did today was powerful. You have a mountain of courage inside of you. My Sioux ancestors rewarded bravery. My dad gave me this knife after I hunted and killed a cougar that had gone on a killing spree.

"Now I give it to you. Never forget that bravery is powerful. And as you walk into your new life as an agent, know that you have what it takes on the inside. The rest is just learning."

With both hands, he presented her the knife. She took it, feeling the honor, and held it to her chest feeling like there was no greater reward.

Smiling, he said, "Director Washington wants you to report to the academy at nine a.m. on September 1. And I leave tomorrow for D.C. – for two weeks, maybe less."

She said, "Two whole weeks..."

Pulling her into his lap, he kissed her, rolling till she was under him. And the feeling of being between her legs set him ablaze. He groaned and rolled again. Now she was on top. He slid his hands in her back pockets and pressed her closer as passion burned them both. He sat up with her in his lap. Her legs wrapped around him.

Breathless, they looked at each other. Flaming. Raging. Hot.

He held her face and said, "Come on Switzerland."

She groaned and said, "Hurry and finish in D.C., Agent Man. I can't wait much longer."

***

When they galloped back to the house, Kerry and Chancy were there. Sean shook hands with Kerry, as Samantha and Chancy hugged.

Chancy held up her wrist with the bracelet, and said, "Thank you for doing this. I love it. I love you. You're a special lady."

Smiling, Samantha said, "I like my family happy – which includes both of you."

Kerry interrupted them with hugs for both women, and said, "Assure me, Samantha. Are you really, ok?"

"I am."

Sean said, "She was a real hero, Kerry."

Kerry said, "I hear you, man. That's the truth," and glanced at Chancy when she giggled.

Chancy said, "I'm sorry, but Kerry was eating when the news bulletin came on. He almost choked when he jumped up from the table."

Laughing, Samantha hugged him. Sean just laughed at the image. What are friends for?

***

By ten p.m., Sean and Samantha waved as the last vehicle left the ranch. They headed inside and sat with a cup of coffee and watched the news showing all three attacks. After the wreck. Suzette's attack. And the hostage situation in court today. She gasped in shock the first time she watched the bait-walk. They had of course blurred parts of her body for public TV. Then she watched it objectively, contemplating how she could have done it better. Faster. Sean smiled. What a woman.

***

The next morning, Sean checked the house since he would be gone a while. Then they loaded his SUV with their bags. Lastly, they sat at the snack bar and checked their to-do list.

Sean said, "Have you decided what to do with your apartment after we're married?"

"Sell it. It's too small for both of us. I'll move my stuff out this week into the big house mom left me."

"I can't wait to see it."

"It's great. Oh, I forgot to tell you the insurance adjuster emailed me and said my SUV was totaled in the crash. But I think

255

I'll wait and buy a car when we get back from Switzerland. I'm not sure what I'll need when I'm in Virginia. I'll just rent something for now."

"Why don't you use my SUV? I'll be gone anyway."

A few minutes later, he armed the security system and they left.

He said, "Well, here it is. Our new life begins."

***

He drove to Samantha's apartment first and checked it since she had been gone a few weeks. Everything was fine so they headed to the airport.

Before they reached the security gate, he handed her his keys, and they took a few selfies.

Sean said, "Since the next time we're together will be our wedding day..." he pulled out a black box and knelt.

Samantha screamed and danced.

He said, "One more time...will you marry me?"

She launched herself in his arms with a thrilled, "Yes!"

He laughed, pulling her on his knee and slipped the ring on her finger. It was a princess cut solitaire encased in diamonds, with a diamond band. Completely feminine. Gorgeous.

She whispered, "It's exquisite. I love it, Sean."

Lowering his lips, he said, "Just like you."

A moment later, he said, "I love you...but my flight's going to leave me if I don't run."

And she watched, smiling, until he faded in the distance. Which didn't take long at the speed he ran. In a few minutes, she sat in Sean's SUV and looked at her ring. She hadn't thought about engagement. Just elopement. And engagement wasn't a secret. She grabbed her phone and took a picture of her ring and opened a group text.

***

Sean proposed. Photo enclosed.

Gabrielle: Scream! Look at that rock!

Jade: Scream! Scream!

Gabrielle: When is the wedding?

Samantha giggled: Soon.

Jade: That isn't an answer.

Samantha: You've been around Dakota and Sean too much.

Jade: LOL. Strip for anyone today?

Samantha: The day is still young.

Gabrielle and Jade: LOL.

***

In southeast Baton Rouge, Samantha pulled up to her mom's…no, her house. A beautiful place. Two-story white brick with black shutters. Great landscaping. Tall black rod-iron fence. It had the feel of New Orleans to her. Inside it had an open floor plan, white tile floors, and painted brick columns. The back wall contained huge windows that overlooked the patio, backyard and…the dreaded pool.

The house had a simple layout. Social rooms were downstairs. Bedrooms were upstairs. It all had a clean, spacious, and welcoming feel to it. Sean would like it. She called Olivia, her self-proclaimed aunt, nannie, and wonderful housekeeper. She would take care of getting it ready for her to move in.

Then she prepared a Fed Ex envelope and inserted Sean's check. A little later she left for the office.

***

The commotion was immediate when she entered the building. Everyone surrounded her – with love, concern, and humor as they imitated her bait-walk. The D.A. joined them, laughing. The noise faded to a slow roar as Samantha followed the D.A. into his office.

He didn't waste any time, and said, "I heard a secret."

"Ah. Which one?"

"Director Washington contacted me."

"Oh. That one."

He said, "Go for it. You have what it takes, and I couldn't be prouder. You left your mark here – that's for sure."

"Thank you, sir. I think."

He laughed and said, "You can call me Jack now."

"Well, Jack, you will be calling me Mrs. Nash in a couple of weeks."

He said, "I knew that was coming. So today is your notice of resignation?"

"It is. A short notice. Confidentially, we are eloping and only you and Director Washington know."

"I love knowing what other people don't know. That's why I'm good at my job. Where's he taking you?"

"Switzerland."

"It's clear that man wants you to himself."

She laughed, then said, "I apologize for the short notice. I can clear my office and case load by close of day tomorrow."

"No problem. You have worked above and beyond the call of duty."

"Thank you. However, I do need a favor."

"What do you need?"

"What can we do for Spencer at Angola?"

"We've already begun the review with the affidavits from both of you. He's already served twelve years. That should be enough to cover crimes his silence caused. Besides, the anniversary cards were key to the Chicago cases. He's in a position for a life change."

"Thank you. Would you give him a letter from me when you see him?"

"Yes."

Samantha stood and shook his hand. "It's been a pleasure, sir."

***

Suzette was hard at work on a brief when Samantha knocked and walked in. With smiles, they hugged.

Samantha said, "Are you past what happened?"

"I am. What about you?"

"Glad it's over. Moving on. Free at last."

Suzette said, "You have a special strength, Samantha. I watched the news report last night. Most women I know couldn't have done what you did. I'm awed by your courage."

"All I can say is – God uses what we go through. I didn't know – or appreciate that concept at sixteen. But I recognize the bigger picture now. In fact, I'm leaving the D.A.'s office. I start in September at the FBI Academy in Quantico."

Suzette shook her head in amazement, and said, "The criminals won't know whether to flirt or run."

Laughing, Samantha said, "Surrender is safer."

Chapter 29

Sean boarded flight 801 to Washington D.C. and settled back in his seat. Smiling, he sent a text to his brothers.

***

I proposed.

Dakota: When's the honeymoon?

Adam: I knew that was coming! Dakota. The wedding comes first.

Dakota: Yeah, yeah. That too.

Sean chuckled: I'll keep in touch. Heading to D.C.

***

In downtown Baton Rouge, Samantha sorted stacks of case files. Her paralegal noted deadlines on each. Then Brian disbursed them to other attorneys. A knock at the door made them all look up.

The receptionist held a giant bouquet of red roses, and said, "Ms. Rutledge..."

Smiling, Samantha thanked her and carried them to her credenza. She opened the card. *Red roses. Red lips. Red hot. It's all about you, Counselor. I love you, Agent Man.*

She could see him saying it.

Then once the stacks of work were gone and she was alone, she took a selfie of her red lips and texted.

***

Red lips are only yours. The red hot too. I love you.
Picture attached.

***

Afterwards, she sat to write a letter she never imagined she would write.

Angola
Louisiana State Penitentiary

Dear Spencer,

I can't tell you personally, but I wanted you to know the anniversary cards provided evidence and closure for many grieving families. Thank you for being the better man. I won't forget you.

The District Attorney is looking into your case to see if anything can be done to help you. I know you don't expect, or even want it, but justice is for all victims. Including you.

Bless you, Spencer. May your future be bright.

Respectfully,
Prosecutor Samantha Rutledge

***

Samantha left the letter with the D.A.'s secretary. Then dropped Sean's Fed Ex in the pick-up box. And headed home for the day. As she merged into traffic on the interstate, Samantha heard her phone ding. She would have to check it later - Baton Rouge interstates were a nightmare.

Later, exiting the interstate, she stopped at a red light and opened the text. She smiled.

***

Sean: Do you like this one?

261

A picture of a very risqué black negligee was attached.

Samantha: Of course, I do. What are you doing?

Sean: Shopping.

Samantha: Will I wear it long?

Sean: No. That's the point.

Samantha laughed: You're supposed to be working.

Sean: Layover in Atlanta. About to board again.

Samantha: Shop for G-strings.

Sean groaned: You're killing me.

**

An hour later, Samantha left Wal-Mart with boxes, tape, and food, then headed to her apartment. After a shower, she dressed in her favorite LSU jersey and shorts and ate while she watched the news. It seemed odd to be back at her place. But…it wouldn't be hers much longer.

After the news, she hit her Salsa playlist and began pack preparation. First, she had to weed out what went to Goodwill versus what she planned to keep. The Goodwill box was filling up fast. She liked current things. Things she used, enjoyed, and wore based on her activities and preferences in the present time. Her favorites were filtered down sparingly to I-can't-imagine-not-having-them favorites. Like her last LSU jersey she wore now. Priceless, soft, and filled with memories.

Hours passed. When she yawned more than she packed, she turned everything off and headed to bed. Phone in hand, she flopped on top the mattress and was out. The phone rang during the night. Fumbling for it on the bed, she rolled on her back and answered the video call as she blinked to wake up.

**

Sean's tired, but smiling face popped up on the screen. She smiled and propped the phone in the stand.

He said, "I hated to call so late but I had a break."

Her voice sleep-husky, she said, "I can sleep anytime. I would rather talk to you."

Sighing at the sight of her snuggled in the bed, he said, "You make me wish I was there."

"I've got the same wish. Is the case finished yet?"

Chuckling, he said, "In hours? I'm good, but not that good." She giggled. He said, "Did you have a busy day, Counselor?"

"You can't call me that anymore. I handed in my notice. I'll be out of my office by tomorrow."

"That's good since I have a surprise for you. We plan to work around the clock to finish the case by the end of this week."

She sat up and said, "You mean, in two more days - like Friday?"

"Yes. But I can't give you much notice at all. When I get word that I'm free to leave, I'll book your flight to D.C. and call you. Just pack enough for a couple of days and bring what you need. We can shop there."

She touched his face on the phone and said, "Just a few more days."

"That's it, baby. A few more days."

Someone called out to Sean, and he said, "I have to go. Get some sleep. I love you."

***

The next morning in New Orleans, Jade rummaged in moving boxes for her shoes. That wasn't surprising since boxes were everywhere. She had finished moving into the third floor flat of their building yesterday. She spent last night on a mattress on the floor without sheets. Exhausted. Angel had done the same in his flat on the second floor.

They would save a bundle living, working, and remodeling all in the same building. It would be an inconvenience, but well worth it. She finally found the sandals she wanted and headed to the bathroom to brush her hair.

A couple of minutes later, she heard Angel on the stairs.

He knocked on the wall and called out, "Morning, sunshine. Are you dressed?"

She stepped out of the bathroom and said, "Lucky for you or you would be in deep trouble."

He grinned as he said, "I couldn't have seen you with the mountains of boxes in here anyway."

He pointed at her hair, and said, "Are you about to braid it?"

"Probably. It's the only way it behaves. Why?"

"With three little sisters, I learned to braid hair." He nudged her back in the bathroom and took the brush.

She laughed and said, "I didn't expect this perk. I'm impressed."

"There will be many perks. I'm good with my hands."

Meeting his gaze in the mirror, she said, "Have you heard about subtle, Angel?"

"Who cares about subtle? You keep wearing those white jeans and I'll…show my appreciation."

She rolled her eyes with a grin but was totally aware of his fine body right behind her. He laughed and made quick work of her braid.

Kissing her cheek, he said, "I'll meet you downstairs. We have so many priorities - we need to prioritize the priorities."

As she turned to face him, she said, "Ok. Give me ten—"

He kissed her. And it went from warm to sensual quick. Like their Salsa dancing. Lost for a moment in the feel of him, she struggled to break the spell.

Finally, she pushed back, and more breathless than she cared to reveal, she said, "You seem hungry. Breakfast is on the first floor."

He laughed going downstairs, not fooled at all.

Jade watched him go. And groaned. Sharing a house with him was going to be a lot different than being a partner, on top of what was happening between them. He was bold and would press her. She knew it. He refused lukewarm and wanted passion-sweat. Sighing, she knew she had to keep the heat at bay. Slow it down. Now, she just had to figure out how.

***

Angel reached the first floor of the building – still smiling. He was pumped they were close and personal under one roof now. It would make it way more difficult for her to play it cool. And he planned to make it very difficult. He wanted to be her husband by Christmas. He was past ready to be in one bed doing a lot more than sleeping.

***

A few minutes later, Jade joined him in the office. After being gone over a week on the case with the FBI, they had plenty to do. Deadlines. A pile of mail. Emails. Voice mails. Texts. Especially, since they had been on the news regarding the task force. That had been an unexpected ad campaign.

Angel brought her a cup of coffee and headed to the giant Louisiana map hanging on the wall. Several job locations were already pinned on the map. Colored pins for cases and locations.

The door dinged as it opened, and their regular Fed Ex delivery guy handed Jade an envelope. With a quick smile he was gone. She opened it while Angel checked the map against his list – and screamed. Angel spun, spilling coffee. She stared at the paperwork in her hand. Speechless.

"Jade! What is it?"

She handed him the paperwork without a word. He read it in shock. What? Then laughing, he looked at Jade. Sean had sent them a check for services rendered. A quarter of a million dollars.

***

In Washington D.C., Sean stepped out of a meeting to take the call he'd been expecting.

Smiling, he answered, "Hey Jade. Angel."

Jade said, "You and Samantha. What's the deal? We almost had another heart attack!"

Sean laughed, and Angel said, "Sean. Really, man. Expenses would have been more than enough. We had to be there for Samantha. You know that. You would do it for us."

"I know. But I insist on this. You worked hard, and the rest is a gift. Now you can remodel and work without the pressure."

Jade said, "I don't know how to thank you."

"You already did. Neither of you hesitated. Not for a second. Now, go celebrate! I need to run…"

***

In Baton Rouge, Samantha's phone rang. She laughed at the caller's name, and said, "Hey sweetie."

Jade said, "I screamed when I opened the Fed Ex. And I recognized your handwriting. You sent it. You knew."

Samantha said, "Come on, I'm into secrets. Besides, that was a great one." Then hearing Angel laugh, she said, "Again, thank you. Both of you. We needed you. No…I needed you - and you were there. Now go get engaged or something. I have a call coming in. Bye!"

***

Jade froze at Samantha's engagement comment, then glanced at Angel. Of course, he had heard. He was already coming. Heart pounding, she stepped back until there was nowhere else to go. He pressed against her. Intentions blatantly obvious. He ran his hands up her hips to her waist. Watching her. Determined to make her face it.

Her dark almond-shaped eyes betrayed what happened when he touched her. She knew they did. She licked suddenly dry lips at the look in his eyes – hoping her knees didn't buckle.

He pressed closer, and voice husky, said, "Tell me how you feel."

She swallowed. Shook her head no. She couldn't.

He lifted her chin, and said, "Come on. Tell me. I already know."

266

Eyes awash with emotion, she whispered, "I...love—"

And he didn't let her finish. Groaning, he lifted her so fast, she gasped, and his mouth covered hers. She wrapped around him, finally releasing the truth she had tried so hard to hide.

He said, "I've loved you for so long. I've waited. Marry me, Jade. Come all the way to me."

"Yes..."

***

Back in Baton Rouge, Samantha loaded the last box from the office in her car. Goodbyes had been said. A party. Lots of hugs. Her phone dinged as she shut the hatch. She got in the car and flipped the AC on, then checked the phone. Sean had texted.

***

Sean: Working hard to finish by six p.m. tomorrow. Want to marry me Friday?

Samantha screamed: Yes!

Sean: Be ready. Love you. Gotta go.

***

At five-thirty the next morning in Washington D.C., Sean ran his hands through his hair as he headed to the coffee pot. The team was pushing to get the reports done and case closed on Maxwell by five this afternoon. In eleven and a half hours. He fixed a strong cup of coffee and heard the elevator doors open.

Director Washington called out to Sean, "Follow me."

Once they were in his office, the Director said, "You're going to be worn out before you leave to get married."

Sean smiled without reply. Never.

The Director laughed, and said, "Wrong choice of words."

Sean said, "My goal is to finish and leave by five this afternoon."

"Leave by three instead. The team can finish the rest. Now get back to work - you don't want to miss that flight to Switzerland."

267

Sean hurried to his desk and called the travel agent. It was done. Samantha's ticket to D.C. was booked to leave Baton Rouge at noon today. Then they would fly out of D.C. at seven tonight headed for Graubünden, Switzerland. And twelve hours later they should be dressing for their wedding. He messaged the hotel to make sure his packages had arrived. Then he called Samantha.

***

Samantha answered, "Hey..."
"Morning, beautiful. Do you have your tennis shoes close by?"
"Somewhere in here."
"You better hit the ground running. Your flight leaves Baton Rouge at noon."
She squealed, sitting up, wide awake now. She could run in any shoes.
He laughed and said, "I'm emailing the tickets and boarding passes. I will be there to pick you up when you fly in."
"I'm heading to my computer."
"I've got to go, but I'll be waiting. Be safe. And hurry."

***

Jumping out of bed, she ran downstairs to start the Keurig, then grabbed pen and paper. Forcing herself to focus through the excitement, she jotted down: Suitcase. Carry-on. Sean's wedding suit and ring. Phone/chargers. Computer. New lingerie. Thank goodness she had packed last night. She just hoped she hadn't forgotten anything.

Then doing a happy dance, she picked up her mug of coffee and headed back upstairs. An idea occurred to her. Stopping, she looked over the balcony at the social setting below, then outside across the patio and pool. They could have the reception here! Smiling, she added that to her list to ask Sean.

Then it was on. Shower. Hair. Makeup. Perfume. Jewelry. Then she tried to make up her mind what to wear for the flight. Even though it was summer, it would more than likely be chilly on the flight. Then it would be freezing in Switzerland. But the most important element for what she wore - was Sean. They had a twelve-hour trip, and she wanted his every moment to be filled with anticipation for what was under her clothes.

She decided on all black. Skinny jeans with designs on the legs and pockets. Leather stiletto boots. A cashmere one-shouldered crop top sweater. She left her hair down – then tucked a jacket in her carry-on with her computer and phone.

She was ready.

By ten a.m. she loaded the car.

At ten-fifteen she left for the airport.

And promptly at eleven forty-five she texted Sean.

***

We are about to take off. I'm coming.
***

Chapter 30

Sean left the FBI just before three in the afternoon. At the hotel he showered, shaved, and slipped on jeans he knew Samantha loved. Soft. Worn. Fit him like a glove. He pulled on a stretch denim and leather pullover. V-neck. Tight. A touch of Indian. A touch of white man. Then tied up his boots.

Looking in the mirror, he ran his fingers through his hair and added cologne. Then put the wedding ring and documents in his carry-on. Samantha's wedding outfit had been shipped to the hotel. Her new lingerie and their snowsuits as well. He checked everything off his mental list and glanced at the clock.

The door closed behind him.

***

Samantha watched D.C. come into focus as the plane lowered through the clouds. Before long, they touched down. She texted Sean: We landed.

***

Sean saw her first and started toward her. She looked gorgeous. Deliciously female. His. She glanced back to pull the carry-on off her shoulder – and when she turned back around, she saw him. Sexy. Handsome. Smiling, she ran, then leapt. He caught her and his smiling lips found hers.

Then with cheers following them, they waved and ran because the flight left in less than an hour. After check-in and security, they reached the international terminal with little time to spare. And in minutes, loaded the plane.

The first-class stewardess showed them to their cubicle and said with a lovely accent, "Is this your first trip to Switzerland?"

Samantha smiled with a glance at Sean, and said, "Yes. We're eloping."

Delighted, the Stewardess said, "Then obviously you will enjoy your stay!"

Sean and Samantha laughed, and the Stewardess said softly, "I'll be sure to look away as I pass by your area. I think the bride and groom earn a little extra privacy for a long flight. My gift to you." And with a wink she left them to settle in.

Two large recliners sat side by side with a small console between them. The cubicle had a privacy wall in the front and back of them. Only the aisle seat was partially open to the public with a half-wall. Two televisions hung on the front wall. They had table trays, a shelf for their bags, plugins for devices, and a fluffy pillow and blanket.

After a soft kiss, they settled in their seats. Sean by the window and Samantha by the aisle wall.

Smiling, Samantha looked at Sean, and said, "If your intent is to spoil me, then it's working very well."

He ran a hand behind her neck, caressing, and said, "Baby...I aim to spoil you...please you. You have no idea what awaits you on the other side of the ocean. But you will love it. I will make sure of that."

Samantha felt the sexual impact. Her toes curled in her boots. Thighs clenched. He knew it and leaned across the console and whispered in her ear. The image his words left behind matched the sizzle she felt.

Her eyes roamed him from head to toe. Lingering on his lap. And she smiled...it was her turn. She sensuously ran her hands down her hips. Thighs. And crossed her legs as she leaned on one hip toward him. Then watching him watch her, she slid a hand between her thighs as if to keep it warm…and nestled it against what he very much wanted to touch.

His eyes went from her hand to her eyes. He could taste the desire. Liking this sensual game, he leaned back against the seat and spread his legs. Then slid his hands down to rest on the inside of his thighs near what she wanted. He shifted suggestively.

Fiery eyes met sultry eyes. Her turn. She sat up, facing him, and raised her arms like she was stretching. Her crop top slid up, exposing lots of midriff. No bra. He watched, wanting to touch, and met her gaze. She smiled as she lowered her arms, brushing her hands over her chest – and spread her legs.

Groaning low in his throat, he leaned over the console and motioned her closer. Sparks flying between them, she came close.

He said, "We're going to catch the plane on fire, and we haven't even left yet."

She burst out laughing as the captain announced their departure.

Once they were in-flight, Sean pulled his phone and showed her pictures of the hotel they would be at for three weeks, the mountain ranges, and activities they might enjoy. Skiing. Snowboarding. Lift rides. Glass saunas. Heated pools. Carriage rides. Snowmobiles. Plus, shops, restaurants, and entertainment.

She said, "Is the wedding at the hotel?"

He laced his fingers through hers, and said, "Yes. It's a gorgeous wedding chapel. I can't wait to see you in it."

"Sean, really. Eloping with you is the ultimate romantic adventure."

"It is. But honestly, I wanted you to myself as quick as possible. I didn't want to wait."

"Like I said…ultimate romance."

After the Stewardess offered refreshments, Sean said, "Did you get moved into your house?"

"I did, and I didn't keep very much from my apartment. Just personal stuff. It's bound to seem odd to you that I didn't live in my own house, but it's big. A lot of memories to live with all by myself. But you'll like it. Here, I took a few pictures."

272

As he scrolled through them, he said, "That's a great floor plan. It's beautiful and perfect for entertaining."

"What do you think of having our reception there?"

"I like that idea…especially the part where I get to sleep in your bed."

Most passengers began to turn off their lights and go to sleep about ten, but Sean and Samantha talked till about midnight before laying their seats back. Snuggled with blankets and pillows, they were comfortable even divided by the console.

He leaned across and gave her a soft kiss, then said, "I love you. Get some rest. Tomorrow is almost here."

"I love you…"

He watched as she dozed off, then in no time at all, he slept too.

***

It was late in New Orleans. Jade straightened her flat enough to function, though most of her belongings would be forced to remain in boxes until construction was complete. Satisfied with what she had accomplished, she turned to the unmade bed now in a frame. In no time, she had the bed made and her exotic floral black and white comforter and pillows set up. Hands on her hips, she surveyed the bed.

Angel said, "That's beautiful."

She jumped, then laughed and said, "I didn't hear you come upstairs."

"I'm barefoot. I called out, but you were shuffling something."

She said, "Did you get your bed together?"

"Not yet. But I thought of something else. We probably should make some decisions before the contractor arrives tomorrow for the remodeling."

"You're right."

He said, "Have you thought about a wedding date yet?"

"Pretty much. What do you think about December?"

Relieved that it wasn't more than six months away, he smiled and said, "December is great. I recommend early December."

"How early?"

He said with a grin, "December 1st."

She laughed and said, "That's barely December."

"Exactly. And now that the date is decided, what are your ideas on remodeling since we won't need two self-sufficient flats in a few months?"

She thought about the years ahead and said, "What about having the living area on the second floor and bedrooms on the third – except for maybe a guest room in the living area?"

"Sounds perfect. And we have plenty room to create the open spaces you like with a few private rooms that I like."

She turned, looking around, still contemplating the layout. He gently drew her back against him, sliding his hands around her hips to cover her stomach, then kissed her neck. She leaned back, covering his hands with hers.

He said, "Will you have babies with me?"

Heart melting, she turned, slipping her arms around his neck, and said, "That's a yes. How many do you want?"

"As many as we can have. And…you know we're going to burn up in bed, right? Smoking hot. And I have to tell you, I can't wait to see that look on your face - knowing I put it there."

***

Thirty-six thousand feet in the air, Sean smiled at the blonde beauty sprawled across the recliner bed close to him. All he could think about, was that the next time she laid down she'd be his wife. In his bed.

He touched her cheek. Her eyelids flickered and she smiled when she saw him.

He said, "Morning, beautiful."

Smiling, she said, "Hey baby…where are we?"

"Over France. It won't be long till we land. It's almost six-thirty in the morning."

They heard other passengers moving around so they took turns going to the restroom to freshen up. When Samantha returned, Sean watched her put on makeup.

He said, "That's a lot of work."

"So is shaving."

"Touché. But I'm going to kiss all your work off."

"I hope so. I'd hate to go to all this effort for nothing."

Grinning, he said, "Wanting you has nothing to do with makeup."

"Yeah. I get that. But…it sure doesn't hurt. All girls want to play dress up when Prince Charming is around."

The captain interrupted with an announcement they would be landing in an hour and a half.

Samantha asked, "Are you going to give me a hint as to what my wedding dress looks like?"

"It's white."

She laughed and said, "And?"

He kissed her hand and said softly, "I couldn't find anything as beautiful as you. So, I bought the next best thing."

She felt his words. They wrapped around her heart, and she wanted to cry. Fighting tears, she said, "Oh…Sean…nothing like knocking my feet out from under me. I'll never forget you said that."

He smiled, and she said, "Do you want a hint as to what I got you to wear?"

"No."

Surprised, she said, "Why not?"

"To me it's just in the way," and she laughed.

He said, "This is all about you, Samantha. Nothing else matters."

She didn't care who saw her public display of affection, PDA as classified by the airlines - and kissed him, then whispered, "I will reward you for that."

An hour later they began the descent into Graubünden, Switzerland. A perfect winter wonderland. After they disembarked, they went through customs, baggage claims, and followed the waiting limousine driver. Once inside the Hummer limo, the driver began the trip on snow plowed roads to the hotel.

After days of being apart, restricted for hours on the plane, and steamy anticipation, Sean drew Samantha on his lap and covered her lips with his. Pulling a blanket on the seat around them, he ran hands up her thighs. Hips. And cupping her bottom, crushed her against him. Samantha groaned at his touch - loving that her cool agent man was losing it. She liked that. A lot.

Sean growled low in his throat and broke the kiss. He looked at her body and slid a hand up the inside of her thigh. Close. Closer. She groaned at the heat of his hand through her jeans and closed her legs, trapping his hand. He squeezed her as he met her gaze. His eyes like boiling chocolate. Hers like blue lava.

He said, "You're hot for me."

Breathless, she said, "Yes…marry me quick."

After that, it was the longest, short ride in history. Samantha gasped at the scenery and Sean's roaming hands. And Sean could have cared less about the terrain outside the window. The terrain in his lap was his goal.

Then finally the driver turned into a large stone-lined entrance. Fabulous snow-draped trees led the way through the woods until the resort rose out of the snow like a woodland castle. Carved columns. Gorgeous windows. Gas lanterns everywhere. It looked like a winter dream. As the limo stopped at the entrance portico, door attendants assisted them, and in short order, they were checked in and riding the elevator to the master suite.

Samantha slid her fingers in Sean's waistband. He picked her up and kissed her – warning her with a glance she was playing with fire. She reached in his back pocket and squeezed. He pressed her against him.

Then the elevator dinged as it stopped, and the doors opened. The bellman led the way to the master suite, and in a couple of minutes, the door closed as he left. Alone at last, their next embrace almost singed the carpet where they stood.

Then stepping back, he took her hand and said, "Come see…and then…the minister is ready when we are."

He led her through a beautiful den. Romantic. Music playing. Fireplace lit. And stopped at the central focus of the room. A huge set of double doors - and pushed them open. Samantha exhaled in amazement. A glass bedroom overlooked the mountain range. A fabulous bed sat in the middle of the room covered in multicolored fur and pillows. A chandelier hung overhead. Velvet benches followed the windows around the room.

She whispered, "You made it magical. I never dreamed…"

Cupping her face, he said, "It's just the beginning…come…the minister's waiting. And so am I."

He carried the luggage to the dressing rooms. It was split as a private him and her dressing/bathroom combination.

Sean said, "Your wedding outfit is in your closet. If you need help dressing…"

Smiling, she handed him the tuxedo garment bag, and said, "I'll be ready in less than an hour…I promise."

Chapter 31

Sean showered. Shaved. Dried his hair and put on cologne. He heard the blow dryer in her room and knew it would take her a while with long hair. Opening the garment bag from her, he smiled. Samantha had gotten him a slim fit, black pin-striped tuxedo. Black silk shirt. Skinny black tie. Sexy.

He slipped on just the pants and walked to the windows thinking about Samantha. He had a raging hunger for everything about her. Sex would be flaming wild, and he knew it would be weeks before he even took a breath. But he wanted all of her. He wanted to enjoy her mind. Her drive. Her desire to challenge. Her taste of wildness. The feisty...and the purr. And he absolutely wanted to see her hunger for him. Anything she wanted - as many times as she wanted it.

**

Samantha applied eye makeup to make her blue eyes pop. And extra liner for an exotic edge. Red matte lipstick that would last for hours. She dabbed perfume on her wrists. Neck. Cleavage. A long string of diamonds hung from each ear lobe.

Now it was time to see what type of dress he had bought her. She opened the long garment bag. Gasping in awe, she lifted out the dress. A white, crushed velvet halter dress. Low back. Deep V-neck. A slit exposing one leg. Gorgeous. Sexy. Sensual. Like him. She loved it. Smiling, she stepped into it and pulled the dress up. His taste was extraordinary.

She turned to the large box that sat on a chair. She lifted the lid and smiled. White patent leather dress boots lay there. Fabulous. Feminine. Perfect for winter and a velvet wedding dress.

After putting them on, she turned to the mirror. Emotion locked her throat. Tears threatened at the bride that looked back at her. His bride. Long blonde hair. White velvet dress. Long bare leg. White high-heel boots. Diamond earrings almost to her shoulders. She was ready for this once-in-a-lifetime moment with Sean. And all the ones that would come after.

***

He was standing by the bed when the door opened, and Samantha stepped into the bedroom. Their eyes met and held for a forever-moment. Smiling, he joined the woman who set him on fire. Always had.

Slipping his arms around her, he said, "You're a gorgeous dream, Samantha. A burn in me beyond any words. And before long you're going to feel what I mean."

She smiled at the man she loved – bold, gorgeous, and magnificent. Everything in her ached for him. Anticipated what would come when they returned to the room.

Leaning into him, she said, "Sean…loving you does things to me. Down deep. I…feel you already."

He groaned and slid his hands along her thighs, pulling her against him. She had nothing on under the dress. She was pure naked fire under his hands. She saw him flare. Felt it.

Huskily, he said, "We've got to go now or the honeymoon's going to come first."

Swift minutes later, the elevator doors opened. Hotel guests inside exclaimed over their formal attire on a Friday morning in the mountains.

Smiling, Sean explained, "She finally said yes. We're making it official."

279

As everyone congratulated them, an elderly woman who must have been hard of hearing, leaned to her friend and said in a loud whisper, "Holy smoke! He makes my mouth water." And as the elevator reached the ground floor, everyone was still laughing.

Sean led Samantha toward the chapel. A growing crowd followed them, enjoying the excitement. They reached a staircase that led to a stunning nook, for want of a better word. It was small, but romantic. The minister stood in front of giant framed windows that overlooked the mountain range. A burning fireplace and elegant seating area framed both sides of the windows.

They ascended the steps to meet the smiling minister. They spoke a few moments and completed paperwork - and the wedding began. The minister read beautiful scripture about the power of passionate love out of Song of Solomon. He prayed a blessing over them. Led them through their vows as they promised themselves only to each other for life. Then they exchanged rings – sealing the commitment.

As Sean heard, "You may kiss your bride," he drew Samantha close, his eyes brushing over her face at this long-awaited moment. Samantha smiled at the love shining from his eyes, and he kissed her. Claimed her. Then dramatically, dipped her. Cheers filled the air.

Following the kiss, the minister announced, "I now introduce to you, Mr. & Mrs. Sean Nash from Baton Rouge, Louisiana - on the southern coast of the United States."

Fifteen minutes later, they stepped off the elevator. He scooped her up and carried her down the private hall. She reached for him, and his passion unleashed as he touched what she offered.

In seconds, he had the door open, then kicked it shut – his jacket outside in the hall. She slid down his body like liquid sugar. And as her feet touched the floor, she backed toward the bedroom. He jerked his tie loose as he followed. Watching. She touched her body.

He groaned and yanked his shirt out of his pants. His body tight. Hungry. She turned, her back facing him, and unclasped the single hook holding up her dress. She glanced back at him as it slid to the floor. Leaving her naked. In boots. Legs apart. He ripped his shirt and buttons flew.

She spun to face him as he stepped out of his pants and came for her. Wild and gorgeous, she jumped. Handsome and raging, he caught her. And they didn't make it to the bed.

***

About nine hours later, Sean kissed Samantha's shoulder and turned her in his arms. She smiled sleepily and kissed his chest.

He said softly, "Room service just delivered a light dinner and dessert. Come eat a bite."

"What time is it?"

"About nine p.m."

"What did you order?"

"American fare - as defined by the Swiss. Grilled chicken salad with all sorts of great veggies, cheese, and dressing. It looks delicious - and you need to eat."

Her stomach growled and he smiled.

She giggled and said, "I'll meet you by the fireplace. Let me grab a robe or something."

"Don't bother with that. This is a come-as-you-are dinner."

"Right...Agent Man. And you know we'll never eat."

"Excellent point. I'll get the food ready while you attempt to distract me with a robe."

After dinner, they curled up on pillows in front of the fireplace.

Rubbing her back, he said, "Baby, we've been beyond active. Wild defines it better. And I don't want you in pain. Tell me...are you too sore? Hurting?"

Smiling at the beautiful intimacy of his question, she turned and saw the worry in his eyes. She kissed him and said, "While I do need a good hot soak in the tub, I'm not really hurting...just sore. A little tender. That's all. I promise. I'm...uh...rather fond of wild as it turns out."

He nuzzled her and said, "And I'm all about that. But…the tub is next on the agenda – even if we get water-logged taking baths. I don't want you hurting. And to clarify your comment, *rather fond of wild,* is an understatement. We barely made it past the door for our first time. Literally, your first time. And you're so small. I should be—"

She untied her robe, interrupting his frustration at himself, and said, "You should be rewarded. It took us three times to make it to the bed. I'm impressed…"

He impressed her again.

It was midnight by the time they got out of the tub and cleaned up. Water was everywhere.

Watching her climb into the massive bed, Sean said, "I have another surprise. Hang on, let me cut off the lights."

Once it was dark in the room, he opened the curtains. Samantha sighed in wonder as she looked out the windows. The Alps were gorgeous in the moonlight. They took pictures, then sat looking outside. It was truly magical. Like a glass balcony.

His phone dinged. Then hers.

She said, "Why don't we send an announcement, so they quit looking for us."

"Good idea."

They scrolled through the pictures the photographer sent and chose a few to send a group text.

***

We introduce to you Mr. & Mrs. Sean Nash in Switzerland.
You are invited to the reception in three weeks.
Please leave a message.
Photos are attached.

***

In Lake Charles, Gabrielle opened her text and screamed in joy, dancing around the kitchen. She heard Dakota laughing in his office.

After a second, he joined her, and said, "No long engagement for Sean. Well wait, that's not entirely true. He had to wait over a year, so I don't blame him for eloping now."

Adam came down the hall with his phone, and said, "I guess you—"

Gabrielle raised her phone, and said, "We did."

Raven and Lance rounded the corner. She said, "Are you okay, Gabrielle? I heard you scream."

Adam showed Raven his text.

She said, "They eloped to Switzerland. Oh my gosh…that's fabulous."

Dakota said, "He fooled me. They both did. When he said he proposed, I was waiting for a date."

Gabrielle said, "Sean's got some very steamy hidden skills."

Raven said, "And it seems like Samantha's into them."

Dakota leaned on the snack bar, and drawled, "You know, you're next, Adam. Last one of the brothers that's single."

Adam nodded, catching a whiff of Raven's perfume.

Raven knew better than to look at Adam after that remark. He didn't need any encouragement.

Dakota had no qualms at all about stoking the fire, and said, "You know, both of you would make beautiful children."

Adam laughed, and said, "No one can accuse you of subtlety, brother."

Raven glanced at Dakota like he had horns, making Gabrielle and Dakota burst out laughing. Adam winked at Dakota, then watched Raven escape, taking Lance outside. Or so she thought.

***

In New Orleans, Jade checked the text from Sean and Samantha. She ran upstairs and met Angel coming down holding his phone too.

She said, "One, I would never have thought of eloping. And two, I would never have thought of Switzerland. I'm in awe – and thrilled for them. Their pictures are gorgeous, but then how could they not be."

Angel said, "This was perfect for them. It fits. I couldn't be happier that they jumped right into the wedding."

Jade touched his arm, and said, "Would you rather elope, Angel? Without all the tradition?"

"No…well, yes…but more than that, I want you to have all the bells and whistles. Church. Invitations. Shopping. Showers. Planning. Celebrating the whole time. All while building the anticipation for me in your bed."

***

In Baton Rouge, Samantha's parents smiled at the pictures and text.

Jonathon said, "I'm not surprised in the least. That man loves everything about her. I couldn't be prouder to have him for a son-in-law - and know that she's in his hands."

Sara said, "Oh honey. Why don't we offer to handle the reception, so they don't have to worry about it? Her housekeeper can help us."

***

In east New Orleans, Kerry and Chancy were walking into an appointment with a real estate agent when their phones dinged. Chancy checked hers first. She gasped in shock, then began to smile.

He said, "What is it?"

She showed him her phone.

He fist-pumped and said, "Yes! Sean, you are the man!"

Chancy said, "Samantha's going to keep Sean hopping for the rest of his life."

Laughing, Kerry said, "And he's going to be one happy man."

***

The next afternoon in Switzerland, Sean chuckled as Samantha came out of the bathroom red like a lobster.

284

He said, "I bet you used all the hot water for everyone in the hotel."

"I was trying to warm up. It's amazingly beautiful outside - but freezing!"

"Agreed. What did you enjoy the best?"

"I loved everything. The lifts. The carriage ride. The tubes. Skiing. Even the snowball fights with you! But flying across the snow on the snowmobile is fabulous. Exhilarating."

"That's because you make everything a race."

"I can't help it. The thrill draws me."

"I get that. But be careful and stay with me. We don't know the terrain at all. Something could be wrong or dangerous and we wouldn't recognize it."

"Ugh. I know you're right. I'm trying."

He lifted her chin, and said, "I love you, Samantha. Try harder," and kissed her.

Before long they relaxed by the fireplace with hot chocolate, blankets, and phones to read their messages. They thanked, and agreed to let her parents handle the wedding reception, decorations, and catering at her house.

They texted Jimmy, Kerry, and Chancy to see if they would sing for the evening. Then they sent Adam a message asking if he would pray a wedding blessing over them.

Then Sean's phone rang. The director.

***

Sean answered, "Hi, sir. How's the heat in the states?"

"Hot. Congratulations! And the answer to your request is yes, your transfer to Quantico while Samantha is in training, has been approved. Report by August 15."

Sean smiled at Samantha's curiosity, and said, "Great news, sir! Thank you for calling."

***

After Sean ended the call, Samantha said, "What news?"

"I have a surprise for you."

"Obviously! What is it?"

"I applied for a temporary transfer to Quantico, Virginia while you're at the academy. It was approved."

Cheering like she was at a ballgame, she jumped up, dancing around him.

He laughed and said, "I report on August 15."

Squealing, she threw herself on top of him. He laughed and rolled with her, enjoying her enthusiasm.

He said, "But...that means we've got to leave Baton Rouge just a few days after we get back from Switzerland. No lingering. It will be fast and furious."

"I don't care, Sean! I'm just thrilled you will be near me, not back in Louisiana."

Feeling her excitement. Seeing her fire. He slid his hand under her robe and said, "So...show me...just how thrilled you are...future Cadet Nash..."

***

Two weeks later, at the Louisiana State Penitentiary, Spencer was hard at work when a guard called him. He followed him to the visitation area.

The District Attorney watched Spencer walk in. Even though he knew Maxwell and Spencer were identical twins, it was still shocking to see the serial killer's face walk toward him. But as Spencer sat down, the D.A. could see that looks were where the resemblance ended. Spencer's persona was respectful. Peaceful even.

After the D.A. introduced himself, Spencer said, "May I help you with something?"

"I'm sorry for the loss of your brother."

Spencer nodded. He was still praying about his role in that.

The D.A. said, "But that's not why I am here. We reviewed your case."

"I told Samantha not to fret about that. My coward silence was crime enough."

"Funny thing, Mr. Chance, is that the law has a mind of its own. Rules. And in your case, the Governor has commuted your sentence. Prison is over."

Spencer stared. Stunned at what he heard. He choked out, "But why?"

"Evidence proved you didn't commit the attempted rape and murder of Samantha, or the murder of Mary Beth. Time served took care of the accessory after the fact."

He slid the clemency release signed by the Governor of Louisiana across the table. Spencer's mind swirled, trying to grasp that life as he knew it, was over. With one finger he pulled the formal looking paper closer so he could look at it. There it was in black and white. He was free.

He said, "What now? This is all I know."

"The warden is setting your clearance in motion now. A few organizations have people ready and waiting to help you start over. There are people on the outside who care. I also have a letter for you from Prosecutor Rutledge."

He slid the envelope to him. Spencer slowly opened it. Read it. One tear rolled down his cheek. He said, "She's an amazing woman."

"You have no idea how true that is, Mr. Chance."

***

Late that night outside a Salsa club in New Orleans, Angel and Jade headed to their car.

Angel said, "How about a walk on Lincoln Beach? There's a nice breeze and we can cool off."

Jade lifted her thick hair off her neck, and said, "That sounds fabulous. I've been sweaty for hours. We ought to wear bathing suits to dance."

"That's what I'm talking about. Why don't we start practicing that way at home? Let's go bikini shopping in fact. I'll buy."

Her laugh echoed as they sat in the car. He set the air conditioner on high, and they groaned in relief. After a moment he pulled her lips to his. Searing. That never cooled off. Ever.

Before long they were at the beach. Jade kicked off her heels and stepped barefoot in the sand. Angel rolled up his pants. They walked toward the waves. As they got close, Jade spun, laughing in the breeze. Angel watched her ruffled sundress mold to her body in the windy moonlight. Her dark hair wild and sexy. He ached for her. Then surprising him, she ran into the water. Then thigh deep, she turned to face him.

He had followed her in. His powerful thighs causing a wake as he pushed through the waves. She yielded when he reached for her. Groaning, he kissed her, his large hands caressing, wishing December 1 was tomorrow.

Passionate. Wet, in the warm waters of the Gulf of Mexico, they were hotter than they had ever been dancing.

Later, walking through the surf, cooler now, Angel said, "How about a beach honeymoon?"

"A private beach?"

"It would have to be, or we'll be arrested for indecent exposure."

"But we can't swim nude. Divers. Drones. Boaters—"

"Who's going to swim? I'm talking nude-water-sex Salsa."

"Angel…"

"Look Jade. I will be your first. The only man you'll ever know between your legs. But we will do it all the time. Everywhere. I'm on fire for you. Which means—"

She kissed him. Then whispered, "I know what you mean. No, I've never had a man between my legs, as you so eloquently put it. But…talking about it is…arousing to say the least. Blunt. And makes December seem way too far away."

"My thoughts exactly. And Jade…this type of communication is me. I want you to know what you mean to me. All of you. From here," and he pulled her mouth to his for a quick hot kiss. "To here," and he possessively touched her between the legs. Then said,

"All the way down," and kneeling, he slid his hand all the way to her feet - and drew her to his knee.

Shocked. Sizzling. Breathless, she said, "I can't believe you did that."

"I'm just staking my claim. Marking my territory. Why? Do you want to mark me? Come on…I dare you."

"Angel…"

"I'm teasing. But listen. Your mind will know me before we enter the honeymoon bed, but your body will be as pure as the day you were born. I swear. Now, I have a gift for you."

"Out here? What is it?"

He pulled a ring out of his pocket, and smiling, said, "Thank you for saying yes," and slipped it on her finger.

***

Across the ocean, Samantha sorted through the shopping bags on the bed.

Talking over her shoulder, she said, "Sean, really, I'm thrilled! When you told me we would go shopping here, I didn't realize you meant multiple shopping trips for a new wardrobe. You're in trouble now that I know you like to shop."

Chuckling, he said, "I enjoyed *you* while we shopped. You have great taste beside the fact that you will look gorgeous in everything you picked out."

He stepped behind her, slipping his arms around her and said, "How about putting on a fashion show for me?"

She turned and pulled him down for a kiss, then said, "One fashion show coming up, Agent Man. Go make yourself comfortable. And pick out a playlist. I need some music to make it…memorable for you."

Sean sat on the sofa facing the bedroom doors and kicked back nice and cozy. He propped his feet on the stone coffee table with a smile. He knew Samantha would have fun with the fashion show and he intended to enjoy every minute of it. Glancing out the window at the mountains, he couldn't believe this was their last day. Three weeks had flown by.

Samantha called, "I'm ready! Start the music."

He played *Brick House* and hit speaker.

Both doors opened and she posed. Red lips. Black boots. And a wild swirl minidress. He sat up and whistled. She laughed and began to groove toward him. Spinning. Dancing. Working it. Then she stepped on the coffee table in front of him.

He swayed to the beat himself as he watched her. Beautiful legs. Teasing lips. And hips that sure knew how to move. And he doubted she had anything on under the dress. Then with a quick twist and squat right in front of him, it was confirmed.

When his expression switched from playful to fire, she stepped off the table. Away from him. He got up to follow and she held up a hand – stop – and danced all the way back to the bedroom. Then shut the door.

Sean gave her a minute to change. Took off his shirt. Unsnapped his jeans. Changed the song to *Lady Marmalade* and hit repeat. The sultry groove filled the room. He laid on the sofa and waited. Hot already.

The bedroom doors opened, and Samantha stepped out in a short pink leather strapless dress. Stilettos to match. Hair in a high ponytail. Full pink lips. She smiled. Her man was ready. So, she worked her body to the groove and stepped on the coffee table again. Working the song. Giving him a lot to see. In seconds, he slid a hand up her leg and got on the table with her.

Two hours later they took off on snowmobiles for their last ride. It was gorgeous. Blue sky. Majestic mountains. Great trails. Nothing but miles of fabulous snow. Samantha pressed Sean – revving the engine, jumping forward – taunting him to race. She motioned to him impatiently. He shook his head no and pointed to the trail. She slowed down and stayed just ahead of him.

Around the next corner, she noticed a huge pile of snow off the trail past a group of trees. She wanted to plow through it, and darted off the trail, leaning low and flying. Sean saw the snowbank and knew what she was going to do. He hit the throttle, and just before she entered the wall of snow, he grabbed her snowsuit and yanked her off the bike. The momentum caused his snowmobile to tip over, tossing both in the snow.

Sean stood and wiped his mask, glancing at Samantha silently. She jumped up, covered in snow, and trudged through deep fluff toward him, ready for a fight. He leaned over and brushed the snow off his suit and faced her. He pulled his face mask up.

She snapped, "What is wrong with you? Why did you do that?"

"I told you not to leave the trail."

"I was just going to plow through the pile of snow."

"And what's on the other side? Stop being careless. I mean it, Samantha."

She blinked at his tone. Then noticed his expression. She said, "You're mad."

He paused, jaw clenched, and said, "I love your fire – there is no doubt about that. But you have to be a controlled burn too, not just an out-of-control blaze. Don't waste your courage and bravery on things that don't even matter. You are going to step into a dangerous job that needs you to stop and think before you act. Lives will depend on it. And you have a husband who wants you to come home at night. I've got to know that you will choose wisdom over a thrill."

The impact of his words hit her. The power. The truth. The depth of concern. The fear. Her throat tightened, and she said, "I scared you. I'm so sorry, Sean."

He pulled her close. Held her tight and took a deep breath. Then a brief rumble shook the ground and a loud crack split the air. Samantha screamed as her snowmobile and the whole wall of snow it was buried in, slowly broke off and fell into open air down the side of the mountain. Sean grabbed her and ran.

Once they were back to the trail, Sean piggybacked her. He refused to go back and see if his snowmobile was still there. Before long, others picked them up. And in less than an hour, Sean unlocked the hotel room. Silently they changed. Then he pulled back the fur comforter and drew her into bed with him to warm up.

Snuggled together, Sean felt Samantha's tears drip on his arm. He understood. He could still see that part of the mountain where she would have been…fall away into nothing. Jesus, he thought…thank you for mercy. Then kissing her, he took them to a warmer place.

That evening, they entered a dinner club and were seated at a cozy table overlooking the snow-draped garden. A man played the saxophone on a small stage. A smiling waiter took their order. Before long, they sipped French wine and nibbled on fresh fruit and Swiss cheese waiting on their dinner. Samantha had ordered a Swiss cheese and pasta specialty that was toasted in the oven. While Sean had ordered a steak with a popular local cheese and potato dish.

He said, "It's hard to believe we leave tomorrow. And that I report to work in a few days."

"I know. Time flew by so fast. We haven't even talked about where we will live. Do we need to find a place when we get to Virginia?"

"Not unless you want to. A friend has a great cottage close to Quantico. I thought we might stay there until you graduate."

"That sounds great. I love cottages."

"Me too. But I don't like that you'll only come home on the weekends. I can assure you most cadets aren't on their honeymoon."

She grimaced and said, "I try not to think about that part."

"I know. But with me working at Quantico, we can at least see each other during the week. However, no private time when you're there. And no cell phones in their controlled space. I'll think of some way for us to connect during the week."

Late that night, they sat on the velvet benches looking out over the mountains while they checked their phones and talked about the trip.

Samantha squealed after reading a text, and said, "Dad won the election! He's the new mayor of Baton Rouge!"

"Go Jonathan! I'm not surprised at all. He's intelligent. Determined. He'll do a fantastic job."

As she texted congratulations, a new text alert popped up. It was Sean.

She bumped him and said, "Why are you texting me?"

"Read it."

She gasped and slapped his arm. He laughed.

She said, "I can't believe you texted that. Take it off! Right now!"

Laughing, he said, "Why?"

"We used to subpoena phone communications all the time. I don't want anyone reading that."

Amused at her insistence, he said, "Samantha. Really. No one is going to subpoena our phone records."

She narrowed her eyes, and said, "If you ever want me to do what you asked for in that text, delete it."

He frowned and said, "Are you kidding me? Isn't that a bit extreme?"

"Do I look like I'm kidding?"

No. She didn't. She meant it. Shocked, he said, "Give me your phone. I'll delete it. I'll take it off my phone too. Or better yet, I'll throw our phones away and buy new ones. Ok?"

She giggled. Then got up, backing away from him.

His eyes sparked as he laid his phone down. He'd been played. Following her, he said, "That was a mean trick to play on your new husband."

She shrugged and said, "I'm sure I owed you for something."

"You're keeping score?"

"Well, aren't you?"

He scooped her up before she could run, and said, "Threatening me with that was not funny."

"Yes, it was."

Chapter 32

They landed in beautiful, but humid, Baton Rouge, Louisiana, at noon the next day. The plane taxied to the terminal.

Sean kissed her and said, "I get to carry you over the threshold again."

"And we have two houses."

"Which means I'll be very busy."

The couple behind them laughed.

By the time they disembarked and got their luggage, their phones were vibrating like battery operated toys. Samantha ignored hers, digging frantically in her purse.

Sean said, "What are you looking for?"

"Your keys. I hope I didn't lose them in Switzerland."

"Baby, you gave them to me in D.C."

Breathing a sigh of relief, she smiled.

He said, "But do you remember where you parked?"

Wide-eyed, she stared at him. The memory of parking only a blur.

He grinned and whispered, "No problem. I've got a tracker on it."

"See, you paid me back for last night. You are keeping score."

He winked.

She said, "But do you really have a tracker on your car?"

"Yeah."

"Why?"

"Because I can."

She groaned, and said, "I can't wait to be an agent."

He checked his GPS tracker on the SUV and before long they were driving to the ranch. Samantha made notes on her phone as they discussed packing.

Before they got to their turn-off, she said, "Wait. Will we need to rent a moving trailer to haul to Virginia?"

"Maybe not. While you're at the academy, I suggest we just bring personal items. If we do that, I can probably fit at least ten totes here in the SUV. Can you make do with five or six of them?"

"Sure. I can always have things shipped later if I need them."

"We're good then. It will probably take me two or three hours at the ranch to pack my office and personal stuff, then we'll head to your house to get you packed up."

Then with a sudden concern, he glanced at her and said, "With the reception tomorrow and us leaving the next morning—"

Touching his leg, she said, "No. Don't apologize. Fast works for me. I want all of this with you, Sean. Everything."

He glanced at her hand on his leg and pulled it higher. Holding it there. They were almost home.

***

An hour later, Samantha packed up Sean's chest of drawers while he sorted and packed clothes from his closet.

She said, "How many pairs of socks does one man need?"

Laughing, he said, "Right. And how many pairs of shoes does one woman need?"

"Gotcha. Point taken. But…my shoes are fine. Socks are…just socks."

Sean said, "I love your sense of humor."

"What humor? That's just facts."

Then they worked quietly for a while. Glancing at each other. Saying all sorts of things without words. The language of love. Familiarity. Intimacy. Marriage.

Samantha taped the lid on a tote and labeled it. Then grabbed an empty one. She sat on the floor and opened a bottom drawer. Pictures. Old pictures of Sean. Albums. Formal photographs as a baby.

She struggled to breathe as she reached for the studio picture, hands shaking. Sean had been a beautiful baby. So beautiful. Then tears blocked her vision as the pain came. From somewhere deep inside, razors ripped open her heart. Her belly.

She screamed, rolling into a ball, lost in the misery.

Sean almost had a heart attack getting out of the closet. Hitting his knees beside her, he tried to make sense of what had happened. She was rolled so tight in a ball he couldn't pick her up without hurting her, so he laid down and pulled her toward him. He saw the open drawer. The picture she was clutching and knew. His heart broke.

He said, "Oh Samantha, baby...I'm so sorry. I'm so, so sorry. Let me help you. Please." He consoled. Rubbed. Held her as she rocked the picture. Grieving.

Kissing her head, a moment later, he tried again and said softly, "Show it to me. Let it out, honey. Share it with me."

Brokenly, she whispered, "You...were a beautiful baby. But I can't give you babies, Sean."

She rolled back and looked at him, eyes filled with torment, and said, "I won't be able to feel your baby in my belly. Ever. I won't be able to see eyes like yours look back at me. Ever. I'm broken. You've seen my medical records."

Knowing. Understanding. And feeling the painful truth that they would live with, a tear slid down his face. Ignoring it, he caught a tear that dripped off hers.

He said, "I know. I get it. I grieve the loss with you. But the true miracle is that you made it. That you're even alive. You're not broken - you're a survivor. An overcomer. And there are lots of babies in this world that need a champion mother like you – that will fight for them. Love them. Protect them. Teach them. We'll know if that season comes for us. If not, life with you is perfect just like it is. Every second of it. I mean that, and you know it."

Wrapping her arms around him, she whispered, "Perfect answer, Agent Man."

By the time they finished loading the car two hours later, four totes were full. Six empty ones waited for her house.

Sean said, "Come see the video I put together for our reception before I packed my office."

Excited, she sat cross-legged next to him on the sofa. He hit play and their selfie at the D.C. airport came up first as *Take My Breath Away* began to play. Then all the remembered emotions passed through her as she watched their flight. The limousine ride through the mountains. Their room. Their wedding pictures. The crowd watching. And all the activities in the days that followed. Selfies galore. And the last picture was when they landed in Baton Rouge.

She said, "It's amazing! I can't believe you put that together so fast. Oh wait. That's not true. Of course, the Drone Master can. He can do—"

And he kissed her, carrying her to the car. It was time for the next threshold.

***

Less than an hour later, Sean backed into a large garage in southeastern Baton Rouge and hit close on the remote. The door closed behind them.

He said, "This is a great house, and the property is gorgeous. Who tends to all this?"

Samantha said, "The boss. Olivia. She's way more than a housekeeper I assure you. And if you happen to forget, she'll remind you. But honestly, I don't know what mom and I would have done without her."

She got out and began to gather her luggage to bring inside. Sean came up behind her, running his hands across her hips as he kissed her neck. He unsnapped her pants.

He said, "Why don't you wait on that…while we take a shower."

And leaving her shorts on the floor of the garage, he carried her inside. Totally distracted with his roaming hands and hungry kisses, Samantha pointed toward the staircase as they left a trail of clothes.

By evening, Samantha's totes were packed and loaded. And they had confirmation that family and friends would start arriving in the morning for the reception. Now it was time to relax. So, for their last night alone in Louisiana, they ordered a seafood platter loaded with shrimp creole, fried crawfish, and stuffed crab - and ate on the patio.

After eating, Sean glanced at the pool and said, "I'm surprised you haven't mentioned wanting to swim. It's a fabulous pool."

Glancing at the turquoise salt-water pool, she nodded, and said, "Yes. It is. Mary Beth and I used to live in it."

Whoa. He hadn't seen that coming. Glancing at her, he waited. Samantha had so many hidden issues from that day. She must be ready to reveal another.

She said, "Did I ever tell you it was my fault we went back to the waterfall by ourselves?"

With a silent groan for having to live with that, he said, "No. But tell me about it."

"Oh, that's right. I told Gabrielle and Jade."

She waited for a few moments, and said, "Waterfalls were my thing, not Mary Beth's. But like all best friends she encouraged me. We had left with the others going back to the bus, but I wanted one more picture. So, we snuck back to the waterfall. And for one stupid picture we got Maxwell."

"Baby..."

She said, "Mary Beth was so beautiful, Sean. So smart. A fabulous gymnast. I always knew I would see her one day in the Olympics. Touching the world. But...now I can't get in the pool. I can't do it without..."

"You know she wants you happy, Samantha. You know that. Your life mattered to her. Otherwise, she would have run away from the attack. Instead, she loved you enough to stay and fight. She was the best kind of friend. She wanted you to live."

"I know that in my head."

"Then make new memories in the pool. I'm not talking making love. I'm talking loving the water again. Finding that joy in God's creation."

She gave the tiniest grin, and said, "You keep reminding me how brilliant you are."

"Then come swim with me. Show me what you love."

Samantha could see Sean swimming when she came downstairs in a pink glitter bikini she'd bought, but never worn. He stood and pushed back his hair. Tall. Dark. Handsome. Water running down his body. He turned and saw her, then smiled, and started toward the steps. She motioned him to stay there and stepped into the water. She closed her eyes as sensations and memories flooded her.

Sean watched as she dropped under the water, then pushed off the side. She glided along the bottom. What a swimmer. Fluid. Graceful. Hardly moving at all. After a bit, he realized she had been underwater awhile. He dropped underneath catching her attention. He pointed up. She smiled and shook her head no. He surfaced and watched her.

Samantha felt the sadness falling away as she remembered the beauty of her friend. The strength of her sacrifice. Her laughter. Her joy. And finally felt peace. Sweet peace. Smiling now, she swam close to Sean and slid up his body, ever so gently, till she broke the surface in front of him.

He whispered, "You're a mermaid," and she giggled.

"No really. How long can you hold your breath?"

"It used to be a lot longer than I can now."

"Just how many skills do you have?"

"Look who's talking, Special Agent. Drone Master. Flash. And Magic Sean." He frowned at Magic Sean, till he realized she was talking about the stripper movie and laughed.

Then she pulled him under the water.

Early the next morning, Samantha woke up excited. Their reception was today. Family and friends would be here by mid-morning. And they would leave for Virginia tomorrow. She couldn't stay in bed another second and glanced at Sean. Sound asleep. She'd go start coffee.

As she rolled to get up, Sean pulled her back against him.

He said, "No. You have to kiss me before running off to play."

"You make me sound like I'm ten years old."

He insisted, "You have to play with me first."

"Now you sound like you're ten years old."

Smiling, he kissed her. Then followed her downstairs. It was five-forty in the morning. Olivia arrived at seven to take care of all the reception needs of the day. Deliveries began arriving at eight-thirty. Tables. Chairs. Linen. Flowers. Wedding Cake. Rental decorations. The caterer arrived at ten and set everything up.

Sean was setting up the TV for their wedding video when the Lake Charles gang arrived. Dakota, Gabrielle, Adam, and Raven in one car. Gabrielle's parents, Jimmy, and Serena in another. Then Angel and Jade drove up behind them. After congratulatory hugs and feminine screams of excitement, Samantha took the women on a house tour while the men helped Sean. Not that he needed help.

***

Later, Gabrielle and Jade pulled Samantha off to themselves.

Gabrielle said, "I don't know anyone that's eloped. I mean, away from everyone and everything you know. That's a very hot adventure."

Smiling, Samantha said, "It was crazy exciting. Sexy. Intimate. And gorgeous. I can't wait for you to see the video Sean made of the trip."

Jade said, "Your pictures were unreal. You found a fabulous dress."

"Believe it or not, we bought each other's outfit as a surprise. His taste is scrumptious! The dress is a dream. And the boots were the perfect touch."

Gabrielle said, "I'll say! And what's with the new grin I see between you and Sean. It's like you have another secret."

Samantha said, "We do. It's called out-of-this-world satisfaction, topped with amazement that I can still walk."

They screamed in laughter.

***

Sean glanced upstairs with a grin.

Laughing, Dakota said, "I bet a hundred dollars that was related to your honeymoon and sex."

Sean said, "I can think of a million reasons it would be about that."

They laughed, and Angel fist-bumped Sean.

The conversation made Adam glance at Raven on the patio. She was gorgeous. Intelligent. Passionate. And secretive. One very hot enigma he was into.

Dakota bumped Sean, and they watched Adam. Little brother was zeroed in on Raven. Countdown.

***

By noon, all prep for the reception was complete. Olivia would make sure the caterer handled the rest. Fifty guests were expected. Early arrivals would get here around three p.m. and the reception was scheduled for four. First the social. Then dinner. Wedding cake. Pictures. Special dances. Followed by entertainment with Jimmy, Kerry, Chancy, and Misty.

By one-thirty Samantha met up with Sean, and said, "I'm heading upstairs to get dressed."

He saluted the guys and chased her upstairs to the sound of everyone's laughter.

***

Sean wore only unbuttoned black slacks as he leaned against the doorframe watching Samantha. Her legs spread. Leaning forward.

Mouth open as she concentrated in the mirror. And in seconds, she went from gorgeous to exotic, in a few flicks of a pencil and brush. With smoky eyes and red lips.

Smiling at his expression, she said, "You see me do this all the time."

"And it's always sexy. It's your body position. And the look on your face. Like you're anticipating my touch."

"She stood in panties and brushed her hair – leaving it down like she had at the wedding. And sprayed perfume.

He said, "You didn't wear those under your dress in Switzerland."

Walking by him she said with a smile, "Because I didn't want to waste time taking them off."

Heat flared and he pulled her against him, contemplating making them late to their own party.

She knew, and said, "Come help me dress."

She sat on the bed and held up a leg. He put the boots on her, then pulled her up. He tugged on her lace panties. She pointed at the dress. He touched her instead, then smiled at the flash of desire on her. Satisfied now that they both had to wait, he handed her the dress.

***

In minutes, they stood at the top of the staircase and looked down at their guests. Family. Friends. Co-workers. Bosses. Fellow professionals. The den and living areas were decorated with tall tables and stools. Glittered candles were centerpieces. The wedding cake was white with glittered designs in three tiers. The wedding video played on the TV. The buffet was filled with crabmeat au gratin, filet mignon, stuffed mushrooms, and shrimp hushpuppies. The patio was decorated with more tables and candles, and magnolias floated in the pool. Samantha and Sean smiled at each other. It was perfect.

Kerry noticed them and played the wedding march. Everyone clapped and cheered as they descended, and the social began.

Samantha's family waited eagerly to hug them. The D.A., and several co-workers were there. Director Washington came to congratulate them in person. FBI Agents Kent and Sylvester were there as well, still telling stories about the bear. The time was sweet with lots of laughter. Pictures. Stories. And hugs. It was a time of congratulations as well as goodbye, since they would leave for Virginia in the morning.

Before dinner, Sean called Adam to the bride's table to pray a wedding blessing over them. Smiling, Adam stood. No boot or crutches now. And all the women in the room watched the shockingly handsome man – beautiful actually – walk across the room. Those that didn't know, quickly realized he was Sean and Dakota's brother. Long black hair. Black slacks. Black dress shirt. Fine body. Smooth sensual moves.

A woman's incredulous voice said, "Mercy sakes alive. Someone. Anyone. Please tell me that delicious man is single."

The entire room, including Adam, erupted in laughter as he joined Sean and Samantha.

***

Eyes twinkling, Gabrielle leaned over and whispered to Raven, "You better hurry. A lot of hungry women are here tonight. He is a hunk."

"Right. And he knows it."

Gabrielle shrugged and said, "All three brothers do. It is what it is. But you and I both know *he* has eyes for you. If I had to guess, I'd say he's about ready to make a move you can't laugh off."

***

At the bride's table, Adam said, "You are the perfectly created union from God. Embrace your oneness as a couple. Communicate creatively. Build each other up. Pray together. And guard this gift."

Then he prayed, "Lord God, empower Sean and Samantha to ride the waves of everything you have for them. Vibrant with love. Flaming with passion. Walking in wisdom. Massive in strength. Surrounded in safety. Increase them in every way – all the days of their lives. Surprise them. Bless them. Anoint them. In Jesus' name."

And amens echoed around the room as Adam hugged them, then headed back to his table.

Samantha whispered in Sean's ear, and he said, "All single ladies, front, and center. My wife wants to throw her bouquet."

Removing the bouquet from the table centerpiece, Samantha waited as the single ladies joined in the middle of the room. Gabrielle insisted that Raven go. Misty, at fifteen years old, wanted to go - but her dad refused, and her mother laughed.

Once the women were in place, Samantha tossed the bouquet behind her. It rose high and dropped right into Raven's hands. Her cheeks flushed as everyone cheered.

Samantha hugged her and whispered, "Stop fighting it. Nash men are fabulous husbands."

Raven, thinking it was a conspiracy, walked back to the table. She looked at Adam's grin and said, "Don't you say a word."

He winked.

Sean called all the single men in the house to the floor. Several from the attorney's office as well as Agent Sylvester joined the group. Dakota looked at Adam and pointed to the floor. Adam grinned and joined the guys.

Samantha whispered, "But Sean, I don't have a garter."

He pulled one out of his pocket and she laughed. He knelt and drew her on his knee.

Smiling, he called out, "Double the fun! I get to put it on and take it off!"

There were a lot of whistles as Samantha had to hold the slit together so Sean could pull it on and off.

Then standing to toss it, Sean paused with a sudden idea, and said, "Sorry guys! I changed my mind. This one is spoken for."

And with a smile, he headed to the group of men and tucked it in Adam's pocket.

***

Grinning, Adam walked back to the table to join Dakota, Gabrielle, and Raven. He sat next to Raven and laid the garter on the bouquet she had caught. A few laughs later they moved on to another subject.

Gratefully, Raven glanced away. Could it get any harder?

Adam said softly, "Raven."

She groaned silently. Yes, it could. She said without looking at him, "Hmmm?"

Pulling her chair closer, he said, "Do you want me to do something you can't ignore?"

Turning, she said, "Adam…"

But he had turned to face her, spreading his legs. And now her chair was up in his personal space. Intimate. He was so close. So…fine. She felt like she was in his lap. She glanced away, avoiding his look. Trying to ignore what she felt.

Watching her fight the attraction, he ran a hand softly along her shoulder, and said, "Look at me."

"No."

He whispered, "I don't bite."

"But I might."

He laughed, and said, "You rock me. You're driving me crazy. I need more of you. I know you feel it. Why do you fight it so hard? You know you're safe with me."

"I'm not ready to be more than friends yet. It's too much too fast. You're already in my life. We see each other every day. We're going to be neighbors for heaven's sake."

"You are ready."

With a touch of anger, she turned to respond, and his face was…right there. Barely an inch away. His eyes emphasizing his words. He looked at her lips. Awareness pulling them to ignite and let it go. She tried *not* to look at his lips. She tried hard. But failed…and her gaze dropped to his beautiful mouth.

He said, "See how easy it would be to kiss me?"

Her mouth went dry with desire, and she wanted to hit him for pushing. Gabrielle had been right. He was tired of waiting.

***

The music started and Sean drew Samantha to the floor for their wedding dance. Kerry sang *Make You Feel My Love*. Sean danced slow with her. Romantic. Intimate. Gorgeous. Him, tall and dark. Her, petite and fair. Then he picked her up, carrying her for the rest of the song.

Afterwards, Samantha called her dad to the dance floor. Kerry sang, *Isn't She Lovely*. Sean's heart was full as he watched Samantha waltz with her dad. Then the dance floor was open as Kerry motioned everyone to dance. Dakota pulled Gabrielle out on the floor. Jimmy drew Serena out to dance. And before long, lots of couples were on the floor.

***

Adam whispered, "Dance with me," and Raven met his gaze.

She nodded, knowing better - but didn't want to say no. Besides, they should be safe enough with other dancers on the floor. He led her to the area overlooking the patio and drew her closer. One hand on her lower back. She stopped, making sure to leave space between them.

But smiling, he pressed her in. Body to body. Feeling her. Watching her. She was more than beautiful. Long red hair like sexy silk. Dark eyes. Red lips. Black spaghetti strap dress. Long fabulous legs in heels.

Determined to break through her defenses right up front, he whispered, "It feels good, doesn't it?"

She groaned inside. Good was an understatement. She warned, "Adam…"

306

"Answer me," he said, and ran his hand under her hair to caress her neck.

Going for nonchalant, she said, "So what if it does—"

His mouth closed over hers – and she was delicious. Everything he thought she'd be. He groaned as she opened to him. Tasted him. And let herself go. At least until she remembered where they were. She pushed back to meet his gaze. Then the song changed, and he drew her outside to a private area on the patio.

Dakota and Sean high fived. They'd seen the kiss.

Adam drew Raven against him, moving to the music. He touched her lips and said, "Quit over thinking. You knew this was coming."

He was right. But Raven knew she had to think of something to slow it all down. But how in the world did she slow that kind of heat down? Maybe she could put the brakes on a little and play it cool.

She shrugged and said, "It was just a kiss."

He laughed and said, "Not hardly, but good try."

"What makes you so sure it's more?"

Pulling her lips to his, he said, "Because we burn…and you know it," and he kissed her.

***

Three hours later, the reception was over. Overnight guests - Dakota and Gabrielle, Jimmy and Serena, Kerry and Chancy, all went to their bedrooms. Jade, Raven, and Misty shared a room. And Angel and Adam would sleep on sofa beds later. For now, they visited on the patio.

Sean carried Samantha over the threshold for the fourth time.

***

At seven in the morning, Sean and Samantha were making sure everything was loaded. They would be on the road to Virginia before long.

Samantha looked around and said, "I've seen everyone but Chancy. Is she still asleep?"

Coming downstairs, Kerry said, "No. She's been nauseated the last couple of mornings, but she'll be down before y'all leave."

Serena passed by and asked, "Is she pregnant?"

Kerry blinked. Stunned. It never occurred to him. Not once.

Jimmy slapped Kerry on the back and said, "It might be a boy this time."

Kerry ran back upstairs.

***

Chancy had just cleaned up from being sick again when Kerry barged in the door. He scared her.

She said, "What's wrong?"

"Baby, are you on birth control?"

She stared at him. Eyes wide. Gasping. Then she got sick and ran back to the bathroom again.

He said, "I'll be right back. I'm going to get a pregnancy test."

***

Kerry ran downstairs and said in passing, "I'll be right back."

They watched him tear off down the road.

Angel said, "I bet I know where he's going," and everyone laughed.

Sean and Samantha walked to the patio windows and watched Adam and Raven talking by the pool. Dakota and Gabrielle joined them by the window to watch the couple.

Samantha said, "Ok. Gabrielle, your baby girl is due in December. Angel and Jade get married in December. I wonder when Adam and Raven will get married."

Gabrielle said, "Their first kiss was yesterday, so not long," and everyone laughed.

Jimmy hugged Serena, and said, "We waited three weeks to get married."

Dakota said, "We waited six."

Sean chuckled and said, "From D.C. to the hotel in Switzerland we waited, twelve hours and forty-five minutes."

Dakota fist-bumped Sean.

Gabrielle said, "Samantha, why are you thinking about Adam and Raven getting married already?"

"Well, when I start training at Quantico I have to live on campus. No phone even. I can only go home on the weekends. So, I'm not sure how to fit another event in."

Dakota said, "That's right. I forgot that."

Sean said, "I didn't."

Dakota said, "No wonder you eloped."

Misty walked up and said, "Has anyone seen dad?"

Sean said, "He ran an errand, sweetie, I promise, he won't be long at all."

A few minutes later, Kerry ran in and went back upstairs.

Jade said, "This is better than a soap opera."

Angel chuckled and said, "Stay tuned."

A few minutes later, Kerry and Chancy walked downstairs. Everyone knew the answer but waited for the announcement.

Misty walked in from outside and asked, "Where did you go, Dad?"

Kerry glanced at Chancy, and she nodded.

He hugged Misty and said, "You're gonna be a big sister," and she screamed.

***

After goodbyes, Sean and Samantha hit the interstate northbound to Virginia. Samantha was too excited to sit still.

Sean said, "Go ahead, let it out."

Raising her arms, she gave a victory yell as Sean laughed. Then she pulled up her GPS and said, "Where are we going first?"

"I plan to get most of the driving behind us today. We won't stop to sleep till we cross into Virginia, so it'll probably be late."

"I'm good with that."

They talked a while, then Samantha turned the music on and rolled her window down. Her blonde hair whipped in the wind. She put on her favorite red lipstick and sunglasses. Then glanced over the top of her glasses at Sean and smiled.

They stopped for lunch about five hours later. They had just gotten seated at a table when Samantha's phone dinged with a text.

***

Gabrielle: We are the last ones to leave. Be safe, I love you sister-in-law.

Samantha: I always wanted a sister.

Gabrielle: Me too! And I think we have another sister around the corner.

Samantha: LOL

***

Samantha told Sean, "Everyone's gone. All is well."

They both checked messages before their food arrived. Samantha sent Sean a text. He read it, then raised hungry eyes to her. She batted her lashes at him.

He said, "I have to drive after reading that - for hours. But if I had room in the car, hot stuff, I'd give you what you're asking for."

"I know. Just think about the anticipation though. Isn't it great?"

It was after midnight when Sean pulled the big suitcase out of the car. They were tired but excited they were finally in Virginia. Samantha grabbed a couple of small bags, and they headed inside the hotel.

She said, "This is a nice hotel considering the small size of the town."

He said, "Thank goodness. I want you, and a bed. And I haven't forgotten the text."

"I hope not."

He unlocked the door and turned to her.

She said, "Stop. Sean, you don't have to carry me across any more thresholds. I'm coming. I promise," and he laughed as she ran and jumped on the bed.

He kicked the door shut and followed. They only had three weeks before she started the academy for five months. She would only be home for weekends. Forty days out of one hundred and fifty. He wasn't wasting a single minute.

A few hours later, Samantha yawned as they got back in the car. She said, "We should have just slept in the car. I can't believe we got here in the dark and we're leaving in the dark."

Sean chuckled and said, "We don't have far to go. I have a surprise for you."

She perked up at that, and said, "Give me a hint."

"No, let the anticipation build."

She narrowed her eyes at him, and said, "Is this payback for the text?"

He laughed and said, "Only you would think that. We both got what we wanted out of that text. And you only have to wait thirty minutes. Chill."

"Ok. But I'm watching the clock."

Thirty minutes later they saw a large sign in the headlights that read, Trail hours: Open 10 a.m. – 10 p.m.

Sean turned into the dark, empty parking lot. Samantha looked at him incredulously.

He held up his hands, and said, "Just wait. Stay right there."

Going to her side of the car, he opened the door and handed her a flashlight. He said, "Come with me."

They walked in the dark.

Before long she said, "Isn't the point of hiking to actually see the sights?"

Laughing, he said, "Come on, it isn't far."

"I've never hiked with a flashlight before."

"Quit it. I don't want to laugh the whole way there."

"Will we be able to see it when we get there?"

He laughed, and she said, "I'm not that funny."

"You absolutely are," and he kissed her.

She said, "I prefer witty."

"All the above fit. And watch your step, it will get rugged up ahead."

They followed a well-worn path through the forest and Samantha began to hear water. Sean glanced and saw the eastern sky beginning to lighten. It was going to be perfect.

Samantha, knowing what she heard, said, "Sean…"

"I know, baby, come get your surprise."

It was a waterfall. She knew it was. She pulled him to a stop, where they could see each other in the glow of the flashlights.

Eyes filling with tears, she said, "I can't believe you did this."

He touched her face, and said, "Hurry, the sun will be up soon."

Minutes later, Sean walked with Samantha to the edge of the waterfall as she looked over. Probably at least twenty feet high. It was magical. The pool was huge. Clear. Glorious. Colored rocks along the edges…and in the bottom. Flowers falling from the trees, floating. The water playing nature's music as it dove below. Morning sunlight danced everywhere.

Samantha's face was lit with a childish wonder Sean knew he would never forget. He said, "There's a trail we can follow down to the pool. Or…" and he waited to see what she wanted.

She whispered, "Or we can jump."

He smiled and kicked off his shoes. Before long they were stripped down to shorts.

She said, "How deep is it?"

"Thirty feet. Plenty deep."

Smiling, Samantha backed a good distance away from the edge. She wanted a good jump. A victory jump with the man she loved. With the man who loved her. They glanced at each other and ran. She leapt with arms lifted high. Laughing. Blonde hair flying.

They hit the pool with two splashes and entwined underwater. He broke the surface first, then she popped up in front of him. In moments they were naked. And Sean showed his mermaid just how magical the waterfall really was.

The End

Epilogue
FBI Academy: Three Weeks Later

Samantha parked at the FBI Academy in Quantico, Virginia. Pulling the mirror down, she checked her red lipstick. Perfect. Then gathering her briefcase and backpack, she stepped out of the car in fabulous red heels.

Grinning, she remembering Sean's delighted laugh this morning when he realized she was wearing her famous red suit to orientation. She brushed lint off the skirt and had a passing thought about her bait-walk – and knew you do what you have to do to get the bad guys.

She made her way to the entrance where other trainees – or cadets – were filing in. In no time, she was seated in a large auditorium about six rows back. She crossed her legs and waited for her next new life to begin. The auditorium filled quickly with approximately two-hundred-fifty cadets.

A man in khaki pants and a navy polo shirt walked to the podium. Everyone stilled and watched him.

He said, "Welcome cadets. I'm Special Agent Lance Livingston, your lead instructor for this class of trainees. So, for the next five months, I'm your boss. Get used to it."

Laughter echoed around the room.

He continued, "Now, let's get gossip out of the way. How many of you have already heard the tale of a new trainee from Louisiana that ran from a bear and was saved by the Black Avenger?"

Samantha froze. You have got to be kidding. Many cadets raised their hands in response to the question.

He said, "It's a true story. And the hero was a giant-sized black man named Kerry Hart that has the scars to prove it. Special Agent

Kent and Special Agent Sylvester witnessed the attack and killed the bear."

"Next, how many of you have heard about the trainee that distracted a serial killer by creating what we now call the bait-walk to save the life of a woman he held hostage?"

Samantha thought. Well, nothing like starting out with a bang.

The instructor smiled and said, "It too is the truth. So, would former Prosecutor Samantha Rutledge please advance to the platform."

Samantha stood and walked down the aisle, ascended the platform, and jointed the instructor.

Smiling, he said, "Just flow with me, Samantha."

"Yes, sir."

He motioned for her to face the cadets and said, "This would be the trainee for both tales."

The trainees clapped with disbelieving looks on their faces. Expecting that, the instructor knew some – or most – were dismissive of a tiny blonde woman being a warrior. An agent.

He said, "The most important thing you will learn here at Quantico is to assess what is going on around you in an operation. Make intelligent informed decisions. And meet the goal of your team, so ultimately lives are saved, and criminals are stopped.

"Valuable team players aren't always big, strong, or tall. Powerful people are men and women in all sizes. Don't forget that. Intelligence and skill are key."

The instructor said, "Video, please."

Samantha watched the video of the courthouse attack with Maxwell pop up on a huge screen.

He continued, "Samantha is the woman that you will witness in the video. What you don't know, is that Samantha survived this serial killer's first attack when she was sixteen years old. Then became driven to go to law school to prosecute criminals and defend victims. Then he came after her again. What you saw on the news or heard about was an edited version. On the wall behind me is the whole story.

The lights dimmed and the video began.

But Samantha knew the video by heart. She watched the cadets. Their faces. The surprise. The flinching at seeing the terror of the hostage. Their glances at her as she stripped and called out to Maxwell. Wooing him. Teasing him. Dancing barely dressed. Then they jumped when Sean hollered, and she ducked. Gunshots rang out in the room. Echoing. Ending with the thud of the body.

Now their faces were filled with respect.

***

The lights came back on, and the instructor said, "She was able to make this critical choice because she knew the two agents had her back. They were on a task force, and this is how a team works. The person sitting next to you could be on your team. They could have skills or perception that you aren't aware of. Be respectful to each other. They may save your life, or someone else's while working a case. Now, Special Agent Sean Nash, please join us on the platform."

Samantha hid a grin as Sean walked on the platform and stood next to her. He discreetly nudged her.

The instructor said, "Sean and Samantha, the FBI commends you, and your task force, for removing this serial killer off the streets. It was a job well done."

The cadets cheered.

***

In the back of the room, Director Washington and the Attorney General of the United States leaned against the wall.

The Attorney General said, "That was a creative, gutsy move on her part."

The Director said, "She has amazing instinct and courage, and she is smart as a whip, feisty too."

317

The A.G. said, "She'll be the smallest powerhouse here."

"Don't tell her that."

"That's what I hear. Let me see if I can give them a little reward since they interrupted their honeymoon for training."

***

The A.G. called out, "Lance, hold on, I'm coming up there."

In total surprise, Sean watched the A.G. come on the platform.

The instructor announced to the trainees, "Please welcome the Attorney General of the United States."

The trainees stood and clapped in excited honor.

The A.G. shook Samantha and Sean's hands and said, "That was impressive work. Thank you."

"Thank you, sir."

He grinned and said, "Sean, I understand you two were married six weeks ago."

"Yes, sir."

The trainees started whispering at that news.

The A.G. smiled and said, "Then I am going to do something that's never been done here at the academy. We congratulate you, Mr. & Mrs. Sean Nash on your wedding. Sean, you may kiss your bride. Again!"

Sean smiled and drew Samantha in his arms, then dipped her in a heated kiss as everyone whistled and cheered. Then he escorted her back to her seat, tucked something in her hand, and left the room.

***

A moment later, Samantha peeked in her hand. A note. She read the first few words and quickly crushed it in her fist. Swallowing a gasp, she glanced around. Shocked. What if he had dropped it? Or someone had read it? They were at the FBI Academy for heaven's sake! He knew—

And then she grinned. Impressed. Intrigued. He had found a way to connect.

The game was on.

Romantic Suspense Novels by Patti Corbello Archer

***

Double Target

Louisiana Secrets: Series
Bloodline - Book One
Obsession – Book Two

Book Three pending summer 2023

About the Author

Patti was born and raised in Lake Charles, Louisiana, surrounded by lakes, rivers, and bayous. She loves the Cajun culture and cuisine and is always ready for a road trip to the Gulf of Mexico or other scenic areas. Family, faith, reading, writing, and research fill most of her days. She loves the holidays, nature, movies, and dreams of living in the mountains.

She published her first novel in June 2022. Her fourth novel is pending publication in Summer 2023 – Book Three of the Louisiana Secrets series.

You can follow her blog at PattiArcher.com – and her author page at amazon.com/author/patticorbelloarcher.cajunlady.

If you enjoyed the story and encourage others to read it, please leave a review on Amazon. Simply go on Amazon – search Patti Corbello Archer – and all her published books will populate. If you click on the book you have read, then scroll to the bottom, there is a place for you to enter your review.

She would love to know! Thank you!

www.ingramcontent.com/pod-product-compliance
Lightning Source LLC
Chambersburg PA
CBHW030928260626
47169CB00002B/399